OF STRANGERS AND BEES

TRANSLATED BY

OF STRANGERS AND BEES
A HAYY IBN YAQZAN TALE

HAMID ISMAILOV

SHELLEY
FAIRWEATHER-VEGA

TILTED AXIS PRESS

The novel you hold in your hands is not the first to boast the name *Hayy ibn Yaqzan*. Our present tale spans centuries and half the globe, but it is mostly the quite modern story of a writer in exile in the tumultuous waning days of the twentieth century. The very first Hayy ibn Yaqzan, on the other hand, was the eponymous protagonist of an eleventh-century allegory by the Persian philosopher Avicenna. Or shall we call him the Uzbek philosopher Abu Ali ibn Sino? However we think of him, this great thinker tended to write sweeping tracts covering all available knowledge on a topic: *The Canon of Medicine; The Book of Impartial Judgment*; essays on the nature of scientific inquiry, physics, psychology and Islamic theology; poetry, even. But one of his more neglected legacies is a short story called 'Hayy ibn Yaqzan', a name which translates to something like 'Alive, son of Awake'. Ibn Sino's 'Hayy' features a wise old sage telling a curious travelling narrator about the nature of life and the world around him. Major sections of *Of Strangers and Bees* – this current *Hayy ibn Yaqzan* – open with quotations from the original, as translated from Persian to French, then to English, and later revised by me with an eye to the Arabic-to-Russian translation by Artur Vladimirovich Sagadeyev.

The next writer to seize on the name and the title was the Moorish philosopher Ibn Tufail, in the twelfth century. This newer, longer, Arabic-language *Hayy ibn Yaqzan* posed a thought experiment: what would happen to a man raised by a deer on an island uninhabited by people? Ibn Tufail's subject teaches himself science and logic. Later, when he encounters a castaway from the civilised world, he has the opportunity to compare his own pure way of life with the experience of most human beings as they interact with society and material things. The European Renaissance discovered Ibn Tufail's tale and produced a Latin translation called *Philosophus Autodidactus*, published in 1671. This seems to have influenced a whole swath of Enlightenment thinkers who conjured up political philosophies based on their ruminations of mankind in a state of nature.

A Moorish physician named Ibn Tufail makes a passing appearance in *Of Strangers and Bees*, too (though there is a decent chance that this particular Ibn Tufail may simply be a double). More prominently featured is Avicenna, Ibn Sino himself, who, you are going to have to believe, did not in fact die in the eleventh century, but has instead been condemned to roam the world. The hero of this story – whose friends call him The Sheikh – is also consigned to wander as a writer in political exile from his native Uzbekistan. His search for Avicenna, combined with his attempts to earn a living and a little respect in the wider world, sends him on a quest through Western Europe and the United States. Everywhere he goes, he finds traces of Avicenna, and with them, traces of his own ambiguous cultural and religious heritage.

Hamid Ismailov's imaginative iteration of *Hayy ibn Yaqzan* tackles big, important ideas of man and society, art and philosophy, but it is a deeply personal novel, too. It's impossible to forget that this story of an Uzbek writer in exile was in fact written by an Uzbek writer in exile, one who has had to reconcile a Sufi upbringing with a post-Soviet political reality in a multicultural and materialistic Western world. The episodes in this novel that examine late twentieth-century life in exile are plainly written, full of small triumphs and humiliations, and remarkable for their strange mixture of absurdity and banality. Then

there are the episodes in between, where the thinking, the magic, the passion in this novel are sunk into
its fables and parables and brand new tales from the
Arabian Nights. Here you will find talking animals,
beautiful princesses, conniving kings, and, of course,
a mysterious wandering Stranger.

And then there are the bees. Ismailov has an apparent affinity for the hive insects, and in this book, they
take centre stage. Do the bees represent the swarming
Soviet (or post-Soviet) masses? Are they humanity,
working according to patterns and towards goals of
which they have only a dim awareness? If we're all
bees in a hive, then who is in charge? On the other
hand, the bees in this novel are part of a larger cultural and religious tradition. Avicenna (and Aristotle)
wrote extensively on bees, with the Uzbek philosopher especially interested in the nature of bee venom
and the healing properties of honey. The Quran has a
whole chapter called The Bee. They must have something to teach us. But you will have to discover what
that might be for yourselves.

ON SUFISM

Like Persian literature, alongside which it is often
nonchalantly classified, Uzbek literature was once

essentially Sufi in nature. Sufism was mostly born in the Persian and Turkic world, and expressed and transmitted from there in literary form. Ismailov tells me that Sufism was in fact a way of adapting Arabic-born Islam for the Persian and Turkic world. Great Sufi teachers such as Jalaluddin Rumi (Persian) and Ahmad Yasawi (Turkic) retold the Holy Quran and Islamic religious thought in a literary, poetic form in their own languages. There's a famous saying about the *Mesnevi*, Rumi's main work: *Masnavii ma'navii Mavlaviy / Hast Qur'on dar zaboni Pahlaviy*. Or, in English: The Mesnevi and its meanings by Mevlevi (that is, Rumi) / Is a Quran in the language of Pehlevi (Persian).

One could read this novel as Ismailov's return to the roots of Uzbek literature with a multilayered Sufi parable, in which the narrator, Avicenna, and the bee called Sino are all on the path of searching for something bigger than themselves. In this *Hayy ibn Yaqzan*, Avicenna's lonely spirit is present at the turning points in world history, inviting us to reconsider their significance while applying both logic and intuition, knowledge and emotions, the conscious and the subconscious, the rational and the mystic. Here, the ancient polymath's presence as the Stranger serves one of the main maxims of Sufism: the idea of annihilating the ego and experiencing one's own life through the eyes of the Other. That, in fact, is the core principle which shapes this *Hayy ibn Yaqzan*, just as the others which preceded it.

ON DATES

Time is marked in Hijri years, which begin with Muhammad's move from Mecca to Yathrib in 622 AD and go on from there following the lunar calendar. Avicenna's (first) death is dated here as 18 June in the year AD 1037. Contemporary passages take place in the mid to late 1980s; the first contemporary episode, dated Year of the Hijra 1409, is AD 1988.

ACKNOWLEDGMENTS

This novel came to me in several versions, some Uzbek, some Russian. What you have here is a new English alternative that mostly follows the Russian, and which is more complete, and that has been checked against and altered to fit the Uzbek in which Ismailov originally conceived of the tale. This novel is arguably at least as Uzbek as Avicenna. The translation was partly financially supported by a grant from

Arts Council England, and morally supported entirely by Hamid Ismailov, to whom I am eternally grateful for entrusting me with his work.

The quotations from Avicenna's original *Hayy ibn Yaqzan* are adapted from those in Henry Corbin's book *Avicenna and the Visionary Recital*, translated from the French by Willard R. Trask (New York: Pantheon, 1960). A copy is available online at http://www.fatuma.net/text/Corbin-Avicenna-and-the-visionary-recital.pdf.

Lorenzo the Magnificent's poem is entitled 'Trionfo', and the English translation provided is by Lomade Lucchi.

The line 'I'd tear like a wolf at bureaucracy' is from a Mayakovsky poem translated as 'My Soviet Passport' by Herbert Marshall.

One excerpt from this novel, 'Events of the Years of the Hijra 1410–1414,' was first published in *Chtenia* no. 40. Two fables, under the titles 'The Fable of the Fox and the Flies' and 'The Fable of the Crow and the Bee', first appeared in the online journal *Underpass*.

Shelley Fairweather-Vega
Seattle, Washington, 2019

For Professor Ilse Cirtautas, who taught so much to so many, and who set me on this path.

There are three regions on this planet. The first is the region intermediate between West and East. It has been thoroughly studied, and the things that take place there, and the motivations and reasons for those things, are all rightly understood. But two regions are unknown: the first is the region beyond the West, and the second is the region beyond the East...

Avicenna

PROLOGUE

There is one episode from my childhood that I will always remember. At that time we lived in a village called Afshona, in the Rometan region of Uzbekistan's Bukhara province. On the particular day I cannot forget, they had sent us out from school to work in the fields again, though I can't recall whether we were supposed to be picking mulberry leaves for the silkworms or whitewashing the trees to keep pests away. During a break, I wandered off alone, and I found myself in the garden of the collective farm.

I had never seen this garden before, and I thought it must be the paradise my grandmother had told me about. Clear water gurgled through a canal at my feet. Everywhere, fruit fell to the earth in a hymn to creation. The ground was so soft the fruit was unbruised and untouched by worms. Half of the expanse was a flower garden, and aromas warmed by the midday sun surrounded me on all sides, intoxicating even the air, not to mention so small a person as myself.

I wandered down the paths of baked mud through the roses and, as I had seen my grandmother do, I sniffed cautiously at first, then plucked just one bud and tucked it behind my ear. Before moving my sun-seared head back into the garden's cool shade, I caught sight of the most majestic flower of all, and I thought I would pick that one for my grandmother. Suffering the pokes and scratches, I pushed further into the thicket of roses.

But when I reached that flower, I froze. It would have been a shame to pluck such a thing.

There are many shades of the colour red, but this red rose had none of the paleness of pink, none of the yellowness of orange, no velvety notes of darkness, and no deep shades of burgundy. This one was the clean scarlet hue of a young child's blood.

It's only now that I'm finding these words, of course. Then, as a boy, I saw all of this with unsullied eyes and a pure heart.

That was its colour. Now for the shape.

There are certain types of roses that resemble wide-open tulips, except with no seeds. There are others that look like mushrooms from the outside, or imma-ture bolls of cotton. There are roses that resemble curved teeth, some are like sets of coquettish lips, and some look like something caught and splattered in a mill. But this rose was like a road leading to another world. Or into the very depths, the very core, of this one.

So, instead of taking a sniff, I tried first to penetrate that flower with my eyes, right to its magical centre. And that was when it struck: the most impressive instant of all... I remember seeing a nuclear explosion once, on television. This real-life blast hit my eye with the exact same sort of impact. I didn't scream. I howled like a wild beast and flung the flower away, cast it straight out of that garden paradise!

I am no longer a young man, but every time I remember that moment, I feel a chill take over my body. I took off running at full speed, flying full throttle, but even then, my childhood curiosity won out and I opened my eye, the eye a bee had flown straight into, and I saw — this you will never believe! — I saw my own eye staring back at me.

Twice as terrified as before, I sprinted away even faster. My eye was starting to swell, making my head feel heavier on that side. Who can say which is more powerful: pain, or the fear of pain? When I think of it now, I also had no idea of where I was running to: if I went back to school I'd get a lecture, that was certain, but if I went back home I'd get a thrashing. So I fled instead onto the open steppe.

Who knows how far I might have run, had a white-haired old man not stepped out of nowhere and into my path?

'Where do you run in such haste, my son?' the old man asked. I removed my hand from my eye. My healthy eye was weeping, and the injured one was burning. All the time I was running, I must have been pressing to my eye the bee that had pierced my eyelid. The white-haired old man removed the creature, spread its wings, and blew a puff of air at it – and the bee, wishing me no more harm, soared off on the breeze. The man blew onto my eye, too, and as he led me home the lid began to open.

But I began to feel a surprising affinity, both bitter and sweet, with the bee that had flown away. Maybe our closeness stemmed from having beheld the same majestic flower, or from the moment our eyes had met. Or maybe it was sharing a love of free flight, over an open road...

I could articulate nothing of this at the time, and speaking it aloud seems beyond me even now. Maybe that failure is why I am a writer.

***

On the first Friday of the holy month of Ramadan in
the Year of the Hijra four hundred and eight, the divine
spirit of the bestower of all wisdom, Master of countless realms of secret knowledge, flew like a bird away
from its nest, quit its sacred refuge, departed its bodily
prison, and, submitting itself to the will of the Almighty,
ascended to the heavenly paradise, that blossom of
eternal purity. At the time, His Radiancy's age was fifty-
three years.

'From now on the Creator of my body will be indifferent to my flesh, and for that reason no attempt
to heal it will be of any use.' After those words were
uttered, in the Zambur district of the city of Hamadan,
under the dome of the heavenly arch, a miraculous
vision appeared in bright rays of light: an angel, which
unfurled its wings, and proclaimed to the people that
the mourning had begun for the death of Avicenna, the
Sheikh-ar-Rais, and this news took flight throughout the
whole world.

The death of His Radiancy was a staggering blow
to all who were present at his departure, and they fell
prostrate before his body. At this moment of truth, there
was just one person missing from His Radiancy's bed-
side: his colleague, student, and confidant Abu Ubayd
al-Juzjani, who got there just a little too late. This true
friend of His Radiancy, who was also a physician, had

the audacity to bend over the hand of the Sheikh to remove from his lifeless fingers a sheet of paper, on which was inscribed not any secret knowledge of healing, but rather some remarks about life in the material world and the soul that, though residing in the body, remains always connected to the heavens, rushing back to that realm after it leaves the body behind.

This unfortunate physician, distressed, grieving, and feeling alone, repositioned His Radiancy so that his head pointed north and his face turned to Mecca, and looked again at the piece of paper. He took from a shelf several glass vials containing potions of reanimation, healing oils and creams, and he sat down at the feet of His Radiancy and began to rub them all in turn over the holy yellowing body of the Sheikh.

Lo and behold, the spirit of the man lying there revived. Tears flowed from his eyes, and his body produced a sound like a young soldier crying out in his sleep. This miracle roused everyone who had fallen prostrate there, but when they recovered and saw what was happening they bowed their foreheads to the earth once again. The blood had come back into the face of the corpse, and his eyelids had come alive.

The physician did not know whether to praise God or ask Him to forgive his sins, and he wavered between the comfort of the present company and his own solitude. Casting one final glance at the piece of paper, he was just extending his hand towards the last little glass vial, which held a floral nectar intended for a queen bee, when in swooped the brave servant of another queen, a villainous bee which thrust its stinger right into the physician's hand. The priceless vial leaped from his grasp and shattered on the floor, splintering into a thousand tiny shards.

The devastated physician would have liked to take his own life, though what would be the point? He had very much wanted to bring His Radiancy back to life, but it had all come to nothing. The bird that was the Sheikh's soul began to stir, and it sprang away from its shelter in that weakened body. But perhaps the doors of the everlasting abode had swung shut by the time it reached them, because it returned to the room in search of a new existence, and chose for itself the body of that lone, unfortunate bee.

This journey, in fact, began in a different place. It simply came to me in a dream one time that, reading between the lines, the news seemed to be reporting that the Sheikh-ar-Rais, Avicenna, was alive, and being held in a hangar in some Western country. The information felt so reliable that, as I slept on, I thought of how many centuries had flown by, and wondered how they had kept up the lie for so long. In my dream, I turned my attention back to the news. It seemed that even now they were holding him in prison under a code name, maybe Warsworth, maybe Huggins, maybe Vissens, in some outlying region of Provence, or failing that of Bavaria or Philadelphia, maybe, and doing experiments on him. You probably know the story of Hangar 18, where the Americans keep the UFO... Half-asleep, I was tormented by doubt: how could this wanderer, a stranger everywhere he went, have survived unnoticed all those years? And not just years, but centuries! Where had he hidden himself? Who had he pretended to be? And how on earth had he managed to bear it?

It was then, in that dream or half-dream, that I understood clearly that from now on this secret would not only occupy a particular place in my own nomadic life, but would actually become that life's central meaning, as well as, incidentally, the contents of this book. So that's that.

EVENTS OF THE YEAR
OF THE HIJRA 1409

The one who walks before you is a deceiver and a windbag, who beautifies what is false and forges fictions. He will supply you with stories you never sought, made murky with falsity, in which the truth is overburdened with lies. But still, he will serve as your secret eye and your watchman.

Avicenna, *Hayy ibn Yaqzan*

It was 1900-and-something AD when that dream knocked me off balance. Perestroika had unfurled its wings, and those wings were starting to stir up a storm, but all my thoughts were tangled up in that dream, leaving me with no interest or strength to pay attention to anything else. Eventually, I couldn't stand it any more. I knew I had to find him, and that meant finding a way to travel – first of all to Provence. Only then did I get to feel for myself the refreshing breeze from perestroika's wings.

And in fact, a way was found. One day in the autumn of that year, I was in Moscow on business when I got a phone call from Sabit Madaliev at the Writers' Union. 'Sheikhov! You speak French, don't you?' Sabit-aka asked.

'Yes, a little,' I answered, somewhat confused, remembering that it had probably been ten years since I last picked up a book in French. 'What's going on?'

'It seems that we have some guests coming from France, and we need someone to go with them to Tashkent,' Sabit told me with a sigh. 'I thought of you.'

To make a long story short, two days later I set off for Tashkent with two Frenchmen. Since they had come to discover the world of Uzbek poetry for the benefit of the good folks back home, the big-name Uzbek poet and dissident Muhammad Solih met us in Tashkent. I won't bother you with the details of the thorough inspection the KGB agents gave our visitors at the airport, nor how they tailed us throughout our trip. I'm sure you get the picture. Instead, I want to start with our arrival at the Solih family home.

We walked in, washed up, and sat down at a lavishly set and draped dasturhon. Then there began the snatches of individual conversations and the long exchange of polite comments, the simple meal and the extravagantly long sojourn at Solih's table. Not to mention the endless toasts. First we drank to our guests' safe arrival, paying them tribute for having arrived at all. Our visitors mumbled something just as florid in praise of their hosts. Ah, how fine and elegant was the French that flew from my lips that day! And how hard my tongue had to work, as though it was juggling a hot potato in my mouth, back and forth from one cheek to the other.

Once he was nice and drunk, Solih-aka summoned me quietly into the kitchen. 'These guests of yours are serious about their drinking! They haven't refused once! I pour, they drink, I pour, they drink... Is it some sort of national custom?'

'The French, you know...' I managed to say with a shrug.

The next day, Jean-Pierre – the one who woke up around one in the afternoon – called me over politely. 'Such strange local customs you have here! Does everyone drink so much? The host kept pouring more, and we didn't want to offend, so we kept drinking. We're here in an unfamiliar country, with unfamiliar customs, after all...'

There you have it – the clash of civilisations.

—

The next morning we left for Samarqand. Riding along in the Volga sedan that belonged to the Writers'

Union, we talked about how one day there would be a Sąjūdis here in Uzbekistan, too, just like they had in Lithuania. You can imagine how the mountains looked, just coming into autumn. The poplars standing straight and tall, their leaves plunged into a deep yellow like so many paintbrushes dipped in paint; the red, and saffron, and blue, and deep grey leaves of the apricot trees... Every five kilometres we got out of the car and were delighted all over again.

We visited Bukhara, and then Afshana.

And, believe it or not − we surely didn't! − the French visitors promised to invite *us* to visit *them*. To assuage our doubts, they wrote out the official invitation letters before they left, and handed them to us right there and then.

Then the craziness began. As the founder of the Birlik movement, Solih was buried in work, so the job of making the return visit to Paris basically fell to me and Sabit Madaliev. It was true that the Frenchmen had issued strict orders not to come without Solih. But no matter how hard we tried, we couldn't talk him into it. In any case, we thought we could handle it ourselves. Sabit-aka agreed to talk to the Soviet Writers' Union, and the Union finally gave us its blessing, along with two thousand French francs.

According to our calculations, and based on what

our knowledgeable colleague Inga told us, it would cost three hundred francs per night for a decent hotel room – one hundred for each star in its rating. We made an agreement with the Hotel Lafayette, in some Paris quarter or other, for three hundred francs each night.

Finally the time came that made our hearts beat a little faster: in the bitter-cold Moscow winter – it was December – we got in a taxi and told the driver to rush us to Sheremetyevo Airport. And wouldn't you know it, on the way there the car slid and spun on the ice and then, while it was getting hauled to the shoulder, ran into another vehicle that had been put out of action! We narrowly missed getting run over by yet another one as we sorted that out. Still, God took pity on us, except that when we were boarding the plane I realised I had lost my hat. Not such a catastrophe, I decided. At least my head was still in one piece; everything else would work itself out.

–

We landed in Paris pretty well sloshed. Paying to get on the bus sobered us up, just as if somebody had poured cold water on us. That was the effect of spending our first seventy francs. This, we told each other, was capitalism.

Sabit-aka had all the money, so he was the one to worry the most. We decided we'd let the bus take us into the city, and after that we'd get where we needed to go on foot. We got off at Place Charles de Gaulle. It looked simple enough on the map, but every passer-by we asked for directions shook their heads and told us to take a taxi. How the hell could we take a taxi, if even a bus cost us seventy of our two thousand francs! So we set off on foot, lugging our suitcases and draped in our Moscow winter coats. We trudged along for five hundred metres before stopping, thoroughly worn out. There were plenty of hotels on both sides of the street, and right in front of us we spotted a three-star place, less expensive than the already fairly cheap Lafayette room we'd reserved by phone. A room for two hundred and fifty francs. We thought we had better check to see if this was one of the hostels Inga had mentioned. It looked nice enough from the outside, we thought, and in we went.

'Any rooms?'

'*Oui.*'

'Can we have one?'

'Of course!'

'Could we take a look first?'

'Certainly, *messieurs.*'

We saw that it was no worse than the Hotel Rossiya

in Moscow, where they put up the writers who come for the annual conference. A television, phone, refrigerator — just a regular room. We decided to stay.

First we arranged in the refrigerator all the chicken and snacks our wives had packed for our trip. To do that, of course, we first had to rearrange all the little bottles holding beverages of various potencies (the fridge was full of them!) to make room for our chicken, as snug as if in its own little nest.

Then we walked out into the city.

'Listen. No more public transport! From now on we walk,' Sabit-aka warned me. We crossed the street, strolled straight ahead, and came out at the river. Following the notes we had made on our map, we headed back to the hotel and the tea kettle we'd brought with us. We served ourselves boiled water sweetened with four pieces of hard candy.

Then we took a walk in the other direction, this time towards the city centre. We marvelled over the Tuilleries, and the Louvre, and all the narrow streets. Tucked away in a corner we came across a hotel offering rooms for one hundred and five francs. One star. (Only then did it occur to us that the cognac back home was labeled with exactly the same star system.) We ventured inside.

'Excuse me, but would it be possible for us – two Soviet writers – to share one room?' we asked.

'Yes, of course,' they answered. 'Would you like to check in right now?'

'No, tomorrow morning, please,' we requested. Believe it or not, the gloom of evening had already set in.

'All right, we'll be expecting you. Just one thing!' they said. 'There's one double bed, and one single.'

'We'd be fine sleeping on army cots!' we told them happily. But what could these silly Frenchmen know about army cots?

—

That night, tired, we returned to our hotel. Trouble awaited us. Those French hoteliers had decided to turn off the refrigerator! Two of our roasted chickens were sweating out water. The whole room stank. It was Soviet chicken, after all, so not the freshest. We toiled at it diligently, hoping to find some unspoiled pieces, but once that smell hit us (*merci, messieurs!*) we knew they were rotten head to tail. We had to throw it all out, wrapped up in our unwept tears. Again we drank our hot water sweetened by candy, dipping some biscuits in it this time.

We assessed the situation, and decided it couldn't

last. If we went on like this much longer, the Writers' Union money would evaporate into the exquisite Paris air, and we would have to return home empty-handed.

'Well, we've decided about the hotel. Now we need to address the problem of food,' I said. 'Let's call Jean-Pierre. We're here, after all. Could the two of us together really be worth less than Solih alone?'

We called. Jean-Pierre did not even sound surprised. He just told us that he would be busy tomorrow and the next day, and asked if we could meet him on Tuesday on the Champs-Élysées. All right, if we survived till Tuesday, we could go back home with a nice report for the Writers' Union. Did you meet them? We did! Because we had an invitation!

Now we needed something to occupy us until Tuesday. There was a Jewish man from Tashkent who had given us the name and address of a Jewish man in Paris, and we telephoned him, too, just to say hello, of course. His wife was a millionaire, they had told us in Tashkent, another good reason for delivering our regards. Only after that courtesy was complete did the millionaire wife burp a little and pass the receiver to her husband.

This Yasha fellow was a Soviet, too – well, a former

Soviet – but in any case, back in Uzbekistan, he used to translate Abdulla Oripov's poems for pocket money.

Yasha asked about Oripov. 'He always drank so much... is he still alive and well?'

'Yes, he's fine. Before we left he asked us to say hello, and he sent us off with a do'ppi to give to you. So we've been trying to find you,' we said, hitting on a trick.

May God and Abdulla-aka both forgive us, but when Yasha heard we'd brought him everyone's favourite Uzbek skullcap, he promised to meet us the very next day. In Abdulla-aka's honour, we would dine at a well-regarded cafe called the Apollinaire. Yasha told us to be there at eleven sharp. With the revered Abdulla Oripov looming there between us, how could we refuse? Our agreement was taken for granted; we didn't need to say a word.

—

When the sun rose the next morning, we decided to move to our new hotel. Our meeting with Yasha was at eleven, and we were resolved not to fall from the saddle, even if we fell off the horse; we would haul those heavy suitcases to the new place, and then make our appearance at the Apollinaire, before all those high-born people, with our hearts pure. So out we walked from that three-star hotel.

It's not easy to describe in words the race we ran with our suitcases, and how we lost our way. Basically, after tramping along for seven or eight kilometres, dripping with sweat, we finally arrived at the hotel from the day before, at around ten thirty in the morning. It was a great street. The very centre of Paris, constantly teeming with people.

Gasping for breath, we managed to haul ourselves up the curved staircase to the second floor. 'We're here,' we announced to the desk clerk.

'Passports, please,' he asked unexpectedly.

Sabit-aka and I exchanged glances. They hadn't asked us for our passports at the last place. We handed them over silently. The clerk, busy with whatever he was writing, asked us another question without looking up. 'This evening we've got a girl named Natasha coming from Russia. Two hundred francs. Shall I sign you up?'

Since I was acting as our interpreter, I translated what he had said to Sabit-aka, word for word. 'Seems a Russian girl named Natasha is coming tonight, two hundred francs. Do you want to sign up?'

'Well, couldn't we do it without the two hundred francs? I mean, I meant to say, without the Natasha?'

stammered Sabit-aka. He was the official leader of our delegation, remember.

'Without the two hundred francs…. no, the price is standard, there's nothing cheaper,' the clerk told me.

'I meant, without the Natasha?' I continued interpreting.

The clerk pursed his lips, offended, peered at us quizzically, and declared, 'If *messieurs* want to do without Natasha, then certainly, as you like.' Finally he finished drawing up our invoice for a three-day stay, handed us our passports and a receipt, and called a maid and told her to see us to our room. The maid led us to the third floor and opened a door there.

We were assailed by a familiar but mysterious odour.

'This bed is for two, and this is for one,' the maid told us as she went to open the window, muttering curses at the previous occupants. 'Now the two of you can let your hair down a little!' she told us, and bestowed on us a smile that made us exchange another glance, trying to figure out what exactly she meant it to signify.

'Well, we haven't got much time. We need to head downtown to meet Yasha,' said Sabit-aka, and he started to fold the receipt the clerk had given us in half. But first he glanced down at the paper, and froze as though he had been struck by lightning.

'What, did they cheat us on the price?' I panicked.

'Achhh, what have we done? Look at this!' Sabit-aka told me, the sweat again pouring off his face.

'What is it?' I took the receipt and saw the price was what we had agreed, one hundred and five francs per day, saving us 600 for three days. Not bad.

'Look at the top of the page, up higher.'

'What? Oh, no! No fucking way!'

In the upper corner of the receipt, in red letters, there was the logo: SEX-HOTEL. So that's what. Now I understood about the Natasha they were offering. And those smells…

Sabit-aka was a mess. He had gone completely pale and was drenched in perspiration. Just imagine it! The head of an official Writers' Union delegation, submitting a receipt from the SEX-HOTEL with his expense report! I really felt for him. 'Sabit-aka,' I said, 'It's all right. We'll think of something. We still have our receipt from the last hotel. Let's leave our suitcases here for now, and after we meet Yasha, we can go ask them for an extra receipt.'

We stared at each other, and then, avoiding the quizzical look from the desk clerk, we whizzed like a pair of bullets out of that hotel.

'Now the most important thing is not to get distracted. We meet Yasha in half an hour,' Sabit-aka
declared in his leadership voice. That meant it was
time to run all-out. All seven kilometres! It turned
out to be much easier to run without our suitcases, as
we checked the street signs out of the corner of one
eye, and kept the other eye glued to the map. Not
to mention that the part of our gaze concentrating
on the streets might just have caught, in some other
alleyway, a hotel room for only a hundred francs.

'Sabit-aka!' I called to him. 'Without our bags we
can get there in ten minutes. Should we check out
this hotel first?'

'Onwards!' my leader shouted in response. Maybe
I interpreted his command incorrectly, but by that
time, I was getting used to sprinting up spiral staircases to the second floor. Sabit-aka was close behind
me.

As soon as we got the clerk's attention, I panted
out my question: 'This isn't a sex-hotel, is it?'

This young man gave us a quizzical look. 'Would
you prefer a sex-hotel? You may use—'

'No, no!' I interrupted him. 'We need an ordinary,
decent, simple hotel room.'

'Then ours is just the thing!'

'Can we move in right away?'

'Certainly!'

The sheer joy evaporated the sweat off our bodies, and we sprinted back to the sex-hotel. 'You know, a certain professor was supposed to have met us. We finally found each other, and now his car is waiting downstairs,' we clamoured to tell the same clerk as before.

'You've got a professor in the mix too, now, have you?' he asked us, in a taunting tone.

'No, not like that,' we spoke over each other, getting ourselves even more deeply confused.

'*Messieurs*, in this country, one does not act this way,' he declared, finally losing his patience. 'I don't know what you did up there today, after you moved into that room, but you're going to have to pay what you owe in any case,' he said decisively. We could have eventually come to peace with the loss of the cash for one night's stay, but what he said next to the maid – 'Go look things over, and check these gentlemen out of their room!' – was much too embarrassing. And sure enough, this pretty little maid had us stand at attention, staring bug-eyed while she inspected the bed sheets. Now there was no trace left of the smile that had been attached to her face only an hour ago. In the end, the stain she did not find on the sheets was etched into our hearts instead.

We trudged back downstairs with our suitcases
and walked out into the notorious Rue Saint-Denis.
As soon as we rounded the first corner, we tore the
receipt with the SEX-HOTEL logo into shreds.

——

At a quarter to eleven we two humble writers strode
out of our original three-star hotel with Yasha by
our side. 'Listen!' he told us. 'I'm taking advantage of
perestroika and organising an international committee! You should join, too! Now we're going to the
amazing Apollinaire, in the Latin Quarter, you know.'
He talked non-stop the whole taxi ride.

When we finally got to the cafe, Yasha told us,
'Today I'll order my own favourite Parisian dishes for
you.' But wait, Yasha! First the wine! We swallowed
the red down into our empty stomachs. Maybe after
the sugary, syrupy, jam-like wine we were used to –
the kind a fly would get stuck in if it happened to land
in your glass – the French wine seemed much too
bitter, or maybe it was just because my stomach had
already broken down in hunger, but as we took gulp
after gulp, we waited impatiently to see what kind of
food there would be to chase it down.

Should I tell you or not?

For the main dish, they brought out raw snails!

'Here it is!' Yasha went on lecturing us. 'The most beloved dish in all of France, look at it, here it is: a bit of sauce, then you swallow it just like that!' We swallow them down, slime and all, like swallowing snot. My empty stomach had difficulty coping with this essential element of French cuisine but, at a loss for other options, we persevered. We were so ignorant and naïve, and things only got worse.

'Here she is, my lady friend has arrived!' said Yasha, and when we looked in the direction he was waving, we saw her – a pudgy Russian woman!

'This is Natasha, from Abakan, in Siberia,' Yasha was saying. All Sabit-aka could do was wipe something slimy onto his napkin. When graced with discerning taste, a poetic character, and a refined nature, and especially over a meal, one can only withstand so much. As if the movie were over, Sabit-aka asked, his voice tight, whether they had any ordinary potatoes in this place.

I translated, my napkin pressed to my chest.

Fortunately, the Russian mistress backed us up. Yasha was left with no choice. He ordered us potatoes. Then we ate our fill! And we finished off the French wine, too. That beverage, even after we had eaten the raw snails, complemented the potatoes perfectly, from the very first taste, and the next tastes came quickly, one after the other. Our tongues rejoiced, and so did our spirits! If only that persecuted Apollinaire could have been there with us.

A time long ago, the city of Kyoto stood under the clear blue sky. This city was built on thirteen hills, arranged in such a way that one of those hills was always obscured from view. On those thirteen hills there were thirteen flower gardens and thirteen monasteries, one of which always remained invisible. In each part of this city there was one teahouse, and out of the thirteen geishas that served in those establishments, twelve remained in plain sight, while one was always hidden, though she made no attempt to hide herself.

One day a Stranger arrived in this city. He went to a teahouse to spend an evening with the geishas, and he heard this story of the seen and unseen from another foreigner, and he found himself burning with desire to find answers to these riddles. From then on, he took all the money he earned each day, from hauling heavy loads or sweeping dirty streets, and spent it on the geishas. Every evening a new geisha came to meet him, and she amused him all through the long night with clever conversation and languid gestures, from which he derived the pleasure of a short period of calm. Then he returned to his room, and compared this geisha in his head with the previous night's geisha, and with many others, but instead of solving the riddle he wrapped himself up ever tighter in a sleepless knot. At first it seemed to him that that day's geisha was just the same as the previous one; but they were different. Then it seemed to him that this was in fact a new one, but still just the same as all the rest. And the poor Stranger soon completely lost count.

One night, when he was returning from an evening with his latest geisha, he suddenly heard the sound of sobbing coming from under a tree in a dark corner of a rock garden. The Stranger hurried in the direction of the voice. What should he see under the weak light of the crescent moon but a weeping white-faced girl sitting by a corpse, trying as best she could to stifle the sound of her voice, but not able to hold back the sobs bursting from her bosom.

'A samurai!' she said, and nothing more.

The Stranger understood that there was no salvation for this brawler, stained all over in his own blood, his stomach ripped through with a dagger. That night the two of them carried the dead man to the foothills and buried him there among the sandstone, then turned over the top layer of gravel to conceal the blood-soaked side. The young geisha uttered not a single word, although the Stranger, who had come to be quite familiar with the people here, expected nothing else. He simply helped her, perceiving that was what she wished.

Whether shivering in the predawn cold or sobbing out again in fear, the geisha trembled from time to time, and when she did, crumbs of white powder fell from her face. Before they landed on the ground, they scattered onto the hem of her garment, and when they did fall, they mixed imperceptibly with the sand and the thorns. Who could know whether to laugh or to cry at all of this? When they returned to the stone garden, the geisha pulled a single long feather from her fan and handed it to the Stranger. And she herself, moving with her teeny, tiny steps, disappeared among the stones and the trees. The Stranger returned to his own humble quarters.

Now he held in his hand the plume from the fan, and saw it was decorated with a lotus design, perhaps one of thirteen blossoms; and in his soul, he held something which might be either a blessing or a sin. The strange events of that night stirred in him now anxiety, now hope.

By the next day, the whole city was overrun with samurai. They detained people, they interrogated people, and all the city streets and squares were overtaken with shouting and chaos. On that day, the Stranger did not leave his room. And he spent the night deeply worried, looking at the lotus decoration, frightened for himself and for the girl.

When the moon had risen high and the dim moonbeams reached his windowsill, he heard a quiet knock at the window. The Stranger, looking out in trepidation, saw that outside his window stood that very same girl, her fan spread wide. He quietly opened the window, and the geisha handed him a scrap of paper before melting away into the night, just as she had done the night before. The Stranger lit a candle and, still uncommonly agitated, directed his attention to her message. Among some mysterious characters there was a map charting a route through the city, to a destination the significance of which, no matter how hard the Stranger tried, he could not seem to grasp. How many guesses he made as he pored over these characters and this path!

'Would she come to meet me herself?' he wondered. Then he looked again at the perfumed paper, and tried to commit the route to his memory. He blew out the candle, slid the letter and the lotus ornament into his satchel, and stepped outside.

From not too far away he could hear the voices of the wakeful samurai, as cruel and terrifying as a sword being sharpened on stone; but the girl had known what she was doing when she sketched out his path, and the voices coming towards him from all sides gradually faded as he passed. Finally, having left danger behind, he walked out of the city itself. As morning dawned he came upon a bridge over a small river, draped with fog. He passed one more hill and soon stopped before the door of a monastery.

'Have I lost my way?' he asked himself, looking around him, but in that dawn hour only the unexpected voice of an owl gently rent the silence. In the haze of the fog, the sound seemed to be coming from the garden in front of him, and the Stranger, sensing something, moved in that direction. He drew close to the trees, and he noticed that emerging from the rocks was not a girl at all but a monk, who took him gently by the elbow and steered him towards the monastery. The monk said nothing, but his soft, careful movements won the Stranger's trust.

He led him to a small house by a pond, and then in the same silent manner pointed him to a low table, laid with a woven mat and set with tea. And then the monk stepped outside, sat down on a rock near the water and, directing his gaze to an unmoving lotus, sank deep into his own thoughts.

That day passed, too, in the grip of thousands and

thousands of different thoughts, worries, torments, concerns, fears, and expectations of the worst yet to come, in panic, in vexation, and in a darkness and turmoil of the very soul. But the monk went on sitting just the same. Evening came. The water, nourished by the last rays of the sun, took back its drapery of fog before the night set in. When the silhouette of the monk and the stone he sat on had blended into the trees all around them, there came the sudden sound of a horse neighing, and the door to the little house opened. Still without saying a word, the monk placed a crust of bread and some tree nuts into a small bag and passed it to the Stranger, then led him to the horse and handed him the reins. The Stranger heaved himself up into the saddle. Steering the horse by its bridle, the monk led them through the garden and the rocks to the gates. He pointed one hand at the road leading to the ravine, and at that instant he disappeared from view.

The Stranger froze still for a moment. The wind blowing from the hills filled his lungs. His stallion was prancing, impatient. So the Stranger set out. Where did he ride? From where had he departed? Or from what? And why was he riding at all? Everything he had left behind him, the thirteen hills, and the thirteen gardens, and the monk and that geisha, yes, the girl herself, and all the murky waters streaming forth from these things all crashed together, and blended, and dissolved in a stream of water that was pure and transparent, and then became fixed together in these incoming streams. What had the Stranger sought, and what had he found? Or was the road, now, the most important thing, the road and the silence which enshrouded this world, a world as abrasive, senseless, and mysterious as a dream?

One day on Earth, one day long ago...

I kept my secret mission — find a way to Provence, and track down Ibn Sino! — in the back of my mind, and meanwhile the French went right on inviting Sabit-aka and me to visit them. We even gradually got used to French cuisine. The owner of the hotel where we had finally settled turned out to be a man named Hassan, originally from Morocco. When we put one of our souvenir skullcaps on his head, Muslim to Muslim, the consideration he showed us then was just as exceptional as that we had experienced from our Jewish compatriot Yasha. Hassan brewed our tea himself, and he personally stopped by to see how we were doing.

We spent the daylight hours wandering around Paris, walking out the tiredness in our legs and the hunger in our bellies. Thinking of our families, Sabit-aka still refused to spend a single kopeck, and I contributed as well as I could to this endeavour, like the obedient dog of a good master, never straying a step from his side. Some evenings Jean-Pierre would come for us, and take us to his home town of Fontainebleau in his luxury automobile. Or we'd visit Henri. Henri was a staunch communist, 'the last communist among poets, and the last poet among communists', whose communist granddad had diapered him with a red banner; Henri was a modern-day Louis Aragon. Yes, Henri sometimes invited us to his place, his library of a house in a working-class neighbourhood, where we gave ourselves up to a really sinful extravagance: leg of lamb. We ate our fill, practically swimming in its blood and juices.

Unfortunately, though, there were far too few of those evenings. For the most part, we spent our days measuring, step by step, the breadth and depth of our voluntary, obligatory starvation. On an empty stomach, even Paris pales. The Louvre looks like a bone picked clean, gnawed over by hungry human eyes for so many centuries. The Centre Pompidou is nothing but a house where all the world's freaks get together, and Sacré-Cœur, the Church of the Sacred Heart of Jesus himself, seems to have been placed up high on the top of that hill just so that the blind wretches of the world won't trip over it. One of those days, though! – one of those days, we finally came out on top.

We had walked to Luxembourg Garden, carrying a free tourist guide. A handful of vagrants, huddled over against the morning chill, just like us, had gathered here, in a less populated part of the park, to play chess. Now, our Sabit-aka was a renowned chess player, who had even studied with Erkin Vakhidov, the chief rival of the chess master known only as U. Elbekov. Chess master U. Elbekov, incidentally, was the son of the poet Elbek, executed during Stalin's time. In other words, the roots of this tree were very deep.

'Think I should take them on?' Sabit-aka asked, stopping to watch.

'If they're playing for money, you might lose everything we've managed to save,' I told him, to give myself a little insurance. But once he caught sight of a chessboard Sabit-aka was a little like a stallion that has laid eyes on a mare – gripped by an unmanageable fervour, impatiently awaiting his turn. The first Frenchman he challenged somehow stumbled over his own feet on the forty-eighth move. My hands were shaking and my heart was thumping, but things were easier with the second opponent, and Sabit won on the thirty-seventh move. He used a tricky combination on his third contender. His fourth opponent fell to a simple scholar's mate. The audience were rooted to the spot, like so many tree trunks in Luxembourg Garden.

'Sabit-aka! You should play for money,' I whispered in his ear like Kara-batyr's sister. Just when I had managed to talk him into it, the other players refused to play against him any more, saying he hadn't been honest about how good he was, and talking about how he must've learned from Karpov and Kasparov.

Idiots! They didn't know this was a different tree they were talking about, with roots in a different place! From an old city, too, from the Xuvaydo district of Tashkent!

We didn't earn a centime from those games, but Sabit-aka took his revenge for our hungry hardships. It was a moral victory, but it felt like payback. Our Waterloo.

Long ago, in the land of Mongolia, there lived a king by the name of Qorud. He was the king of all winged creatures. One day, King Qorud decided he wanted to taste the most delicious flesh in the world, no matter to whom it might belong. He summoned before him, from among all the flying beasts, the Crow, the Swallow, and the Bee, and this is how he greeted them.

> *Swallow with his forked tail*
> *Swallow in the spring,*
> *If you see a swallow sail*
> *Blessings he will bring.*
>
> *Crows are eaters of the dead*
> *They pick their meat with care*
> *If a crow flies past your head*
> *Misfortune you will bear.*
>
> *Honey bees to honey pray*
> *Let them fly before you.*
> *Gather nectar through the day*
> *And ne'er a false word for you.*

After he pronounced those words, King Qorud gave his three winged soldiers their instructions. 'There are three dimensions to this world: the height of the heavens, the length of the land, and the depth of the deep blue sea. Fly now in all three directions, and find me the most delicious meat of all!' The three winged creatures bowed to the King, and flew from the royal chambers.

As they soared together, the oldest, the Crow, cawed out: 'King Qorud spoke of three dimensions. I will go perch at the edge of the water and watch its surface, and perhaps I will see something interesting. You, Swallow, fly up to the sky. You will be in your element with all those insects! And you, Bee – you take the surface of the Earth. After three days, we will meet back here and make our decision.'

Each of them agreed that this was a very good plan, and the three winged creatures flew off in three different directions. The Crow settled down by the water, but other than a dead toad, all he saw on the surface was his own reflection. The Swallow flew up into the sky and started chasing flies and mosquitoes, while he himself was chased by hawks and falcons. But we will leave the two of them for now, at the edge of the water and in the blue of the sky, and hear some more about the Bee, flying along just over the surface of the Earth.

When she went out collecting nectar, the Bee flew from flower to flower; now, in the same way, she flew from beast to bird, and took a bite of each to find out which was the tastiest. She sampled them all: the Goat, and the Elephant and the Tiger, and the Porcupine and the Snake, but none of them had a flavour that was anything at all compared to the taste of Man.

The three days had not yet passed when this news had already spread, from the Butterfly to the Magpie, from the Magpie to the Hedgehog, from the Hedgehog to the Rooster, and from the Rooster to the whole wide world. So of course the news also reached the ears of the Swallow in the sky and the Crow sitting on the shore. The two of them conferred, and when the Bee returned to the meeting place, they asked her, quite casually, 'Who, then, has the tastiest flesh in the world?'

'Man does,' answered the honest Bee.

But the Crow sighed, and pretended to be hard of hearing, and complained to her, 'I'm an old bird now, and my eyes and ears are not what they used to be! Come a little closer, and repeat that again a little louder!'

The bee buzzed up closer to the Crow, right up to his open beak, and when she started to say loudly, one more time, 'The most delicious thing in the world is the flesh of Man!', the Crow snapped his beak shut and cut off the Bee's tongue.

And now, back in the court of King Qorud, the three winged creatures had to make their reports. The Bee tried to speak, but could make no sound other than a buzzing.

'What is she trying to say?' the King finally asked.

And the Crow answered, 'If Your Majesty permits it, I will tell you what she says.'

When the King graciously permitted him to speak, the Crow said this: 'She is saying 'poison'. She is trying to explain that the taste of poison is superior to everything else. And her own honey, she says, is made of poison too.'

To which the King replied, 'In that case, I will try this poison,' and he did, and in that very instant he died.

Ever since then, people like you and me have never again been food for bees; but King Qorud became food for the crows. And that is how the King becomes lunch, and our story comes to its end.

EVENTS OF THE YEAR
OF THE HIJRA 1406

The one on your right is greatly violent: when the passion
arises within him, it may not be appeased with advice, nor
moderated with courtesy. He is a fire in a dry woodpile, a
torrent rushing from the heights, a lioness who has lost her cub.

Avicenna, *Hayy ibn Yaqzan*

One fine day, the Institute of Oriental Studies where
Sheikhov worked (his friends called him the Sheikh),
signed, to its own detriment, a partnership agreement
with the Sorbonne in Paris. To its own detriment,
because how else could you describe a process by
which the whole partnership boils down to the fact
that the Institute is obliged to take in Parisian profes-
sors, and hang its head and offer homage? Everyone
at the Institute has to listen to their purring speech-
making, satisfy their constant need for drink, copy
their ancient manuscripts and then translate them for
small change, and in the end, after they've published

their works of worldwide importance on nice glossy paper, they come back and purr a very personal *merci*. Then there's a new cycle of 'partnership' and the Institute is back in the same mess all over again.

It just so happened that, on the winds of perestroika, in flew a professor by the name of Grammon, or Kilogrammon, or something like that, bringing with him a whole catalogue of books from the Orient which were being stored most graciously by France. Naturally, this was because there was nobody in that country who could read them. The Sheikh was perplexed. 'Nice job collecting that whole pile of books, but now we're supposed to read through every one of them for you?'

It's a good thing the Sheikh didn't say that to them outright, because this particular catalogue contained some manuscripts hitherto completely unknown. These were kept in a Benedictine monastery in Paris, which was connected to the Sorbonne by exactly the same type of agreement that bound the local Institute of Oriental Studies. The manuscripts had been carried West to France by Benedictine monks, way back when, all the way from the Orient, as proof of their missionary feats. And these manuscripts were not on a single list published by any of their Blochets! Nobody

knew they had even survived, except for those secretive monks.

—

Not four months passed before the Sheikh found himself in Paris. When had he been here last? Ah, Paris,
Paris! Eternal Paris! Do you remember releasing the
doves into the clear blue sky in the summer garden
of Louis XIV? If only we knew who finally received
the missives they carried! Or the prayers offered up
to Allah in the darkness of Notre Dame, the words
pouring through the stained-glass windows with their
gold leaf and shooting straight to the top of the vaults?
Paris, ancient Paris!

Strolling around the Latin Quarter, the Sheikh
looked over all the buildings that seemed so familiar to him. There was the library of the Sorbonne
with its vaulted ceilings, where voices were amplified
and echoed as if centuries-old thoughts were being
brought back to life. The Sheikh roamed the city for
three days without tiring, and the stones melted before
his gaze, and the air between the buildings crystallised
like diamonds. Paris was reflected in his eyes just as in
the antique etchings sold by the men hawking books
by the Seine. Only after that did Grammon escort

him to the Benedictine monastery, located right in the middle of the city.

Beyond the front gates there was a door, then another, and then yet another smaller one, and then, finally, they entered the quarters of a very nice-looking, very pious-looking monk. 'Pater Guillaume!' the monk introduced himself, in a voice like a prayer. They completed a few formalities, and then Grammon, as if delivering a child to an orphanage or a boarding school, handed Sheikhov over to the monk with nary an apology and disappeared.

Pater Guillaume turned to the Sheikh and said, 'My son, our lunchtime meal will take place in *this* chamber, but before lunch, you must visit the Chapel.' (That's what they called their church.) 'The library is over *here*, and *these* keys are for you. Use them wisely to seek mercy from the Almighty!'

After which Pater Guillaume (who was the same age as the Sheikh, though his title was Father), his long garments trailing after him, his steps small and neat, showed the Sheikh his cell for sleeping and the way outside, and after that, pointing out to him the signs that hung on the walls, said, 'My son, here among us, silence reigns.'

Silence! Silence! read the signs.

'Speaking out loud is permitted in only two places

here,' Pater Guillaume warned him, his voice more jovial now. 'In your own cell, and in the room of reconciliation, the confessional.'

The Sheikh was not sure he understood those last words. But not having to speak would actually make things easier for him.

'That's all, for now,' Pater Guillaume told him. 'Next week, here in this tholos, the abbot will read St. Benedict's Rule, and then you'll have a chance to learn more.'

Now it seemed to be supper time, and Pater Guillaume led the Sheikh to the refectory to dine. Before they entered the dining hall, though, he gestured towards his brother monks who had gathered for prayer. 'My son, now you can go and join the ranks of the laity, the novices. Copy what they do, and I will explain the rest to you later.' He moved off towards the tables for the higher-ranking monks.

The prayer began. The abbot, a monk dressed all in white, led the prayer, and then his assistants were seated. They wore capes with triangular hoods like bags that flowed downwards into their collars. Then came the attendants, monks dressed in the same sack-like outfits, and at the very end the green-clad novices. The Sheikh tried to stand up and sit down when everyone else did.

'Allah forgive me!' he thought, but the only thing that appeared in his memory was one line from the Quran: *Lakum deenukum waliya deeni*, 'You have your religion, and I have mine.'

After this solemn service began a grander cere-mony. Led by the head monk in his snow-white garments – the brother of all brothers! – they moved in procession to the refectory, filing out in strict order of importance, with the monks of aristocratic heritage and superior rank, in their unusual clothing, prancing in the lead, and then their attendants, and then the ordinary lay brothers at the end. The Sheikh gingerly attached himself to the rear of this procession. Once they reached the refectory, all the men removed their sack-like hoods, tossing them back on their shoul-ders. One of the brothers was still tirelessly reciting a prayer, and the rest were finding seats befitting their rank. The attendants sat on chairs with backs, and the lay brothers at ordinary oak tables. Two of the broth-ers began to pass around some food.

They tested the food first by throwing some to a dog that lay in the doorway, a cur who resembled the devil himself. Then it was the lay brothers' turn. Seeing that neither the dog nor the laity were suffer-ing, the attendants and the nobility joined in the feast. The meal stayed loyal to the French cultural canon, with the food followed diligently and closely by wine. The wine flowed in streams, in rivers, in floods. Wine is the blood of Christ, after all, and so its bitterness is often diluted with water. This wine, however, must have been chosen especially for this select company, because no matter how they diluted it, they were all turning as red as their beverage. Not wanting to offend this superior *vin*, the Sheikh dribbled only a few drops of water into his glass, just enough to be polite. He also drank of the blood of Jesus, light, like a sigh, and he drank of it in such a way that nothing would surprise him; he could turn into a Jew and it would seem perfectly logical.

These monks formed an order in which every concept seemed inextricably mixed up with all others. Physical needs blended with spiritual needs, even when it came to the need for food and wine. The Sheikh was convinced of this when he sensed a certain strange lightness after the meal was finished, and when he rose to his feet with the attendant monks, and felt, through the sheen of his own perspiration, how this lightness had travelled to his legs as well. Again they praised the Lord, the earlier ceremonies were all repeated, and they left the high-domed tholos and walked in a circle several times, one after the other, before eventually going their separate ways: the more elevated individuals went to rest, still rejoicing, while the simple folk set off to labour for the glory of God.

—

In this monastery, the Sheikh's life was devoted to work mixed with pleasure, and the pleasure was work, too. As he handed him the keys to the library, his spiritual benefactor Pater Guillaume told him, 'My son, to be safe, simply note down here the books you take,' and with that, granted him permission to bring books into his own room. Now the Sheikh spent all his time outside the refectory reading as many books as he wanted, or he took strolls through the city, where he could drink of the blood of Jesus, light and tipsy as the air, just to stretch his legs. But this fate was his alone. The other brothers got up some time past midnight for the dawn prayers; then, keeping to the prescribed schedule, began each day with chores, met five times for common prayers, and after sunset, having received a blessing in the chapel from the Father Abbot, marched off to their own cells, untalking and grim, and continued their prayers in silence and solitude.

Every so often the Sheikh would be invited behind the metal-grated door of the confessional, where, under the gaze of the candlelit Virgin Mary, Pater Guillaume delivered lectures that reminded the Sheikh of nothing more than the old Persian morality tales in the Qabus-nama.

His words poured forth like a melody performed by a virtuoso singer. The Sheikh would have to kneel and place his hands on his breast. Pater Guillaume's shadow loomed over the Sheikh's bowed head like a hovering hawk, and the flickering candlelight seemed to cleave through the ancient stone walls. 'My son!' said he. 'For us, silence is the manifestation of spiritual purity. If you are pure, then like our Christ, you may pass not just over the floor but also over the water, leaving no tracks behind you.' And on he went, pronouncing other similarly splendid words. Not fully understanding what was being said, all the Sheikh could do was to nod his head in the darkness and think his own thoughts.

Later in the day, reading through the *Book of Travels* after one such lecture, he wondered whether the travelling Father Paul d'Assisi had gone through something similar. Could it be that he too had been subject to scoldings and admonitions in a language he only partly understood, when he came upon a dervish village or a den of hashish smokers on the trail of Friar William of Rubruck? Now the Sheikh dove into the *Book of Travels* with more curiosity than ever. The Gothic letters were a puzzle in their own right, and when he somehow managed to tease them apart and read the word that emerged the mystery only deepened, with the dictionary providing a dozen possible meanings.

The sun had long been rolling over the rooftops of Paris, its rays like axles, carrying him away in his mind to the distant historical past. In this book, Paul d'Assisi described how, having escaped the Inquisition, he journeyed first to Frankfurt, then through Nuremberg to Austria, and finally to Constantinople, the capital of Byzantium, which is of course to say the great Roman Empire city of Istanbul. It was in this city that he first wrote to his monastery, a letter addressed to his friend Jean-Jacques. Picking his way through that letter, the Sheikh believed he was starting to understand the reasons Paul d'Assisi had fled the monastery. In every phrase, in every topic, he could sense a particular affliction, perhaps even a passion, scabbed over but not yet healed. Paul wrote:

> *Wiping from my brow the sweat from Istanbul's summer heat, I feel, through my delirious ravings, the sweetness of your fingers.*

And in another place:

> *As this evil fate constantly pursues me, so the distance grows*

between us, and yet I feel the threads connecting us, stretching
out to the very edge; and they seem to me the threads of my very
soul, singing praises to your countenance.

The Sheikh would have liked to share his suspicions
with Pater Guillaume, but the lecture he had received
about spiritual purity had tired him out.

—

The next morning, the Sheikh was woken by a gentle
whisper. 'My son! Today is the reading of the Rule,
a very happy occasion indeed.' And Pater Guillaume
invited him to visit the *chambre de chapitre*.

When the Sheikh arrived, alarmed and amazed,
preparations for the ceremony were already well underway. As always, the brothers were lined up according
to their rank, heads covered by their sack-like hoods,
from inside which they could see only the back of the
head in front of them. Once the initiates fell in at the
end of the line the procession headed to the Chapter
Chamber at the same tempo as on the way to the
dining hall. The Most Superior Abbot occupied the
place of honour there, as the nobility filed in along
the wall behind him, and took the places ingrained in
them by years of experience. Under three windows
arranged like a candle – the symbol of the Trinity
– another ten hooded figures sat, five on each side

of the Abbot. The rest arranged themselves according to status, not in the places along the walls but on long polished benches. In the centre of the Chamber were individual chairs between four white marble columns, and across from those was a sconce holding a candle. One monk, who recited prayers better than the others, walked over to the sconce and took out some sort of book from under it. The brothers tucked their hands inside their billowing sleeves, rested them on their knees and bowed their heads, and there in the mixed light of the sun outside and the candles they concentrated their attention on the words of the sermon. The soft glow of the candles played, barely perceptible, on the vaults of the arches connecting the columns to the walls, and the voice of the orator touched those arches, too; in fact, it seemed to crash right into them, then float calmly back down again.

First he read stories from the life of Benedict of Nursia and offered a prayer in the saint's honour. Then he moved on to read the Rule itself, written by the founder of the monastery.

A sermon delivered in Latin provides a particular kind of pleasure. The Quran is read in a sing-song sort of way, with the words and music of the verses blending together. But when you read a prayer in Latin, each element sounds separately. While the ceremonial speech was being made, the Sheikh sat and waited for the organ in the corner to start playing. But the only sound that disturbed the ceremony was the cooing of a pigeon, which had flown up into the domed ceiling. And the Sheikh slipped deep into a sweet dream.

When you turned to look out of the Trinity windows you could see the twentieth-century sky and the contrails of passing planes. But here in this Chamber time had stood still since the sixth century, and it seemed that St. Benedict himself would walk in at any minute, wrapped in his garment of coarse fabric, to say, 'I found solitude not in solitude, but among my brothers,' delivering the Rule not to the Monte Cassino monastery near Naples but to this place, right here in the very centre of Paris. Then the Sheikh truly felt his own estrangement, and realised how long it had been since he last spent any time alone.

—

The Sheikh went on studying the *Book of Travels*. Paul had come to Constantinople with another crusade, another war hot on his tail. The Sultan's turban was better than the Pope's hood, he remarked, and in his last letter from Constantinople he really let his heart cry out.

*We have truly fallen victim to Latin jaws. Churches and palaces,
monasteries and libraries, grand buildings and tiny huts, have
all alike fallen before these soldiers, who have iron helmets where
their heads should be. The innocent maidens of Byzantium have
been violated, and in the basilica of St. Sophia, some harlot
sang and danced lustily for a crowd of drunken louts. Under the
feet of these iron-clad beasts, the pictures of girls' faces have been
turned into kettledrums for dancing. Alas, this poor city! This
unfortunate city, once the eye for all others, a fairy tale for all the
world, a legend for all to tell, a place of faith and conviction, of
concentration and contemplation, bathed in the light of learning,
witness to the wheel of supplication! Have you truly drunk of
the Lord's wrath, and torn asunder the curtain of thundering
perdition?*

Fleeing from his bloodthirsty fellows in faith, Paul
soon came to Angora, then held by the Muslims, and
moved from there to Iconium and finally to Antiochia,
after which the letters seemed to have ceased. All of
this appeared before the Sheikh's eyes as the preacher
read the saga in the Chapter Chamber. Thanks be
to God, the crusaders turned back, having no interest in Antiochia and Iconium. Paul the Benedictine,
who had travelled an uncharted path with nothing
but the Gospel in his hand, stayed for several years
in Anatolian territory, among the Muslim and Syrian
teachers at the madrassa where they were translating
the books of Aristotle.

It was there that Paul related how in the Seljuk
capital Iconium he had come across a cloister of

dervishes, founded by a certain man of God called Mevlana of Balkh – but here, some pages had been torn out of the *Book of Travels*. The Sheikh, perturbed, had grabbed the manuscript, dropped his manners, and rushed over to the library to find Pater Guillaume. When he found him dozing in a separate room there, he grew even more agitated, and couldn't control himself – he even raised his voice.

'*Silence!*' Pater Guillaume told him, his lips moving without sound. '*Silence!*'

But after Sheikhov had explained, he raised his eyebrows and said, 'My son, do not worry. It is not your fault. The numbering continues uninterrupted at the top of the pages. Those numbers were placed there in the sixteenth century by a Franciscan monk.'

The Sheikh had not even thought of blaming himself, and he was confused for a moment, but the Abbot's calm spread to him. 'So the missing pages had already been removed before then?'

'Yes,' Pater Guillaume confirmed, and nodded meaningfully at the iron door behind him.

The Sheikh's suspicion that even the library was segregated by rank had been confirmed by Grammon, the atheist scholar, the first day he arrived. And now here in the Chapter Chamber, as he looked over the silent parade of ranks and files, the Sheikh suddenly burned with desire to get himself into the section of the library reserved for the attendants. Every time Father Paul got to something interesting, he had been silenced. His thoughts were constantly being cut off mid-sentence. The conversations he had with the Mu'tazilites and the orators from the library in Damascus, and his talks with the Jewish rabbis; the story of how he travelled to Qom, where he met with the Shiite ulama and secret members of the Ismailite societies; and, finally, his description of the Sufi orders, from when civilisations had flourished in Khorasan and Transoxiana. And then there were his stories of the marketplaces, of amusements with young boys, of canings, not to mention a tale from faraway Mongolia – all trailing off in unfinished chapters. Who had taken those missing pages? How could he find them? And if he did, what might they have to teach him? The words of the Rule rang out in all their pomposity, but the Sheikh, off in his own world, could not stop tormenting himself with these questions.

Few people know that bees have names of their own. This particular bee's name was Sina, and on the second day of the month of Ramadan (it seems to have been a Thursday), jostled by a shaking that jolted the whole earth, when the sun had just climbed up and swept inside the hive, Sina burst from his cocoon, which was the size of a kernel of wheat. That was his birth.

Sina was a little dumbfounded, surrounded on all six sides by melon-shaped midwives who were buzzing, and pressing honey to his mouth, and waving their arms and whiskers. Amid this clamour and commotion, Sina did his best to straighten his crooked legs, smooth and extend his crinkled little wings, and use his front legs to feel his face and his middle legs to feel his body.

Sina's mother Pasha had left the old hive when spring arrived, and worked hard to build a new place for them to live. But, whether from an illness that developed during their resettlement or from the weight of all her accumulated years, she died, and the family hurried to appoint a new queen. The swarm of bees in their communal hive told Sina all about it. His mouth full of honey and his stinger full of poison, Sina tried to think over what he had heard, and meanwhile he failed to notice how he had involuntarily started scurrying around in all six directions, tidying things up. But how could anyone stand still for long in a place where everyone was hustling and bustling about, working away? Constantly bumping into the other bees around him, Sina swept the crumbly bits of cocoon and strings of dried honey from his untidy little cell. He gathered the stray strands of wax and pollen, and he wiped all traces of nectar from the walls, but he was distracted as he worked. You know how young people are, after all.

Then a smell crept in around him that made Sina's heart squeeze tight, and his nurse burst in – the same nurse who had come to see him a thousand times a day while he was still in the cocoon, feeding him honey from her own mouth. Pushing the other bees aside, she came right up to fawn over Sina. 'Oh, my little one, you're awake! Oh, what a sweet titbit you are!' The nurse brought with her the fresh aroma of the sweet wildflowers and mint which grew on the banks of the stream, and she carried a whole basketful of pollen. And her dance, expressing all her joy and merriment, also announced the news of flower petals and the sun's warmth.

Even her words – 'Hello hello, and how are we today? Everything all right, is it?' – went harmoniously with her dance. Because young ones can be rude when they are confused, and a little rough around the edges, Sina mumbled that things could be better. His nurse laughed and told him, quietly, so nobody else could hear, 'Ah, what a clever little tongue we have! But things could be worse, too, couldn't they? And thank God for that!' She said it in a way that was so pure of heart, and so ambiguous in meaning, that her words stayed in Sina's heart for a long time.

A pure heart is like a clear mirror. Sina may have heard the story from his nurse, or maybe it was reflected in his own heart, but whatever the case, he learned that one day, a bee had brought back to the hive not a blossom's fragrant nectar but the juice of human flesh, an atrocity which the drunken guards should never have let into their home. Then and there Sina's mother had decided to move. But her efforts exhausted her and she died; and a small part of that juice, bitter as poison and sweet as honey, infected Sina as well.

That was probably why, throughout his daily work among the humming of thousands of his brothers and sisters, unexpected images would sometimes pop into Sina's mind. At first he thought that they must be old folk tales, stories his nurse had told him when he was an uncomprehending infant. Soon it became his habit to compare those tales with the visions that kept appearing in his mind.

—

Not wishing to dismay His Excellency the Shah of Khorazm with the news that was to come, the Head Vizier Abulhussein ibn Muhammad al-Suheil took it upon himself to receive Hoja Hussein ibn Ali ibn Mikoil, who brought a message from the Sultan of all Sultans, Mahmud Yaminud-Davla. Having read the missive, the Head Vizier summoned a council of religious ulama and learned men. They gathered in the throne hall: Abu Nasr Mansur ibn Iraq, a mathematician many compared to Pythagoras; Abu Rayhan al-Biruni, an astronomer as good as Ptolemy; Abu'l-Khayr ibn al-Hammar, a luminary in the healing arts; Abu Sahl al-Masihi, a philosopher unmatched and unequalled; and one man who had achieved perfection in all the sciences, the Protector of the Truth, the Sheikh-ar-Rais, Avicenna.

In this assembly of wisdom and insight, the letter in which the Sultan of all Sultans ordered that every learned man residing in Khorazm be sent to his palace in Balkh was read out loud, and al-Suheil said: 'Sultan Mahmud Yaminud-Davla has vanquished his enemies in Khorasan and India, and obliged them to pay tribute. If we do not comply with his request, he may send his army to confront us next. Which path shall we choose?'

The youngest among them, Abu Ali Avicenna, spoke first. 'We will not go!'

Abu Sahl agreed with Avicenna.

The rest, imagining what suffering the Sultan's army might bring upon the people, decided it would be better to go to Balkh.

After thinking for some time, al-Suheil spoke to all those present. 'I will relate our discussion to the Shah of Khorazm, the Conqueror of the World, Ali ibn Ma'mun. Let his great will be done!' Leaving the men to their debates, he went to bring the news to His Excellency.

—

Had Sina's nurse really told him that story? 'There is much for you still to see, my sweet, but even in all this variety, you must never settle for too little. That is the law of flight! He who stops falls to the earth,' she said. The maternal love he would never know, the closeness he desired with all his heart, the gentle, teasing whispers of his nurse, and bittersweet memory itself – childhood, the open fields, the hive, the warmth – Sina wondered whether he would ever be strong enough to bear it all, to raise all that up and carry it on his still-feeble wings. In this troubled spirit, he left his cell and began tidying the next one over. Maybe instilling cleanliness all around him would clean his own soul and renew it.

Childhood is innocent, really. A time when no contrition is necessary.

A translator who translated a work by Andrei Platonov into a foreign language wrote down the recollections of one of Platonov's female relations.

Platonov recalled, she wrote, the following.

In the period between the 1920s and 1930s, the native population of Moscow, mostly ethnic Russians and Tatars, started to change. From all four corners of the Soviet Union, they began to gather them in, to gnaw upon the granite of science, as Comrade Trotsky said. From up above came the Chukchis and Nenets, from the right, the Mordovians and Chuvash, from down below the Uzbeks and the Turkmen, and from elsewhere, the Moldovans and the Latvians. It was a brilliant and furious time!

It was in that period that I made the acquaintance of a man named Nazar, and we became friends. He told me all about Khiva and Ustyurt, Sarikamish and Karakum. In this lonely, disconsolate world, I did not know how to soothe the burning in the muscles of my heart. It turns out that children of man will latch on to almost anything when their overburdened hearts have no room left for life.

This Nazar had a whole pile of friends, but his face was loneliness incarnate, and as a result, it seemed that his friends resided in one corner of his loneliness, sometimes popping in, other times disappearing again. One evening, solitary and lonely as all the others, he cooked up some plov in his dormitory and invited a few friends over, including me. That night there was a full moon, and a light breeze trembled the warm air. And

*when night set in, all the shortened shadows began to interlace,
extending their hands to one another to preserve what remained
of the light.*

Among those gathered there was a sad-faced poet by the name
of Cho'lpon, and someone named Sheikhov, a resident in the
internal diseases department. They were seated on either side of
me, enabling us to get acquainted. While we dug into the plov,
Sheikhov toasted Nazar. 'You are a piece of history,' he told him.

The poet, Cho'lpon, interpreted for me.

'In an era of revolution and class struggle, in order to bring about
a new dawn from the shards of history, I read a particular book.
In that book, Nazar – which of course means 'the human gaze'
– travels the path of the world and strives to find the purpose and
source of life. You, Nazar, were born at the end of that path, and
you live within this meaning. You turned yourself into a person
who makes no effort in vain.'

Nazar's only response was to sigh from the weight of the gloom
that filled him. But Sheikhov continued, undistracted by
thoughts or mood.

'Happiness is historically predetermined, but a human lifetime is
not enough for anything. And you, Nazar – not from the years
of age, but out of social responsibility – are achieving, with your
nation, exactly what I read about in that book!'

But Nazar, who let these words into his ear solely for the sake of
listening, felt he could remember, through a strange bodily grief,
his own land, and his mother. And this sadness, and the words
that had been said, seemed equally pleasant to him.

I asked the poet, 'How well-known is this book he describes?'

'Books like this one are fairly well-known, and well-distributed,'

answered the poet, and immediately mentioned that he was
working on a novel at the moment himself. Then he told us
about Avicenna's book, Hayy ibn Yaqzan, or Alive, Son of
the Awake. I remembered a book by the same title, by ibn
Tufeil, and the poet responded, 'After Avicenna and ibn Tufeil,
others, like Attor, Jami and Navoiy, and Bedil and Nishati
(those names I scribbled down on a paper napkin) all tried
writing things with similar names.'

The poet was really an interesting sort. An aura seemed to
emanate from his pale face that made it seem like he was living
through an everlasting illness as he told me about the story
he was planning to write about Nazar. But I, watching a fly
wander the corner where the ceiling met the wall, grieved over the
glaring deficit, in this world, of things not said out loud.

Sheikhov took up his favourite topic again. 'Nazar,' said he, 'I
have wandered this world for a long time. Everyone has found
their place in the geography of the world and its climes. It is only
the Uzbeks and the Russians' – when he said that, I took it
personally – 'who reside in limbo. Settling in the desert is not
really hell for them, but putting up a tent in the blossoming forest
is still far from heaven. The mixed mongrel peoples are the elect
of this world,' he concluded.

Then he added, 'Take a look into my soul. You'll find many
books there, but what I have just told you cannot be found in
any written tome. That is probably the reason that the corner
of my heart always feels pinched. These words come from that
corner.' And with that, he poured a glass of vodka into himself.

The poet sighed, readying his face for a smile, but then he
suddenly switched tracks, and said to me, 'I translated Pushkin.'
And, as if he were drawing it out of his heart, he released a
piece of paper from the pocket inside his jacket, and tickling my
ear with his breath, he began to read Pushkin's verses in the

*unfamiliar Uzbek language. I did everything I could to improve
my reception, even letting my mouth drop open to listen more
carefully. You know, I once had the opportunity to hear Pushkin
as performed by a Chinese translator. It was all clinging and
clanging, which of course did not get through too well. In Uzbek,
however, the words were even more melodious and grand than the
Pushkin we know. In this language Pushkin sounded less like
the cannon that his name implies and more like some sort of fire-
breathing machine launching fireworks into the heavens.*

*Finally the poet reached the end and stopped, as if he had
collided with an immovable barrier. I told him what I had been
pondering. The medical resident Sheikhov, taking my words to be
a national, collective compliment, said, 'Speak boundlessly! We
have got a long time ahead.'*

*Nazar opened a window, swinging it into the space of the night.
The wind billowing in his heart reached out for its freedom.
Nazar kept his hold on the window frame for a moment. The
moon, already low to the horizon, had been returning all the
rays it had borrowed in a lavish fashion, but the light from
our human lamps raced towards the stars and led our souls to
darkness.*

*'Tomorrow I will return to Ustyurt. Come with me,' he said
into the silence. 'There the sun sets, running up against swamps
on its way. The desert is too wide to be measured by numbers,
and it answers to nobody, except to the people whom fate has
cast out there.' His words were coming out in a rush from the
gloomy depths of his own thoughts. 'Darkness does not restrain
itself on the surface of the desert, and strangers can barely catch
a few tiny rays and sparks at sunset. Under the sand the soil is
salty, and as much as the people who come here try to tame it,
the earth overthrows them, it depletes the seeds of the men who
work the land, and no matter what they build, it all crumbles*

and collapses...'

'*He's quoting Avicenna,*' *the poet told me. As his words landed in my thoughts, having swept together the stupor that had seized those gathered there, Cho'lpon exclaimed that Nazar had just recited an excerpt from a tale not yet written.*

*Sheikhov, who had spent all this time watching alertly over the meaning of life as it sprinted past his eyes, cast aside all the pettiness of unclarity and said, '*Go, and answer the call of the new life! Let us start living, and planning to live! Your people have been given back life and are striving for life; you deliver to them the meaning of existence and our purpose!*'*

The agreement was unanimous. Nazar, leaving the dust of life in his tracks, walked out into the hallway. At that moment, the bells of the Kremlin clock tower rang out twelve times, gongs marching in the night.

EVENTS OF THE YEAR
OF THE HIJRA 1411

O unfortunate one, it is to these evil companions that
you have been bound, so that you may free yourself
of them only by fleeing your native country to such a
land where the likes of them may never set foot.

Avicenna, *Hayy ibn Yaqzan*

I wedged myself as best I could into the cabin on the
plane, with thirty dollars to my name, all generously
provided by the Writers' Union. I squeezed past the
passengers in their best squirrel-fur coats and skulked
into my seat near the tail part of the airplane. Would
my friend Zev meet me or not? I had sent him a telegram three days earlier but, strangely enough, there
had been no answer. I was so wrapped up in these
thoughts that I didn't even notice when the plane
took off, or when someone sat down in the seat next
to me. But when the stewardesses started passing out
wine, I drank, the way one does to soothe one's soul.

But it only made my sorrow grow stronger, and I had no friend next to me, no Sabit-aka or any other confidant to whom I could pour out my heart.

After flying across the vast ocean for four or five hours, we reached the other side of the world. We were passing over the islands of Newfoundland, which looked now like land, now like water beneath the wings of our plane. There was no way to tell them apart, pick out the water from the islands or the continent from other islands, and the sun, low in the sky, seemed to have paused in its own hemisphere to wave goodbye to us. In these new-found-lands there was not a single person, not a single living thing, just the swampy turf of dark-green vegetation and the wind racing along off on the horizon, preventing the rays of the setting sun from falling to the earth. I had never seen anything like it, no picture so majestic and so bleak. Newfoundland was a dejected place, where no human being set foot... and I remembered a part of the text I had memorised from my Avicenna:

> At the uttermost edge of the West there is a great muddy sea, which in the Book of God is named the Muddy Source. The sun sets there, and it meets the Muddy Source on its way. The space over which it has spread belongs to an uninhabited region, the width of which has never been measured, and none reside there, except for strangers who happen upon it unexpectedly. Darkness never leaves its surface, and settlers here catch only fragments of light as the sun slides towards its nightly resting place. The soil

*there is a desert of salt, and every time people settle there, trying
to plant their seeds and tame this land, it rejects them, and if
a few nevertheless find a footing here, they never do tame it;
everything comes to destruction, no matter what; everything falls
to dust.*

Anyway, after that we landed at JFK. And nobody
was there to meet me! I got change for a dollar and
phoned Zev's apartment. The answering machine
played a Turkmen melody and then recited some lines
from Magtymguly, the great Turkmen Sufi poet.

*Remember the teacher who gave you knowledge,
Poet, remember the people's acknowledgment,
Remember that esteem is greater than all wealth.*

I practically died right there. A taxi wasn't worth
thinking about, obviously. I couldn't even get halfway
there with the money I had. I stood there and pondered the godless world, the inhuman world I was
confronting, and then I dialled Zev's number once
more, impatiently. There was the Magtymguly again,
mocking me.

*Remember that esteem is greater than all wealth,
Poet, remember the people's acknowledgment.*

There was nothing else to do but to walk over to
the line of waiting taxi drivers. I listened – and I heard

them speaking Tajik. I'd be damned if they weren't all straight from Bukhara.

'*Koru-boreton nagzme!*' I started with a how-do-you-do in Tajik, and I brought out a copy of Pravda for them as a gift from their native land (I'd grabbed it on the plane, thinking I'd use it to line my formal shoes if was rainy in New York).

Those immigrants from Holy Bukhara couldn't get enough of me. 'Oy, braaather!' they said, even their Russian twisted by their dialect, 'You just tell us where you need to go, and we'll do it.'

After relieving me of twenty dollars, the Bukharans delivered me to 42nd Street. From there I picked up my suitcase and went down to the subway. Somehow I managed to locate Zev's address. I found the place, yes, but nobody was home.

It was a big apartment building, and if you made it through the front entrance, rattling off some explanation to the neighbours, you'd never get out again, because the door slams shut automatically, and the lock is encoded with some secret number; you just have to wait until one of the neighbours decides to go out. Sorting this out required so much talk I just about wore out my tongue. Finally, I gave up, tossed my suitcase into a corner by the door and set off down the street. I used half of the five dollars I had left to buy some pizza, and got change for the rest – then, as is fitting and proper in situations like this, I went to call on a Jewish family who had recently moved here from Tashkent.

These folks turned out to have much more human decency, so I didn't have to listen to any Turkmen melodies or to Magtymguly's voice long lost in the drifty desert. Their daughter picked up the phone.

I asked if her parents were at home. She said they were at work.

'When will they be back?'

'This evening.'

I objected, 'It's already evening!'

To which she answered, 'When it's even more evening.'

I ended up giving her some strict orders. 'You tell them Uncle Sheikhov called, and I'll be waiting outside at the corner of such-and-such and such-and-such street. If your father comes back, let him know I brought him something from Tashkent.' (And what might that be, you ask? Another do'ppi, of course!)

But I still couldn't calm down, and I went back to that same address and stood there like a doorman by the glass door, waiting for a wandering neighbour to appear.

If there is a saviour race on this planet, then it is

our post-Soviet Jews! It must have already been past ten – in New York, it's impossible to tell day from night, actually, it's so well-lit around here – when a car white as a bed sheet screeched to a halt in front of my door. When I looked, I saw none other than electrical engineer Edik climbing out, a man who used to fix his neighbours' televisions and refrigerators for free back in Tashkent.

I walked up to him, my arms wide open.

'Mr. Edik, isn't it? Well, well! Finally we meet again!'

As I yanked one of the skullcaps from Chust out of my pocket and went to put it on his head, who should I see emerging from the same car, his eyes overflowing with jealousy, but Zev! Now I, a displaced Uzbek, found myself in the company of two displaced Jews! Out of my depth, I started to introduce them to each other. Good thing I did, too, because neither knew the other, and they had shared the whole ride without speaking.

'You didn't send a telegram, you didn't call, I had to come from the other side of America.' Zev had reread the whole corpus of Uzbek literature starting from the previous century, and when he spoke it was always in shades of the poet Tavallo, for which his Bukharan accent was ideal, or of Qodiriy's *Kalvak*

Mahzum. 'How comes this servant of Allah, of the people of the book, to you?' And Zev pointed his index finger at the almost-Uzbek Edik.

Edik was no slouch in my native tongue, either, and answered in the Tashkent dialect. 'Beats me, bro! And up yours!'

I quoted Magtymguly.

> *Remember the teacher who gave you knowledge,*
> *Poet, remember the people's acknowledgment,*
> *Remember that esteem is greater than all wealth...*

What can I tell you? About how I was too shy to eat at Zev's place, so I only drank tea? Or about how I hiked all over New York? The master of the house gave me complete freedom. If I wanted to eat, he told me, I should find something in the refrigerator, and if not, I could sit there hungry. If I wanted to go out, nothing was stopping me, but Zev himself declined to keep me company. Not a real Uzbek, after all!

The human memory is imperfect, and by now I've forgotten a lot of what I once remembered.

But fine. We'll start from somewhere.

Of course I had my usual investigative mission, to find the elusive Avicenna, but I had come here with a cover story: to deliver a couple of lectures and make a little money. The thirty dollars from the Writers' Union had long since evaporated, but Zev told me,

'You sent that telegram too late. All the students are on vacation. Who are you going to lecture to?' And then he added, 'It's all right, we'll find a way,' and he spent the evenings calling the other side of the country.

Finally he had a plan for me. 'You'll fly to Seattle, via Texas, and you can stay there through the end of the break in a house right by the sea. The owner's a millionaire, filthy rich, and he'll be away the whole time. Then at the end of the month you'll do some teaching.'

'What about my family?' I asked. 'I only meant to come for two weeks, and my visa is only for two weeks, five days of which, by the way, have already passed.' Of course, it was my secret mission that worried me the most. But then Zev managed to make an arrangement for two lectures to be given nearby, at the end of my scheduled two weeks, and including a trip to Philadelphia, for two hundred dollars apiece – four hundred all told, in hard green cash. In the meantime, Zev himself went out to teach every day, and I wandered around the city.

*⁎⁎

One time, when Sina was busy tidying up and observing the life led by the brotherhood of bees, he was summoned for an audience with the Teacher. The Teacher lived in a cell in the very heart of the brotherhood's dwelling. All six walls of that cell were stronger than those of the other cells, and the fixtures were majestic. The irreproachable Sina passed through the ranks of a dozen caliphs, or guards, or servants, to bend low before the Teacher. The Teacher lay his face atop Sina's head, and drew him closer, and stretched out an arm towards Sina's arm. At the same time, without turning his face away, he gave a signal to the twelve who had just licked him all over, cleaning all the parts of his body, and they came to gather around the two, carefully shielding them from any outside observers. The Teacher's elevated spirit made Sina's heart melt, and, from inside his heart, his sadness for his mother and his involuntary dislike for the Teacher suddenly burst to the surface. An enormous sense of penitence had awoken in his tiny heart, and Sina could no longer raise his eyes, which pulsed with tension. The strange loyalty oath he took filled his throat with a bitter delight.

The Teacher could sense all of this. The sermon he delivered from under his beard addressed the oath Sina had just taken and the importance of loyalty to one's native dwelling; he spoke about pure abodes on the path of service and noble deeds, about eternal brotherhood and unity and the goal of spiritual cleanliness.

The Teacher whispered his teachings from under his whiskers, and Sina, bewitched by the fragrant aroma of this sermon, cleansed himself of all his spiritual sins and submerged himself in this warm stream of words. Left to themselves for some time now, the two folded their hands against their breasts, and concentrated their attention on their breathing, and the Teacher's prayer echoed three times in Sina's head.

Finally, the Teacher raised up both his hands and finished his rejoicing, and he grasped Sina by the cheeks and pulled the young bee's mouth to his own. Then the kingly sweetness, like a life-giving liquor, engulfed Sina's tongue in flame, and seemed to tie a knot in a thread linking the two hearts, eternally connecting him to his Teacher. Overwhelmed, Sina bowed down to the Teacher's hairy knees and kissed and embraced them. It seemed to him that the Teacher was secretly telling him, 'The feelings my heart senses, you can see with the eyes of reason. What is in your mind is in my soul.' And he whispered a blessing in Sina's ear.

Then, following the rules of etiquette, the young

bee stepped backwards, squeezed through the same dozen caliphs, and walked out of those majestic rooms. Now he had been set on the Path.

—

Ali ibn Ma'mun, Shah of Khorazm, having built his state on a foundation of justice and humanity, did not wish for his people to suffer in war, and he listened to the words spoken by his irreproachable Head Vizier. The next day, before a meeting with Hoja Hussein ibn Ali ibn Mikoil, he called together the learned and enlightened ones and placed the fates of Abu Sahl al-Masihi and Abu Ali Avicenna in their own hands, ordering them to prepare for a journey. But to Hoja Hussein, he said, 'Those two scholars have already set out on the road to Balkh, and the rest will follow in the coming days.'

Truly, soon after, a group of three scholars reached the fortress of Balkh. Of them all, the Sultan of Sultans, Yaminud-Davla, was most keen to see Avicenna, but he was not among that group of three, so the Sultan ordered Abu Nasr Mansur ibn Iraq to sketch him a portrait. When the portrait was ready, forty copies were made, and they were sent to the four corners of the world with an order from His Majesty: whosoever delivered news of this man would either be richly rewarded, or summarily executed.

—

In this world, someone who has learned something cannot keep that knowledge inside him. He wants to share it with others. It is the same with the bees. Every worker bee who receives the aromatic nectar of the queen bee develops a gland in his larynx that forms a sweet substance, which it then pours out again – just like a nurse giving her love to an infant – into still unformed, headless, stingless baby bees. Sina so loved his family that every day he saw to a thousand infants, fed them, swaddled them, wiped them clean and cuddled them close.

Of course, there was also another way to explain this. Just try to instil order around you, and you will see what your enlightened heart desires next. Out of cleanliness, you will see, grows love for those around you. The generous sun, in a clear sky, is the perfect illustration. On the other hand, what is there to prove here? Glands are glands, after all!

But the textbooks say that one other gland also grows in the bee's larynx, one that generates the royal jelly. This is used in emergencies, when enthroning a new Pasha. The fragment of human breath present in that gland made itself known, at night, when Sina was so tired from his nursing duties that he could no longer feel his arms or legs, and, just for a minute, he fell into a deep sleep in his cell. The pain emanating from that gland was reflected in his dreams. He dreamed of a blue-eyed girl child. Her father had not seen her for a year, and when they met again she kept her distance and would not go near him. But the bonds of blood finally prevailed, and the little girl's heart relented. Her lips pouted, and she threw herself into her father's arms, and he wanted to pick her up and squeeze her to him, this soft, slight, gentle little person, and straighten her wings and give her the feeling of flight...

But as those same textbooks will tell you, worker bees cannot have children. That is probably why their love is so pure.

—

At the end of the book called *Ma'ad*, Avicenna wrote that he had heard the following fable.

Once upon a time, in the inner chambers of the castle of the Samanids, the padishah was talking with a certain healer. And he ordered that a servant woman should bring him a meal. One of them appeared in the chamber, carrying on her head a dish of food, and she lifted the dish off her head and bent to set it on the ground. She bent and bent, but suddenly such a pain seized her that she could not stand up again.

'Lift her up!' the padishah commanded the healer. The healer was beset by doubt. How could he relieve this ailment when he had no medicine or drugs? Unless the very heat of the blood could banish the pain, nothing would help.

So the next moment, the healer said, 'Let her unfasten her cloak and loosen her hair!' Perhaps the shame and embarrassment would make her blood run faster, and increase the heat within her! They did what he said, but it did not help.

'Let her lower her pants and display her nether parts!' ordered the healer. Hearing those words, the servant was so ashamed that the blood rushed to her legs, and the pain released her, and this imperfect creature ran out of the king's chambers on her own two feet.

—

So what inside Sina was glands, and what was the soul of a living creature? There was so much that kept him busy. He cared for the infants, he served his drone brothers, and he worked alongside several other servants to prepare food for the Teacher and wash his bedclothes, so that His Excellency would not be distracted from his weighty affairs.

Those of his brothers who were drones turned out

to be quite strange. Descended from the greats, they themselves did not work. Instead they looked down on the worker bees and treated them with condescension, as though they were slaves and servants. One look at their solid bodies and stern visages was enough to make you want to throw yourself at their feet and ask what they demanded of you. When they felt like it, they'd brag and hog the glory at meetings, paying attention to nobody else. When they felt like it, they'd sit silently, putting on airs, alone, as if their mouths were full of water. They had no time for prayers, or ceremonies, or even customs. They were their own masters.

As spring arrived they flew off through the fields, like sheikhs looking for disciples who had wandered off into nature, but later, at their assemblies, one of them – one with long whiskers – would pronounce, 'Just think of it! There is not a single female I've left unsullied! I've stripped every single one of her virginity! How can we look at them, raising their sabres and stingers over yonder, without laughing? Look how stupidly self-important they are! Now check out this tool of mine! When I thrust this one in, it goes right to the hilt!' Then came their buzzing, roaring laughter as they rolled on the ground in mirth.

Sina was cleaning up after them when he

overheard this; not knowing where to turn, he suddenly remembered his own mother Pasha. But he tried to find in himself the strength to forget what he'd heard, and focus on his broom and bin, his shovel and scrubbing brush, his washing and waxing. So much work, and life was so short...

Bored of sitting around Zev's house, I ventured out to look for compatriots of mine (one in particular, as you know).

The first address I got from Zev himself. It turned out that a particular Uzbek merchant owned a store on a central avenue in Manhattan, a place called Nurata Ladies' Fashions. I went straight there, because its name reminded me of the Nuratau mountains. The good merchant, a man by the name of Ubaydullah Nurata, seemed quite used to visits from guests like me – barely pausing as he worked, he was able to order a cup of tea and some pizza over the phone, watch over his employees, and, at the same time, take an interest in his guest with a series of polite questions.

Now, you know us Uzbeks. We try to make ourselves bosom buddies, always ready to hoist a log up onto our friend's shoulder and then rush to help out

from the next region over. In just that way, I tried
with all my might to find out what Nurata's problems
might be, but the only thing that seemed to worry
Ubaydullah Nurata, Fashion Master, was that he was
getting distracted from work. He kept his answers
short: 'Yes. Maybe. We'll see.'

'Probably these capitalist Americans are clobber-
ing you with taxes?' I asked, as if speaking straight
from the heart. But in fact it was thanks to capitalism
that this merchant was earning his bread at all.

'Yes,' he agreed, out of respect for a fellow Uzbek.

I sat a while longer, and as if to pay him back for
the treats he had ordered me, I said, 'You should really
come open a store in Tashkent! They'd sweep your
shelves clean!'

'Maybe,' answered the sultan of style, not paying
too much attention.

'Okay, I'd better go — so much to do — need to
prepare for a lecture at Columbia University,' I told
him, inflating my own value a little.

'Okay,' came the profound response. But in the
end, the Uzbek mentality prevailed within him, as
well. 'Stop in again when you have time, all right?' he
said as he waved goodbye.

I did in fact go back to Nurata's store, and there I
met an Uzbek who had been born, as it turned out,

in Kattakurgan: his name was Sharaf Alibek, and he was sitting in Nurata Fashions wrapped up in an overcoat. Unlike me, he wasn't trying to be helpful at all. He was too occupied with his own thoughts. And now, leaving the owner of the store to carry on with his business in peace, he and I got down to talking like the do-nothings we were.

For hereditary Uzbeks like Nurata, born in the US, or in Afghanistan, or in Turkey if they're lucky, Uzbekistan is just a distant legend. But Sharaf-aka had been drafted into the war in Tashkent in 1941, and he knew things I didn't know about Uzbekistan. So it was interesting for me to listen to him, and my stories were interesting to him, because after all, he had left our mutual homeland before any of the events I had witnessed.

What a conversation we had! He warmed to his role, singing songs he had heard in a teahouse from Mullah Tuychi Khafiz in the 1940s, while I took the high notes from the repertoire of Nasiba Abdullayeva and Munajat Yulchiyeva. Our conversation seemed to have expanded enough to breach the walls of that little shop, and finally Sharaf-aka said, 'Well now, let's go to my place. I left the cart around the corner,' prompting a vivid image to appear in my mind of a horse-drawn cart parked on Lexington Avenue.

Nothing of the sort! His cart turned out to be a Ford, the very latest model. Seeing the dumbstruck expression on my face, my blue-eyed compatriot explained, 'I was a car salesman, once, in my time.'

I rode around all afternoon with Sharaf-aka, and truly, there was no language he did not know. On top of everything else, he was an exact match for a character from my novel *The Railroad*, the green-eyed Mullah Ulmas! 'Ya, onara!' he said, starting a conversation with the Koreans we wanted to buy cabbage from. With the Chinese selling rice, he chatted away in Chinese. And with the Persians, a people close to us, he opened with some memorised lines of poetry. I only had to mention once that I needed to call home, and he took me to a payphone, dialled a particular number, had a quick, lively exchange with some woman from Guyana, and convinced her to put aside all the international rules governing telecommunications – after which I was connected with my wife. Bravo, my Uzbek, bravo!

—

I remember those cold December days. I think about the life of that Uzbek man I met that day in Nurata's shop, full of days with as little warmth in them as these. He has a house, and two young daughters, sixteen and thirteen years old, who live with their mother. He has a car, he has a girlfriend, some Pole or Czech woman, even though he's past seventy now, but despite all that, it seemed to me that his heart remained all too full of sadness, just like these December days. And when it came to me, there was no burden he would not bear! He would pick me up at night and take me somewhere to play pool, or use my arrival to justify collecting his daughters from his wife's house and treating us to strawberries and cream, or drift around among the local Uzbeks – but whatever the case, no matter what he was doing, his heart remained somewhere else, far away. Where his heart should have been there was an emptiness, one even I could feel. Even a country like America was an alien place for him.

At night, when we were getting ready to sleep, he always handed me a pair of pyjamas, in the American manner. 'Here you have to give your guest pyjamas,' he told me as he directed me to the shower. And once I was showered and getting into bed, he would sigh heavily, and say, 'Maybe you can find me a girl to marry. I don't even care if she's from a backwater like Kattakurgan, just as long as she's from our native country.' In those words, there was not a single drop of derogatory feeling, and not a particle of passion − nothing but a longing for his homeland, a bare, naked sadness.

And what stories he used to tell! 'One time I travelled to the sea, the ocean, they call it, and we were swimming in it, and there was a fish, a whale, they call it − throwing out water just like that. A fountain, they call it. Oh yes, I have seen such things! And then one time we were in a land called Australia. They've got real Lilliputians there, you'd never believe it, just four feet tall, barely up to my waist. They're called Bushmen. Look and see if you don't think it's a miracle! I've made the Hajj fifteen times. Once during a pilgrimage, on Mount Arafat, a snake crawled out right in front of me, a cobra. It unwound itself and looked at me. As soon as I prayed to God to protect me from this devil − *A'udhu billahi min ash-shaytaan-ir-rajeem!* − away it crept!'

This same man brought me to a demonstration that took place in front of the United Nations building before Turkestan Day. But more about that later.

It is boundlessly difficult to be a stranger. Your usual ways of behaving bear no fruit: if your habits are not fit for purpose, you might as well be a wheel off its axle, alone over and over again. In a country where working men and women make up the whole foundation of society, one corner, just for form's sake, is given over to them by the masters of the land. If they feel like it, they can turn it into a gymnasium, or perhaps a place to relax after a visit to the museum.

Gymnasiums, like Soviet workers' clubs, are the same everywhere. There are no chairs to sit on, just plank benches hung on hinges that give out an unforgettable squeal. As you walk inside this structure, closed off on three sides, you think you've finally found a place where you can recover your breath, begin to nurture your own heart, in hopes of at some point dissolving into this uncomfortable disorder, into this grey, colourless semi-darkness, among these discarded piles of clothing awaiting the bodies of their owners. But in the end, you begin to understand that this is a place for prayer, specifically for the women who work here. And this feeling of awkwardness is even more terrifying than your fear of being among women, as a Muslim, as a servant of God from the long-suffering East...

You draw back from this unsuitable place, and you hide behind a column, but now your prior experience dictates that you should subtly look around you. The place you have retreated to is in the men's section, but that makes it no easier; the men have already formed a circle. In the middle of that circle, as if in a dervish's hut, there is a servant, half sitting, half lying down, accompanying every beat with a word of some sort – maybe in Arabic, common to all Muslims, maybe in his own language, now splintered off – now he bends low, now he claps his hands, now he touches his palms to his forehead. The others are equally unfamiliar. You've never seen them before. This circle, in a corner of the gymnasium itself, starts to spin, faster and faster, like a grain mill, regardless of the fact that in some other corner of the gym there is an old television barking out the news. The cycle of their joint movements is reaching a crescendo. The words fly apart and collide together, like the last drops in a centrifuge. They complete their rejoicing and are carried towards heaven, and from one side comes the head trainer, or head dervish, into the circle, who blows on these bodies lying supine and lifeless, covering them with incantations as if sprinkling water on their faces.

And you do not know what to do. Join them? Go back? Or cut right through this corner of the workers' club and emerge again outside?

Now of all the things to happen, at this very point in writing my notes, I came across a diary, my notebook from those days. On the one hand, what is written is

written, and I do not have the slightest desire to go
and cross anything out. On the other hand, the notes
I made back then now seem much too raw.

2 December

Endless discussions over poetry... Coughing...

*Discussion of theoretical ideas began with Naili and ended in
Hindi style.*

Partial complication...

*A method that analyses change in syntax. For the Turkic
languages, every change in syntax is an extraordinary event,
leading to a higher level of change in semantics. As a consequence:
the syntax of the language of poetry (the divan) and prose (the*
Baburnoma, *Navoiy's* Munshaat).

*

*Where lies the chief principle of composition in Farsi? What
surrounds it: the synthesis of meaning, or style?*

To decide, let's compare the dialogues in Navoiy's Holoti
Pahlavon Muhammad, *which make no claim about 'style' and
are endowed with no functions of 'style', with the syntax in the*
Munshaat, *which strives for 'immortality' at the very highest level
of quality and quantity.*

*And the unification of all of this in Turkic and Urdu poetry.
Striving of isolated bits of poetry to conceal their beginnings and
ends. In that case, perhaps the best bayt (or ghazal) is the one
that has nothing in common with any other? Then where are its
borders, and what are they made of? If we are going to violate
syntax and mutilate words, then perhaps the most Uzbek verse of
all is a verse written in Russian?*

*

As I've already said, a border is a wall: the presence of a beginning and an end (birth and death, original and final).

Isn't it the case in Urdu that when the authors of ghazals begin their works from the middle, there is a striving there for the illusion of overcoming that border?

★

But that is in fact the impetus for poetry. We can say it's the same as the very worst qualities of Russians, their ignorance of all their bad qualities...

Poems and coughing...

The presence of the absence of money...

★

'In illness it is for health we strive,
In secretive love we lust to survive.'
—Naili

★

Coughing...

7 December

So I have still not written about how I went to the library, or about how annoyed I was. I should never have dredged up the memory, because now I'm angry again.

The thought had occurred to me to make my present whereabouts official. I hoped that I wouldn't have to be a twenty-dollar guest of any one person, but instead would be a real guest of some state institution, a guest with some use.

But they put a damper on that hope right away. Instead they turned the whole thing around in the other direction — to their own benefit. As if I'm a prisoner here, rather than a guest. A twenty-dollar prisoner.

I'll never set foot here again! And where is that anger that had managed to settle down? Now my heart is turning to stone! Could I also act on principle, and effect a 100% change in my own status?

I went to the library. They had none of my books there. I asked them to send me some. They gave me a request form.

Where was that governmental support? Where were all the institutions that needed me? Or maybe I shouldn't be getting so hot under the collar. Maybe I should just blow it off. But I was well and truly pissed off. I didn't have the strength to think any more. I couldn't. And I can't get back on my feet, I'm like a boxer laid out by a knockout punch!

The next day I occupied myself with a lecture or something else. Is this really what I'm worth?

I've quarreled with America. Goodbye, America! Goodbye, voice of America! I'm going home, back to my family. What's done is done!

Respect! Human dignity! Ha!

Maybe I should learn to write about made-up joys. 'Hey!' I'll say, 'At least I'm in America!' America is deaf.

The night before 16 January, while the US was attacking Iraq, the prophet Jesus sat down across from me. In fact it was nearly impossible to tell whether the person was a woman or a man, but his face shone with the light of a kind, gentle smile. Some of that light came from the slightly narrow eyes, and a second stream poured out of the thin lips to merge with his words.

'Yes, it is I. I have come to help you. I want to help you. I will help you.'

His words were as simple and even as light, clear and precise as day, so much so that it seemed to me there was no need to have faith, not even faith in the very concept of faith. And so on, and so forth.

EVENTS OF THE YEARS
OF THE HIJRA 1350–1411

So you must be satisfied with the journey, and with the stops along the way; this is the time to be on the road and to be occupied with them. If you give yourself over to your journey with zeal, I will join with you, and you will part ways with them; but if you mourn for them, you will return to them, and be parted from me. So shall it be until such time as you break with them once and for all.

Avicenna, *Hayy ibn Yaqzan*

And the Sheikh said, 'Once you purify your outside and inside, the station of the seeker is asceticism.'

Then they asked Junaid of Baghdad, 'What does it mean to be an ascetic?'

He answered, 'It means to keep your hands free of possessions, and your heart free of envy.'

Sari al-Sakoti said, 'What the hands are forbidden to touch is also forbidden to the heart.'

Other Sufis have reached an even higher station. About asceticism, Ruvim bin Ahmad said, 'It is a separation from everything that gives pleasure to your carnal soul.'

But more perfect still was the definition of the elect brothers. When Sheikh Abu Bakr Shibli was asked about asceticism, he answered, 'Asceticism is the state of ignorance, because our life in this world is nothing. And abstention in nothingness is indeed ignorance.'

At that level, asceticism transforms into selfless devotion.

———

A bee grows up bodily, step by step. Feeding jelly from his own larynx to a thousand infants every day had its effect, and the glands in Sina's honey stomach grew larger and stronger. This was reflected both in his outwards appearance and in his inner state: inside his body, his wax glands matured, out of which there began to flow a wax reminiscent of the rays of the sun. For this reason, Sina began to feel he was a builder.

In his innermost thoughts, he interpreted these changes in the most magnificent light: inner purity was naturally being reborn in love for those around him, and love requires action. It demands that work be done, for its own protection.

Just look at the dark-eyed little Uzbeks. No

sooner have they learned to wipe their own noses than they've begun toting their younger brothers around. The big brother lays his little sister in the pram, and sets about kneading mud to lay bricks, and finds a way to drag that bucket of mud, which weighs more than he does himself, across the yard, and soon he knows how to erect, if not a whole house, then at least a wall for the kitchen.

Sina, too, built cell after cell, room after room. It was easy to distract himself with everyday business, and it was an interesting thing to do. But every type of work has a progression of difficulty. First, Sina took part in preparing the wax for the walls. Next he started using that wax to fill gaps that appeared in the cells. When his eyes could remember everything and his hands had got the hang of it, he put up a wall himself, under the supervision of an older bee. After that, he evened out a corner between two walls. By the end of the first day, Sina had already begun building six-sided rooms all by himself, and later he would suspend the arches over them. When somebody told the story of Bibi-hanum and the architect, to keep their work moving along, Sina imagined himself as that architect, and he blushed. In a word, the young, blossoming Sina worked as if he could never grow tired.

———

Now let us return to our main purpose. Abu Ali Avicenna and Abu Sahl al-Masihi travelled a path of fifteen farsangs. In the middle of the desert, Avicenna turned to the most miraculous of the arts, astrology, and used the stars to predict their fate. After he had determined the locations of the constellations he needed, and the axes around which they acted on destiny, it became clear that their path was not without danger. Abu Sahl occupied himself with measuring the heavenly bodies that shone in the sign of Capricorn, an omen of separation and parting. 'God is great, and even hope in Him enlightens the mind. The most important thing is for our spirits to remain as one,' said Abu Sahl. They continued on their way.

On the fourth day, a hot summer wind arose. The sky darkened with a blackness impossible to describe in words. Though their guide was a resident of this desert, he lost his way. Everything was covered with sand, and their food and skins of fresh water were lost.

Out of these unprecedented sufferings, the strength was sapped from Abu Sahl's body, and in the hour before sunset he stood before his Creator. They bathed his body in their tears, and began to dig a grave for him in the sand, which was constantly refilling, because all the sand they dug out simply flowed back into the hole.

Finally, Abu Sahl's body, which they had wrapped in the cloth from his turban and laid on the leeward side of a dune, was carried to the grave and placed inside it, and covered with yet more sand. Avicenna led the burial ceremony, strictly according to the rules. After the rites were complete, they paid tribute to the deceased man by spending the night alongside his grave. Only after the morning prayers were finished did they continue on their way.

The guide headed in one direction, and Avicenna in the other. But at noon – praise be to Allah, who showed them the way! – they met again, at the only well along their path. After that incident, it was eight days and eighty-eight hardships later that they finally reached a village by the name of Bavard, and from there the guide joined a caravan and headed back towards his own home country, while Avicenna took the road to Tus and Nishapur.

Then the Sheikh said, 'The road from danger to hope is the same as moving weights from one pan of the scale to the other.'

—

Only later did Sina recognise that, without realising it, he had also been building himself.

But if you don't trust the bee's interpretations, then perhaps you will trust a psychologist like Jung.

—

According to Jung, what you see in your dreams – majestic palaces, medieval buildings or even huts and hovels – symbolises your entrance into your own subconscious, into your own fears and your own reason. What you have built consciously remains on the outside, but what you build quietly, secretly, imperceptibly gets hidden deep inside you. Here is what I myself see, most of all, in my dreams: always exactly the same stone palaces, in which the staircases stretch towards the ceiling in a high, heavenly arch. And truly, those staircases always break off at the same point; after all, *you* are not the one who built them. After that, you need to either launch off the ground to continue along your path, or break out of the dream back into reality – but in either case, that means flying. One choice is full of hope and ecstasy, and the other means the imprisonment and diminution of the soul. But the beam linking those two pans on the scale is your own interrupted, yet righteous, path to the heavens.

Soon I want to tell you about Bamberg, but for now

I'll start with how, in the month of Mizan in 1411, I left Bamberg and travelled to a village by the name of Balrechten, where there lived a Frau Arlette, the friend of one of our acquaintances. My wife and daughter had already arrived, just a bit before me, and I was about to be reunited with them. We stayed here for five or six days, during which we paid several visits to Freiburg. Then we went for a picnic on the hilly slopes of the Black Forest, dense with legend, and we went boating on the lakes, and only after that did we decide to leave that generous Frenchwoman who had adopted the German way of life and head for France ourselves. When I said that she had practically become German, I was thinking about her thriftiness. She would turn on the hot water, for instance – but since the water doesn't flow hot right away, she would collect the initial, tepid water in a pot, saying, 'Let nothing be wasted! We have to pay for it, all the same,' and she would use that to water the flowers.

I made the decision to go to France under the influence of my latest dream about the Sheikh-ar-Rais. But, as often happens with Soviet people, there was a problem: our daughter didn't have a visa for France.

Well, that's all right, we thought, as we loaded a suitcase the weight of a shipping container on top of

Arlette's tiny car, making the vehicle sit a little lower on its wheels like a neglected rubber ball, and somehow crammed ourselves in the car, too, and took off towards the border. In fact, we had learned a little trick on our trip to visit Arlette. People had told us that the train stations and airports were well-secured, but that the secondary roads across the borders were not supervised all that strictly. So that is the kind of road we took that day.

German roads! What would you rather hear about first, the avenues or the pavements? Shall I mention the autobahn, and how once you drive on, you can't get off until the next town? Or the rural roads, winding around the curves of the mountain slopes, as bendy as a grapevine growing in the foothills? Or the dark forest highways, wide enough for only one car at a time? Ah, German roads...

We arrived at the border between Germany and France. We had seated my daughter between me and my wife, and as if nothing were happening at all, we began singing the Marseillaise at top volume. Since the car had German plates, and there was a German citizen at the wheel (actually a blonde Frenchwoman), the border guards satisfied themselves with a single glance inside and one look at the suitcase secured to the roof. Obviously thinking we had nothing to hide, they decided not to pester us, and let us through.

So there we were in France. It felt like coming home. I told you about the German roads. But the French roads are just like ours, uneven, and full of ruts, as if last year's fallen leaves had already been covered up with a new layer. So we may as well have been back in the motherland! Soon we arrived at Mulhouse, the first small city past the border.

—

Now let me tell you one story connected with the border that will not in fact happen to me until later.

Two and a half years after these events, in the spring of the year of the Hijra 1413, during a time when I was working in Germany, in the city of Essen, I had to return to Germany in order to extend my German residency permit.

Let me explain. On the surface, the law said I no longer had the right to extend my stay in Germany. That being the case, the Germans, taking pity on me, said I would have to re-enter the country – it didn't matter from where. Then I'd be able to get a new residency permit, for a year or maybe even longer. If I were to go home, then obviously I'd never get back in again. I thought it over and decided to go to France.

(You understand, by now, what was inspiring me to keep moving from country to country.) But I didn't have a guest visa for France, either. Oh, who cares, I thought, and I set off. As usual I scraped together all the cash I had, and comforting myself with the thought that it was all for my family's sake, I got on an express train.

Once aboard I put on one of my most stylish suits, knotted a tie around my neck, and sat posing with a book in my hand, all very chic. A couple of times I bought coffee and drank it down, even though it was expensive. I can still remember those little cups. Basically, for all appearances, I was a serious business-man.

As we approached the border, German border guards strolled through the moving train, looking us each in the face. I sighed, but kept up my serious expression.

Again the door opened, and now some French border guards walked through. That's when I put my head down to work. And maybe because I was the only one in the whole compartment working, they headed straight for me. '*Votre passeport?*' they asked, the good-for-nothings.

I dug around extravagantly in my pockets, and pulled out the red passport that caused me so much embarrassment. No, it was not just red — it was as scarlet as my face. It was their turn to do some digging, and when they were done, they asked me one polite question: 'Where is your French visa?'

'Isn't it in there?' I asked, as if much surprised, and I decided to start off with derision. 'I'm on my way now to put my documents in order. They are in, as you say, *la stade de regularization*.' I even tried scaring them. 'I am a famous writer, and I am late for a meeting with my readers. If they are inconvenienced, you will have to answer for it!'

But all that had no effect whatsoever. They grabbed my bag and, in front of everyone, very impolitely, they kicked me and some sorry-looking Arab off the train. We turned out to be at the last German station before the border.

There we both sat in a room belonging to the border guards, or maybe the police. The officer in front of me was filling out a report about my attempt at an unlawful border crossing. When they began the personal inspections, they found a powdery substance in the Arab man's pocket — so the French started assuming that we were drug smugglers! 'That's it, Mr. Famous Author! Sheikhov, you called yourself? Next we'll lock you away in jail with your brother Muslim, and you can chew up whatever is left of those drugs!'

But do you know who came to my aid then? The writer, poet and translator Hamid Ismailov. That's what it means to be famous! But actually what happened is that after they failed to find even crumbs of that garbage in my pockets, they decided to search my bags, and there they found Ismailov's French translations of Alisher Navoiy and Boborahim Mashrab. No offense to my friend Hamid, but to be honest, I had brought along those books he had given me so I could sell them and use the money to maybe cover some of my expenses on this trip.

'What's this?' the border-police officer suddenly asked me.

'Books,' I replied.

'Whose books?' he asked, leafing through one of them, and probably he came to the part with the foul language in the poem by Mashrab (who, legend has it, called opium 'the shit of the pharaohs'), and he looked at me and smiled.

'Mine,' I replied.

'You wrote this yourself?' he asked, thinking perhaps I had been honest when I claimed to be an author.

'Yes!' I shot back, as if offended by such a question.

'Then why is your name different?' he asked, pointing to the names of Mashrab and Navoiy.

'Those are my pseudonyms,' I retorted.

Trying to hide his rising interest, this cheerful book-lover in an uncheerful place told me, 'I'm confiscating these books.' As far as I was concerned, he could do whatever he liked in this game of ours, just as long as he didn't stamp my passport.

He pointed at the Arab, and asked, 'What do you need that guy for?'

'He's my apprentice,' I lied, a sudden sense of Muslim solidarity arising from who knows where. In the final analysis, this orphaned Arab also found salvation as an apprentice of Mashrab and Navoiy. But to be fair, I'll say that they still put a stamp in *his* passport.

It turned out the Arab was a bit fanatical by nature. 'Let's go, we'll cross that border on foot!' he said, exhorting me to join in his escapade.

'No, my friend,' I said. 'I think I'll go back to town and call my friends. Maybe one of them can pick me up or has some pull with the border guards.' At that, I parted with my coreligionist, and we went our separate ways. I rode the border guards' train to the lovely city of Saarbrücken, and he, after pulling out from his jacket pocket a clump of some dried substance and tossing it in his mouth, headed off towards the swamp in the direction of France.

I arrived in Saarbrücken after sunset. Everywhere I looked, billboards were gleaming and vendor stalls were beckoning. I walked all through the city. When you look closely, history aside, all German cities are exactly alike, especially right in the middle of town. Where I come from, when we talk about the city centre, we mean a mosque or a marketplace, or, in Soviet times, the square where the district committee or city committee or provincial committee had its offices. But the centres of all German cities begin with a train station. The starting point is the train station, and the end point is the market square. Between those two points, traditionally, there is a pedestrian walkway, lined on both sides by an endless procession of every possible type of small shop. Sometimes, as I've said, you can look up above the stores and see a historic church or cathedral rising up into the sky, but then, after that, there are more stalls and kiosks. Saarbrücken turned out to be just the same kind of town.

At six in the evening, according to German tradition, all the stores closed, with just a few sex shops and a couple of cinemas remaining open. I had no money to see a film, so I had no other choice – I had to walk into one of those shamelessly indecent stores. In the best of them, on the walls up near the ceiling, television screens were hanging, showing a thousand scenes of sexual intercourse. It was the shopkeepers, mainly, who were watching them. The more modest stores only sold magazines. With nothing else to do, you might as well ask them for some rare book, like the old Indian *Minutes of Delight* or the *Ananga Ranga.* 'We don't have those,' they'll answer you, surprised. But it's a good way to justify walking into the inferno; now you can leave the store at ease, having touched nothing. But you can goggle over this kind of contagion a thousand times, and it never stops being attractive.

Again, completely inappropriately, your thoughts turn to Avicenna.

> *The man on your left is a sloven, a glutton and a lecher; only dust will fill his bowels, only the earth will satisfy his lust. Licking, lapping, devouring, desiring, he is as a pig long kept starving, then released into the dung pile.*

There might be some bars open, as well. But you have no money for them. In short, after you fill a couple of hours walking around like that, you figure it must be a good time to go to your friend's place, the friend who lives on the other side of the border, and you phone him. And how infuriating it is to learn that just today he left for Paris.

That is the state I was in, as I walked, not knowing

my destination, cursing myself for having sinned by
entering that filthy store, something God was clearly
punishing me for now. But here I sensed that next to
me, alongside me, somebody was walking in the same
direction I was headed.

Well, I thought, I'll ask him if he knows where
I can find a cheap hotel. I made my best effort to
explain myself in German. He seemed happy enough
to speak with me, and in his own broken German, he
asked, compassionately, 'Are you new in town?'

I looked again and realised that, although he
looked just like a German on the outside, this man
was a genuine Turk.

Overjoyed, I switched to Turkish. 'Are you
Turkish?' I asked him.

It turned out his name was Rishat, and he was
just about of an age to retire, and we had met while
he was on his way to see his mistress. 'Come along
with me! My girlfriend is a communist, and she'll be
delighted to see you!' my new arkadash exclaimed.
'And you should taste her belyashi!' old Rishat went
on, showing off his knowledge of communist vocab-
ulary.

So we went to her place. A one-bedroom flat,
cozy, no particular luxuries. When I saw the books

we all used to read, I let it slip that I was a writer – and then the conversation really took off.

It was midnight before I had a chance to tell them my reason for visiting this town. 'I want to cross the border into France,' I said, my voice sounding as decisive as good communist style would dictate.

'Then you will certainly cross it!' Gerta announced, brimming with proletarian hatred for borders of all kinds. Knowing full well that communism had started with her countrymen before it spread to the Turks and all the other people like us, this enterprising woman took all the organisational matters upon herself. 'You call Mehmet,' she told Rishat. 'Have him get his car ready by morning. Meanwhile I'll make the beds, and then I'll study the map. We'll leave at six o'clock sharp!'

True to the ideals of communist morality and human justice, this miniature woman made up three separate beds in three separate places. In this adventure, even poor Rishat's amorous interests had to be put to one side. In revenge, the old Turk snored all night, enough to make you think he wasn't allowed to do it at home.

The next day we got up with the sun and headed out to see this Mehmet. And so I had the honour of getting better acquainted with the Turkish working class of Germany. The poor wretches, as I eventually learned, were almost all married to German communist women. Interesting how things worked out. On the one hand, the German bourgeoisie and capitalists were screwing the Turkish working class, while on the other hand, they, the Turkish working class, were screwing the female half of the German population. In the best possible sense, of course! It turned out that Mehmet's wife, too, had been a communist, at least until he divorced her, after her own set of German Turks knocked her up a couple of times. However, in the European manner, Mehmet kept his ex-wife's portrait in the place of honour in his home, there among the dishes in the drawing room. 'So that I'll never forget that bitch of an infidel,' he said.

He shared those memories with us as he filled up his car, which required siphoning some petrol from another worker's car parked nearby. Off we went, concentrated on our goal. The day had started out sunny, but it was clouding over now, and as we approached the border the rain really poured down. Not likely the border guards would be standing out on watch in this deluge, I thought, trying to calm myself, but I was trembling as I sat there in the back seat. Naturally, if I got caught again, no Navoiy or Mashrab would be able to help me. But Rishat and Mehmet told me,

'Don't worry! If anything happens, we'll say we're just showing you around, and we accidentally crossed into France.' As if anyone would trust that proletarian simplemindedness of theirs!

But we crossed the border in an instant, with the swiftness of a true master performing a circumcision. And now either they'd take off after us or we'd dart away nimbly to freedom, kicking the car into high gear. We flashed through the rain over the wet asphalt, but after half an hour we were well and truly lost, and in the end, we found ourselves driving up to a place we'd been before – the border checkpoint! If you could have seen what a state I was in! Worse than a cat soaked in the rain. Under the cover of that deluge, we turned back again. 'This time I won't muck it up,' Mehmet vowed. And the communist hero kept his word! He brought me to some little French village, and there these honourable Turks unloaded me, like a bulldozer dumping its load, and turned right around and hurried back home.

Naturally, the place where I got out was right across from a police station, full of genuine French gendarmes. Taking advantage of the rain yet again, I tossed my hood up over my head and, concealing myself like a woman in the East hides from strange men under her burqa, I ran quick as I could in the direction my eyes led me. So as not to attract any suspicion, after a little while I walked into a Crédit Lyonnais, where I had an account with four francs waiting in it.

I peered around the room seriously for a little while, trying to look like I'd either lost something or found something interesting, and as I left, I asked an old woman, 'Where is the bus stop?'

But fear has big eyes, as they say, and this old woman asked me, out of the blue, 'Are you a stranger here?'

Maybe for the first time in my life I put aside all my French circumspection. 'I asked you,' I hissed at her, 'about the bus!'

After such an unceremonious response, the old lady hurried to show me the way. I thanked her wholeheartedly, and I finally found the bus stop. After half an hour of a rain to end all rains, I got on the bus. It was only after I had ridden to a city named Metz that I was able to sigh in relief. Now I had really been in France!

—

Back in the present, here in the town of Mulhouse, where the German Frenchwoman Arlette had driven us, the very same feelings enveloped me. I was really in France now! France had become like a lover to me. Once you're in her embrace, whether or not you have any right to be there, that embrace washes away all the lies, all the difficulties, all the hardships that beset you on your way there.

10 January 1939
It has now been ten years since we arrived at this place. Today I received a letter from Mariam that tore my soul apart. I dropped my work and left the house. It was snowing, mixed with rain. I walked along the Werke canal, and came out at St. Michael's. I cut through the garden. Despite the slush, it was a picture that enchanted with its orphaned air. Apples not yet fallen sparkled in the tree branches. It reminded me of our mountain valley. The Domplatz, Cathedral Square, was deserted. Soldiers were swarming around the Rathaus. A loudspeaker at the market was broadcasting the Führer's speech from the previous day. I walked off to one side, pretending to be on my way to the university. Helga has still not returned.

14 March 1939
It seems that war is imminent.

15 March 1939
I found a document at the Stadtarchiv. It said that in the early seventeenth century, a group of emissaries arrived in Coburg from the Ottoman Empire. According to that document, the mission included a certain Muslim from outside the Empire, whose native land was called the country of the Turks. This stranger parted

ways with the travelling embassy and headed for one
of the monasteries located in this land. I requested
more documents to review tomorrow. The archivist
suggested that I have a look at the documents in the
city library. I remember reading somewhere that in the
late nineteenth century, the Hungarian scholar Vámbéry
brought a Muslim man to Europe with him, allegedly to
find out whether a man from the East could acclimate
himself to the culture of the West. Some have the same
attitude today to students from our country. Surprisingly
enough, while Nazism is gathering strength, I have seen
no racism against Turkestanis, since they classify us
neither with the Russian Slavs nor with the Jews, and
even say they'd like to free us from their control, as if
rescuing a beloved pet... Helga takes the same attitude
to me. Her father, who forbade her from marrying an
evangelische Protestant, had not a single cross word
to say when she brought me home with her. He only
mentioned the work of Vámbéry and Radloff, and asked
whether they had mostly written about us or about
the Tungus in Siberia. In response I told him about our
Avicenna and al-Marginoni, and also Ulugbek and Abu
al-Ghazi. To that, he had nothing to say. Four years have
passed since then.

From the Stadtarchiv building, I walked downhill to
the riverbank. A pair of willow trees grow there, their
swollen buds ready to burst. I strolled by, remembering
our Anhor canal in Tashkent. Higher up the hill, lining
the river, the houses were hung with clean laundry that
waved in the breeze. From there, I walked down the
narrow alleyways to Domplatz. I would have liked to go
into the city library and request those documents, but
it was closed. All the employees had been called up for
military training. At that point, I summoned up an image
of that Muslim stranger. What had brought him to these
parts?

On my way home, I stopped by the post office and

mailed a letter to Tohir Chagatay. Today I must write to
Uktay.

17 March 1939

I spent all day yesterday at the Stadtarchiv, straight
through till evening. One document says that this
Muslim stranger met two Jesuits, and had a long
conversation with them about religion and faith. The
Jesuits mentioned that conversation in the letters
they sent to their central office. But they were here
in Bamberg on a secret mission, and they feared the
Inquisition, and as such, they begged this Muslim man
to be careful, and tried to bring him over to their side.
This document has the inventory number XZ 703.
Another document (numbered F 103-21) mentions the
monastery at St. Michael's, where these two Jesuits
appear among the monks using Catholic names. At the
same time that they surfaced at the monastery, a deaf
and dumb gardener was hired to work there. I found no
information about this gardener yesterday or today, but I
have reason to suspect he is in fact the Muslim traveller.
Today I went to the city library and sifted through books
and documents pertaining to St. Michael's, but I found
nothing worthwhile other than a book dating to the
nineteenth century.

Before now I had no idea of how these monks lived.
They awoke before sunrise, at three o'clock in the
morning, and began their prayers. At nine o'clock, after
an hour's nap, they devoted themselves assiduously to
their prayers once again. Aside from their three daily
meals, everything revolved around prayer, with any
remaining time dedicated to chores, and again, after
sunset, there were the evening and night-time prayers,
with the next day beginning just three or four hours
later. So inspiring is all of this to me that I've decided
I, too, must begin sleeping as little as possible. I
remember when I was in Berlin. I used to wake up at six

o'clock, if not five, and begin work on my German, then after a small breakfast I would leave for the institute, spend all day at lectures and seminars, then move on to the library. Other than two meals, it was nothing but studies, studies, studies.... Those were such happy times!

Then Madjidovich arrived, and my friends returned to Tashkent. At first we received no replies to the letters we sent them, and then we learned, from fellow Uzbeks who had left for Turkey, that they had been arrested. Uktay and I were supposed to return, ourselves, very soon, but we now had little doubt that we would be arrested as well. That was when Vali Qayumhon interceded, and we received a letter from Paris. When I read that letter I was terrified at first, because it was written in such a nationalistic spirit that merely casting eyes upon it seemed equivalent to treason. But it was extremely difficult to refute anything written there. Uktay and I, and Tohir Chagatay who had come to join us, spent that night in heated, indeed flaming, argument. I expressed my feelings about universal education, while Tohir brought up how our poets, like Cho'lpon and Fitrat, were living out their days at present; and Uktay spoke of our women, who now, by revolutionary tradition, went about with their faces uncovered, and Tohir pointed out how the new alphabet had torn us away from our past. We had reached no agreement by the time morning arrived.

In the end, Vali Qayumhon himself came into the room and handed us a telegram. It said that the Bolsheviks had executed the nationalist Munavvar Qori. Now we knew our way home was cut off for good. That man, after all, had played a direct role in sending us here to Germany.

But I've strayed off track. The woman working at the city library gave me a letter of recommendation for the cathedral library. I arrived there just after noon, and stumbled across a document that made me think I needed to write an article immediately and send it to Young Turkestan for publication.

According to this ancient document, the road from the cathedral to Michaelsberg Abbey was divided into seven stations, and I could match those stations with the seven steps of Sufism. These seven stations also signified the seven stops Jesus Christ made on his way to the cross. They were as follows: first Sandstraße, supposedly coinciding with the house of Pontius Pilate in Jerusalem, the starting point of the Way of the Cross. There was a second station in Aufseßstraße, where Jesus was said to have met the Mother of God, the Virgin Mary. At the third station, he receives help from Simon of Cyrene, and at the fourth station, he meets the weeping women. At the end of that street, Veronica wipes the sweat and blood off Jesus's face. That was the fifth station. At the sixth, Jesus, carrying the cross, falls. This was on Mauer Street. And finally there was the highest and most important point on this path, the Tomb of the Lord, across from the Church of St. Getreu.

Today I followed the whole path in sequence, and looked all these points over. The reliefs on the walls were carved by an unknown sculptor in the sixteenth century. Probably due to the fact that stone is a material which does not reflect light, it all looks surprisingly animate, and the pale winter light falling on it gives off a dim, sickly shade. At that moment it truly seems as if Jesus is there, moving under the weight of his cross.

The feelings that arise in response to these episodes are comparable to the states arising from the seven steps of Sufism. Climbing higher and higher, high enough to take my breath away, up into the flower gardens of Michaelsberg Abbey, I felt so free that it seemed I too could rise up into the heavens. Perhaps that was my brush with the spirit of Jesus Christ.

Or on the other hand, perhaps not.

3 August 1939

Troubling news has been reaching us. German troops have crossed into Poland. Could this be the start of a real war?

Today I received a response from Tohir about the article I sent. 'This is not the time for this sort of query. Please understand the political problems involved,' he wrote.

I think I may soon drown in all these documents. Here are the results of my queries so far. According to the documents, on 27 April 1610, Michaelsberg Abbey was beset by fire, and it almost burned to the ground. Everything was incinerated, except for the tomb of St. Otto, the first Abbot of the monastery. The Abbot at that time, Johann Müller, rebuilt the cathedral from the ground up, bringing in the Munich architect Georg Niedermeier for the job. At the very same time, the Italian master Lazaro Agostino led a group of four artists, whose names were not known, in painting the *Garden of Heaven*, or *Himmelgarten*, on the cathedral ceiling, a work still famous today. What I found indicates that two of those artists were from the Jesuit order, while one was a Muslim from foreign lands, who left his name nowhere.

These Jesuits had certain confidential letters which I managed surreptitiously to read. Their missives say that five hundred years previously, meaning at the beginning of the twelfth century, during Otto's abbothood, alongside such personalities as Tiemo and Burghardt from St. Michael's, Heimo from St. Jacob's, and Tuto from the cathedral, there was also an individual widely known as Ibn Barat from Andalusia, honoured among them under the name of Bernhardt, who had taken refuge from the Black Plague in the monastery at

St. Michael's. He participated in debates about the scriptures, arguing with those Christians over Greek philosophy, astronomy, medicine, and theology.

Following that same pattern, in the seventeenth century the two Spanish Jesuits and the Muslim from another corner of the earth discussed and debated over the Weltchronik, compiled after those historic discussions and stored in the cathedral. With the beginning of the new construction work after the fire in 1610, under the leadership of the Italian Agostino, they first painted the ceiling of the cathedral with plants and vines. The Jesuits wrote that it was the Muslim foreigner who convinced them to cover the dome with greenery, rather than images of maidens and idols. Their motives included Abbot Johann Müller's fondness for botany. As they did so, they created interlacing patterns of remarkable flowers and birds, where someone looking closely might just discern, among the twists and turns, the word 'Allah', the symbolic depiction of the Islamic faith. And in another place, a swatch of material is sewn into the clothing of an abbot, allegedly as proof of victory in the Crusades, and no Christian knows, or at least does not acknowledge, that it contains the words 'There is no God but Allah'.

In another book in the city library, I found pictures drawn in Bamberg in the seventeenth century. There is only one road leading to the newly built city. When the Crusades began, monks and city dwellers took this road upwards, all dressed in black and white clothing. And in another picture, off to one side of a group of pilgrims walking to the tomb of St. Otto, I caught sight of a man, palms clasped in prayer, and my heart skipped a beat, and I realised that this must be a countryman of mine... If only I could learn something about his life.

23 August 1941

The war has rolled onwards as far as the Soviet Union.
They say that in just a month or two, Moscow will be
in the hands of the German forces. Our countrymen
have leaped into action. After the death of Mustafa
Bey, Young Turkestan ceased to exist. That means the
articles I've sent them will never see the light of day. Vali
Qayumhon sent a letter urging me to write about the
sufferings of the motherland for his publication National
Turkestan, and he says that someone is forming a
Turkestani Legion. But I could not muster up any desire
to respond to him. One day, I saw a whole train full of
prisoners being transported, among whom there was
one who caught my eye, who resembled a countryman
of mine. For some reason I turned away, and averted my
gaze. When I turned back, the train was already moving
off towards Schweinfurt.

9 September 1941

Yesterday was Helga's birthday. The Germans got
together. I made plov. They ate, and showered me with
compliments. 'Soon we will liberate Turkestan!' they told
me. 'Just a bit longer, and we'll be eating plov in your
homeland. Your country will be autonomous. And we'll
turn those Russians into slaves,' they said. But mostly
they talked among themselves. I walked out, and sat for
a while in the kitchen. They laughed loudly. They danced
the tango. At night, after we bade them farewell, Helga
and I took a long walk, just the two of us, along the
banks of the Regnitz. I thought my thoughts, and she
thought hers.

Today I again spent the day at the Stadtarchiv. I
found a picture drawn in the year 1628. It depicted the
refectory, or dining hall, in the monastery at St. Michael,
where among the monks praying before their meal
and those listening to the service, there was St. Otto

himself, in the ranks of the servants carrying the dishes. A wooden spoon, fork and brass plate lay on a napkin before each monk. Deep inside the room there were seated three honoured monks, of whom the one on the right was busy reciting a prayer. It seemed that the hero of my novel was also seated there among them... Relying on this picture, I have just written a scene about the refectory of the Benedictine monks.

12 January 1942

One question has been torturing me for some time now. What are they saying about me back in my old village? Before, all was clear; everyone could see and hear what was happening. But now, everyone who has returned from Germany has either been arrested or shot. And now the whole village, the whole motherland, is on one side, and all that is left to me is the other side. The war has separated us.

I wrote to Tohir about this, and in his response he wrote, 'When our country is cleansed of Russian Bolsheviks, our people will judge us according to our worth.' I'd be surprised if such a thing were truly possible. Or would these 'poor wretches', as Tohir called them, consider us traitors?

All day long, all around Bamberg, the radio has only been reporting news about Moscow and Stalingrad. I walked up to the Villa Kügel. A cold wind was blowing up from Bamberg. Once the city began succumbing to the winter darkness, and the dim street lamps were lit, I could stand it no longer. Where could I turn to find peace?

7 September 1942

I've begun some interesting work: translating all sorts of stories, fables and tales from different Turkic languages into German. As it turns out, all this was written down

from the words of neighbouring clans and tribes, all
now taken prisoner: the Tatars and Chuvash, Altai and
Kyrgyz, Kazakhs and Uzbeks. I am supposed to work
through all of their folklore and make a book. It was
extremely good timing, as I've now almost finished work
on my novel. Helga's father found the job for me through
his friends in the Gestapo. All that I need to do is listen
to them, and compare. The Chuvash pronounce /s/ like
/kh/.

12 October 1943

It is autumn again. I walked along the edge of the
woods, up to Altenberg Castle. I wandered alone
through the forest. Not a soul anywhere around. I felt
strange sensations. As I approached Altenberg and
saw the frescoes there, another memory came to me:
Albrecht Dürer once came to this fortress, and he
stayed here for some time. As I pondered that fact,
another idea unexpectedly flashed through my mind – to
make it so that he met my Stranger here! Maybe I ought
to write another couple of chapters? When I returned
home, that desire still burned hot within me, but there
is no task more difficult than reviving a finished work. I
still cannot find an episode where I might fit this story
in. And I keep thinking that this is a novel about how
one stranger turned up in a strange land, and given
that human nature is such that he would nevertheless
try to put down roots, even in a foreign environment,
that must be why I want to connect him with someone,
anyone at all. Perhaps I shouldn't be trying to invent
things. One invention could ruin the whole piece, after
all, a work based on my study of so many genuine
documents. I sit here and I ponder all of this.

3 February 1944

In such devastating times, what can help a man?
What can heal his soul? When the meaning of life has

disappeared, when even the concept of 'meaning' does not remain in this life, even in words... Only the window, and the eternal, unchanging picture attached to it like a seal... Life has not succeeded, and in the face of this inalterability, everything that has been done has no substance; but for some reason, words once spoken, sometime, somewhere, appear as a moment of warmth, of hope, in this eternally frigid world. You could turn a person into firewood and toss him in the furnace to burn up, and even then he will never thaw out. It is sometime between four and five in the morning. Inside me, it is cold. Inside, it is empty. Nothing but my frozen soul. Knowing it is pointless, I nevertheless persist in this pointlessness. As if this enormous pointlessness might serve to conceal the hopelessness of this life. Here there are buildings, one white, one black. Both are lifeless, and seem not to differ one from the other. What was supposed to have happened is happening, and will continue to happen. The frozen world, a world where there is no love. The world torn up, consisting of small pieces unconscious of their own desires. The world unlit by day, the night unwarmed by flame...

What am I doing here? What am I doing in this world? Here today, gone tomorrow. Or even here today, gone today... What truth has been proven, what lie has been exposed? Even my novel means nothing. Its only possible justification may be that life is no better than the book, in fact much more sordid. Maybe that is the justification a man can use to stand his ground?

3 April ...

This is the day of my death. Tonight there will be a full moon. Today I stopped by the barber shop on Langestraße. As he shaved my head, the barber asked, 'Where are you from?' When I responded, 'Turkestan,' he said, 'Isn't that Russland, too? Land of the swine?' and he started swearing and cursing, maybe at them, maybe at me. He had only managed to shave half my head, and he was still holding the razor in his hand, but by then he was worked up into such a frenzy that – well, I would have rather he cut my throat at that moment than go on experiencing such shame and humiliation! People had started to gather around. They joined right in with him. 'We should have destroyed them all!' they said, 'Put them all in the gas chambers!' What could I have done? Even if I had wanted to fight back, what would I have been fighting for? For the Soviet land of the Bolsheviks? But I also feel hatred for those Russians. Or should I have fought for my own offended dignity? 'Cut my hair!' I yelled at him. But he did nothing to curb his rabid attack, and eventually he simply collapsed, literally frothing at the mouth. Everyone rushed towards him. There was nobody left who I could fight with. My head was still half covered in shaving cream. I wiped it off with a towel and stood up, completely humiliated and offended. Wouldn't it have been better to burn in a furnace than to go through all this? I am a stranger at home, and I am nobody abroad. To whom can I ever be of any use? Right now, not knowing what else to do with my half-shaved head, I am sitting here holding it in my hands.

Last night, I had a dream. In the dream a childhood friend of mine was sitting at the wheel of our car, and he brought my child inside with him and said, 'I'm going to make a run to that corner up there,' and then he disappeared from sight. When I went after them, worried, it seemed to me that in the place where they had turned I could see flashes of barely noticeable child-sized silhouettes in the crowd. And when, in order to close in on them, I got on somebody's bicycle, I found I was not riding along that street, but had somehow ended up on the road to the airport. For some reason I decided that bicycles were forbidden on airport territory, so I turned around, and on the far side of the hangars

I almost collided with a cobra in spectacles, swaying
and dancing, his hood blown out behind his head,
just like the flame on a candle. There were countless
serpents sprawled out all along my path, and I was glad
my feet were not touching the ground. But when the
road came to an end, I rode onto an overgrown lawn,
and the bicycle wheels became entangled in the grass,
and I had to walk over the dirt, frightened all the while
of those beasts. Finally I came to a well-lit house, and
when I walked inside I exchanged greetings with some
old men who came in one after another; they were not
religious leaders of any sort, but simply handsome-
looking old men, wise with a lifetime of experience. After
they were seated, I squatted down, just like the children
and women of the family, next to those old men, and I
felt insufficiently Uzbek among Uzbeks.

Is that when I woke up to this day?

EVENTS OF THE YEAR
OF THE HIJRA 1409

Capable of crossing these deserts are only a few Elect, who
have acquired the strength which nature never bestows
upon man. Assistance in acquiring this strength may be
had from immersing oneself in a certain rippling spring
not far from the lasting spring of life. If a traveller comes
to this spring, and washes himself in it, and tastes its sweet
water, then the force of creation will spread through all
his limbs, giving him strength enough to cross vast deserts,
and he will not sink in the waters of the ocean, and he
will climb Mount Qaf without difficulty, and none of its
guardians will cast him down into the abyss of hell.

Avicenna, *Hayy ibn Yaqzan*

I have been trying to describe life in foreign lands,
but in the end, just the same, I return home. What
might that mean? Just now, the very act of recalling how I was obliged to leave my motherland for
good is returning me, in a way, to Tashkent of the
early 1990s. Perhaps I will not dwell on Tashkent, but
rather begin with how, one day, we were forced to

leave our young daughter with my in-laws, pack our bags, and depart for Moscow overnight. I will tell you how, after arriving in Moscow, we settled down into Valentina Nikolayevna's empty apartment – she was my wife's academic advisor, a musicologist. Valentina Nikolayevna was busy teaching in China, and we whiled away the chilling days of the late Moscow autumn in her tiny two-room flat.

An Uzbek woman we had grown up with also lived in Moscow, and on one of those days fraught with worry, she invited us to her home, and told us that I had been sentenced to death. Who had done such a thing, and why? The young woman could only sob, and she said nothing. I haven't yet told you, but that same year three armed men had broken into our home. Their identities have still not been established. Just imagine how my wife felt after that! Not to mention how I felt. What was I supposed to do? Our daughter remained in Tashkent. Should I grieve for her, or focus my sympathies on my wife, or mourn for myself, now that I was sentenced to hang? The whole Salman Rushdie affair had begun in a similar way. How sorry I felt for the poor man! But at least he was under the watchful eye of the global community. If we, on the other hand, were doomed to die, who would say a word to support us?

At night, in that apartment on the outskirts of the
city, after locking up and chaining the door every
way we could, even barricading ourselves in with a
bicycle, we sat stewing. During the night, if we ever
closed our eyes at all, sleep fled at the slightest noise
outside, and we woke up covered in sweat. A car driving by or a cat jumping off the roof made my poor
heart follow suit, rushing, leaping and clattering. And
during the day, no matter where I was, I called my
wife every thirty minutes, to make sure everything
was all right with her, and to let her know nothing
had happened to me.

We remained in this state of limbo for six long
weeks. In the interim – that year, I understood why
the Turks call December the 'interim' – in that cold,
ice-covered interim, I composed a farewell letter to
my friends and loved ones. And in the interim, old
Jean-Pierre came to my rescue again. In record time,
he dug up a three-month stipend from Montpellier in
France, and as soon as the documents were in order,
my wife and I again departed for Paris.

A person never returns to a place twice in an identical mood. There was not a trace left of the zest and
pleasure of my previous visits. This time, we rode into
Paris knowing nobody wanted us at all. Our daughter
remained on the other side of the world. We would

be spending all the money we had on telephone calls, trying to watch her every step. 'Papa, if you want to come get me, don't! Every day a man comes from the prosecutor's office and asks for you,' she told me.

Our mood must have spread to those around us, because Jean-Pierre seemed cross with us now, or perhaps he'd simply had enough of us, because this time he told me, 'Here's your money. Find yourself a place to live for three months.' But in this France, finding a place to live for three months turned out to be a matter of severe difficulty. Nobody would rent for fewer than six.

One day, or more accurately one evening – most of French life happens in the evenings – we were visiting someone we did not know, and there we met a man from China who spoke French with a strong Chinese accent. And this man, who seemed to have lived through something similar, winked at us, and said, 'There are some vacant rooms where I'm staying. I will try to talk with the old woman.' Two days later, we moved in with that old woman, into a house situated just across from the Château de Fontainebleau, once the residence of the king.

—

Our elderly landlady was no plain old biddy, but a

woman named Mademoiselle de Suze. On the first evening, the evening we met, sitting in the foyer on the main, ground floor of the house, she gave us a brief overview of her ancestry. It turned out that members of the de Suze family had been confidants of the kings, and her grandfather's brother was the one who had shipped from Egypt the column that stood tall in the very centre of Paris, the one they called Vendôme, in the Place Concorde. Everything we learned about the old woman came not from her – she was a noblewoman, after all! – but in the course of conversations with the residents of the other rooms, who came from China and from Spain, and from the one French bachelor. Mademoiselle de Suze herself only nodded, hinting at what could not be expressed.

At first the old woman seemed to resemble my grandmother. My grandmother was from a family which traced its lineage to the caliphs, and she was aristocratic in bearing, with light-coloured eyes and a sleek countenance, and a second chin that hung down like a velvet drape. I even felt struck by love for this old Frenchwoman. And then, when she said that we'd have to pay fifteen hundred francs per month, I nearly wept tears of adoration. Would you like to know why? Because nobody else we had spoken to had even mentioned a sum of fewer than three thousand. 'A granny just like my own!' I thought, in a fit of feeling.

'But first you must make a deposit of a thousand, which I shall return to you when you leave,' she said.

'If that's what is required, we have no objection,' we agreed.

'And now let us go upstairs,' Mademoiselle de Suze suggested.

Can you hear the majesty contained in those words? 'And now let us go upstairs!' As if she had said, 'We shall take our tea on the upper veranda, where the air is fresher!' Our hearts fluttering sweetly, we hiked up the stairs.

When the old woman opened the creaking door to our future home, we beheld a room which must have been set aside for indentured servants in her ancestors' time. A bare light bulb hung from the ceiling, and an iron cooking stove stood in the middle of the room, the kind we used to see in small villages when we were children. 'Firewood is free of charge. You may chop it down below,' Mademoiselle told us. This is what we found, in the very centre of France, at the very tail end of the twentieth century. And there was nothing else in the room at all.

Remember the writer I mentioned, Hamid Ismailov? In one of his stories he recounts how he journeyed around Moscow, from building to building, hoping to find a room. I recalled the tale, and specifically, how the poor man in that story repeated to his weeping wife, like a refrain to a song, 'But you understand, wife...' I remembered it because my own wife was sobbing, shedding bitter tears.

—

A person can adapt to anything, really. Inside that house of French aristocrats, we moved on to a more modest way of life. Thank God I grew up in a village. In the mornings, using just a hatchet — no splitting wedge — I hacked at the crooked logs, which may have been as old as the old woman herself, I stoked the furnace, and, when the boiler had heated, I cooked breakfast. And my wife sobbed, 'Is *this* what we came to France for?' Understandably, of course. Our little girl was far away, and all the money we had saved was going on phone calls, so it's not as if we were out shopping for French perfume.

Since I had come there as a writer, I needed to do something to earn the money we had already received — and our cash was melting away from day to day. Some days I'd translate something or other, other days my wife and I would visit Paris to look for work. They've got a book there called the Yellow Pages, a telephone directory, and I used it to call up every place offering language courses, asking each one, in a very beseeching tone of voice, whether they needed an Uzbek teacher. 'And what sort of language is that?' they all asked. The kindest ones would add, 'Well, all right, go ahead and send us your résumé,' and when I sent it they disappeared without a trace, along with their copy of my life history. And life was ticking along.

To be perfectly honest, we did sometimes seem to be in demand, even in Paris. They have an Oriental Studies Institute there, called Inalco, which houses an organisation called the Friends of the Turks, and that club invited me and my wife to make an appearance. There we drank French wine and paraded around, feeling like the first living examples of the Uzbek people. These people knew nothing about Uzbeks. 'What sort of poetry do you have?' they asked. Clearing my throat remorselessly, I recited something from the folk epic *Bakhshiyon*. They were entranced! They gave us even more wine. 'Can you sing, too?' they asked. After all that free wine and Turkish baklava, how could I *not* sing? I performed some Mamurjon Uzakov, bold and clear as a nightingale. The plates that had been emptied of their baklava reverberated in the sweet tones of the song, and everyone there was speechless.

Caught up in that routine, we never noticed the New Year approaching. But then our friend Semih-bey and his family decided to come visit us from Germany for the holiday. I told him, bravely as I could, 'Certainly, come, and we'll be delighted to have you!' Our Uzbek hospitality would have allowed nothing less. But I looked deep into my pockets and found nothing – no money, and no place to entertain guests, either.

Finding space wasn't necessarily a problem; we ourselves could stay with friends, just like the times we got stuck in Paris overnight and went through the phone book at the Gare de Lyon and phoned every-one we knew at two or three in the morning. Our friends were used to it by now. We were poor Soviet citizens on the decline, after all, so why would we have any money?

But let me put my story in order. The first thing we did was to offer our friends from Germany to our friends here in France, at a very good price. That meant we'd have to do a good job pulling the wool over our friends' eyes. We could say, for instance, that our guest was a great scholar, a philologist, the most eminent expert to be found in all Germany on any Turkic language you could name. After all, the French always prefer a beautiful bedspread to a good, durable blanket. It was most important that everything was resplendent on the surface. What was inside, or even whether there was an inside at all, didn't bother them. They were only interested, we believed, in the outward lustre of a thing. And we were right. They acted quite interested.

I told you: it's surfaces, all surfaces.

I even have a theory about it. Judge for yourself. The Italians speak a Romance language, as do the Spanish and Romanians, Moldovans and Portuguese. Those languages are just languages, simple, no tricks; the letter A sounds like an A, and a U sounds like a U. But the French! I have found sounds in French which cannot be pronounced without flexing your tongue and lips in such a way that you come off like a flirt, sounds that make you twist your lips as if you're making a very erotic noise. What kind of people would casually say so many 'ewwws' and 'uhhhhhs'? The French! Only the French. What I mean is that only a people occupied solely with what decorates and flatters them could so shamelessly alter the blameless Latin tongue!

Perhaps a lack of money is making me overreact a

bit. It's all right. After all, we ourselves were twisting our lips and mumbling through our noses just like them!

Anyway, we managed to make arrangements for five or six meals, with several of our friends deciding to host a dinner at their place. We delivered the news to all the Turks of Paris, and to the Friends of the Turks, assuring everyone that we wouldn't have wanted to leave them out of the loop.

Then, just before the New Year, Semih-bey and his wife and children arrived in Fontainebleau in their Audi. Probably due to the fact that their car was fairly large in size, matching the size of the family itself, and sensing that these narrow streets and narrow houses were not for them, they went straight to the hotel. Perfect.

But instead of leaving them in peace, my Uzbek mentality started putting ideas into my head. 'But you wanted to stay with us!' I found myself saying.

'Well, all right,' agreed Semih-bey. 'How about our oldest daughter and one of the twins stay with you? They know a little French. It wouldn't hurt them to get to know how the French aristocracy pronounces things.'

'He who promises a cart will pull that cart himself,' I thought, making up a proverb on the spot. Renting another room from Mademoiselle would mean an enormous financial loss.

—

Just to be safe, we had already made arrangements with the old lady to rent a small room for four days. Naturally, the world of capitalism is arranged according to its own laws, and the formidable mistress of that ripe old world insisted on one thing: 'If you rent long-term you can have it cheaper, but for only four days, the price is higher.' And so the old woman collected all the money I had left.

And then! The very first evening, in honour of our friends, a ceremonial dinner was held in the old woman's parlour – at our expense. It seems she had not quite understood us correctly. Overestimating the majesty of Semih-bey, she had summoned, from among her old friends, an alleged great-great-granddaughter of the famous Josephine, Napoleon's own wife. In a word, it was a genuine banquet.

The younger Josephine, as old as our old woman, spoke Russian very well. But Semih-bey, who we had of course introduced as Europe's leading linguist, out of what must have been pure spite, could not speak even a syllable of Russian. After all, as Kalvak-mahzum said in Qodiriy's story, 'Is that really a language? If you want to learn that Russky, go get any drunk off the street. He speaks Russky as well as anyone.' It seemed this Josephine was also a devotee of current affairs. She spoke endlessly about her encounters with Brezhnev and Chernenko. But all that aside, Semih-bey's daughters were pretty capable of speaking French, and they knew something about French culture, too. That was a big positive, because after they spent their first night in one of our Mademoiselle's unheated rooms, both the poor girls woke up coughing. So much for French aristocrats and their marvellous mansions.

After that experience Semih-bey seemed to cool somewhat to the noble classes, and instead started taking an interest in our friends from the middle ranks of society. It's simple enough: you go, you chat, you eat, and you leave. No extra exchanges of niceties, no need to smile just so.

—

Why am I so attached to these hours, these days, these months, I wonder? As if every minute and second of that time had some hidden content and meaning, even though this entire period of my life could have been summed up in a single quatrain. But I return to those times over and over again, and I sink into the vortex of meaningless events, and I try, always, to find some meaning in them. Probably I want to use those events, each more vaguely defined than the one before, to hide all the hopelessness and abandonment of those times. And yet.

—

After three or four days, Semih-bey and his family left. All that remained were memories of our time together in Paris and, especially, the memory of how we couldn't ever seem to get *out* of Paris. Not knowing the roads in the big city is a fairly serious problem, and we spent hours wandering in circles. 'I think we've already driven by here,' we'd say, while the Eiffel Tower, looming over us like a giant peg hammered into the city, appeared first on one side, then on the other. Finally we'd get to the road we needed. But the roads here are like the German highways in that once you're on, you have to travel ten kilometres or more before you can get off again. If you happen to miss your exit, you'll be stuck, unable to escape, until you're forty or fifty kilometres past your destination.

—

On the days we didn't go in to Paris, we walked around Fontainebleau Park. The weather was warmer now, and people from every corner of the world came together here. There was noise and commotion all around us, and the chatter of young people, but both the winter sun and this park full of people weighed heavily on us. Our memories were constantly pulling us back to our little girl. Meltwater began to flow in the storm drains, buds began to swell on the trees, there was beauty and freedom all around — and the air was so fresh — but this freedom, and this air, only seemed to welcome our despair, measure our grief, as we thought of our daughter. Every time, we returned again to our cold, empty room, lit the stove, and sat, looking out the window and quoting morosely from Avicenna:

> *If you journey away towards the East, then first will appear a region settled neither by people nor by grasses and bushes, nor trees, nor stones. It is a vast desert land, a flooding sea, imprisoned winds, and the heat of raging fire.*

January, then February. Our money was running out. I was trying to sell one of Hamid Ismailov's well-regarded manuscripts, and had found a purchaser, but he wanted me to write an article about Hamid to explain his place in history. I wrote it, and I waited for someone to offer me a job. I called everyone I knew, but heard nothing in response.

One of those days I got a call from Paris, and when Mademoiselle answered the telephone, they told her that the Ministry of Foreign Affairs had given them the name Sheikhov as the only Uzbek national in France, and they wanted to know if that Uzbek could be found. The old lady was extremely agitated – it was the Ministry of Foreign Affairs, after all! – and as soon as we returned from our walk in the park, she summoned my wife. 'Madame, there has been an inquiry for your husband, from the Ministry of Foreign Affairs!'

You ought to have seen the state I was in after I heard that. My heart was thumping, and I didn't know whether to celebrate or to weep. I haven't mentioned yet that I had written a letter to President Mitterand, asking, as a writer, if I could possibly spend a year or two in his venerable country. Maybe, I thought, this phone call was in response to my letter. On the other hand, doubt gnawed at me. 'What have you done?' I asked myself. 'Now they'll toss you out of the country.' There were about fifteen days left of our stay. By then, we were just waiting, relying on the will of Allah.

On the third day, I was very politely called to the telephone. As usual, the old lady picked up the phone downstairs with a wheeze, and then called out in her ringing voice, '*Monsieur l'écrivain!*' Once I had run down the stairs, panting, skipping every other step, I heard a pleasant voice. That voice introduced itself as Thierry Somebody. But since there is nothing more difficult than the sound of French surnames, he repeated himself, sensing my confusion. 'My name is Thierry.'

He asked, 'How well do you know the Uzbek language?'

'I'm a writer, *un écrivain,*' I answered, copying the old woman's daily pronunciation.

I must have sounded convincing, because he said he had a job for me. I did not have time to ask what sort of job it was before he had already got to the point.

'You've probably heard of the Tour de France?'

'Certainly!'

'The television channel Arte plans to film five- or six-minute videos about twenty of the best racers. Each stage of the race will feature a film about one of them. I need to make one about Jamaliddin Abdujapparov.'

'Is that so?'

'I need you to be my translator.'

And that was the entire conversation.

The very next day, I met Thierry at his home, next to the Maison Blanche métro station. I once had a friend from Yazyavan, in the Ferghana Valley, named

Matrasul. He and this Thierry could have been twins. Roaming the world has taught me one thing: Allah seems to have been rather thrifty. He created maybe five or six types of people, and within each group, certain individuals are practically identical, even though they are created and installed in places thousands of kilometres apart. Now this Thierry had appeared in the guise of Matrasul.

From what he said, I learned that Jamaliddin Abdujapparov was one of the best sprinters in the world. He was able to really pick up speed in the final stretch of a race. I would compare him with a rider in a traditional Central Asian buzkashi match — the game some people call goat polo — who would steal the goat carcass away from his opponent at the last second, and burst free of the crowd of other riders to victory. Usually, the cyclists toil on to complete stage after stage. But there are some racers, like Jamaliddin Abdujapparov, who save their strength through most of the race, and then in the last three or four kilometres (out of one hundred and thirty) they suddenly dart ahead, leaving the others far behind and empty handed. Thierry Matrasulovich explained all this to me.

'When Jamaliddin tried out for the Soviet team, they called him a gook and dismissed him with the other Muslims,' Thierry told me. 'Now he's the best sprinter on Team Lampre from Italy. Last year in Paris, Jamaliddin was in first place in the last hundred metres on the Champs-Élysées, but he crashed when he skidded on the cap from a Pepsi bottle. He broke his shoulder and arm doing that.' Thierry was educating me about bicycle racing just the same way Matrasul might have taught me about an early-spring buzkashi match among the good people of Yazyavan.

King Kabus ruled at that time in Gorgan. He received a copy of Avicenna's portrait, and he sent out his own spies to join the search. When Avicenna arrived in Gorgan, he found a place to stay in a caravan-saray. Since he was a surprisingly skilled healer, he began treating those who needed his help, and his fame spread throughout the region. At that time, the king's eighteen-year-old brother was ill with a mysterious disease. Nothing the healers treated him with did any good.

When he learned there was a healer in that caravan-saray whose excellence was recognised even among other men of medicine, King Kabus sent a rider to find him. Avicenna was summoned to the palace.

He felt the pulse of the ailing young man, and he

said, 'Send me a person who knows this city well.' They did so. 'Make a list of all the quarters of the city,' Avicenna instructed him, keeping his grip over the artery in his patient's arm. After the names of all the quarters of the city had been written down, the healer ordered that they send him a person who knew one particular quarter very well. They did so. 'Make a list of the neighbourhoods and streets there!' this new person was told, and he did. Avicenna continued to hold his patient's arm where he could feel his pulse. Then they summoned a person who knew all the houses in one of those neighbourhoods, and that person wrote down the names of all the residents of those houses. Finally, still feeling for his patient's pulse, the healer said, 'From such-and-such a neighbourhood, from such-and-such a street, from such-and-such a house, send me a girl by the name of such-and-such!' When he heard the girl's name, the sick prince gave a start and jumped out of bed.

Then Avicenna told King Kabus that he had found a way to treat the illness known as love. And King Kabus, who was no less resourceful than the healer, said that he had also found what he was looking for: Avicenna himself. And he handed him the portrait which had been sent to him by Mahmud Yaminud-Davla.

With this portrait and many generous gifts, Avicenna travelled on towards Rey.

⁎⁎

Sina remembered his childhood home. A dark, close, secluded hive. Seven waxen structures, in each of which, as spring arrived, there began a continuous humming and hubbub, from top to bottom. In our times, something like that sort of movement can be seen in the mosques in Kum, and in places where pilgrims throng: somebody is saying a prayer, somebody is learning to recite, someone else is busy with a task, another is reading Avicenna's *Book of Birds*, and yet another is kissing and caressing the grave of a dead woman free of sin.

It was the same in Sina's hive – everyone was busy with their own affairs. As a consequence of his ceaseless labour and ascetic life, Sina began to feel that a certain strength was accumulating not only in the glands inside him, but also in his wings. When he tried, once or twice, to flap them, the air around him was set in motion. Sensing this motion, one of the labour-brigade leaders brought Sina down to a lower level of the hive and instructed him to fill one of the six-sided cells with honey. Sina was a little offended that this labour leader, a cripple who had lost one arm and one leg, was telling everyone what to do as if he were the idle master of ceremonies at a typical Uzbek wedding. After the hard work of construction was over, Sina suspected that the labour leader would use the rooms for his own needs.

On the other hand, Sina felt like the woman at the wedding assigned to arrange all the gifts and presents in some separate room. He was responsible for ushering in all the bees as they arrived humming, and for taking the presents from their hands while they danced the circle dance for others, and talked with him only as an afterthought: 'Here's a little something for you, dearie,' they might say, and slip him some nectar. He took those packaged-up presents, which required a good deal of flapping of the wings, and evaporated the moisture from that nectar, and stored what they brought in the proper places, and it was the same thing all day: boring, monotonous work. The others could enjoy the celebration, while his lot was to sit there and keep careful count.

But other sensations were also stealing over Sina's still-immature body. Sensations similar to the feeling the very young have in the middle of summer, loading watermelons into train wagons. The kids hired to do the job, along with a couple of adults, take melons the size of a football from a farmer's automobile, pass them quickly hand to hand, and pile them into a dark freight car. And one little lad, his hands and face sticky with juice, remains in the very darkest corner of the car, catching the striped fruit as it flies through the air; but sometimes an incoming melon is invisible in the darkness and it crashes into him, and breaks and bloodies his nose. The insides of the ripe melon, and the pulsing pain of the bleeding nose, mix together and decompose in the darkness. In the resting time that follows, the bees fly in, following the scent of the watermelon juice. One of the adults sets a cool rind against the boy's nose, filling his nose and his mouth with the aromatic nectar of summertime...

Memory is consciousness infused with honey.

———

Rumour had it that after the death of Fahr ud-Dawla, his wife Saida took over his throne in Rey, depriving his son Majid-ud-Dawla of the chance to rule. And Saida sent a letter to the Sultan of all Sultans, Mahmud Ghaznavi, which said, 'Would you really send your troops to attack a woman?' All of this cast Majid-ud-Dawla into a terrible despair, which disturbed his thinking and led him to growl at those around him, 'Kill me! Take off my head!'

Some time after these events, Avicenna was called to an audience with Saida, and he found her deeply despondent. The healer said, 'Let the queen not despair! She has a son, and she may yet find a treatment for his ailment.' Saida was surprised. She took courage, and she sent Avicenna to her son.

'I'm insane! Kill me, take off my head!' the prince kept repeating.

Avicenna said only, 'Tell him that the butcher has come.' And, whetting his knife, he approached Majid-ud-Dawla. 'Tie this calf up, and I'll slit his throat!' Avicenna shouted, and he began feeling the prince's limbs and flanks. When he got to his thigh, he said, 'Thin, isn't he? He needs to be fed and fattened up before we butcher him.' And he walked out of the room. For the next month, they fed the prince the most nutritious viands they could find, right there in that cowshed where he lived, and his health returned. Saida conveyed upon the healer the very highest honours, and her son became the heir to the throne.

—

Sina flapped, flapped and flapped his wings over the honey. He felt completely alienated from the world. The honey he had collected and carried on his breast was not destined for him, and in fact, he had already had more than his fill of its aroma. The next winter, the bees who remained in the hive every day, creeping up and down, would feed themselves on that honey, which would melt, drip and drain under the weight of the hive's dense air. And if they could continue in that rhythm till the greenery returned, the hive would again be filled with honey, and it would bubble, buzz and boil with life. Also, perhaps, with the knowledge of what comes from honey.

Today's poverty is tomorrow's hope, says the Sheikh.

*
**

We agreed that we'd place a call to the cyclist's home near Lago di Garda, so the next day I was back in Paris again. As I fiddled away my last centimes, I warmed my soul with the thought that perhaps all these expenses could be reimbursed in the end. We called the number in Italy, and got connected to some sort of restaurant or bar. The hostess picked up the phone, listened to Thierry's broken Italian, told him, '*Uno momento!*' and went off to call Jamaliddin.

I don't know what I was more excited about, the upcoming conversation with a star athlete or the possibility of finally getting a job.

At first, from what Thierry had told me, I thought

that Jamaliddin spoke very little Uzbek, maybe too little to stand in for all Uzbeks in that film, and we wanted to make sure. So after an international '*Allo!*' I gathered my courage, and greeted him in Uzbek. '*Assalom aleikum!*'

'*Aleikum sal-yam.*' I heard a fractured version of my native language in response.

I switched to Russian, just in case. The guy spoke Russian like a native. I stumbled through an explanation of what the film was about, but I gradually began introducing Uzbek words into the conversation so he knew what he was facing.

'You know, Jamaliddin, you're an Uzbek, so you'll need to speak Uzbek in the movie. The Russians are going to be speaking Russian, the French will speak French, and Indurain will speak Spanish.'

'*Mayli,*' said Jamaliddin in a heavy Russian accent. 'Come on down, *gapiraylik.*'

Thierry had kept his ears perked up this whole time, and when I hung up, he asked right away, 'Well? Does he speak it?' It was Thierry's assignment, after all, to convey the image of a formerly oppressed and now liberated, independent Muslim.

'Yes,' I said, 'he does… a little. He says we should go visit him and we can talk then.'

'Maybe we should do it all in Russian, but that

would mean I found you for nothing, since we have a Russian interpreter at the studio.'

'Not a chance,' said I. 'His Uzbek is no worse than his Russian, and plus – *plus*,' I repeated, 'he expressed himself fairly dryly in Russian, but when he switched to Uzbek, his voice really warmed up!' As God is my witness, I was telling the truth. Maybe Jamaliddin was remembering his childhood, or maybe I was the first person he had heard speaking Uzbek since his arrival in foreign lands. But in either case, that broken Uzbek of his radiated a truly spellbinding warmth.

Although Thierry already believed me, I spent another half an hour guaranteeing he was convinced. 'If you want a sure thing, have Jamaliddin speak Uzbek. Then you'll get the kind of film you're looking for. I'll give you the images you need to make your movie the best in the whole series. Can you imagine the game of ulak, Thierry, you Matrasul among Frenchmen? What you told me about this race – it's all ulak! As a good friend, I'm telling you, your work will start with the riders – the horseback riders of ulak! – and I'll read for you what Abdulla Qodiriy wrote about that, and Tagay Murad, and we'll make that film of yours together!' I think that I more resembled a Gypsy, at that moment, than an Uzbek.

Matrasul's French double agreed. 'There are going

to be four other films about Russians, anyway,' he said. 'So come to the television studio tomorrow, and we'll get your documents filled out, and sign a contract, and go to Italy.'

That's how it works. If God shows you mercy, he shows it in full measure. Everything was decided at once. My visa was extended, the trip to Italy was planned, and the next day I learned I wouldn't even have to do all this for free. I could earn five thousand francs! With prospects like those, even daily trips to Paris would no longer be a hardship.

And then Thierry said, 'Take these tickets. They're covered as travel expenses.' Didn't I tell you he was a carbon copy of Matrasul?

I was a little in awe of Jamaliddin, too. He had such an impressive crash in Paris, in his day, that he had become a local celebrity. When we stopped by the gendarmerie for more paperwork, a fifty-year-old woman there nearly shrieked in glee. 'Yes, yes, that's the same Abdu who fell on the Champs-Élysées!'

And now my visa would be extended till the end of our visit to Italy. I actually would have liked to extend it for longer, taking advantage of Jamaliddin, but Thierry told me, 'Be patient. We'll come back, and then we'll think of something!'

Finally the day came for us to depart for Italy. Even

my wife, who usually moped around before my trips, responded differently to this privilege, and she prayed for me and wished me a good journey. She knew this was our ticket back to the charms of the European lifestyle. The rats creeping along, ready to dart into any burrow in the ground, had transformed now into free-flying birds, soaring up into the heavens.

The airport. Air France. We left the Alps below us – by the way, maybe it was my own ancestors who had named them the Alps, since the word means 'hero' in Uzbek – and we landed in world-famous Milan. And here was Italy!

From what he could remember, the Stranger had never been to Florence. One day, certainly, one glorious day, he might, he must, spend some time in that majestic and forgotten place. But he knew of the city from other sources. In his youth he had drawn a map of Florence, street by street, consulting dozens of books.

Now, as he looked at the yellowing piece of paper, his mental journey began at the Piazza della Signoria and moved to the Mercato Nuovo, encountering on the way names that were foreign to his tongue but pleasant to his soul: Pisano's roofs and the Palazzo Vecchio, San Carlo and San Michele, Palazzo dell'Arte della

Lana, and then the Oratoria della Misericordia and the Loggia del Bigallo. All these names felt out of reach, yet they were all rhymes of a poem written in a magical language, and they melted on his tongue, one after another.

Were they coming to life, out of the tales in the books he had read, or was life itself filling the pages of those books?

Two pictures hung on the walls of the room where he was staying. One showed a young man in a red outfit. The other was a portrait of a beautiful lady, holding in her arms, instead of the Heavenly Child, a wild ermine. These paintings had not been placed on opposite walls. Instead, they were arranged so that the lady with the ermine was on the far wall, and the man with the long face was stationed in a recess on the wall to the right. The centuries had frozen their faces in such a way that neither was able to see the other. In the hours just before sunset, one wandering ray of light, reflected off an enormous window at the Biblioteca Laurenziana, shot into the room through the small window. As the Stranger watched, the gazes of these two young people met for just a moment, and the warm flow of light brought tears to his eyes.

—

The first time the Stranger went to Florence, the city was in the grip of the Great Plague. Although check-points had been set up along the major roads, the thinned ranks of the guard and the people exhausted by the plague all awaited salvation, if not from heaven, then at least from other lands, because news about towns where the plague had unexpectedly abated had been arriving like balm for their souls. Therefore, any newcomer introducing himself as a healer was allowed to pass into the city, as long as he was not suspected of coming to encroach upon the property of the unfor-tunate. He was sent on with the words 'God keep you!'

There is no picture more woeful than a city beset by plague. Here is a young woman, staving off death to save her baby, holding the child out beseechingly to the wandering dogs; here are enormous rats creeping out of every hole in the abandoned shops, not chewing on but simply devouring food and supplies. A deranged poet, a stolen marble crown on his head, walks behind the shadow of his love, declaiming ceremonial verses, and behind him flies a crow awaiting the poet's death, carrying over the earth and around the world the bro-ken-off rhymes of his poem.

A house with cracked windows, disconsolate streets, empty churches. Only the inns are full, of people in a kind of ecstasy. In the time of plague, their feasts do a poor job hiding their childlike fear of Death. The perpetual Venetian merchants and Paduan clerks, the local moneylenders and the Genoese sailors, all these people leading their peculiar lives never stick their noses outside, and they greet every man venturing inside like a messenger sent by the plague. But perhaps as a consequence of how the breeze carried out the musty scent of alcohol, or perhaps because the Lord had prepared a more bitter lot for them, the mountain of sorrows, as if squeamish before such a feast, passed this place by.

There is no picture in the world more sinister than a city beset by plague. In the refectory of the monastery of St. Appolonia, at the edge of the city, the Stranger hands out wine and holy water to the sick, who have gathered here from all around. Bereft of all strength but needful of the monks' prayers, the patients barely touch their parched lips to the cups they are offered, and continue to ceaselessly repeat their entreaties.

In this way the endless days continued on and on, and the torments sent down by the Almighty did not end. Finally, a certain madwoman gave birth in the refectory. Perhaps a miracle occurred when the cut sliced her belly and her blood flowed abundantly over the stone floor of the monastery, or else the loud cries of the male infant blessed the city with an amulet of salvation; but whatever the case, the woman, half out of her mind, robed all in black, gave up her soul – not as the latest victim of the plague, but as the Plague itself, and the sky cleared.

That day at the inn, the Stranger used red wine to scrub away the dried blood of the umbilical cord that had stained his hands. And that same day, in that same inn, a certain healer from Granada by the name of Ibn Tufeil[1] bathed his hands in wine for the same reason. If not for the Arabic words he uttered, the newcomer would have considered everything he saw a drunken illusion, but no – a tiny girl infant, consigned to a nurse-maid from Tripoli, pressed herself to a woman's empty breast, and whined in her sleep; and when the woman found she had no milk, she put to the lips of the little child some fermenting dough.

Two children were born that day, and these two orphans, who were named Fabrizio and Cecilia, came to symbolise a new life for the city of Florence.

—

[1] Ibn Tufeil, Latinised as Abubacer, died around the year 1185. He was an Arabic scholar, philosopher, statesman, physician and secretary to the rulers of Granada, Ceuta, and Tangiers, and later physician and courtier to the Almohad caliphate. In his *Tales of Hayy ibn Yaqzan* (translated into Latin in the seventeenth century, and from Latin into almost all the European languages), which he wrote according to themes copied from Avicenna, he paints a picture of the spiritual growth of a man abandoned on a desert island. But this is most likely a different Ibn Tufeil.

Fabrizio grew up in the monastery of St. Appolonia, and Cecilia, left in the hands of the healer from Granada and the nursemaid from Tripoli, found a place in the orphanage of the Innocenti, located just four streets away. During the first two years, when the scars from the plague had not yet healed, many people came from the surrounding area to see them. But little by little, the everyday cares of the world wore this highway back down into the earth, just as a healing scar becomes flush with the skin, and the two children, now walking and talking, were left to their own devices.

As often happens after plague, pestilence or war, life now resounded with a sort of relieved nonchalance. So it was in Florence, as it bade farewell to the days of winter like a carefree girl lying down to daydream in a springtime enchantment of tulips. Everything seemed easier now, from the construction of dozens of new building to the never-ending feasts in the new palace; and at those endless feasts the conversation flowed easily, too, between painters and sculptors, sculptors and architects, architects and poets, and between all of these and the merchants and travellers, the mariners and princes. And there was the instantaneous transition from conversation to dancing, no holds barred, and flitting from flower to flower like butterflies – no, like wisps of flying dragonflies – were the young ladies of Florence, effervescent and radiant as the city itself. And during this new holiday of life, Cecilia and Fabrizio effortlessly slipped away from the weightless memory of the people.

But those times, which seemed to have arrived to stay, lasted only fifteen years. In those years, the children of the plague grew into adults, and they grew close.

In those same years, a famous painter by the name of Alessandro da Mariano di Vanni Filipepi, also called Botticelli, lived in Florence. It was to this man that the adolescent Fabrizio was delivered as an apprentice. An apprenticeship with a great man was as desirable as it was difficult. Not because the truly great are so variable of mood, but because greatness has a shade of alienation about it. Botticelli's business was booming, and as they covered with artwork absolutely everything, right up to the ceiling of the tholos for Pope Sixtus in Rome, the master never tired of nagging Fabrizio, who held the brush. 'Look to the line! Look to it! It is not the colour that conveys the mood, but the line. The lines on your palm determine your fate, and the lines in a painting determine its music and its essence. And determining that essence is the harmony of the lines! Handed down to each person there is a kind of thread. Either you can follow that thread all the way to God – or you can tangle the thread, and stumble and strangle in the knots, and lose sight of the right direction and go astray.'

But when their work was done, and the prayers of Pope Sixtus had been heard, and all the gifts and remuneration had evaporated into the dark corners of the Eternal City in a mere week, Botticelli, now destitute, and lacking the strength to dispel his sadness, resorted to this: he soaked with paint a moist sponge he took from an empty hostel, and flung it with hatred against a white stone wall. 'These idiots could not even paint a landscape... I'll paint you a landscape!' And he dragged a finger through the splash of paint, spreading it so that all the different shades of colour crept over the white wall.

'Learn, while you can!' he shouted. Fabrizio, who held the sponge, watched in confusion, first looking at his teacher's face, then at the growing stain on the wall. The stain on the heart of the sensitive pupil had not yet dried when they saddled their horses and rode back to Florence, where they painted a portrait for one of the Medicis who had lately been disgraced by yet another scandal. To keep the artists focused on their work and to please the teacher's eye, they brought one handsome young lady after another into the palace. And again there was the idle debauchery between jobs, and wine, and women, and suffering... Just as the very greatest of the Medicis, Lorenzo the Magnificent, had said:

> *Quant'é bella giovinezza*
> *che si fugge tuttavia!*
> *chi vuol esser lieto, sia:*
> *di doman non c'è certezza.*[2]

Not trusting in the uncertain tomorrow, life worked to get all it could out of today.

—

In those days in Florence, a new genius was making a name for himself: Leonardo, from the village of Vinci. Fabrizio's teacher saw the paintings that emerged from under his brush in the Medici palace. Botticelli was not angry, like the others, but he kept a profound silence for weeks, until finally, when he was beginning to paint St. Sebastian, he declared, 'It seems this Leonardo has found both God and the devil inside himself.'

One week later, news came that Leonardo, the young genius, had secretly moved from Florence to Milan, to the Sforza Castle. Fabrizio's soul turned to ashes. For when Leonardo left Florence, he took with him, to hostile Milan, the healer from Granada. And the healer took the girl Cecilia, whom he had raised, and whom fate had bound to Fabrizio.

---

[2] 'Youth is sweet and well, / But doth speed away! / Let who will be gay, / Tomorrow, none can tell.'

But life rushed on, panting and chaotic, and a new day followed each night. Returning home late again from some tavern or scene of revelry, Fabrizio cursed himself for a day spent in vanity, and found no reason why he should not go to yet another feast the next day, and let everything start over: his weary mind, his sad thoughts, and his vain pursuits, another day dawning and another night settling in, again and again... You could cry out 'Stop!', but life would not halt for a second. Aside from the work he did with his teacher each morning, Fabrizio felt there was no justification for the life he was burning through. Sometimes it seemed that he would begin his real work, his real career, his real life, his real faith tomorrow; but that tomorrow slipped by just like today, and today turned out just like yesterday.

There is nothing in the world more fleeting that the things which at first glance seem eternal. One day, his blissful life shattered into pieces like the most delicate china in a Medici collection.

—

In the Convent of San Marco, which had been built for the duplicitous penitence of the drunken Medicis, there appeared a monk by the name of Girolamo. And so a danger descended upon the land, its sovereign rulers, and everyone living that life, worse than any plague. In the beginning the Medicis jeered at Girolamo, of course, and laughed at his first, inarticulate sermon. 'Just listen to what he said! All people are born and die equal, so they ought to live their lives as equals, too? Lorenzo the Magnificent and the son of that lame Francesca Paola, sure, they're equals – but only in bed, ha!'

However, it is true what they say: when you call a madman a fool, you may not be pleased with what he comes up with next. No matter how sweetly Lorenzo de Medici tried to bring Girolamo around, no matter how he tried to treat him as an equal ('My friend!' he'd say, 'You mentioned equality, so come now, live like me!'), no matter which people he sent to intercede for him – in the end, no matter what favours he bestowed upon him, all of it came to naught. That bastard Girolamo perverted everything Lorenzo did for him, everything he told him, and turned it against Lorenzo himself.

'Florence is drowning in debauchery and depravity!' Girolamo proclaimed in his sermons. 'Florence is becoming the mother of perfidy, the cradle of deception, the nursery of falsehoods. And there is no man able to trample underfoot these seeds laid in the soil. No man able to tear out by the roots these dragon teeth, sown in this sacred earth! Has the plague not been a lesson to you? Did it not make you tremble with fear? What can remove the blindfold from your eyes? Must the trees stop bearing fruit? Must the road be washed away in a flood? Must the waves of the sea crash into the very mountains? Have your ears indeed grown deaf, your eyes grown blind, your hearts grown empty, before the Word sent down by the Lord?'

Imagine Lorenzo the Magnificent's astonishment when those he loved best, the artists, poets, and sculptors, bowed down before those words. Even Buonarotti broke, Buonarotti, who just the day before had stood up against the forces of heaven, and proven himself their equal in everything he undertook to do.

'You have all become worshippers of idols! What makes you any different from the beasts who feast on their own excrement? The fact that you have renamed your excrement 'art', and yourselves men of art?' How loudly this trenchant, merciless voice resounded under the vaulted ceilings of San Marco!

After that, books were burned on the city's central square, and painters slashed apart the canvases they had taken long years to paint, and sculptors smashed their stone statues. Even Fabrizio's teacher joined them, defying his patron, and he cast Fabrizio out.

But these were not the worst of days. 'The interesting thing,' Fabrizio heard people say, 'is that as woeful as the time of plague was, a time we took as a time of God's wrath, the current times, in which God has shown us his mercy, have been just as treacherous and filled with fear. When you look at it objectively, the fact that the debauchery and feasting moved out of public view, and the festive gatherings travelled to less populated areas and then dwindled away entirely, and the debates and songs and sermons all stopped – this is all quite reminiscent of the onset of the plague. But meanwhile, should we not have tried a little harder to prevent this?'

It was because he entertained doubts such as these that Fabrizio had been cast out of his teacher's favour, and now he spent whole days wandering down the Via dei Calzaiuoli, or around the Uffizi, or the Palazzo Ricasoli. But the alleyways, which just days before had been swarming like a beehive full of grocers and tanners, merchants and cobblers, adventurers and fortune tellers, were now empty, and the occasional monks or nuns who passed through on their way to the cathedral cupolas picked up their black skirts and the shadows mixed into them, and stepped aside, and whispered something he could not understand.

So the young Fabrizio suffered. At the same time, Lorenzo the Magnificent, under the influence of this spiritual plague, was seized by an incurable illness. There was no pleasure in this world he had not sampled, and so there was no sin he had not committed. But even for a sovereign such as he, who had turned the imperfection of the human being into his philosophy and creed, this madman Girolamo, presenting himself as Jesus Christ, was an abomination, no better than if he had been a leper. Certainly, with time, this leprosy would swell to a tumour. Everyone had heard the creeping rumours of Judgement Day – the poets and the scholars, the clergy and the common people. Perhaps all the marble palaces and churches the Medicis had built, all the streets and squares, were only temporary, and there was only one thing of value in the world: an intangible spiritual turmoil. And perhaps, in fact, Lorenzo's era was ending, and his life was coming to its conclusion, and God's wrath would take the form of neither lash nor plague, but rather the extinguishing of his faith in a life able to withstand all trials and defend against all troubles. These were the thoughts which occupied Lorenzo the Magnificent.

Lorenzo believed there was only one person who might be a match for the mad Girolamo. That man had been born in the same year as him, but he was now far away. They said he was in Milan, in the Sforza Castle, occupied with inventing flying bombs and exploding cannonballs. Maybe this was the hand of providence the crazed Girolamo had foretold? Or was none of it worth the trembling of the muscles in Lorenzo's chest? Just at that moment, in fact, something lurched in the sovereign's heart. And so he asked the most reliable of his confidants to make the trip to the House of Sforza.

The ambassador set out. And following after him, as if pursuing its last hope, flew the bird of Lorenzo's soul. That day, Florence lost its most magnificent man. But Girolamo, that hysteric, did not even pay him the proper respect at his funeral service. In his sermon he called upon God and spoke of vengeance, calling this life, and this world, signs of the end of days.

—

At the funeral, the young Fabrizio met his teacher Botticelli. As Pico della Mirandola, Brother Bartolomeo, and several other poets and men of the arts were about to depart after the service, they were stopped at the San Giovanni crossroads by a servant sent by Piero, son of Lorenzo. The new sovereign of the city requested their presence at the Palazzo Vecchio. That crossroads was the point of decision: some, wary of spying eyes, hurried to turn in the opposite direction; some, in hope of praise from St. Girolamo, declared that they had business that could not be delayed; but many, with Fabrizio's teacher Alessandro Botticelli in the lead, made the decision to bid farewell to their former master.

That evening passed in melancholy. It seemed that, before heading off to Purgatory, the soul of Lorenzo the Magnificent wanted to spend just a little more time among friends, host one last banquet and one last feast, enjoy one final, heartfelt conversation, launch one last debate. Though night had long since settled in, he still could not leave this company behind; and remembering the happy occasions of the past which had now disappeared into history, times when they had surrendered themselves to drunken songs and women, they too found they could not leave, perhaps because a whole era was vanishing, or because Lorenzo himself was just about to leave this world – Lorenzo, whose majesty contained this very era within it. Or perhaps it was other, more mysterious, more unnameable phenomena that caused them to linger; but in any case, there was no untroubled, pure tranquility there, only the premonition of the grey and painful sobriety of the day to come.

'Do you remember, Pico, what you said, in the lusty days of youth, in the name of the Lord? You said, "I have created you as neither celestial nor terrene, neither mortal nor immortal, so that you may fashion yourself freely, by your own power, modelling your being into the form you desire." Which one of the books you burned contained those words?

'And you, Alessandro? Were you not the one to craft the enchanting Venus emerging from the foam of the sea? Could it be that this discarded woman has been transformed, now, into the scum of the sewers draining your own past paradise?

'Niccolò! Who was it who once insisted, "Learn from the past, and experience the present!" Why so quiet, like a statue of frozen stone?'

Lorenzo's restless spirit tormented them, interrogated them from every angle, making his guests suffer and squirm. And so the evening indeed passed in melancholy.

Then, at the end of the night, the orphaned son Piero read out his father's last will and testament, addressed to all of them, and before the company gathered there, he tore the black drape off a painting which Lorenzo had bequeathed to all the city.

Imagine the surprise of Fabrizio, Son of the Plague, when he saw on that canvas his own Cecilia, married to him by the Plague itself. There she was, in the pose of a seated Madonna, holding in her arms, instead of the Holy Infant, an unruly wild ermine! In a single instant, the intellectual gathering transformed into a mob. In that frenzy, in that panic of mind and imagination, one man crossed himself, another fell on his knees, another moved close to his neighbour's ear and hastily began to whisper. Only Alessandro Botticelli, mentor to the frozen Fabrizio, looked directly at the painting, and his pale lips said over and over: 'I told you so.'

———

That night, Girolamo, asleep in his stone cell at the Convent of San Marco, had a dream.

He dreamed he was on a ship at sea, but a storm blew up over the ocean, and all the space around him was filled with rats. Girolamo chased the rats away, and when he looked up, he saw that his ship was surrounded by Turkish infidels. They picked Girolamo up by the scruff of his neck, and they delivered him to holy Constantinople. When he caught sight of the Hagia Sophia from far in the distance, tears might have welled in his eyes, but he heard a voice rising up from that sacred cathedral, which seemed to say, 'The heavenly lash is prepared to strike!' And at that very instant, Lorenzo leaped out of the cathedral with a roar of laughter, looking less like those red-headed infidels and more like the rats crawling out of every crack and crevice, and he began flogging Girolamo mercilessly with a whip, its handle gilded in gold, while he lay with his hands and feet bound.

Under the endless blows Girolamo began to shrink, and he shrank until he had changed form to a creature resembling a rat – no, not a rat, maybe a weasel... And when Lorenzo, still bellowing with laughter, picked him up by his tail and tossed him back onto his ship, he rushed for a crack in the floorboards and woke up.

Though the voice from heaven filled his soul with some sort of pride, the humiliation which had followed it lodged like a stone in his throat, one that demanded revenge. But what kind of revenge could be had, when just days ago Lorenzo had died like a stray dog, leaving no satisfaction for poor Girolamo?

That same day an even greater degradation awaited Girolamo. News of an evil painting reached him after his tasteless breakfast. Even if the informers had not forgotten to mention his claims to be a prophet, even if they had not said that he was a modern-day Jesus Christ, even if they had not connected the painting to his name, the fact that the Madonna in the painting held an ermine, rather than the Heavenly Child, and that she had been depicted in the guise of a modern young woman, would have been enough to cause Girolamo to explode with brimstone. But his avid followers, each interpreting his hysterical fervour in his own way, stood before him in obedient silence, as if they had unveiled a vile conspiracy.

It was not for two days, nor even two weeks or two months, but rather two whole years, that the saintly Girolamo held his bitter tongue. He spoke only when the scourge of the end of the world burst into the city – not from the sea in the shape of the Turks, but from the mountains, in the form of the French King Charles. Now his sermons sounded not like a chastisement, but like a command. They had grown potent, like wine kept for years in oak barrels, and they proved this potency by intoxicating otherwise healthy minds.

'An era fifteen centuries long is coming to an end,' Girolamo thundered. 'For what purpose did the Son of Heaven dedicate these years to you? In what form? By whose example? And what harvest do you bring to the Apocalypse? Isaiah's trumpets have ceased to sound. Who among you heard their call? The scourge of the Almighty hangs above you. The time has come to submit! Perhaps we will be allowed another five years on this earth, or six. Our duty is to construct, in this world, the nation that the Creator himself bid us build. But so long as this state, beginning with Florence, is not supported by these pillars, I shall bear no responsibility for it!' That prediction proved untrue. The Black Sforza in Milan aligned with the heavenly scourge King Charles, and in the space of one day, Girolamo indeed became the fully responsible leader of Florence. For the bearded clerics, dressed in white, rose up and seized all power from the hapless, secular rulers.

But even disaster always has another side. One night, something happened that delighted the young Fabrizio. Hoping that the Medicis had lost power, Ibn Tufeil, the healer from Granada, entered the city with his adopted daughter Cecilia.

That winter was especially bleak. The streets were empty of people, who feared the fists of their god-fearing governors, and even the blossoming natural beauty of Florence, now deprived of the human gaze, seemed desolate and alone, like trees after their leaves have fallen. More than those trees was stripped bare; the evergreen cypresses and boxwoods had also gone dry, and the marble and granite of the buildings, which had only yesterday gleamed in the rays of the sun and the moon, was covered in grey; snow, the beauty of winter, seemed to be shunning this place, and only the wind, roaming homeless and inscrutable, wandered the streets of the deserted city.

Florence was preparing for Christmas, and while in previous years this holiday had passed with a joyful clamour of merrymaking, with parties and performances, this year the sacred day seemed to have turned to face despair. The people knew not how to make ready for the holiday. They did not hang pine boughs and colourful garlands in the cathedrals. The homemakers shied away from cooking festive dishes, and those who were not afraid to make them did not share them with their neighbours and friends.

But the holiday did reign in Fabrizio's heart, because while by day he was occupied with copying ancient manuscripts in the newly built terrace of San Paolo, by night, his eyes, tired of the beauty of the letters and words, raced to find another, his double, who had never stopped loving him: Cecilia! They spent the long winter nights talking over all the days they had lived. These stories, while outwardly somewhat sad, were also filled with the fire of youth, and her father the healer smiled gently and meaningfully when he heard their tales.

Fabrizio, who could now see his love while wide awake rather than solely in his dreams, was enchanted. He had entirely forgotten that scandalous portrait of several years ago. Could he ever have guessed that the portrait would intrude into his life again, and in such a tragic way?

—

Two days before Christmas, an announcement was made throughout the city. That year, there would be no carnival, as was the usual custom, but a crusade against vanity and futility instead. The town criers

spread the news that if there was anyone who had in
his home any pictures not depicting Jesus or the Virgin
Mary, anyone who owned a book which did not mention
the name of God, anyone keeping idols that distracted
them from godly thoughts, all these would be consigned to the flames right here in this earthly world.
The fire would be set in the public square across from
the Cathedral of Santa Maria del Fiore, and it would be
fuelled by all the vanity and futility that still remained.

And so they began hauling masterpieces of art out
of every house. Mountainous piles rose of countless
books, gold-brocaded clothing, paintings and sculp-
tures. It just so happened that Fabrizio, with the help of
the healer from Granada, had recently finished a manuscript of Greek philosophy, translated from the Arabic.
Now he did not know what to do with these books. So
that day he went to see his former teacher, forgotten,
and himself forgetful, but still not a stranger to him:
Alessandro Botticelli. Alessandro had been locked in
his room for weeks, alone, painting a picture; but as
the picture that kept emerging had nothing in common
with the vision he held within, he had torn up several
canvases, and he was pacing from corner to corner
when Fabrizio arrived.

'Have I come at a bad time?' asked Fabrizio.

The audible doubt in his voice made his teacher's

rage, already at its limits, finally overflow, so much so that it almost instantly lost its strength, like a pot that had boiled over. 'Do you know what they have decided to use to kindle that bonfire?', he asked. Fabrizio thought of the books he had been rewriting for a year and a half now, but Alessandro, as if reading his student's mind, told him, 'No, not your books. The painting with the ermine!'

'No!' Fabrizio exclaimed.

Alessandro nodded his head in confirmation, and again began pacing from corner to corner.

'You know,' he said, in a voice untouched by passion, 'I would have painted you, holding a giant coat of arms of the city. Florence would have presented that symbol to you, and it would have been as pure as your face, and dazzlingly bright. A red cap on your head, like this one, for instance...' he nodded over to one of his own old hats. But when Fabrizio, perhaps involuntarily, put that hat on his head, his own soul filled with something quite different.

'Would you really agree to such a thing?' Fabrizio asked, looking his master straight in the eye.

'To what?'

Instead of answering, Fabrizio tossed out another question that seethed inside him. 'Do you truly not understand that, after they burn that painting, they will burn *her*?'

'Who, now?' Alessandro again answered a question with a question. Perhaps he was truly a prisoner of his own thoughts and could not understand what Fabrizio meant, or perhaps, seeing no solution, he was simply pretending not to understand.

And so Fabrizio laid bare his ultimate fear. 'Do you want to see Cecilia in that bonfire?'

'No, no, I meant the painting—'

'And this coming from you, who knows more about the divine power of art than anyone!' Fabrizio, infuriated, cut him off almost mid-word. 'Do you remember what you told me? You said, "When God created the world, perhaps he understood something about the artist's condition." And now you are unable to recognise the value of one person?'

'She can take refuge at my estate,' said the teacher, in a voice suddenly grown weary. 'Nobody will look for her there.'

'What about the painting?'

'The painting is just a painting,' answered Alessandro, shrugging his shoulders and slouching like a man who had shed a heavy load, and he walked out of the room. The visit was over.

Not knowing what to do next, Fabrizio looked around

the studio, and when he saw a portrait of St. Sebastian, which he had never seen before, an errant thought struck his mind like lightning.

'Alessandro!' he called. There was no answer. He called one more time. No answer. Then he took the portrait and walked out, towards the Palazzo Vecchio. Dusk had fallen, and there was nobody on the streets except the wandering wind; this Florence seemed to be in a stupor before the holiday, like a widow burying her husband.

Arno, why do you flow so peacefully? Tuscan sky, why are you so veiled in silence? Avenue of the Uffizi, have you truly shrouded yourself under that cathedral? Florence, my Florence! Are these the days of your suffering that Dante, in his exile, foresaw for you?

When Fabrizio reached the Palazzo Vecchio, priests in sharply pointed hoods were hurrying in agitation from room to room, and Fabrizio took advantage of this confusion, and told a monk standing near the door, 'I have orders to deliver this painting to the gift room!' Then he concealed himself in the tumult around him.

The room had been there since the time of the Medicis, and Fabrizio knew it well, but as he approached it, his heart beat ever stronger, threatening to leap out of his chest. 'Is the painting still there?' he wondered. 'Or has it long since been taken to the cellar of San Marco, ready to be burned?' But when he caught sight of the painting from a distance, when he saw his Cecilia and her ermine, he began to worry even more. His hands shook, his knees went weak, and his legs did not have the strength to move him forwards. Fortunately, the only priest in the room left just then, and Fabrizio was able to close the door behind him. Half swooning, as if in a fever, he quickly tore the painting off the wall and hung the portrait of St. Sebastian in its place. Then he drew a knife from his bag, and he used it to slice through the canvas of the newly deposed painting, all around its edge, just inside the frame. He took one more look at his beloved and her ermine, rolled the canvas into a tube and tucked it away inside his tunic. Later, Fabrizio could not recall how he had broken the frame into four parts and tossed the pieces into a fireplace, nor how he had run from room to room and finally down the staircase and out of the palace.

Early the next morning, he was apprehended. After all, very man in the city knew him, and every dog besides; he was the symbol of life renewed after the plague. Accused of treason against his city, his government, and his religion, that very day, he was thrown onto a bonfire raised of books and paintings. But even then, he never uttered a word about where he had hidden that fateful picture, nor about the location of the real Cecilia.

The young man perished as the crowd watched. Still, the death of Jesus had given rise to a new religion, and in a similar way, this death shook not just those present, but an entire people. Perhaps the gale and lightning, splitting the dark winter sky into tiny pieces, rattled the souls of the people that night. Cries rang out from among those gathered: 'Murder!' 'Fraud!' and even 'Ermine!'

The city had fractured.

The next day, the walls of every monastery were covered with charcoal sketches of the ermine. It seemed that another sort of plague had drawn the enormous rodents out of the depths of the city and right to the surface of the streets. The religious nobility tried as they might, but they could not counteract this plague. The whole city was shrouded in fear – and then Girolamo, transfixed, dreamed again.

In his dream, the young man was calling to him from the burning bonfire, his voice gentle, promising him eternal life. As Girolamo, terrified and helpless, walked into the bonfire with the crowd watching, nothing in him burned except for his heart: only his heart hissed in the scorching heat. Finally, the young man extended a friendly hand to him, and when he gripped it, the hand suddenly transformed into his mother's hand, drawing him close. Girolamo sensed with terror that he himself was transforming into an infant, while the crowd shouted in unison, 'Ermine! Ermine!' – and in that instant Girolamo, curled up in an infantine lump, awoke, bathed in cold sweat.

He thought a great deal about that dream, more than he had thought about the previous one. That was because he felt, in his heart, an unjust pain. Had he truly come into this world with ill intentions? Had he not brought it equality, purity, and godliness? Had he not steered the vagrant mob towards their forgotten God? Why was his Lord punishing him now? Why this stubborn pain? For what unknown sins must he atone? Or was the problem that every step and every movement ever made towards a good deed begot enmity and evil in this world? Could the internal fire of this inwards suffering compare to the outwards blaze of a bonfire? Even if those things were comparable, as the man in his dream had said, could a child of man truly be scorched between those two flames?

Alone with his endless doubts and endless excruciations, Girolamo reached a final decision.

'I shall enter the fire. Yet I will not burn!' he boasted. 'I will show you all the power of Faith!'

This particular bonfire was scheduled to take place at a time of equilibrium: noon. It was not to burn on vanities and futilities, but on pine logs and cypress branches. Girolamo ordered that it be kindled with the parts of the broken picture frame that young man had tossed hurriedly into the fireplace.

—

The scheduled day arrived quicker than anyone had expected. The people of the city gathered in the square from early in the morning. The pilgrims' well in front of the cathedral was surrounded by rings of spectators, many layers thick. Every street leading to the square was full to overflowing, like rivers in flood. Noon was approaching.

As the hour neared, Girolamo's spirit wavered and flagged. He could not even summon to his side a trusted wife, because his whole life long the monk had never trusted anyone but God; and now, most likely, God was angry with him, too, and had turned away from him. Or perhaps some devil had pushed him off the path, and it was the devil and the hysteria of his followers that had forced him to consent to the burning of that innocent young man! Or had the days allotted by the Lord indeed run out? Had Judgement Day arrived? If that was so, were the holy infant and the ermine now equals after all?

Girolamo sensed once more, as he had long ago, the absolute ambivalence of the world. But now this world did not seem foreign and in need of conquering.

Instead, it was here beneath his feet, and it had penetrated into his very essence. Yes, this world was his
own, native home. The heat of these thoughts helped
him recognise one more thing quite clearly: whether or
not he burned in that fire, he would not prove a thing.
And woeful as it was, that thought made his load easier
to bear.

In this state of the soul, he walked out of his cell
and into the one next door. All the hypocrites had long
ago escaped, to beat the crowd to the spectacle. He
put his hand inside the cabinet that held the sacred
books, and he suddenly laughed at his own foresight:
but of course, here was a half-empty vessel of wine
at the ready. For some reason, the words Jesus said
when he stood all alone in the Garden of Gethsemane
floated through his mind. 'Let this cup pass me by!' And
with those words, he took pleasure in drinking what
the vessel held, and then he used a knife to slash into
the feathery quilts hidden under the bed-mat, and he
reclined back in the soft down, which billowed up gently
all around him like white flames.

—

By noon they had used the picture frame to kindle the
fire, and the crowd, and especially the monks who were
Girolamo's followers, began to show their impatience.

The fire was raging, and the hot branches crackled. As the heat reached certain hearts, a murmur became audible in the crowd. The monks who heard it tried to mingle with the crowd, out of harm's way, but eventually they decided to send several of their brothers to the convent of San Marco. But just as a few pebbles sliding off a mountain inevitably bring down an avalanche after them, the four chosen men drew after them eight other men with nothing to do, and after those eight came sixteen genuine miscreants, and after the miscreants there followed a group of revenge-seekers, and after them came the whole unrestrictable, unpredictable crowd. The power of that current put the four men in a state of fever, and now they were ready to conduct an interrogation instead of simply posing a neutral query. But when they reached the cell of the holy Girolamo, they let out a cry that all could hear: 'He has fled, the scoundrel!'

When the crowd heard the news, an unease travelled through the crowd that resembled the undulant movement of a serpent's body under its scales. Then one monk, for reasons unknown, went into his own cell, and called some new and disturbing news out into the crowded street. 'Here he lies, the devil, drunk as a skunk! He couldn't even crawl into his own bed!'

Now the serpent had a mouse to swallow, and

the crowd picked up the unfortunate half-conscious Girolamo, wrapped him in mariners' cords, and passed him, hand to hand, all the way to the raging bonfire. Fed with pine logs and cypress branches, the fire would not be extinguished that day, for the people brought all the holy books and religious paintings that remained from the time of Girolamo, and they threw them onto the fire along with their crosses and monk's habits, to burn with the saint of yesterday and the demon of today.

No, no miracle occurred that day. Later, somebody said it was because the fire had not been fuelled purely by pine and cypress. Somebody else blamed it on the holy man's insobriety, and another man thought it was the fault of the spirit, and the hysteria, that had seized the crowd.

Only Alessandro Botticelli achieved what he desired that day. He emerged from the depths of his own thoughts, and he put on canvas a painting which had nearly destroyed his heart and mind when he had first envisioned it. He called this painting *The Outcast*. Others called that painting Alessandro's own orphaned soul. Some were reminded of Cecilia, alone after the death of young Fabrizio. But while some may have thought of the Virgin who had lost her ermine, others went further, and named her using Dante's words, and called her *Florence*.

The Stranger, meanwhile, gazing upon the canvasses, seemed to witness this whole story again as he glimpsed the ray of sunshine which, for a single instant, connected the two portraits. And he felt a certain bittersweet dissatisfaction that he never had been able to visit that city.

⁂

EVENTS OF THE YEAR
OF THE HIJRA 1414

Here, you may encounter any manner of animal
or plant; but no sooner do they settle here, or feed
on its grass, or drink its water, than they begin to
take on coverings most strange to their form.

Avicenna, *Hayy ibn Yaqzan*

Life truly had taken a European turn. As soon as we
landed in Milan, one of us went by a rental place
and picked out a nice little car, another bought some
sweet treats to snack on as we drove, and the third –
that was me – watched everything happen with great
pleasure. We drove from Milan to Lago di Garda. On
the way, I took a good look at Italy. To my eyes, every
little business along the road, whether a cement fac-
tory or window-cleaning establishment, looked like
a museum.

That was Italy!

We feasted on Italian dishes at a roadside restaurant.

I remember how one time in Tashkent we got in the car and drove to the banks of the Anhor to have some lagman. It was the same thing here: a legion of cars travelling by, and this Italian dish as starchy as our own Uzbek noodles. We ate it happily.

We travelled until around noon, when we finally wound up in an old village. I remember how we tried to make a call from there (it seemed Jamaliddin could only ever be found in that one particular restaurant; either the owner was a friend of his, or all the cyclists hung out there in their free time) – we called, but nobody answered. We asked someone, and learned that today was some sort of holiday. There's nothing like these empty little Italian towns, frozen for centuries and centuries; they seem enchanted, and are shot through with those narrow streets. Occasionally a bicyclist would appear, decked out like a real racer, making our hearts beat faster as we continued on our way.

Finally, we found the little town we were looking for, Garda. The town was a paradise, sitting right on a lake where the hills began. We even found the restaurant, but there was not a soul there. You know Italians and their holidays! Everyone we asked seemed to know Abdu like a brother. We decided to find a hotel before doing anything else.

We didn't have to pay because the French government was footing all the bills. That was what had been so nice during Soviet times: a genuine lack of responsibility. You could celebrate Pushkin Days with a group of writers, or take part in a ten-day festival of Uzbek or Russian literature, all with your mind at ease, because the state would take care of everything. It would decide where you spent the night and what to feed you. Now finally I had that kind of life again, in sunny Italy! There was so much to rejoice in. Under my window were the branches of an olive tree, something I had only ever encountered in García Lorca's verses, as translated by Shavkat Rakhman – go ahead, adore them, and the olives truly will tremble, like a bird's tail in the evening breeze! We ate whatever our hearts desired. Thierry begrudged us nothing, including Italian wine. To your health, Jamaliddin, worthy son of the fatherland! It is thanks to you that we are being thus honoured!

Later that day, we found Jamaliddin himself. We went to see him at his house. There we also found his young sister, who had only just arrived from Tashkent. 'My brother's out training, riding his bicycle,' the girl told us. 'If you want to wait, he'll come back.' She spoke Uzbek so sweetly that I found myself thinking maybe we should open the film with her.

About half an hour later, Jamaliddin himself made his appearance, glowering like a thundercloud. To be honest, earlier, when I had first heard the name Jamaliddin Abdujapparov, I had envisioned a sturdy fellow with a face like a Kazakh, a guy from Qashqadaryo or Boyovut in the south-east. But no. This Jamaliddin was a big, strong guy with a sharp nose and an eagle's haughty gaze. And he conducted himself like a genuine Uzbek, indicating with every move he made that we had better have a good excuse for being in his house without him. We talked about this and that until he was in a slightly better mood. Then we suggested we start filming the next day. He suddenly became a great deal friendlier.

'Maybe we could start right now, instead of tomorrow?' suggested Thierry. 'I've heard that you keep pigeons. Could you tell us more about your hobby? And is it true that you brought these pigeons with you from Tashkent?'

'Of course!' answered Jamaliddin, his eyes flashing. 'Want to see them?' So off we went.

Half an hour later Jamaliddin showed up in his red Ferrari. He opened a pigeon cage and sent one flying into the sky, while we filmed it all and interviewed him. Our subject was more of an eagle than a pigeon, of course. He was certainly not a Russian (it was a very good thing the filmmakers had brought me with them), and Jamaliddin only spoke Uzbek before the camera. Still, though, before each shot he asked me, in Russian, how to say what he wanted to say in Uzbek.

—

If you are patient, unripe fruit transforms into a sweet delicacy. The tiny larva, barely flickering to life, grows a body, a head, eyes, arms and legs; in just the same way, the gland puts forth the first drops of love and compassion, drops of treacle, drops of honey, and the wings fill with strength, and the time comes when you sense, inside you, a kind of combat readiness. At that moment, you feel like a warrior ready to rush into battle, and you move outside the hive. Then the story unfolds, the story of a bee and his glory in war!

Is this not how the mind itself develops? The wick of the torch rising up in your consciousness first illuminates the objects around you. And when the light of consciousness is sufficiently disturbed, it runs up against some duty looming dark; and after that, it first shapes the foundation, collects scattered concepts and puts them in order; and then, like a bee becoming a nurse, it feeds and nurtures those thoughts. When that step, too, has been completed, the thoughts are given shape, fed on the nectar of knowledge gathered by others, and they are laid down in beds, and then raised still higher as your confidence in your own power grows. Now it feels ready to discuss things, to argue, to fight and to struggle... The wisest among us understand all this easily.

The steps in the scientific method, and, let's say, the transition from the culture of dialogism to structuralism, and then on to compilativism, or indeed a possible classification system for the human experience: the migration from syncretism to the ethical dimension, and from that to the gnosiological, practical, aesthetic, political and religious dimension, or indeed the concept of *hamsa* in general, was described in full by Mavlan Abdurahman Jami. Not to mention the ideas of the Haft Avrang cycle, consisting of seven poems: truth in 'Subhatulahror', wisdom in 'Tuhvatul-ahror', beauty in 'Yusuf and Zuleyha', love in 'Leyla and Mejnun', power in 'Hiradnama-yi Iskandar' – are not all of these things shoots off of a single branch? Those who are most perceptive will quickly guess the point. This is all merely a sign for those already in the know.

—

Sina could sense, now, that the stinger he wore on his waist had been suffused with poison, and like Alexander the Great, he headed into battle, seeking glory and fame. Words Sina's nurse had once said were spinning through his head. 'A bee's business is flight. And in flight, just as soon as you stop, you fall.' And that is in fact how it happened. After the first step, the second inevitably sprouts in its wake, and then the third. It's like the staircase I mentioned. If you're not climbing or flying up, then you're falling. Therefore, a bee who flaps his wings just once is destined to do it again, and a third time, and a fourth. He who steps onto the road must continue to his destination. That is the rule of flight. The rule of growth. The rule of life.

One time, in just that way, Sina broke through the crowd pressing in around him from twelve different directions, and pushing through the pack, he made it all the way to the exit from the hive.

A bee's first step outside the hive is always a remarkable experience. When your body, accustomed to constant crowding, your five eyes, so used to the dark, and your hive mind itself all suddenly perceive the green clouds and the black, black sun, the yellow, yellow meadow and the violet water; when your lungs, gone moist in the musty air, first fill with a sharp, pure breeze; when your four wings, which had seemed so insignificant before, first toss you bodily up and then down, faster than your own thoughts – any bee might forget, then, his purpose here on earth.

You and I, my friend, have experienced the same thing. We have also been stripped of our childhoods, sent instead to mix the clay to build a house; one summer day we were shaved bare, and sent to concrete buildings three thousand miles from our own clay-walled homes. We too were issued rifles – I myself got an AKM numbered LA 8278 – and we lay down with them every night and woke up with them every morning for three long years. Our heads, too, spun with the distance and with the forests, with our own youth and the power emerging from our hearts. And bees stung us when we spent the nights in the fields and the meadows. But etiquette requires that we not leave those others in mid-thought.

That day, Sina received an order to join the Guard. That word, *guard*, can mean a lot of things, not all of them positive. We might be used to thinking of security guards as idle, immoral old men, standing around at night with their rusty old weapons, passing around vodka. But that was not Sina's task. He was to check the affiliation and origins of every living thing that tried to enter the hive, and allow in only his brothers, and stop all others, even if it cost him his life.

Those entering this place had no need to show ID.

If you look a bee in the eyes – and it's not the same for ants, who resemble the flat shadow inside a small square on the melon-shaped crevice in the hive, or spiders, thin and long-legged, as if they were simply reflected off the surface of a samovar – the bee always backs away, cowed by even the hint of pressure from another of its kind.

But lately, there had appeared a new strain of crossbred bees. Sina's old nurse had told him their story over the long winter nights. It seemed that one hapless bee had come here from a place called Africa, and was captured by human beings who began conducting various experiments on him in their prisons. They poked around in his mouth, then looked him over from behind, then brought him a white-winged beauty from among the local bees and left them alone together.

Thank God those human beasts did not understand the language of bees. The local bee fell in love with the bee from far-off lands, and she decided to try to free him. They made a plan. One morning they both played dead, there in their glass container. The first man to appear, seeing them lifeless, shouted hysterically and called the others. In the hubbub that followed all the doors were flung open, and even the director himself came in. As soon as someone opened the container and bravely stuck a hand inside, the African bee stabbed his stinger into that hand with all his might, and then immediately pulled it back again. Panic set in. Meanwhile, the blonde girl bee wasted no time. She hugged her co-conspirator close to her body and flew with him towards the open doors, and in that way, they both escaped their confinement and were free.

In the virgin forests, they started their family. Their descendants spread over the earth. Ever since then, there has been a breed of bees who are big, strong adventurers, subordinate to no one and trusting no one, either, who make their living exclusively through raids and robbery in the forestlands.

The chronicles say that once, at a feast, someone said within earshot of Mahmud Daudi, 'Avicenna is such a great man that even among the sheikhs there are none to compare with him.' At which the veins in the madman Mahmud's forehead bulged, and he responded, 'Can he even be considered a man? You can compare me with a thousand Avicennas! Why, he has never even fought a tomcat, while I, before the eyes of Emir Doda, fought off *two* young hound dogs!'

———

Sina flew around his hive, keeping a special lookout for those mulatto bees. But every bee that flew by carried the scent of his Mother and the Teacher, so Sina did not interfere with them, and let them pass into the hive.

It was drawing close to eight o'clock in the evening, and the final stragglers, bringing their harvest back to the hive from the fields and the gardens, were returning home in the last violet rays of the sun. Sina sensed that some of them were drunk not on the nectar they had gathered but on the breath of the evening air, but commenting on that was the last thing on his mind. If only he could have shed this guard duty and gone flying off, himself, over the steppe and desert! Probably his opportunity would come, one day.

There was some resemblance, here, to how a soldier posted to keep watch on the bank of a river might glance around him, at sunset, and sink a bit into the languor of his own future.

It was time to change shifts. Sina was just turning

back to the hive when suddenly there arose a smell he had never known before. Flashing through the air quick as lightning, like an enemy fighter plane, dove a creature the size of a hornet, straight at the entrance to the hive, swooping down out of the clear blue sky. Sina hurried to intercept it. The creature, still in a nosedive, collided with him, and from the force of it they bounced off through the air in opposite directions. Both were stunned with the force of that impact. Without his armour and strong thorax, none of Sina's ribs would have survived intact.

As he fell to the earth, his wings broken, one thought flashed through Sina's head: 'Don't let the Teacher find out!' But his instinct for self-preservation, quicker than that thought, made him ready for battle again, and Sina rushed back towards the opening slit in his hive. The Mulatto, not expecting this youngster to move quite so quickly, had spread his wings and was readying himself to demonstrate his full strength. With all his might he rushed at Sina, like an outlaw charging forwards on horseback, his spear aloft before him. But Sina, anticipating the fight, had forgotten everything else, and in the blink of an eye he made himself ready either to prevail or to perish.

His muscles must have been quicker than his

mind, because while the Mulatto was preparing to ram into Sina with the full weight of his twice-as-big body, Sina ducked under his enemy's wing at the last moment, in a way not even he could explain, and thrust his stinger towards the Mulatto's body with all the strength he could muster. His dagger glanced off the Mulatto's armour and did not penetrate his body, only scratching it, and into that scratch there oozed a drop of poison. The poison from his dagger mixed with the blood, and the nectar that spilled between them caused their bodies to stick together, and they both tumbled to the ground. That was when Sina noticed that the huge Mulatto's stinger had got caught in a blade of grass and pulled from its body.

Everyone knows that a bee who loses his stinger dies. So now Sina found himself lying there in a pile with this dead adversary. Sina felt bitterly envious of his enemy's body, which had landed on top of his own. Somehow he struggled out from under the corpse, and placed the enormous Mulatto under a blade of grass filled with poison. Finally, exhausted, he washed himself in the evening dew.

Sina spent that night alone, away from home. That night, Sina walked the thin line that separates life and death, and he began to understand the meaning of what the storyteller had said: to have repentance in piety, desire in love, asceticism in the straight path, humility in faith, and perseverance in all work.

———

I was telling you about Jamaliddin. That night he showed up at our hotel, bringing his restaurateur friend with him. He was clearly curious about our plans for the next day. They're really a different sort of people, these big stars! He wanted to know whether we were well-prepared.

'Well, what can we come up with for tomorrow?' Thierry-Matrasul started off modestly.

'Maybe you could go fishing! That could turn out as well as the bit with the pigeons,' the Italian restaurant man broke in. So it seems the two of them had already talked it over.

'No,' said Jamaliddin. 'I have practice in the morning. I need to ride a couple hundred kilometres.'

'Oh, perfect!' Thierry cheered. 'We'll be able to drive along behind you and film, and when you slow down to take a breath, you can answer our questions.'

Jamaliddin thought a bit and accepted our proposal. 'And then we can go fishing after lunch.' He seemed satisfied with that suggestion, too.

—

I'd like to be able to describe to you how Jamaliddin caught fish. The cyclist lived on the shore of Lago di Garda. 'This is where we should do the filming,' suggested Thierry-Matrasul.

But the cyclist frowned and told him, 'There's another lake, too. This one is sort of… civilised.'

What else could we do? We followed the racer's red Ferrari out towards the wilder, less civilised lake. A racer is a racer, and as soon as we reached the main road, he darted off ahead and disappeared from view. But fate was kind to us, and we had his restaurateur fan with us, who spurred on his more mundane Fiat and eventually got us to the lake. By then, it seemed Jamaliddin had already been out there angling for half an hour. He had probably intended to catch three or four big carp before we arrived, but that day there didn't seem to be any simple-minded fish around, and there were none lying, mouths agape, in his empty net.

'I just got here,' was all that Jamaliddin said.

We started shooting. Maybe it was the light from the cameras, or the dust from the cars, or God only knows what else, but that whole afternoon not a single fish hooked itself on his line. Jamaliddin's face

took on a mournful expression. He didn't want to say
two words to us.

*

One time in New York I attended a demonstration
at the United Nations building. That day, all of us
speakers walked up to that podium ready to either
sink or swim. In those days of quickly shifting political winds, that truly required courage. Even the
American Uzbeks admitted it, and they told me that
nobody had ever agreed to do anything of the sort
before. 'What would be, would be,' I thought!

On that day, the warmer it got outside, the more
people arrived. It would have been great if only the
Uzbeks had come, or, say, Turkestani Kazakhs and
Kyrgyz, although the Kazakhs and Kyrgyz never by
any means describe themselves as Turkestanis – only
the poor Uzbeks and Sarts do that. Yes, if Turkestani
Sarts had been the only people there – but instead,
all sorts of interested people started arriving. A
Crimean Tatar. Two Turks. Three Ukrainian nation-
alists. You'll never guess who it was who opened that
demonstration. A German man! A German, who had
been kicked out of Königsberg by the Soviet Army.
After neither of the Germanies took him in, this little
Führer created the Organisation of Enslaved Peoples,

and became its chairman. This man walked up to the podium, and he began to heat up and practically boil over. You've probably seen Hitler's fiery speeches in the movies. It was just like that. We were almost ready to shout out 'Heil!' ourselves. This German spent half an hour weeping at our funeral, telling us all his terrible problems.

After him the Ukrainians stepped to the podium. They too had suffered, as it turned out. Interestingly enough, they had each experienced a different kind of pain. Every time one of them said one thing, another would interrupt him in their Ukrainian-accented Russian – 'No, Mikola, it wasn't like that, it was like this!' – and then arguments would spring up among the demonstrators. It was a good thing the Crimean Tatar was there to break it up.

Apparently the Ukrainians distracted him, because he missed his turn and a Turk climbed up to the podium and set it trembling like risen dough, and with remarkable eloquence he began to sympathise with us and our sorrows. 'My friends!' said this Turk, with nary an introductory word. 'My aggrieved friends! Freedom to Turkestan!'

This must have been the spiritual leader we were waiting for, our sheikh, because a furious shout rose up and travelled around in a circle that reminded me of the ring in the Qadiri Sufi order. Naturally, we chanted in English. 'Turkestan free! Russia go home!' And we started marching stubbornly in a circle, like bulls digging a well, and we all entered into some sort of ecstasy. But while I walked in that circle, holding somebody's hand, a thought was marching in circles in my brain: 'There goes your cover, Sheikhov! You've guaranteed your own arrest when you return to Uzbekistan!'

But that was only the beginning. Once our Turkish sheikh stepped down from the podium, none of the other friendly peoples there could bring themselves to take over, seeing that the Turkestanis had struck a particular tone, and due to that it was one of the Sarts who stepped up next – they're a hospitable people, after all – and he had not forgotten, even in that ecstasy, to suck up, so he abruptly announced, 'Dear countrymen! Among us there is the most genuine countryman of all countrymen who have ever come from our motherland. Please, come up here, to the place of honour.'

By that time, thanks to our circle chants ('Huv-va! Huv-va!') a few of the highest windows in the United Nations building had opened up, and a crowd of tourists, photographers and ordinary passers-by had gathered. Everyone stood there and wondered what on earth we were demonstrating for. I walked up to that podium, thinking that if this had been ordained by God, then the outcome was also in God's hands.

'Brothers!' I began. But somehow I could not find in my memory the oratorical style of Erkin Vahidov or Abdulla Aripov.

'Dear friends, brothers and sisters!' I tried again, and then stopped, flummoxed. Because I realised then that I sounded like Stalin giving a speech before the war. If I kept on in this vein, it was entirely possible that a phrase like 'the invincible Red Army' might come out of my mouth. Which would be as good as jumping into a boiling cauldron.

We writers, you know, we understand the masses. That may be the reason that I suddenly felt sympathy for these countrymen of mine, young and old. They had left behind their shops and their affairs for two hours, maybe even for the only two hours they could leave them that whole year, and here they were, in a completely alien country, worlds away, and they were worried about their nation, they were thinking of their people. I felt so much sympathy for them that tears almost came to my eyes.

'My dear ones!' said I. 'You and I are just a small sprinkling here. So our voices will not be heard behind those windows, and if they do hear us, nobody will listen or give it much thought. But in that place where I came from, there are twenty million of your people, and when the voice of an entire people rings in tune with your voice, then that voice will be heard by all. Whether they want to hear it or not!'

I spoke on and on. It turned out that we, too, had suffered quite a lot, only we hadn't been paying attention.

The demonstration was over, the passion had died down, and we were standing around catching our breath, like neighbours steaming in a bathhouse. The people who had just been demonstrating, flaunting their bare nationalism, had now put their civilian outfits back on, and they looked like level-headed American citizens again, and off they rushed, some back to man their stores, to make up for the volume of commerce they might have missed in this time before Christmas, and some consulted with each other on what to have for dinner.

I also stood there, sad, on the windy square before the UN building, feeling that I had made that speech to myself, like a little boy left all alone after his circumcision ceremony. Then a very old man, very venerable, probably a hundred and two, walked up to me. 'You must be the nephew of Pasha-Khan-Tura?' he asked.

Although at that moment my thoughts were occupied with something completely different, he and I still managed to talk a little about this and that. 'Son,' the old man said, 'You surprised me with all those serious things you said. What do we Uzbeks need, after all? For our stomachs to be full, for business to be brisk, and... and... well, take a look at that girl photographer over there! You think I have a chance? Yes yes yes, look at that figure! Why isn't she snapping in two under that heavy camera she's holding? I'm a hundred and two years old, you know, and I still can't deny myself a little taste! All you need to do is eat well, then you won't have any trouble below the belt!' And with those words, the venerable old man headed off, a youthful spring in his step, making a beeline towards that girl photographer.

EVENTS OF THE YEAR
OF THE HIJRA 1415

Then follows a kingdom the residents of which are people
of handsome and charming mien; they are people who
love gaiety and merrymaking, and who know nothing
of grief or regret; and they are fine players of the lute,
of which they possess a multitude of variations.

Avicenna, *Hayy ibn Yaqzan*

We wanted to leave Jamaliddin in peace with his fishing and pigeon-raising, his bicycles and prizes, so we
quickly wrapped up our film and returned, through
Milan, to Paris. So now we can return to our main
purpose, too, and of course to my own secret mission, because I still had not found Avicenna, nor
Warsworth, nor Huggins, nor Vissens.

We had a friend in Paris named Hélène, an
opera singer. This opera singer of ours told us, one
time, 'I have a student who is a single woman. Go
and move in with her, and you'll pay only six-zero-
zero francs.' She didn't express herself all that well in

Russian, so she pronounced each digit individually. 'Six-zero-zero' meant six hundred francs! That was nearly two-thirds cheaper than the one thousand five hundred francs (one-five-zero-zero, as Hélène would have said) we were currently paying Mademoiselle de Suze. This new woman, whose name was Martine, had a mother who lived in some distant corner of France, and recently, ever since her mother had fallen ill, Martine had been obliged to visit her more frequently. During those visits, she needed somebody to water her flowers.

To make a long story short, immediately after my return from Italy, Hélène decided to come in her car, along with her husband Lionel, to help us move from Fontainebleau to Martine's house in a commune just outside Paris called Nanterre. The day came. We had announced the news to our old woman at the last possible moment. But the real beneficiary of the new arrangement was that old crone, not us. You might remember that when we settled in at her house, we paid her a month's worth of rent as a deposit. And the old woman decided to withhold that from us.

We tried to appeal to her better nature. 'Come on! We're foreigners, after all, and you're someone who knows how the world works by now...'

'No!' she cut me off. 'We have laws for this sort of

thing. I won't be able to find anyone to replace you, and that room will be empty.'

To which we objected, 'But you've already got ten empty rooms as it is.'

'That room is a special room. There's great demand for it,' the old woman insisted.

The bourgeoisie have learned something over all those centuries! How could we have prevailed over her? We had to leave that empty house completely empty ourselves. We loaded our suitcases into Hélène and Lionel's small car and we headed for Nanterre.

As it turned out, that very day Martine had in fact left for Vichy to visit her mother. We walked in. This was a real house, two storeys tall. You might call it a cottage, but after that eighteenth-century hole-in-the-wall in the old lady's mansion, it felt like a real palace! The first floor was all set up for us, and that's where we went. We arranged all our things in a civilised way, and then sat down to take a breath. Downstairs, we saw flowers, a television, and a piano. My wife tried playing right away, and Lionel joined in, imitating the way Hélène sang, and we all laughed. Really, for a place like this, we would happily have paid a bigger sum in any language – fifteen hundred, one-five-zero-zero, or anything you like.

'Now let's find a restaurant!' Hélène suggested.

'Our treat!' Hélène's was a life of amusements. She had no time for boredom. Her father had been a Russian nobleman, which is why her last name was Vasilyev in a Frenchified form: Vassileff. She brought us to a Chinese restaurant that day, but other days, if she had a concert to take advantage of, for instance, she'd take us around to all the little receptions that happened before the big event, and afterwards there were always Japanese or Indian or Thai restaurants where we could count on a long feast around the table.

Two days later Martine returned. Let me tell you a little about her. We Uzbeks are not a grateful people, and I remember mostly how she tormented us. She was about forty-five years old and had never been married, and so she had put her whole heart into this house and the things inside it. All those things – tables, dishes, ashtrays – had been passed down hand to hand to her over four or five generations. If you touched any one of them without thinking, or you put a teacup or even a sheet of paper down on the wrong table, you'd get a scolding. 'Now what is this! How could one put something down here? It came from my aunt's eldest cousin, after all! Do you know how priceless it is?' And on and on. It was enough to make you lose your will to live. Of course, it's our Uzbek character that was responsible.

But to speak more substantively about Martine, I'd have to admit that this woman had allowed complete strangers into her home, trusting them with her life. In what century could you ever have found something like that among the Uzbeks? She stayed for two days, then always got in her car and drove off to Vichy for weeks at a time. When she returned, she would sit and translate articles from German or English for some Catholic magazine. That's how she earned her living. She earned a thousand francs per month, fifteen hundred at best. Even university students probably make more than she did. But despite all that, she went out for a nice *déjeuner* every day with a friend or niece or aunt.

Once in a while she would invite them to the house. Then we would cook up some Uzbek plov or samsa for them, and she could introduce us to her friends in the best possible light: 'These are my friends from a country called Uzbekistan.' Everyone was very jealous of her, since they didn't have any friends like that. For Martine, that was enough. That was her wealth. That was her popularity.

She took us once to a club devoted to eking out similarities between different religions. 'They'll have a free lunch!' she said, so we went. Sitting there was one Jewish woman and one Arab-looking man. The

Jewish woman was there out of boredom, and the Arab was there for the free food, like us. They told their life stories. It turned out the Jewish woman's daughter had started dating a black guy. But the father of the family was categorically opposed, on religious grounds. That's what this woman told us about. Everyone nodded their heads. They even repeated a few slogans, like, 'If only we could bring our religions closer together!' If there was any hint of argument, it mostly fizzled out when they started bringing in wine and cheese. After the wine had been distributed all our differences were forgotten, the fraternal feelings took over, and Martine asked us to recount Rumi's legend about the grapes.

Wine came from grapes, after all. So we told them the story.

> *Once upon a time a man gave an Iranian, an Arab, a Turk, and a Greek some money. In doing them this kindness, he said, 'Buy whatever you like with this money.'*
>
> *One of the four, the Iranian, said, 'Let's buy some angür with it.'*
>
> *The Arab disagreed. 'Don't be stupid! I don't want any angür. I want some inab.'*
>
> *The third person, the Turk, didn't like either of those ideas. 'I don't want any angür or inab. Let's buy some üzüm,' he said.*
>
> *The Greek, who had been watching what was going on, cried, 'Stop this foolishness! I want some istafil. Let's buy some istafil with this money!'*
>
> *Soon the four of them started arguing, each man yelling that*

they should buy what he wanted. Punches flew and there was a big fight. Before long a scholar who was passing by broke up the fight and asked what their problem was.

The Iranian said, 'I want to buy some angür with the money we were given.'

'No, we're going to buy some inab,' protested the Arab.

'I say we should buy some üzüm,' shouted the Turk.

'We're going to buy some istafil with our money,' insisted the Greek.

The scholar understood that these four people speaking in different languages actually all wanted the same thing. He said, 'Be quiet and listen to me. I'm going to buy what all of you want with this money. Trust me!'

Then he went and bought some grapes. He gave them the grapes, made all four of them happy and settled the senseless argument.

A good person remains good, wherever he or she may be. It turns out that kindness remains kindness, and does not choose nationalities.

—

Every morning, when we woke up at Martine's house, I put on a record with some wonderful song – *Ave Maria*, maybe – and got down to work. I was writing a novel. In fact it was pouring out of me, being ladled directly out of my heart. I had tried experimenting with Uzbek music, but it hadn't worked. Your own native music ends up distracting you, sucking you in, making you forget what you're writing. It can make you think of the little daughter you left in Tashkent, and every word in the song takes on a meaning just for you. When you hear an Afghani song with the words 'I will take your child, Majid', or you hear a woman from Andijan singing 'Friends, I have parted with my only blossom', then that's it, you can't take any more. You start to think they are singing about you, and you succumb to panic or confused perturbation, and you rush to use Martine's phone to call Tashkent, and you can't even begin to relax until you hear your daughter's voice.

This was the beginning of spring. We had used up all our money paying off our debts, we weren't sure if our visas would be extended, life was battering us in different ways from all directions, and the sense of separation was always dragging at our hearts. When I walked up to the Leclerc store with the pennies I earned here and there, I saw the soil had already dried out, and the children – healthy children from healthy families – had come outside to play football on the fresh spring grass... and meanwhile, nothing about my own situation had changed. I still faced the same complete lack of clarity, and had the same uncertainty inside me. So I returned again to the lonely house, sat down to work on my novel or some poetry, bathing them in the blood I might as well have wrung out of my heart, like juice from a pomegranate, and when it became intolerable to sit in that house any longer, or sulk around the garden in front of it, I escaped to walk down the road. I used to drive to the Oriental Studies Institute, wallowing in the songs that were eating me up inside all the way there. I might end the day in the library, distracting myself with something or other, and then return home again, back to the loneliness, the homelessness, the melancholy.

—

I told you how we made that movie about Jamaliddin. I made some money in other ways, too. I gave lectures in a couple of places, I discussed Uzbek songs on a Turkish radio station in Paris, I transcribed the words from old ghazals that had been used to record a CD of Azeri songs one of our friends was putting out, and did some other jobs in that vein. Basically, if there was any way to make a little money, I put my pride aside and did it.

One of our friends, a sculptor named Boris, mentioned he was remodelling his studio and asked if I could help. 'I can pay you what the work is worth,' he added.

'Well, of course!' I agreed. Is there a single Uzbek in the world who has never built a house, or at least helped remodel one? Since we were little kids we've been mixing up clay, setting bricks, wearing ourselves out dragging buckets full of mud around in circles like whirling dervishes.

I went to that studio. And what a studio it was! A mansion! Not to mention that this studio was right next door to the castle where Proust wrote *Swann's Way*.

The job got under way. First we decided to use sandpaper to remove the old plasterwork. It was hellish work. We got covered head-to-toe with the dust from the alabaster, and the powdery stuff even got inside us. Everything went white, even our shit. I started to think I was turning into a real saint.

That job went on for three days. All day we worked hard at that, and then in the evenings, after showers, we wolfed down the food Boris's wife Madeleine graciously prepared and got to talking. We'd talk about poetry, about Zionism, about the great thinkers of world philosophy like Plato and Avicenna. When our conversation ran out, I would leave Boris with his family, and go out to stroll around the quiet neighbourhood. French forests and fields... The open spaces... Deserted churches, and haystacks appearing out of nowhere... Empty roads... In these places, you can always sing the same song, at the top of your voice:

I once wept in sympathy for every sick man I knew,
Now the sick are weeping for me, so many, their hearts so true...

When you realise the only one hearing your voice is your Creator, you get fed up with yourself, tired of yourself, and you want to scream in frustration, with the sort of strength that could match the scale of these fields and wide open spaces.

But then we started on the plasterwork. After that came a base coat and then paint, and things got a lot easier. The dust was gone, so the paint roller could just fly over the ceiling. The walls were no problem – the paint seemed to leap onto the walls of its own accord. We didn't get as tired, and we could pay more attention to our conversation. There were no great questions we did not address! Boris might declare he knew the first lines of the first verse ever composed, and cite the words of Ezra-nabi from the Bible, the things he told his sons; then I would up the ante and bring up Adam's poem, penned in *Tales of the Prophets* by Nasriddin Rabguzi. Then Boris would say he knew the latest thoughts ever thought, and bring up a certain Jacques Derrida, and I would cite examples from the *Treatise on the Question* by our philosopher

Sokrat Sharkiyev, who discovered our own Hamid Ismailov in this very city of Paris where we stood.

I keep talking about Boris. Let me tell you how I met him. Previously, I wrote that I had a friend working at a French international radio station. He was the one who interviewed me when Uzbekistan first declared its independence. Once, on his birthday, we used some money we had saved up to buy a bottle of expensive wine, and all us Uzbeks with nothing to do went to his house. That's where we met a fellow countryman of ours who had married a French poétesse ten years earlier and left our motherland for her. He was a sculptor, and his name was Boris.

Another time, that same friend decided to bring us to Boris's house for a visit. 'Boris,' he told us, 'is thinking about starting a new journal. If you've got anything interesting, you might be able to put it in.' That was why we were meeting at his house. Boris's home and studio were about one hundred and fifty kilometres from Paris. When we arrived, Boris introduced another grand plan to everyone there. 'An evening of Russian literature!' he declared. During the process of choosing participants, it was decided that on the list would be Nobel laureate Ivan Bunin, translated by Boris's wife Madeleine; Anna Akhmatova, translated by my radio friend's wife Marie; and finally,

as a living exhibition, there would be yours truly,
never translated by anyone, my own wife sitting there
next to me. I could think of no reason to object, and
feeling more cheerful, I struck a proud posture.

It was only our former fellow countrymen who
gathered together to organise that event. Who would
remember the poor Russians if not for them? All
sorts of artists, conference planners, sound and lighting engineers, assistants – the generous Boris forgot
nobody when he handed out pieces of this pie. After
all, some serious money had been allocated to organise the festivities, which were to take place in a town
name Laon, just outside Reims, which is the capital
of the province of Champagne. This would be the
first evening in the town's history ever to be devoted
to outstanding representatives of the Russian literary
world. An evening of historical personalities *and* one
living writer!

On the appointed day, my wife and I put on the
most fashionable clothing we had, boarded a train, and
set off. It's no joke going to meet a crowd of admirers
as a living classic of Russian literature. Within two
hours we had arrived at the Laon rail station.

The minister of culture of Champagne Province
met us there, and suddenly announced, 'We're going

to a primary school first. There's a group of students waiting to meet you.'

On the way, this minister of culture, who was in fact a friend and sponsor of Boris, warned us, 'You can tell them a little about yourself, of course, but they're expecting a lecture on Russian literature.'

'And how long is this encounter supposed to last?' I asked.

'One hour,' he answered.

Oh God, have you truly decided to punish me? An hour's worth of material on Russian literature! Classic or not, I doubted I could even speak for a whole hour in Russian about Russian literature, to say nothing of doing it in French.

We rode in the car, and my thoughts spun along as fast as the tires. Now what was I supposed to do? What could I possibly come up with?

Then we reached the school. If only you could have seen the reception we got! Never had I experienced such consideration. It's nice to be a classic. Flowers, kisses, autographs... All the people at that school, aged four to fifty-four, treated us with unmatched respect and attention. On the other hand, they were filming my every step with a film camera. It's tough to be a classic. They must have assumed Ivan Bunin was my best friend, and Anna Akhmatova my mistress, so they were showering me with the kind of attention only those two deserved.

Ten minutes floated by on the waves of ceremony. After those ten minutes they announced my name, very loudly, and after some enthusiastic applause, a dead silence settled all around me. Now I was supposed to start my speech. Let me say it again: it is tough to be a classic. It becomes especially tough when you have to earn enough money to support three people. Next to me sat my wife, who was blushing red as a tomato.

'Dear friends!' I began. 'Dear devotees of Russian literature! Some people have earned the kind of respect and honour you have just expressed, and some people have not earned it.' (Shades, you might have noticed, of the Uzbek poem 'Some Have Survived to These Days, and Some Have Not Survived'.)

'Please allow me, on behalf of my teachers Ivan Bunin and Anna Akhmatova, who have not lived to reach these days, to thank you from the bottom of my heart, and to consider this ovation you gave me to have been delivered in their honour!' More jaw-dropping applause followed – and that gave me time to get my thoughts together.

'Russian literature is a vast ocean, but I will begin on the far shore, with Uzbek literature,' I started with

confidence. (More verse was nagging at my conscience, though – 'Your hands caress her body, but
another beauty is in your heart...') But now there
was a nice, clear road before me. The lecture rolled
onwards, like a wagon with well-greased wheels. I
started with the great Navoiy, and I just happened to
have in my hands a book put out in Paris by that same
hard-working Hamid Ismailov you've heard so much
about. As evidence for each thought I laid out, I read
to them from Navoiy, either his *Dark Eyes* or *Out of
the Bath Unclean*. It was a good thing the world had
Uzbek literature! And thank God it had promoters
in French, like Ismailov, because here again it wasn't
Bunin and Akhmatova that came to my rescue, but
Navoiy, Mashrab and Ismailov.

When I stopped to look, I had already been talking for almost an hour. And they were all sitting there
spellbound.

'Now let's get back to the beginning,' I told them.
'Russian literature is a vast ocean. But even an ocean
is measured by its shorelines. It *starts* from its shorelines. If it has no shorelines, it does not exist. What
gives an ocean its shape is its shorelines.

'I mentioned Navoiy's *Hamsa* to you. But note,
please, that four hundred years later, this phenomenon
repeated itself when Russian literature was at the very

peak of its development. Take Pushkin as an example. Or Dostoyevsky's five novels. They are essentially nothing other than the *Hamsa* written over again. But all that is another story,' I declared, wrapping it up, turning into the homestretch of my lecture.

By the time I was done, things had developed in such a direction that I was not, in fact, the student of Bunin and Akhmatova; no, historically speaking, they were students of *my* national literature. It was probably for that reason that as soon as I spoke my last sentence, a storm of applause rang out to praise me, and I was named an honorary teacher of that school.

But then I learned that honour came at a price. According to the school rules, anyone named an honorary teacher had to lead one lesson with the school's most gifted students. Even the provincial minister of culture who tried to intercede for us did not have the power to violate that two-hundred-year-old tradition. So I had to stay for a lesson.

But there is such a thing as inspiration, a thing that, once it appears, cannot be got rid of or chased away, until you finally give up on everything and go and get a good night's sleep. And I let inspiration gallop free.

'Children!' I began. 'My young brethren! A talented person has original talents all his own, and so in most cases, he never even needs a teacher. Let's test this idea. I'm going to give each of you two lines of verse, and I want you to try to supplement them and expand their meaning and write them out to a quatrain. I'd like some of you to write in some antique style, like a troubadour, and some in a more modern style, like a clown tossing thoughts around randomly. Ready? Good! Let the games begin!'

I gave each student two lines from well-known Uzbek poems: 'I too walked past', 'My heart, filled with blood, hurried to her', 'A simpleton rushed to rebellion', 'Much to my surprise, I saw a moon-faced beauty'.

Although it was not easy to go about disguised as a classic, I believe I pulled it off just fine. You should have seen how much more respect and regard that minister of culture was showing us now! Immeasurable amounts of respect, simply immeasurable.

Maybe the minister sensed that we were getting tired, or maybe he didn't want the authority of his province to deflate before us, but whatever the case, he drove us straight to a restaurant which deserves its own, separate description. Restaurants are usually notable by the variety of dishes they have on offer. But this one was built to collect champagne. Just imagine: they handed us a menu, and on that menu there was nothing but different types of that bubbly beverage! You won't believe it, but there were three hundred and fifty-four names listed. One variety had been bottled back in 1864, and a single glass cost five thousand francs. Almost as much as I earned working on that film!

No, the minister did nothing to cast doubt on our authority. He started ordering us champagne that cost found hundred francs per glass. I'll just say that the value of two glasses of champagne amounted to a significant increase to the salary we were receiving for our two-day journey here. 'I would have preferred cash,' I almost said, drunk on the aroma of that champagne. I'm whining, I know. But it was some very good champagne. It was just as nice to swallow as it was to smell, as if everything inside you was being draped in fine silk, from your liver to your stomach. And your brain, stationed up higher, sank into the luxury of that softness.

Then, late in the evening, the minister let us know we were receiving extra-special treatment. 'We reserved a hotel room for you, but you will stay with me at my house. You'll be my guests,' he told us, and took us home with him.

We had never seen a house like his. From the outside it looked like a haphazard heap of a building, all turns and angles. But we walked into the lift and rode up to his apartment. The minister opened the door leading out of the lift using an ordinary key, and we found ourselves in an apartment on the fourth or fifth floor. There wasn't so much a terrace there as a genuine courtyard, with trees and flowers growing, green grass all around, a fountain reaching for the sky... and more rooms than I could count. One of those rooms was assigned to us. There was as much space in that room as in Martine's whole house. It was intriguing. No neighbours on any side, the sky all around us, and even the trees growing below seemed to be stretching upwards to get themselves a better view of this paradise.

The minister's wife left their children in our care and sequestered herself in the kitchen. One hour later she had some exquisite dishes all ready for us, and it was time for another long banquet. Here in this paradise, under the naked stars, we talked tirelessly of literature, and we recited poetry and told stories late into the night.

—

The next day was the big event, the long-awaited Evening of Russian Literature. From early morning on, artists, translators, scholars, and other like-minded

supporters began arriving from Paris. Our own unpar-
alleled uniqueness and superiority began steadily to
wane. By noon, we had all been given rooms in a chic
five-star hotel. Martine arrived close to dusk in her
car, its tires bald from her many trips between Paris
and Vichy. Finally, evening fell. And so many people
had come! In fact they were still coming, with no end
in sight. Perhaps events like these are all too rare, or
maybe, on the contrary, they have been held so often
that people were simply in the habit of attending. But
whatever the case, I never would have guessed that
there was so much interest in Russian literature here
in France

The event itself got off to an excellent start. Each
of us was supposed to speak. We wanted to start with
Ivan Bunin, but because the man himself had long
ago left this world, my radio friend Vitaly spoke
for him. I've already told you he can speak forever.
So now his lecture on Bunin began. He must have
collected facts very carefully from an encyclopedia.
What sort of family Bunin was born to, when, and
what fruit was in season then; what sort of school he
went to, which little girl's braids he used to pull, and
on and on. It took him half an hour to get about halfway through the great man's life. Signs of impatience
were beginning to surface among the audience, and

when I looked, I saw Boris starting to sputter unhappily. I don't know if Vitaly sensed that impatience, or if he caught Boris's whispering out of the corner of one ear (Madeleine managed to put a stop to that), but over the next three minutes, Vitaly successfully moved poor Bunin and his entire creative life on to his deathbed and pushed him on through the pearly gates. Boris was the first to applaud, and he couldn't help exclaiming in relief, 'Bravo! You do good work when you set your mind to it!'

We heard some of Bunin's poetry, delivered in a style beyond reproach by a French actor. The way he pronounced the phrase, 'It would be nice to buy a dog', sounded so natural that probably every person listening felt like a little dog himself, and spent a moment trying to nuzzle the actor's hand.

Then it was Anna Akhmatova's turn. Seeing that due to Boris's hissing the flawed life of Ivan Bunin had only been partially revealed, Akhmatova's translator did not even try to bring her unhappy subject back from the dead. She only shared a few of her poems. More verse filled the air. Then a friend of Boris's, who happened to belong to a rock band, began giving us an inspired reading of Akhmatova in translation. In the process he was practically reborn as the poet herself, so much so that we started wondering whether he was actually a woman or a man.

And then it was my turn. I won't elaborate here, except to tell you that, truly, it's much better to still be alive! Again it was up to me to collect all the glory and honour that was due to the people who had spoken before me. Even our musician friend, during the banquet that followed, admitted, 'Honestly, man, I liked what you wrote the best. That wasn't a museum – it was real life!'

*
**

'He who has never lived through a war has not been acquainted with death.' This proverb does not appear in any books. This proverb is a motto of the bees, known by only the most devout among them. Struggling against his pitiable condition by sheer force of memory, Sina awoke in the predawn darkness of that night and found that a spider had woven a web all around him. The bee had just narrowly escaped death, and now things were worse than before. He tried to free himself, but the strands of that web were sturdy, and the spider herself was sitting in one corner, waiting for the bee to lose strength and succumb as her prey. Only the dead know how it feels to be caught in a trap like that, because nobody has ever come out of one alive. But Sina could tell you all about it. How?

Because at that moment the wind gusted, tossing the spider and her web, along with the bee inside it, up into the air, and in the next instant it struck so hard against a tree growing there at the edge of the forest that the mulatto bees, who had barely managed to jump out of the way, buzzed towards the poor spider in a full rage. There was no room left in life for her; judging by the hundreds of protruding stingers, you might have mistaken the creature for the corpse of a young hedgehog or small porcupine. But the strange thing was that none of the bees attacked Sina, who had already looked once into the face of death, and this time, unafraid, looked it proudly in the eye. It was not his bee brothers or bee solidarity that saved him, in the end. Fortunately or unfortunately, most probably because of the spilled nectar of their dead brother, these mulattos adopted Sina as one of their own – though not without some mistrust. They took him in, having decided that a bee so similar to themselves must be a relative on their father's side.

Life in exile! May it be cursed. Once you have become a stranger, a stranger you shall remain; you may endeavour to make friends, but the task is a difficult one, full end to end with uncertainty. You must keep your mind always vigilant and wary, live where others have lived before you; everything is temporary, everything costs your heart dearly. In exile, you may be closer to the meaning of life. Some whom you meet, when they catch the whiff of that nectar, will consider you one of the elect, and they will want to make you a minister, if not a king. But not all are destined for majesty, a fact many know to be true due to their own mercenary motives and greed.

Among the bees there is a law: all females are born with the potential to become the queen mother, but of ten thousand young bees, only one is cultivated in such a way that she might become the sovereign. And after that, is it any surprise that among the ten thousand, there are some who are envious? It was those envious ones, from among the mulattos, who decided that Sina was unworthy of a minister's glory, and did not even have the right to dine with them. But still there was one kind bee who took him into her own cell, apart from those others, and in the evening, distracting the guards, she dressed Sina in a mulatto's clothing and set him free.

And Sina soared off, with all his strength! He flew with passion and inspiration. In that flight he collected no nectar from flowers, but rather the elusive nectar of his own thoughts.

—

O brothers in truth! Rouse yourselves, and tear aside the curtain of your own spiritual contentment, and fly off in search of the perfection in each of you!

O brothers in truth! Cast aside your scales like a snake, grub in the earth like a worm, prepare your stinger like a scorpion. The temptations of the devil lie in wait! He who gathers the poison shall live, and he who awaits death shall shrink and cower!

Do not build a nest; that is a job for the birds. If you have no wings, then cower quietly; the best of your leaders have cowered, as well!

Be an ostrich, swallowing a hot stone; be a snake, digesting a bone; or a flaming salamander, unharmed even in fire. Become a bat escaping the light of the sun; there is a reason bats fly better than birds.

O brothers in truth! The richest of the rich have seen into the future; the poorest of the poor are not worthy of their fate!

O brothers in truth! Every morning, an angel disavows evil, and a beast drowns in sin; and surprisingly, only a man, falling into the trap of his own avarice, loses all traces of humanity. Surprisingly, the man who

falls into the trap of avarice is the man with only indo-
lence in his soul!

O Allah! A man can ascend as an angel when he can
conquer his unquenchable avarice, but if he drowns in
it instead, he falls lower than any beast!

———

Flying from blossom to blossom, he dove headfirst
into the pollen of each and, once he had satisfied
not his own avarice but his duty to his hive, Sina
again continued on his way. When his mouth, arms
and legs were full to overflowing with pollen and
nectar, when his thin wings began to bend under
the weight of his body, he committed to memory all
of this blossoming bounty and turned towards his
hive.

A bee's flight is a remarkable thing. When you are
drunk from the scent of the flowers and are full of
this blessing in body and soul, and you are returning
to your people, you take note of all the places you
stopped on your journey for the benefit of other travellers. Along the way, Sina sampled the seven levels
of the sky, the kingdom of the angels, and in it, the
twenty-eight degrees of existence; then finally he
reached the gates of his own hive. New keepers and
guards were buzzing around the gates. Probably as a

result of the previous day's events, they numbered nearly a thousand, and their mood was hostile. Two of them came to meet Sina, and they gave him a good sniffing, as insistently as if they were demanding to see his passport. They must have found something they did not like, because they both started speaking louder. 'Who are you? What are you doing here? You think you can just knock on the door and we'll open those gates?'

After the bliss Sina had so recently experienced, hearing this sort of talk was especially dispiriting.

—

I have one Russian friend, a gifted artist. Everywhere he goes he's inventing things, whether anyone needs them or not. Not long ago he decided to make a movie about the life of a Christmas tree, after the holiday was over. It's interesting, isn't it – the tree which people go to such lengths to procure as the holidays approach, the tree that stands at the centre of attention in your home in all its celebratory finery, gets tossed on the rubbish heap right after New Year's Day. That's the end. Nobody has anything else to do with it. But it's a living thing, too, isn't it? Now, my friend gave that some thought, and he went to the dump and filmed one of those trees.

While he was filming a huge bin lorry drove up, and the chief rubbish collector got out of it and shouted at him. 'What are you doing here, you son of a bitch?'

'I'm filming these Christmas trees,' my friend responded calmly.

'What are you, Jewish?' the idiot replied, and showered him with layer upon layer of curse words.

My friend did not know what to say.

—

This was the story that flashed through Sina's mind now. It was a story he had overheard somewhere before. Sina wanted to stand up to the guards. 'Do you know where I've come from? Do you know who I am?' he would demand of them. But in the end he decided it wasn't worth the trouble trying to match wits with these errand boys.

Sina was using his front arms to wipe his eyes, feeling distracted and empty inside, when from behind him he caught a scent which could never be confused with anything else. He could hardly believe his eyes, but there, coming wheezing out of the dwelling, was his own nurse, older but not yet despondent. Though the guards shouted at her to get out of the way, and not to block the road, the nurse waited till they were distracted checking somebody else, and then she gave Sina a very brief account of what had happened in their hive.

It turned out that there had been a rebellion against the Teacher. There had come to be more and more uneducated and uncultured bees among them, like those standing guard now, who had never tasted human flesh, and as a result, the plots and the chaos had multiplied. When the signs of unrest first surfaced, they fanned the flames, saying, 'The Teacher no longer has any power! Not even a hint of magic, no matter how hard he tries. The time has come for us to crown a new padishah!' After that, the Teacher collected his closest advisors, and told them the following.

> *A wise man said, 'This is my advice to you: die like the fox did when it was being bitten by the flies and mosquitoes.'*
>
> *They asked him, 'How did that fox behave?'*
>
> *And he told them.*
>
> *'Once some hunters were trying to chase a fox into a trap. The fox jumped into a river and swam clear to the other side. When the hounds came rushing after her, the fox had no choice but to climb up on the opposite bank and hide in an overgrown ditch. The fox was injured and scratched all over. No matter how she tried to climb out of that ditch, she could not do it, and she gave up. Then the flies and mosquitoes fell upon her, and they bit her.*
>
> *'In that ditch lived a porcupine. When he saw how the fox had fled from the hunters only to end up a prisoner of the flies, he said to her, "Fox! Shall I chase the flies away from you, and pull you out of this ditch?"*
>
> *'And the fox answered, "Not under any circumstances!*

Your sympathy only hurts me, and your generosity is even less helpful!" The porcupine asked her, "But why?" And she answered, "Now that the flies and mosquitoes have claimed me, they will not give up their prey to anyone. They've drunk so much blood that they are docile now. If you chase them away, others will descend on me like starving hounds, and suck the rest of my blood from my body!"'

When they heard that tale the bees wept, ashamed of themselves, and the Teacher pronounced his final verdict: 'The time has come for a migration.'

You might be familiar with how bees migrate. Once the decision is made, scouts fly off in all directions in search of a new place to live. All those who find something promising return to the hive and begin to boast of the discoveries they've made. They gather together, and one might say, 'What I have seen is a hollow in the trunk of an oak tree. Nice and dry, no ants!' The next might interrupt him, beginning, 'But my place is located right at the edge of a garden. No need to fly far to collect nectar!' And in that manner each of them tries to tip the scales of the debate in his own direction. Factions begin to take shape around these messengers. In order to confirm or deny what is said about other options, they are not above flying to the locations their competitors praise so highly. But if those words turn out to be true, then they switch to their opponent's side, with no pangs of conscience.

Finally, when the choice comes down to two places, the padishah herself dispatches one of her advisors to see them, along with representatives from both factions. On their return, they present their final report and recommendations to the assembled court. Only then does this swarm of bees, having chosen their future home, move as one body, with the old padishah in the lead, towards their newly chosen abode.

This was what Sina was now experiencing. Crowds of settlers had begun swooping out of the hive. The place in front of the hive was as chaotic as a scene from the Day of Judgement. Someone attacked someone else, someone screamed for a lost child, and the escorts pushed right and left, clearing a path for the Teacher. As he emerged from the hive, the Teacher met Sina's glance from a distance, and although hundreds of ranks of guards and sentries closed in around him that very instant, his easy, barely noticeable smile lifted Sina's wings, so much so that he too was able to transform into another small element of this crowd, this swarm, this horde, and this enormous humming, buzzing, unified living thing floated into the sky like a black cloud.

Never in his life had Sina felt such beatitude, such happiness. The pleasure one receives in solitary flight seemed to him only a pale shadow when compared to this group voyage. There is nothing in the world more joyous than the feeling of being a drop in a flowing body of water. No matter where you might be flying, no matter what might await you, no matter what you have left behind, none of it has any meaning, it is all nothing; the only thing that matters is this company in flight.

Maybe love hides a similar pleasure inside of itself. But isn't love, indeed, a flight of the conscious and subconscious mind?

EVENTS OF THE YEAR
OF THE HIJRA 1419

Next comes a kingdom whose residents are very tall
in stature and even more fair of face. They are unusual
in that keeping well away from them is beneficial to
the health, while close proximity is harmful.

Avicenna, *Hayy ibn Yaqzan*

The Stranger remembers the day of his arrival in
Istanbul. He recalls the cart descending down the road
to Uskudar, and the fog or cloud that covered the hills
and suddenly draped the whole world in white snow.
There was a strange feeling of alarm, constant alarm.
As if a man who seemed to have reached his goal
suddenly found that, no, he had not received Allah's
consent, and in a single instant was left without any of
the things he had been striving for.

Lower down, the sea, too, like a dark trepidation,
torments itself and your heart.

The rafts tied up on the shore slip and slide, seemingly trying to escape two sources of misery at once. They give out a screeching sound where the water meets the sky. When you mutter a prayerful *bismallah* and scramble aboard one of the rafts, your feet slip against every wooden beam, as if you were traversing the bridge of trials that leads to the heavenly tabernacles. You slop along through the slurry of water and snow covering the leather cords that bind the boards together. The raftsman is a Greek and an unbeliever, dour as Charon in their Greek stories; this man seems fully prepared to conduct you to the kingdom of shadows.

The Stranger does not wish to remember this sea, this terrible gulf. The underworld is probably more welcoming than these waters. Soon, the shore must appear out of the snow which the wind heaves in different directions, there in the direction of the Kaaba; but whether he was nearing his goal or moving even further away from it, only God knew for sure.

—

Three or maybe four hours after he had set out on his journey, the Stranger found himself slipping and sliding again down towards the estuary leading to the Galatasaray promontory, with its narrow alleyways, filled with a hodgepodge of merchants and tradesmen in rows of shops. He knew that he did not have the strength to bear more of the hellish sufferings that he had witnessed. But what could he do? Especially when, stretched out against the red wound of the setting sun and the broken clouds of a sky that seemed to resemble a dead thing, Istanbul glittered in all its majesty and wonder!

He looked in awe at the opposite bank, where enormous dark mosques and minarets thin and straight as cypress trees loomed in the middle of the snow-covered land. In that moment the city, holding tight to the slopes and heights it scrambled to climb, seemed to him sweeter than any passion or any clever ruse.

No, it proved simple to conquer the estuary. When the Stranger came out at the shops of Eminönü, the muezzins' enchanting voices were floating down from the minarets, calling the faithful to prayer, and joining the merchants and their customers. He hurried to the big, central mosque. He had seen mosques here built like cathedrals, the likes of which he had never seen in Anatolia. It seemed that after the Roman cathedrals had been converted into mosques, the blueprints for new mosques had undergone certain changes.

He wandered around the bazaar. Despite the natural brotherhood among Muslims, he still sensed a certain difference between himself and the people he saw. This bazaar and its shopkeepers resembled the bazaars of Margilan and Isfahan, yet at the same time there was some unique quality here, elusive and alien. Not in the people's faces, or in their garments, so similar to those of other Muslims, but in their particular variety of dexterity, levity, and agility. There seemed to be no end to the shops and stalls. The snow was still falling, but it never reached the ground, melting instead on the tall hats and burqas, the robes and turbans, in the motion of the indescribable crowd. The Stranger made a complete circle of the bazaar and then set off, first towards the Bayezid Mosque, and then, walking down a sloped street, towards the palace.

Although it had already begun to grow dark in the city, the shops were not closing yet, and the grocers and the weavers, the hawkers of goods and the chefs, were shouting loud invitations to passers-by, hoping to tempt the last customers of the day to step inside.

The street lights had not yet been lit, though it was difficult to tell whether that was the habit here, or if it was a consequence of the suddenly descending snow. He walked where the road led him. Some sort of unconquerable trepidation was rising up in his soul. Which would end first, the road or this trepidation? – and as a fork in the road materialised before his eyes, so too did the suffering in his soul split his heart in two.

He chose one path, and soon emerged onto a dark square. Here, the snow had no walls to collide with, and it fell especially strongly; in fact it did not fall so much as press downwards, in a terrible assault, incommensurate with its actual weight. The wind, meeting no barriers, carried in all directions the madness with which the sea had infected it. Hiding his face in one corner of the cloak that covered his body head-to-foot, he unexpectedly found himself before some sort of wall. He turned right and followed it, and came up against a madman, huddling frozen under a small arc. The Stranger asked, 'What is this place?'

The madman may have been trying to state a name, or, hoping for a handout, he may have been loosening the reins on his tongue, but in any case, he pronounced two syllables – 'A-ya'. And he paused, and then mumbled something else.

That word seemed to make the Stranger shudder, and he tossed the last chunk of dried bread he had saved from his journey to this ruffian wrapped in his own filth, and then he stepped through the gate. Once inside the inner courtyard, he encountered a marble staircase. Under their covering of snow, the steps gleamed with a white light, and there was no way to distinguish them from the snow falling upon them. It seemed that with each step he took up, he was ascending into the heavens. He did not even notice when the stairs ended and he was left standing before an immense and very solid archway. There he stood in the snow which connected the heavens to the earth, seemingly under the vaults of a celestial palace. Every step he took towards that colossus now seemed as smooth and even as the snowfall. He passed under the archway.

Dark as the night was, in the glow of the snow that had already fallen he could just make out gigantic stone walls marching away in both directions. It seemed to him that he was entering a stone dungeon, one from which he would never escape. Suddenly he realised where he was. Looking ahead, he shuddered again. Before his gaze a view opened up in which the earth was covered completely, all the way to the sky, with an amazing web of cupolas, resembling the many strata of heaven, or maybe the empty, overturned cauldrons of hell. And stone walls wrapped all around it, locking that magnificent web in place, and created the sensation that all routes of escape were closed, that the sky would always remain dark with night, that the earth would always remain frozen in stone.

All of this flashed through the Stranger's mind with the speed of a vision before death. He took two steps, then stopped stock-still, because his thoughts had paralysed his legs like an axe slicing through a poplar trunk. He was so small, and this colossus so great, that in response to any one of his ant-like steps this stone horror might turn and crumble away, and the scale of its fall would be something like the collapse of the sky itself.

Perhaps it was the effect of these thoughts penetrating his trembling body, or perhaps it was the Christian origins of the cathedral, but it seemed to him that all the demons of the world had focused their attention in one direction, while he had ended up on the other side. Or maybe everything was much simpler, and this was simply another manifestation of dread before Allah. But whatever the case, if he fell into despair, feeling as a speck of dust, before these great rock walls, then how could he ever answer to the Almighty? How difficult it was to overcome that despair and take one step, under the stones and the cupolas that resembled the heavens, which now seemed ruined; and all around, it was darker than dark, and the snow lay as bare as his nerves.

Human beings, as it turns out, find open spaces frightening. The same goes for uncertainty within them. His ears caught a voice, which he thought somehow similar to the scraping of the rope over the boards that had conquered the terror of the sea. 'Hallo! Anyone there?' he shouted then. Receiving no answer, he tore his gaze from the sky and turned it to the ground beneath his feet, to step more confidently towards the room for ablutions. He went all around it, but once he reached the end of one wing of the cathedral, he understood, seeing the drops of water that drained (like his nerves) and fell onto the floor, that the heavenly dome had disappeared from his field of sight. Now he was again in the ordinary world. Through the enormous doors of the Aya Sophia, he walked inside. In the light of a lonely candle, a single shadow recited an evening prayer. What he saw prompted a new thought – 'My shadow is drinking a shadow of milk!' – which sprang to life out of nowhere and then immediately disappeared.

The Stranger gathered his thoughts, and he too said a prayer, then walked outside, but this time not through the door through which he had come, but through another. As he walked away, he fell into the grip of the buffeting wind blowing off the sea, and the snow struck without mercy, but the view of the world felt more familiar than that colossus with its silence and stillness. Now he strode confidently through the darkness towards a venerable building just across the way: the Sultan's Topkapı Palace.

—

That day a north wind began blowing across Istanbul

in the early morning, a gentle, clean breeze from the Black Sea, providing this city, at the centre of four climates, with a glimpse of the approaching spring. The physician Ajjam Ahmed-effendi from Palace Street, in an upbeat mood, had invited his guest to join him in his garden with a view of Liman, asking that the table be set for breakfast; but up till now the guest, having travelled from a warmer seaside climate, had been sitting there in the open air purely out of respect for his host, looking out at the clouds which raced by faster than the water. Like the clouds, their conversation never settled on any one topic, and their thoughts rushed around and wandered off. At noon, the Stranger and the master of the house were to visit the Imperial Palace, to be received by Mehmed-effendi, His Majesty the Sultan's chief healer.

Not two hours had gone by when, like a dirty stream of water flowing into a clean river, under the snow-white clouds there appeared mysterious billowings coloured not just black, but dirt-black, and the wind, blowing first from Anatolia, then from the Sea of Marmara, smeared the sky and the earth together in this blackness with its drying breath. The sea in its perplexity knew not where to cast its waves, and the downy clouds, panicked, began to hyperventilate, and they gave out what seemed nothing less than the howl of the desert, now approaching a heart-rending screech, which, as it neared, could almost be interpreted as a single word: 'Fire! Fire!'

The two men broke off their breakfast and rushed down to the street. People were running in all directions, terrified, echoing the fear of the clouds and the noise of the sea, forced, it seemed, into a state of panic. Nothing could be understood other than those cries of 'fire!', and while some were yelling about Cibali, others mentioned Kichikbazar, and still others said it was Kantarci, while somebody else fretted about the Suleimaniyeh. That meant that fire had besieged the entire city. Now there were even greater numbers of people rushing from Aksaray and Altimarmar. Everyone was running towards the palace or towards the sea in hope of salvation, and it would have been impossible either to stop them or to bring them back to their senses.

Naturally, the two men did not make their appearance at the palace that day at noon. There was no hope of pushing through the crowd, for one thing; and Ahmed-effendi was a doctor, after all, so he saddled two swift horses and they rode off to where the fire raged. As if testing its strength against the piercing wind, the fire launched itself into an embrace with a whirling funnel cloud, and even if both felt their backs breaking, neither the fire nor the wind would ever release its grip: the whirlwind knocked the fire down again and again, but then the fire overtook the wind and brought the battle to a new house, to a new arena. There was nothing but screaming and confusion all around, as terrible as a scene from Judgement Day. Those who tarried fell victim to the flames, but those who rushed upwards had a chance of saving themselves from the deadly embrace of wind and fire. Ajjam Ahmed-effendi and his guest managed to pull several families out of the inferno, and in the process the heat singed away every hair on their bodies, sparing neither their eyebrows and lashes nor the horses' tails and manes. The two men pondered what the infernal flames of hell would look like once they had set the whole world on fire, given how much terror this fire had instilled by seizing just one city. They provided aid to those who had suffered burns, and put others into wagons, and they moved further away from the fire, which still had not stopped, despite all their prayers and curses; the fire seemed to be playing an evil game of tag, pushing them closer and closer to the sea.

Somebody had the idea to build a firewall to counter the oncoming flames. They tried, but the ungrateful blaze only redoubled in strength, as if to show them what it thought of their efforts. Thanks to the light emanating from the fire, or perhaps because the evening had been so dark, nobody noticed when night fell. House after house went up in flames, street after street, neighbourhood after neighbourhood.

It was only the next day, when the fire had reached Zayrak and Atbazar, that the black clouds which had come to fill the sky, perhaps due to all the weeping and tears which had ascended to the heavens, began to release such a downpour that black streams of mud and debris swept down the hills of Beyazit and Cerrahpaşa; and the fire, finding itself caught between two watery barricades, could no longer resist, and it surrendered to the city.

It was extinguished with water sent down to the people, a miraculous gift. But there is a reason they say that there are two sides to every coin. In the ash mixed with rubble from the mudslides, tulips rampaged into bloom, two hundred and eighty-six varieties of the very choicest tulips. In just one week the ruins of Istanbul were blanketed by tulips, and a new era, of sorts, began.

Unfortunately, while tulips may flourish even in black ash, they never can grow out of human hearts. On that day, Ajjam Ahmed the healer had intended to visit the Topkapı hospital, but early that morning some sullen soldiers knocked at the door to his home and came inside. They swept up his guest by the scruff of his neck and, paying no heed to the desperate pleas and sobs of the physician, they took the Stranger off to prison.

They took him, allegedly, to verify his guilt, his culpability for that fire. In the predawn darkness, after they shoved him onto the cart and started off to the Yedikule Fortress along the road leading towards Aksaray, they stopped by the house of a Turkish woman who began to weep hysterically, and they dragged out, by the scruff of *his* neck, a half-dressed Armenian man. They shoved him in the cart, too. This unfortunate soul, straw stuck all over his hairy body, knew his case was hopeless. He hid his palms between his knees, and repeated the name of Allah over and over for a time, and when he caught sight of his cartmate he fell into an even deeper despair and muttered some sort of curse, this time in his own language. 'They must suspect him of culpability for the fire, too,' thought the Stranger; but that man was not the only one he met on that journey. Not long before they reached Yedikule, they hauled a blue-eyed Jewish man, who had landed in this city from God only knew where, out of some Roman man's house; and fettering them all together with a single chain, they finally rolled on to Yedikule itself.

When terrible events occur, layering one atop the last, men may begin to experience an atrophy of the emotions. On the streets and squares, on the rooftops

of houses and in window boxes, the tulips were bloom-
ing; but these men, covered with straw and tossed onto
the stone floor of a grey prison cell, could only remember the days gone by. In prison, regardless of how much
time passes – a day, a week, or a month – time transforms, all facts aside, into an insuperable adversary,
which, whether you try to spend it thinking about your
past or about your future, will never release you from its
cruel embrace, leaving you with only one option: your
dreams. It is your dreams which begin to rampage and
rise up, just like those two hundred and eighty-six varieties of tulips. And all because there is no way to stop
them!

   In the days that stretched and clung to them like
glue, a military officer came and questioned each prisoner about something called Iran, and its Padishah
Tahmasp; in fact he did not question them so much
as tell them stories, as if delivering a sermon. He mentioned an Afghan rebel by the name of Mirwais, then
moved on to a Hussein or Mir Mahmud, who murdered his own father-in-law, Mirwais, in Isfahan; and
then he forgot all about that and began to ramble on
about Ashraf, who was said to have joined forces with
Tahmasp and seized Hamadan, and then, as if inviting them to take part in the legend, began searching
for evidence of their guilt. But after a while even that

officer, as if he had drowned in his own stories, stopped coming. And again they were left with their dreams.

There is one thing we know about dreams: as soon as you speak of them, the truth flies away from them. Therefore the Stranger began to read the dreams of his cellmates from their faces, closed off to the world while they slept. He behaved much like the now-vanished interrogating officer, ceaselessly droning on about his own endless thoughts and visions, but on the other side of the door, whether in hopes of cracking the conspiracy or out of sheer boredom, the sharp ears of the eavesdropping soldiers realised that this chatter was nothing other than the interpretation of dreams, and they began to apply what was said to their own lives.

One day, when the Jewish man awoke with tears rolling from his blue eyes, the Stranger began to recite, allegorically, the 'Source of the Pure Well'. How was he to know that just an hour later the Emperor's messengers would spread the news, throughout the city, of an order about the Fountain of Sultan Ahmed? 'Marble stones are required to build a new decorated fountain in the middle of the ancestral imperial palace! So demands the Imperial Edict!'

The royal guards informed the asasbashi of this coincidence, and the asasbashi conveyed the news to his lieutenant. And at the moment the lieutenant was passing on that interpretation to the judge, the Stranger had just seen or imagined a spider creeping around and weaving a web on the hairy body of his Armenian cell-mate, and he spoke in fear: 'Time to expose a plot!' But he could not have known that at that very moment the judge had just read another imperial order, a report of a plot revealed. 'Men who have admitted their guilt and have called for disorder, acting for Christian Europe, and who have lured many to their side...' it began.

Soon the Stranger's auspicious interpretation of the spider's actions was reported to the Imperial Chancery, in the same way as it happened in the story of the prophet Joseph. And then – because the Grand Vizier was away on a journey – this news was reported directly to that valiant individual, the worker of miracles, the loving, powerful, but merciful effendi, the Sultan and Emperor.

At that time, the Sultan of all Sultans of the world, the third Sultan named Ahmed, was dwelling on unhappy thoughts. There was the surrender of Tabriz to King Tahmasp, not approved by His Majesty, by Mustafa-pasha's troops, and their retreat; there were Baku and Derbend, conquered by the Russians; there was rebellion sweeping the land... And on top of that, despite the fact that the sons of Osman had graciously entrusted the country to his son-in-law, Grand Vizier

Ibrahim-pasha, rumours were afloat that poisoned his heart: they were saying that the Grand Vizier had personally given orders to dismantle the defence of Tabriz and quit the city. In fact, Ibrahim-pasha had left for Uskudar, the fortress where new troops had been gathered, and that made it look as if governmental affairs had been left improperly unattended.

It is no easy matter, being the twenty-third sultan in a dynastic line. What more could one man do in this world, once the victories have been gained, and half the world was under the control of the Emperor – from Algeria in the south (where, by the way, he himself had brought down Oran, the last stronghold of the Spaniards!) to Bessarabia in the north (captured from Peter I); and the new buildings, each one more majestic than the last, were transforming Istanbul into the world's most beautiful city; and all men, not just on land, but also on sea, bowed before the sons of Osman, from the Benedictines down to the Swedish King Carl XII, who had himself been defeated at Poltava by Peter I.

Sitting with quill and ink in his library, the Sultan tossed a glance of a poetic nature at the *Dictionary of Vankulu*, which had been printed right there in Istanbul and just recently delivered from the typesetters. Now there was no need to write a thing. In this state of spiritual turmoil, His Imperial Majesty gave himself over to reminiscing about his childhood.

By a tradition originating from the time of Sultan Fatih, one of the founders of the dynasty, all princes of every generation, except the eldest, were put to death in childhood. This was an attempt to eliminate intrigue and conspiracy. The practice, though abolished, had not been forgotten, and the fear which was passed down from generation to generation had not been dispelled. But the princes who had once spent their lifetimes fearing either the executioner's axe or their stepmother's poison, who had withered away out of sight of the sun in the dark rooms of Topkapı Palace, now rode fearlessly to Edirne or to Konya or to Eskişehir, where they learned from the best minds of their times; some mastered fencing, some learned calligraphy, and some studied astrology. And yet Ahmed had not been the eldest brother, and therefore he could not help treating this life as a temporary, transitory phenomenon.

Then, one night, he dreamed of tulips growing out of the spilled blood of the murdered princes, and he counted, and found that there were precisely two hundred and eighty-six varieties of these astonishingly wondrous tulips. No matter what else came to pass, he knew that these new laws could not be trusted, for they resembled the crust of ice that forms over a puddle when a cold wind blows. And that was probably the reason he grew up very nonchalant by nature, and with a fine appreciation for the elegant.

In fact, when his brother Sultan Mustafa, who had rightfully acceded to power as the eldest son, was overthrown by the janissaries – new soldiers who moved against him – it was thanks to the carefree way little Ahmed had of passing the time that he was chosen to be put in his place as Sultan. Once on the throne, the demonstrations of weakness in his nature did not wane, but rather grew more prominent. It was then, by his command, that wherever Sultan Ahmed's ambassadors were sent, they began bringing back tulips, and all of Istanbul came to be covered with them. Now this resplendent city, blessed with its year-round greenery, was drowning in red and scarlet, pink and pearly blue, and that carpet with all its colourful comfort and joy gleamed and brimmed over like ruby signet rings, with the light of good fortune, and warmth, and delight. Like a cup of good wine served up by the universe, this splendour stirred the senses. Time, as it surged in and out like the blue sea, pulled along in its waves drunkenness, wastefulness and luxury. The life of ease, unjustly denied to those innocent, murdered princes, now seemed to be claiming what it was owed.

His Majesty thought again of what he had read in the newly printed *Dictionary*.

> *Most of those who took our side gave themselves over, day and night, to revelry and pleasure, music and dance, feasts and fine decorations. But even if his enemies intended to fall upon Ali Osman, could we leave aside our revelry at the time of his lamentable demise, or during the forty-day period of mourning?*

And what was there to say, then, about the present?! An inexplicable feeling of alarm besieged the Emperor's soul. Perhaps it was because of a vision he had had while drunk, a vision like intoxicating tulips: it was as if all the innocent tulips had gone dry and transformed into arrows, piercing the earth, and among them walked a person, lighting them all like candles.

'O Grand Vizier, my constant friend and respected son-in-law, the most august, and most aromatic, he who puts the whole world in its rightful order!' he had whispered, early in the morning as he lay in bed. Now, reclining on a cushion in the library, he was in no condition to issue an order to his son-in-law to return home, and nor could he put his disturbing feelings down on paper under his pseudonym Najib, either in the form of a ghazal or even half a line of verse.

Then another image flashed through the mind of His Imperial Majesty – the foreign prisoner who reminded everyone of Joseph! The Sultan of all Sultans issued

the command for that man to appear before him immediately.

Perhaps it was the wrathful tone in which the order
had been issued, but the prisoner was brought to the
palace before the spit had dried in the corners of the
Sultan's mouth.

The prisoner's manners were amusing to behold. As
soon as he entered the Emperor's presence, he fell to
his knees, and then prostrated himself in a deep bow.
However, in this bow, His Majesty did not sense any hint
of sycophancy; on the contrary, he saw only a modest
sort of humility, and a tradition from a foreign land.
His Majesty enquired as to whether he had any com-
plaints, and then told the Stranger about his dream.
We do not know what interpretation the prisoner might
have shared then, because at that very moment, in a
noisy flurry of ceremony and surrounded by a crowd of
noblemen and dignitaries, into the inner sanctum of
the palace strode none other than the Sultan's son-in-
law, the Grand Vizier, the very backbone of the state,
Ibrahim-pasha.

When the guard announced the Grand Vizier's
arrival, the words raced from the reception hall to the
library – 'My glorious effendi, worker of miracles, the
beloved, all-powerful, but merciful Sultan Emperor!' –
and the much-respected son-in-law appeared. Such a

pompous and overly ceremonial appearance on the part of the Grand Vizier had become something of a tradition between the Emperor and his son-in-law. The Grand Vizier, however, was surprised to see an unfamiliar man in the Emperor's presence. And what do you think the Stranger was feeling! The Vizier's flashing, hawklike eyes, his moustache like a pair of sabres held against his chin, his bulging chest and his flowing cape that nearly reached the floor – all of this bore witness to an unsparing certainty which inspired alarm in the soul of every man he met. Tucking his hands behind his back, he tossed his heavy gaze at the Stranger for a moment, and that man, sensing a token of destructive power in that look, dared not even glance in the direction of His Imperial Majesty, but instead stumbled out into the reception room.

As soon as the four emerald columns and blue cupolas of the library were hidden behind the door, the guest shuddered as if emerging from a state of enchantment. In the reception room a pair of courtiers were waiting. One of them, younger and more welcoming, gestured for the Stranger to come and sit down next to him. Oddly enough, he had wrapped his turban up and around a layered fez which peeped out from the midst of that turban, lending his face a playful expression. The edges of his moustache, which turned up towards the turban, intensified that playful aspect into laughter, and the laughter in his sharp eyes and his inattentive gaze combined to reveal the man's poetic nature.

'Heir to the knowledge of the prophets from the sacred books, head of religion, Sheikh-ul-Islam, the great Abdullah Effendi,' he said, by way of introducing a respectable-looking nobleman who also sat in that room. The Stranger bowed in his direction with due respect.

The Sheikh-ul-Islam then returned the introduction. 'The young face of our national verse, the confidant of the Grand Vizier, Nadim.' And in those words, the guest sensed a hint of flirtation, as if between those two acquaintances an easy smile had spread its wings. The guest observed all this, enchanted. He could not have predicted that the door through which he had come would at some point open again, and that this time his quick glance would see the expansive decorated cushions lying there. How could the Stranger have known that the Grand Vizier, as he crossed the reception room, would tell the guard, 'Throw that one back where you found him!' – and that just half an hour later he would be back on the straw bedding in his damp prison cell, dreaming of those pillows?

—

If for an innocent man being arrested is a misfortune, then a repeated arrest, for no reason, is a double tragedy. Now the Stranger had lost interest even in his dreams; what had happened in real life seemed a mirage, as murky and mysterious as a dream. So therefore the three believers, all detained on the same charges – the Armenian, the Jew and the Muslim – offered up three different prayers, all beseeching their common God for mercy. Just as they had a God in common, these three suffered in common, too; and more than that, they shared the joyful news that their suffering was coming to an end. Sultan Ahmed had decided to hold a grandiose celebration, quite possibly to distract the people's attention from the lacklustre results of his military exploits. The town criers strolled down every street, announcing that the heir to the throne of the Ottoman Empire, the Sultan's own beloved son, Prince Abdul Hamid, had reached the age of majority and was ready for his ceremonial circumcision. This time, for the first time ever, children from poor families would lie side by side with the prince on the long bed where the circumcision ceremony would take place.

That evening, fireworks boomed and trumpets blasted music in all corners of the city, all brought over from Anatolia. The fireworks flashed in the darkness as if tulips had been tossed into the night sky and disappeared on the straw strewn over the stone floor.

The sultan's effort to distract the people extended not just to these ceremonial rites. He also declared an amnesty for prisoners, announced on the third or fourth day of the celebration. The Stranger emerged from prison to an interesting spectacle: jesters and puppeteers, cockfighting and battles between larger beasts, races on all the main squares, and candy-sellers and confectioners everywhere. They were enjoying the biggest holiday of them all, demand for their wares unceasing as crowds of women, no matter if they had been invited to the feasts or not, handed out sweets to throngs of children. Without a penny in his pocket and not knowing what to do with himself, the Stranger looked first towards the sky, then towards the sea, and then at Istanbul itself, laid out between them. Perhaps his apprehensive stare was interpreted as that of a beggar in distress, but someone, without a glance at his own hand or the hand of the beggar, passed him a whole silver coin, a gracious act of charity, as is the tradition among Muslims.

The Stranger immediately felt ashamed of what he must look like. His uncombed beard hung in clumps and looked gnawed over from his long spells lying on the damp floor; his tortured body, deprived of fresh air and good smells, emanated only the stink of sweat. Now where in this perishable world was he to go? He did not wish to bother Ahmed the healer again, and the sultan's palace, to the glory of its Creator, was evidently occupied with the festivities and had forgotten all about him. Then an idea occurred to him. In this cold and filthy world, the idea occurred to him of a bath, and not just any bath: the famous hammams of Istanbul. And that is where he went.

By the time he reached the biggest hammam in Beyoğlu it had already started to grow dark, and here the snow, which elsewhere in the city the celebrating crowds had stomped upon and turned to mud, lay soft as a white carpet. The old man guarding the place came out and lifted his lantern. He must have been taking advantage of everyone's preparations for the festival, catching up on his sleep when he should have been awake, because he grumbled, his tone surly, that it was a holiday; but when the light of his lantern fell on the shine of that silver coin, he got straight to work and warmed up a separate chamber in the baths. They brewed and drank tea over a fire lapping with blue tongues of flame which looked especially lonesome amid the snow and the cold. Far in the distance, like shooting sparks, fireworks poured into the sky, and the spirit of the festivities waxed and waned on the wings of the wind.

By the time they poured water over the hot stones, night had fallen. For the Stranger, this was the warmest and most peaceful of all nights. Then the steam rose and warmed his flesh straight through to his bones, and it softened his whole body, and he lay down in a bed made up for him in a hallway, and there, wrapped in a blanket, he slept like the dead. His slumber went on and on. The Stranger slept through the predawn prayer, dreaming of being in that bath in the company of a beautiful woman.

But early in the morning he awoke to a knock on the gate, and the elderly guard resumed his perpetual grumbling. The Stranger's heart, which had grown so much calmer, was beating hard once more. 'Not again?' he thought in terror. The next thing he heard was a familiar voice. But he knew nobody in this city, other than those who had brought him grief! In this panicked state, he entertained the thought of fleeing. But could one really escape one's fate? Imagine his astonishment when, in the midst of the turmoil of such ideas, he saw the poet Nadim, the close confidant of the terrible Grand Vizier, enter the room. He was glowering dark as a thundercloud, and his eyes saw nothing before him, and while the Stranger had just begun to wonder whether things had reached such a state that they now sent a poet after a prisoner, Nadim disappeared behind the doors to the sauna room which had been warmed up the night before.

Terror released the Stranger from its grip. The calm comfort of sound reasoning, and even a fervent sort of gaiety, came to take its place. It was in fact the force of the merrymaking that had brought this man here. As he sat down to breakfast with the old watchman, his spirit calm after he had washed and said his prayers, the poet came to join them, in just the same state of spiritual cleanliness. Nadim began to tell them how he had once come to a hammam to mend his health, and there a beautiful woman had met him, who laid hold of all his thoughts in a single instant.

Giving himself over to the purity of that joy, Nadim began to recite poetry, and the Stranger and the old man sat stunned into silence in the face of his inspiration. In his verses the poet conveyed, word for word, the Stranger's dreams from the night before, and this awoke in the Stranger's soul an immense feeling of alarm, greater than he would have thought possible. Was a soul truly so transparent that a kindred soul could see through it with a single glance? Or was this poet a special case? Surely the baths were not to blame for all of this! Still, the poet was setting the Stranger's dreams

to verse, and not only that; he was also not the slightest
bit surprised that the two of them had met again here,
under these circumstances, and like a guardian angel
always sitting on the shoulder of a believer, they picked
their conversation, interrupted a few days earlier, right
up again. Only the Stranger, remembering that feeling
of trepidation that had seized him then, seemed to suspect that the door would suddenly open and the Grand
Vizier would materialise, and shout 'Throw that one
back where you found him!' And he looked slantwise at
the old watchman.

Yes, that was it! Only now did he realise whom the
old man resembled. If you disregarded the cloak covered in ash from the fires he tended, the man was a
perfect copy of the Grand Vizier. Or was this simply one
more game of fate? Were they toying with this foreigner,
reconstructing the whole earlier scenario for him?

The very next morning the warm sun rose after a
snowy night, and as if the lovely lady from Nadim's
poem was sweeping his heart clear of grief, the sun
cast a cover over the whole world with its caresses, its
gentle rays, summoning them all to purer, more time-
less ideas. Under these soft rays of sunshine worries
were swept away and the snow melted, and under that
blanket, like snowdrops, tiny shoots of new tulips raised
their heads.

'Now let's ride to Sadabad!' the poet announced all of a sudden, and newly inspired, he began reciting verse:

> *Come! The feast and the games begin,*
> *My beauty, let's ride to Sadabad.*
> *Three pairs of ships in the waves and the wind,*
> *My beauty, let's ride to Sadabad.*
>
> *We'll sing and play and find all we require,*
> *We'll drink in great gulps and get drunk as we desire,*
> *We'll find the fountain from the dragon's mouth pulsing with fire*
> *My beauty, let's ride to Sadabad!*

Could it be true that this world was made of the fantasies of poets, and run by thoughts as vagrant as gypsies? Why should he go? Well, because the Stranger had no will left, and no desire, other than to surrender to those entreaties, all the more so because a chariot was already waiting for the poet beyond the gates. Once he settled inside it, the poet gave a wink to the old watchman, and this strain of reality continued. But now the Stranger was resolved, and in an unusual attitude of reconciliation, he looked straight ahead – to the future.

They approached Sadabad, the City of Gardens. A place of legend. A valley that stretched from the bay upwards, along the river known as Kagaz-khan. A gap between two green mountain ranges, and a palace that rarely tossed a glance beyond those forests.

Sadabad! There were mansions there, too, between the water and the woods behind them, woods that ran all the way to the hills. It seemed that winter could never break into this garden, nor could autumn ever penetrate there. In this garden, spring reigned eternal.

Everyone here knew the poet, right down to the maid; and more touchingly, every flower greeted him, too, opening its blossoms; and the astounding tulips which grew along the pathways bowed their heads to his feet. The fountains prostrated themselves, the springs began shooting forth water, and as for the palace itself, as the poet neared, its doors opened miraculously of their own accord. And when he and his guest stepped over the threshold, the doors closed again, soundlessly, behind them.

Unsure whether he was actually visiting Sadabad that day or whether it was only a dream, the Stranger tried to wake up and force his way out of this reality, but he returned to this palace of mirages every time, so that eventually he grew angry; but this sweet vision was so persistent that the Stranger lost the will to resist, and he overcame all his fear, and again he surrendered to this dream.

This seemed to be the place for people to gather to

recover from the drunken revelry of the Sultan's feast. Guests were arriving constantly: soldiers with their sabres hanging from their belts, young men in their sheepskin hats, older ones with tassels hanging down from their caps, and loudmouthed senior officers, but every single one of them, for some reason, a military man: janissaries, the new troops, young budding men collected from Christian lands and brought up here in the Islamic faith. Their conversations were unpleasant, their jokes were vapid, their laughter was uproarious and their behaviour, overall, was disgraceful. That might have been the reason that the poet held his tongue, a thoughtful smile on his face, and the Stranger made not a sound, instead only looking, first at the agitated military officers, then at the dismayed poet.

Then he sensed it, with his whole body at once: a whisper was spreading throughout the feast. 'The Admiral! The Admiral, Patrona Halil!' – and then, through the newly opened doors and the hall where they stood, there strode a gaunt, bewhiskered man.

This effendi, named Halil, was the head of the Sultan's navy, and two oceans and ten seas were under his command. The man seemed rather small for his glorious station, and he took long steps as he walked, as if attempting to match his stride to his rank. Even his voice sounded more heroic than one might have guessed, leading one to believe there was more to him inside than out. The whole package resembled a bottle floating on the ocean waves, with a genie inside it just waiting to be released. In any case, the entire assembly immediately fell under the influence of this Patrona. Nobody there seemed capable of fending off his caustic allusions; his jeering provoked no laughter, and his sneer seemed to hang, like a chandelier, in the middle of the hall, casting a shadow of fear on the faces of the men sitting there.

Then another man entered the room, accompanied by Abdullah Effendi, Sheikh-ul-Islam: the watchman from the sauna – or, in other words, the respected son-in-law, the most august, and most aromatic, he who puts the whole world in its rightful order, the Grand Vizier Ibrahim-pasha. At that moment the Stranger realised that he was not the only person experiencing unconquerable fear. Every person present felt the same way. Even Patrona Halil, who up till then had not given any other man a chance to open his mouth, faltered and stood quiet. Everyone, right down to the Sultan Emperor's hound master Dervish Mehmet of Zagar and his head armourer Haji Husein, now hearkened to every word the Son-in-Law uttered, giving their ears and faces fully over to him, just as one minute ago they had hearkened fully to the words of the Patrona.

Ibrahim-pasha, who acted exclusively out of concern for his country's well-being, naturally began his speech with admonitions and rebukes. He declared in no ambiguous terms that the state was sustaining losses in Iran, and if the necessary measures were not taken, both Tabriz and Nakhchivan would be lost; meanwhile, he said, the men of the country were living in wastefulness, spoiled by the sweeter passions, showering their wives with gold; and there could only be one outcome, given that everyone assembled there was idly feasting on halva and honey: the country of the Ottomans would very soon cease to exist.

Patrona Halil was outraged, or perhaps he simply thought of himself as a patriot. 'If you had dug that canal, we would have brought our navy to Tabriz!' he declared.

Those daring words infuriated the Grand Vizier. So great was his anger he could find no words to say, and instead made a sound like 'Tffffu!' and spat, in an expression of his terrible indignation. The trail of spit landed right in a goblet of wine.

'Every single one of you ought to be locked up in prison, and tied to a horse's tail as an example!' he said, finally. Then he rose swiftly and stormed out of the hall.

The feast was ruined.

In the long silence that followed, Patrona Halil abruptly grabbed the cup that had been the target of the Grand Vizier's saliva, splashed the drink over the table, then tossed the cup aside, and he set off with long strides towards the other door and disappeared from view.

—

Whom do you suppose they came to arrest that day? Once again, the Stranger, whom nobody knew, along with several of the newer soldiers, ones with no roots in the city. Even the poet, who had flown away from this frail and venal world on the wings of his thoughts, could not protect his guest. In this world, now, the Stranger could do nothing but wait to be tied to the tail of a horse.

The poet, his soul much distressed, was the last to leave the assembly hall. The last boat from Sadabad picked him up and set a course towards the city, through the mysteriously calming environment of the bay at night. The moon in the sky rocked in time with his boat, and he could not have told you whether the moon was floating among the sparse clouds or whether the waves in the sea were spreading into the sky; but the poet's soul, like an island between two oceans, felt in harmony with both the elements, swimming over the watery plane and floating through the air. What was his purpose in this world? Could he not have been born a seagull, to fly and call out cries with no meaning, or at least a fish, to swim in its own mute surroundings? No, better yet, a tulip, to be plucked in the very bloom of life!

So many things had the poet seen in his time! He had held places of honour ever since his youth, but then became a man nobody needed; to his good fortune, Ibrahim-pasha had been promoted to be the imperial Son-in-Law, and he had made Nadim his confidant. Now in this new arena, where he could partake in astounding journeys and wise conversations, the poet grew in stature, and was even showered with gold, himself, head-to-foot, several times over. Yet still, somewhere deep in his soul, a certain sacred desire remained, only just out of reach, as if it were floating right there next to the reflection of the moon on the water. But as soon as his boat carried him closer, the reflection, flashing and teasing, skipped away again...

The poet had experienced the pinnacle of pleasure. Had he not tasted heady delights from the ruby lips of all the beauties? Which intoxicating and mysterious feelings had he not sampled in this world? He had seen it all, except for the saints; he had known it all and lived through it all in this indifferent, ungodly world. Perhaps now was the time for him to retreat to the dervishes' abode?

Suddenly he remembered the foreigner he had spent time with at the baths and at the feast. Riding in the chariot together, he had told him of St. Bahouddin, who said, 'Heart God, and hands to work.' So is that what he must do? But was not this world another manifestation of the Creator? All of this, the palaces and grand structures on the banks of the bay, the sailing ships and bridges, and even Istanbul, this most beautiful of cities – was not all of it His eternal reflection? The mosques and drinking dens were His. The girls frolicking on the swings of Sadabad and the dervishes whirling in their cells in Ayuba were His. His were the neighbourhoods of Galata, with its peoples from hundreds of countries, and Uskudar, with its fortress that housed the valiant Turkish army... All of this, all of his beloved Istanbul.

Yet, like another sacred desire, the wind, gusting through the unbounded space over the sea, just happens to bring with it the dusty breath of the desert... the sun, which blinds with its endless incandescence... nothing and nobody anywhere around... eternal silence... and where, now, was that foreigner?

—

The poor foreign Stranger had been delivered to Yedikule. He did not know whether it was even worth lamenting the inconstancy of the world in this mad city, where there was scarcely any difference between the highest and the lowest of men, in this city which made him want to drown in some wondrous world of his own imagining. He thought vaguely of the poet, too, and as he lay down on his bed of straw on the stone floor once again, he tried to guess which palace he would wake up in this time. But even if a slice of history, once complete, comes to be repeated once, then a third or even a tenth time, there still never seemed to be a hint of rhyme or reason to it. O God, Lord on High, how truly inscrutable are Your ways!

An hour later, or a day, or maybe an entire month later the same sort of hubbub arose in Yedikule that had once arisen in Sadabad. 'Patrona Halil! Patrona Halil!' they shouted – and then all the doors in the dungeon swung open, and through them, along with all the thieves and martyrs, the Stranger was chased out onto the street.

'Mutiny! Mutiny!' called a handful of hooligans, running back and forth among them.

The streets were unrecognizable. Apart from the mischief-makers and rabble-rousers there were no people in sight; all the shopkeepers' stalls and booths were closed, and bars had been thrown up across the gates of all the houses. The city had been emptied.

—

How could the Stranger possibly have known that Patrona Halil and Dervish Mehmet of Zagar, Kichik Musli of Erzurum and Haji Husein the armourer, and several more fortune-seekers besides, had gathered at that night-time sauna in Beyazit, and there developed their plan for rebellion? While the Sultan and his Son-in-Law were occupied with preparing the army for a march on Iran, and while Sadarat Kayim, who filled in for the Grand Vizier in these situations, was busy planting tulips at his summer residence in Chubukli, and while other men of great and noble rank carelessly abandoned themselves to the world of revelry, this group of six conspirators was determined to pull the country of the Osmans out of the swamp of abomination and to rescue it from the covetous grasp of the Son-in-Law Ibrahim. They coaxed a couple dozen more do-nothings onto their side, who went and roused the entire new army, the janissaries, for they were always ready for anything. And then, yes, they broke the prisons open.

Could the Stranger have known that the old man at the baths, his nose to the wind, had not even both-ered to put out the fire under his kettle before he fled to Beshiktash, to the poet's house? Or that the poet had immediately sent him off with a servant to the fortress at Uskudar? The rebels arrived right behind them there at the fortress, putting the fort in a difficult position. The poet's servant saved his own skin only by selling out the hammam attendant, who fled to the protection of the Son-in-Law, and similarly betrayed his own master. And then, when the crowd turned its ire towards the house of the poet who was so close to the Son-in-Law, that servant thought of his master's kindness, and he warned the poet about them just five minutes before the mob arrived.

The Stranger, carried along with that undulant mass, only just managed to catch sight of a silhouette fleeing along the rooftops of the houses, and he heard how the crowd shouted in one voice: 'There he is! Seize him!' A shadow leaped from roof to roof as if reaching for heaven, while an acrid smoke rising from who knows where suddenly clouded his pursuers' eyes; the fugitive increased the distance between them until he finally took one more jump and disappeared from view behind another rooftop. Immediately, in that very same place, a flock of gulls rose into the sky. A single sighing shout rang out from the mob, and then dissipated... could he have ascended to heaven like the soul of Jesus?

Not much time passed before a voice shouted out from somewhere at the front of the crowd. 'Is there a doctor here? Is there a doctor?' The Stranger pushed aside the prisoners clustering around him and began making his way towards the front of the group. They brought him to a particular house. A broken figure was lying on a divan. The blood had not yet congealed on his face, and there was something in this face that seemed familiar to the Stranger. When he wiped the blood away with a damp cloth, he was surprised to see before him none other than the poet Nadim, winking conspiratorially.

Now the poet spoke. 'I do not need a healer! I need the man who fell from the roof. I would like to hear his assessment of my condition.'

For two weeks, the Stranger sat with this body. For two weeks he pampered it and worked to heal it. But what can you do when the soul has escaped its substance together with a flock of crying gulls? The poet never spoke again.

———

On a sabbath day, which was the sixteenth day of the third month by the Muslim calendar, the Stranger put the injured man to sleep with a potion of poppy seeds, left him in the charge of his daughter Luboba, and headed to the congregational mosque for the Friday prayers. On that day, aside from the thousands of Muslims who had come to pray, Jews and Armenians, Greeks and Romans all gathered as well to visit a market in the square. After the service, Ibrahim the Mad read out an order about acts of piety, not missing his chance to insult the name of the scoundrel Ibrahim-pasha from Nevşehir, soiled in the swamp of debauchery and abomination. When he was done it was Chairman Mustafa-pasha's turn to speak, then Sheikh-ul-Islam Abdullah Effendi's, and then, finally, Lieutenant Mehmet's. 'Kill them! Slaughter them all!' screamed the crowd, which had quickly forgotten its own humble station. About that time, a group of riders appeared from the direction of the Topkapı Palace, led by Admiral Halil, evidently late for the Friday prayers. Suddenly someone in the crowd shouted out, 'Allahu akbar!' – because they carried with them the sabre and cloak of our Prophet Muhammad, the Messenger of Allah.

The people were in ecstasy. The crowd pressed forwards. They pushed and shoved as every man worked to get closer to the riders; those who tried to kiss the sabre and lift it to their faces were cut and bled, and soon a panicked shout rang out over the square. Then Ibrahim the Mad called with all his strength, 'Allahu akbar! Allahu akbar!' – and from the black clouds looming over Istanbul, lightning flashed, and in the next instant the crowd fell silent.

From the other side of the mob came the sound of hoofbeats, and the Sultan's emissaries appeared, bearing with them the holy banner of Islam. The two groups of riders met in the centre of the square. Every demand they posed was passed from person to person, from row to row, all the way across the square. The rebels demanded that the Son-in-Law and thirty-seven other people were to be handed over to them, dead or alive. Only after that would they allow Ahmed III to return to the imperial throne.

At those words the Stranger felt a cold sweat glistening on his body, for that fateful evening at Sadabad, with nothing better to do, he had counted exactly thirty-seven people, excluding those who had entered alongside Patrona Halil.

The emissaries disappeared in the same way they had arrived. The rest of the crowd, boiling over with passion and no longer paying attention to the downpour which had followed the lightning, wished those thirty-seven men dead, and never thought of dispersing, despite the fact that the sacred belongings of the prophet had been taken away and the ceremony was long over.

The wind grew stronger, but nobody in that crowd felt its gusting. The wind glanced off the rooftops and leaped from there to the low-hanging clouds. But when dusk fell, swiftly, and the rain turned to snow, the wind shattered into hundreds of splinters which launched a stinging attack. Fires were kindled in some of the merchant's stalls. And the Stranger, not knowing whether to stay or to go, pondered what fate might have in store for him. Perhaps he ought to return to the dying man in Beshiktash? But even if he could restore him to health, he would pay for it with his life. Now that the list of the thirty-seven doomed men had been revealed, none of them would escape their fate!

He hurriedly walked out of the great mosque. The snow was falling mercilessly, and aside from the people all around him, this day, this hour, was turning into an exact repetition of the day he had first arrived in Istanbul. Again that same uncertainty, again the trepidation, again the panic. And the wind. Always the wind.

But the thirst for life pulled stronger than a dear friend. The Stranger turned not towards the poet's house, but towards the home of Ajjam Ahmed the physician, where he had first been snatched and taken to prison. Before he left the city, some strange force drew him again to the Aya Sophia. The snowstorm continued to rumble in from the sea, and under its onslaught even those who had lit fires decided to leave and go home. Soon every street and square was deserted.

Now, as the Stranger approached the stone wall, just as he had the first time, he encountered a half-wit beggar sitting motionless by the doorway, who shuddered and turned his face in the Stranger's direction. The Stranger looked again, and saw that it was the poet himself. Had he come here for a breath of fresh air, or simply lost his mind and fled? He very much wanted to know, but the beggar stood up, and without speaking a word launched himself heavily into the darkness.

Frozen into place for a moment, the Stranger soon hurried after him. He caught sight of his shape, now and then, in the flash of a torch or the light from a window, but the next instant the shadow disappeared again in the impenetrable darkness of the snowfall. For a long time he hunted the shadow through the streets of Istanbul, famously crooked and sloped, but he never overtook him.

Finally the Stranger found himself at the edge of the sea. Here two raftsmen were talking about the danger that threatened all those who ventured out onto the ocean.

'Have you seen a madman?' he asked them.

'We're all madmen these days,' they told him, laughing.

'We need to catch up with a raft that has got away!'
he told them, and he handed over to the raftsmen a
ring decorated in pearl which Luboba had taken off
her father's finger and given to him. The pair of them
started scuffling over the ring, as if they were compet-
ing for control over their own deaths. But finally one of
them came out on top and, putting the Stranger onto
his raft, he joined the mortal struggle out on the stormy
sea.

Was his life repeating itself, suddenly upended top
to bottom? How else could he explain that instead of
feeling fear and trepidation, this time he surrendered
himself with a thrilling pleasure to completely different thoughts, not paying the slightest attention to the
storm, or the black gloating sea, or the wind which had
broken its fetters, or even the snow that resembled the
shattered shards of those very restraints? If everything
were repeating, it would explain why the light of the
full moon flashed between the clouds and why it lit, for
a moment, the other raft and the familiar face of the
man riding it, and it would explain why that raft, after
again vanishing into the darkness, struck the rocks on
the shore and splintered into pieces, and even why the
Stranger, in that same state in which he had been paralysed before, was now sitting on the sandy seashore.

'There's a dervish's residence on this island,' the Greek raftsman told him, his teeth chattering.

The Stranger began searching for a path over the island. The night had come to an end, but it was still an hour when it was difficult to distinguish a white thread from a black one. The island was made up of cliffs, piled high one atop the other, and near the bottom they were covered first by low bushes, then, as they rose upwards, by rare trees, and then, after one more towering cliff, a genuine forest. The road led ever upwards. By the time the Stranger broke through the forest, it had grown light. Now the wind was sweeping the clouds relentlessly from the sky, and as a result the heavens, which had been clothed in rather muted hues at first, finally shone clear and blue, causing even the sea below to change colour in response.

The residence was situated at the very tallest point of the island, in a small courtyard surrounded by fields of wildflowers. Having climbed up here so courageously, the Stranger caught his breath and then, just as courageously, opened the gates to the residence.

The small courtyard that bubbled with springs was empty; above it there was the sky, and on all four sides there was the sea; everything else was sparse, thin air which never seemed to quite fill his lungs. The Stranger felt a little bolder as he crossed the deserted square.

He had left all his trepidation behind, and now, under the pure sky, he feared nothing. Full of that sensation, he opened the door to the stone building without thinking about what he was doing, and then he stopped, as if struck by lightning.

Around a huge table – so big he wondered how it had ever been moved into this small building – people were sitting, about forty of them... no, exactly forty. The thirty-seven from the list, and with them the Admiral, the Son-in-Law and Sultan Ahmed.

The Stranger bowed to greet them. The most venerable old man there, wearing Sultan Ahmed's face, nodded in response, and indicated with a pointed glance the place where the Stranger should sit. As soon as he was seated, he felt some kind of shadow descend upon the room, and the Stranger's heart, here among all these souls that resembled shadows, or dervishes, themselves, began to keen in a way that was both painful and sweet.

You are familiar, after all, with that solitary twilight world. It is a time when you are no longer truly alive, but as you are not yet dead, you cannot move on into the night. Like a sunset swallowing the light, does not your heart, too, yearn for that light, wanting to swallow it up, or plunge inside it? Do you not begin, in that moment, to love those who have been declared your enemies?

In this twilit residence, even the tablecloth was not a tablecloth, but rather a miraculous object, a glass reflecting the whole surface of the earth. There, on the Sultan's orders, many of those named by the Patrona had already been snuffed out – the Imperial Son-in-Law Ibrahim-pasha and Sheikh-ul-Islam Abdullah Effendi, then Chairman Mustafa-pasha and Lieutenant Mehmet. They had been loaded onto a cart and driven to the square just across from Topkapı Palace. The crowd caught sight of the bodies and discovered, to its great astonishment, that the Grand Vizier from Nevşehir and his companions had never been circumcised! Someone in that crowd recognised the hammam attendant was in fact the Armenian; someone heard mention of the poet and recognised the beggar; and in the corpse of the Sheikh-ul-Islam, they recognised a seller of wine. That is when the blood-curdling screams rose up! 'Bring us the false Sultan! We will not be led by an impostor!' they yelled in chorus, guards and prisoners, sinners and rebels.

The Stranger looked around him. In the twilight, the forty dervishes, leaning forwards, gave themselves over to an ecstasy of devotion. They all rejoiced: the old man in Sultan Ahmed's clothes, the fighting man who resembled his Son-in-Law Ibrahim-pasha, the lanky student who looked just like Patrona Halil... the Stranger turned again to the glass.

The crowd rushed to lash the dead bodies onto the tails of different horses and chased those swift steeds across the square in front of the palace and down the stone-paved streets. There, the heir to the knowledge of the prophets of the sacred books, the head of religion, the Sheikh-ul-Islam, the great Abdullah Effendi, was shattered to pieces on the stones, and there the face of the bookprinter Ibrahim Mutafrica was torn open like a shredded book, and there... and there... the Stranger shuddered. Still, though, the forty dervishes in their ecstasy around him did not stir, and they repeated, on and on, the ninety-nine glorious names of Allah.

The Stranger turned his attention back to the square. Yes, it was an unforgettable scene. There he was himself, his arms and legs bound! Could the heavens truly be so indifferent? Could the insanity of the mob truly demand this performance to soothe it? If there are indeed men of art, men of enlightenment, men of purity in this world, then all of them were gone – one had been crucified, one had been scourged and stuffed with straw, one had been tied to a horse's tail, one had been hanged, one had been strangled.

'Ah, what a mob!' the Stranger moaned, and looked one more time into that herd of humanity, and oh, God!

– he saw that there in the crowd, in terrible fear, but at the same time unable to conceal his passionate excitement, he himself was standing.

Then he was running after a horse with one eye and plunging into the crowd with the other, and his skull cracked, and out of that fissure there sprouted an unbelievably beautiful poppy or tulip. It seemed to be suffusing the entire world with its beauty, or its blood, or the black splotches inside it, or its stores of morning nectar, or its youth, or its eternity, or all of this at once. And the Stranger, wishing to pronounce its name, took one last breath and gasped out, 'Allah!' And he choked on the air in his lungs.

⁂

Now, you understand what sorts of things were *actually* keeping me busy, between the little details of everyday life. I had never merely been stripping layers of old plaster at Boris's studio, or paging through a manuscript to translate at Zev's house. What I was doing, layer by layer, page by page, was attempting to uncover the trail of a man named Warsworth, or Huggins, or Vissens. But by all outward appearances, I was continuing to work in Boris's studio, the studio that had already given us so much trouble.

'Do you get the feeling that Martine is a little bit

off her rocker?' he asked me once, not hiding his frustration.

'No,' I answered, feeling protective of Martine.

I didn't want to delve deeper into that sort of gossip, so I turned on the tape player, and, as if to remind Boris to get back to work, I put on songs by the Azeri singer Alim Kasymov and the Uzbek singer Munajat Yulchiyeva.

'That Munajat of yours is much better than Alim,' Boris opined.

'Why?' I asked.

'Alim's art belongs to the Mediterranean coast,' he said. 'He displays his suffering plainly to his audience, as if he's expecting sympathy. But your Uzbeks show a kind of taciturn nobility when they're expressing spiritual torment.'

It was impressive how quickly he had seen what was what!

When we finally finished the remodelling job, Boris paid me four or five hundred francs, refusing all my embarrassed objections about how he shouldn't, how the work hadn't been worth that much. That's how things work in the West. No, I'm not talking about how a friend might hire you to work for him, but about how much higher they value mental labour over physical labour here. You probably remember

how much they paid me in Laon, just for being a
writer.

Anyway, we Uzbeks are not a proud people. It
doesn't take much for us to be happy.

Riding the train back from Boris's place that day, I
saw the earth was dressed in green. It was the height
of spring. I had money in my pocket, enough to easily
survive another ten or fifteen days. And truly, spring
is such a beautiful time in this world of ours.

—

Paris! Paris, a city of banquets and leisure, a place of
pleasure and inspiration! Even the heaviest burdens of
life are easier to bear here. To borrow a phrase from
Hemingway, it's a moveable feast. There's probably no
place on earth quite like it. A city that knows how to
help you along even if you can't pay your own way.
You indulge, you dance and you laugh, and fate will
always toss you a piece of the pie. By complete chance
you encounter a particular professor, for example,
and are surprised to learn he has been interested in
Uzbekistan for a long time – which is to say, he is an
amateur collector of traditional long-necked pitch-
ers. And now, having invited you to his home, and
having shown you a long procession of those pitch-
ers, he treats you to pastries and cold drinks. Then

he shows you books containing photographs of an extremely rare Uzbek long-necked pitcher, and says that his own specimen, preserved since the reign of Mallyakhan, is even older. He draws a pitcher out of a secret cupboard, or maybe it is some other sort of vessel. 'Bravo!' you exclaim, wholeheartedly. Anyone so devoted to his business deserves praise! After all, he has carefully preserved and protected something that we ourselves wouldn't give a second glance.

Your blood is racing pleasantly after the wine you've had, and you are inspired to think out loud. 'In Islam, it's not customary to conserve physical things. It could be seen as idolatry. That's why Islam is a religion of the Word, one for reciting verbal testimony, the *shahadah*. And Christianity is a religion of the Act and the Image,' you say, as if divulging a new theory.

Then you go on. 'That is exactly why material evidence is so important for the West. In the East, on the other hand, what gets passed down from generation to generation is not idols and images, but instructions, which are essentially another manifestation of the Word.'

The professor is carefully jotting down every word you utter.

'Very good!' you say to that. 'Write this down, as material evidence. But at the end of the day they're

still just words!' And you and the professor will both
be content, because neither one of you has had to
back down from your religious convictions.

—

I want to tell you about the day my daughter arrived.

As I've already said, Paris, for me, is directly equivalent with missing my little girl. After living there,
together, for a while, eventually my wife had left for
Germany, so now our family had been split up across
three different countries. During that time my soul,
too, was broken into pieces. Honestly, these fissures
are the reason I so frequently lose my train of thought
while I'm telling this story, and why I get distracted
by details.

One day my wife called from Germany and
announced that there might be a way for our daughter to come to Europe, along with Atanazar-aka, who
was scheduled to fly in any day now, and in order to
secure them a visa, we needed to send them an invitation. As a matter of fact, we had already tried to do
that when we had first arrived in Paris, and the ordeal
had cost us some of our best friends, because when it
came to filling out the documents for the invitation,
nobody would agree to do it.

But now we had friends among the chosen people,

who, no matter what they had lived through themselves, were always ready to help. We confided in them and they came up with some imaginary invitation right then and there, had it signed by a housecleaner working nearby, and sent it off to the Uzbek Ministry of Foreign Affairs. Now all we could do was wait and hope, and call Atanazar-aka every day.

Apparently our prayers were heard, because the decision was made to write our daughter's name into Atanazar-aka's passport as his niece. Some people who ought to know warned us that keeping our daughter in Germany would be very difficult. Still, as they say, he who risks nothing drinks no champagne. Let her come, we thought, and then we'll figure it out.

We closely monitored their every step. Soon we learned that they had already bought tickets to Moscow. Impossible! I rushed to Place de l'Opéra and bought tickets from Moscow to Berlin, and sent them straight to Moscow. They were already supposed to be on their way. Was it true? Be honest with me! I might faint! Their plane took off. They landed in Moscow. I tracked their every move from Paris, my wife watched from Germany, and we conferred with each other about every step they took. We couldn't quite believe it, and we were afraid.

In Moscow, they were supposed to stay with a

journalist we knew. We almost melted down his phone line that day.

Finally, the long-awaited moment arrived. The journalist's wife informed us that the plane had taken off for Berlin! And did our daughter take off with it? She didn't happen to have come back with him? Your husband came back, but our daughter got on the plane? Honestly? Impossible! She was on her way! She was on her way! She was on her way!

That day I went to a park with an Irishwoman I knew and we both got drunk on champagne. She was genuinely happy to hear that my daughter had arrived safely in Berlin. And she even admitted to me, sweetheart that she was, that once, when she had been translating one of my wife's scholarly articles, she had caught a whiff of sorrow over our child in the words.

And then? And then I went back to Martine's house, where I sat down alone in her little garden, and spent a long time thinking and grieving over life. It made my heart beat so strongly that if I had started writing just then, the paper would have been covered in red. Only poetry can contain a feeling like that.

That spring! To be honest, it was during that spring that this novel of mine took root and began to grow. When my daughter had been so far away, while I walked across the red sand that was everywhere in this foreign land, across the street towards the Leclerc grocery shop, through the playground for the neighbourhood children, my face happened to brush against the branches of a tree whose buds had just opened, and when the rays of sun behind them touched my face, I trembled, and my whole body flinched, and I exclaimed, 'Oh! Spring must already be upon us!' The children playing football on that red sand kept right on playing, and I continued on my way to purchase my weekly provisions for the fifty or sixty francs I had just managed to earn, and all of my thoughts were racing towards my daughter, five or six thousand kilometres away.

EVENTS OF THE YEARS
OF THE HIJRA 1410–1414

Next comes a vast kingdom whose residents are endowed to the utmost with moral purity, justice, wisdom and piety, who resolve to provide any country with all that it might need for its welfare; they are renowned for their readiness to lend a hand to men near and far, and to show kindness to friends and strangers alike. And they are of extraordinary beauty and brightness.

Avicenna, *Hayy ibn Yaqzan*

This city cannot be described in words — it is indescribable, beyond any words. Sometimes a person has a dream he would never share with another soul. This city is akin to that dream. This city could, perhaps, be described properly in verse, but even those lines will seem like childish chit-chat compared to the city itself. I would rather not write about this city, only feel it, walk around in it, breathe it in. But human beings are imperfect. I want to try everything. As if this city intends to harness me to its cause, as if its endless beauty might lend colour, in gentle shades, to what I have written here, and then, like the opalescent resplendence of the moments just before dawn, endow with its splendour these outpourings of my soul...

Bamberg.

Very likely, everyone has a favourite city. Mayakovsky, for example, asked to be buried in Paris when he died. I could say almost the same, but without casting any aspersions on Paris, I would name a different city: Bamberg. And if a few people ever came to visit my grave, at least they could benefit from the beauty around them. I don't think I need to say any more.

Now imagine, if you would, how the rivers of this city branch into multiple streams. We settled in a former mill located between two of those streams – Walkmühle, they called it in German. I had never lived in such a beautiful place in my entire life.

I don't know where to start this tale: inside the mill, or outside it?

We had all lived and grown up in the Country of the Soviets, and we were unfamiliar with life in the Western world. We never suspected that life could be like this. Living in Walkmühle spoiled me. I was spoiled by the radio and the clock installed over the heads of the beds, by the kitchen appliances located right there in the room, and by getting to live in such surroundings with my family, instead of all alone, for the first time. That last reason was really the most important. I've been to so many places alone, after all, but without company nothing really makes an impression on you. Places where you go with your family, on the other hand, become firmly lodged in your memory. We watched television when we felt like it, or took hikes to see the nearby waterfalls when we felt like that. And sometimes, when we really wanted to, we took a stroll along the path that led from the mill up into the hills. There was a grand, quiet, calm river stretching out on one side, and a playful stream on the other. The path of gravel and sand passed under a series of archways made of the crowns of the tall trees in the leafy forest, their branches intertwined above our heads.

When you went for a jog in the cool early morning, you set the lazy fog over the river swinging. When you set out in the evening for a slow, quiet walk, you saw ducks swimming, or rather, floating along, making no ripples on the smooth surface of the water and never interfering with your thoughts, either.

Bamberg.

Should I tell you about the sound of the bells in Bamberg? No, everything in its time.

Should I tell you about the first grief we experienced there? Because we were there for a grandiose
event, a conference on Central Asia in general and
Avicenna in particular, and that was coming to an
end, and that whole time, up till now, we had been
enjoying all the pleasures of a cost-free life. We would
drive to a village called Bayreuth, where Wagner was
born, and walk in its parks with the Japanese; to be
honest, I'd never seen anything like those parks. And
we would visit the local theatres and museums. Such
a beautiful life, all of it, and we weren't paying for it.
But that life came to an end. The Japanese eventually
left, the Russians disappeared, and only we Uzbeks
stayed behind. We had to be back in Paris in a month's
time, after all.

As it turned out, we're not the only ones who hold
a guest in high esteem. Nobody ever told us it was
time to leave. But the rent which had been prepaid
for our apartment ran out, and the money we had
been given had all been spent. That was when our
friends appeared to rescue us again. First a Mongolian
man sent me some money, assuring me that I was a
fellow Mongol first; that paid for our rented room
in the mill for another few weeks. Then it was our
friend Inga, who went on a trip to America for a
month. She handed the keys to her house over to us

and left. But still, no matter how things were set up, we grieved sorely. We weren't used to depending on other people. We were used to being our own masters, making our own decisions. When we couldn't, we grieved.

Our life there helped me understand something: for me and my family, September is the most difficult time of the year. Here in this world, it turns out, this transition to winter does not come easily. Every time the calendar turned to September, my heart started to whine and prickle and shrink. Just as the Bamberg leaves that trembled and fell to float down the river Regnitz, yellow stains appeared on my calm heart with every return of September. Either the sky or our souls, losing their transparency, were getting lost in the layers of life, and somehow both were going grey and damp in the endless wet.

That September of five years ago was just the same. We had moved to Inga's house, which was a warm place filled with books, and our wonderful landlady had filled her refrigerator with chicken for us before she left – but still, there was no peace in our souls. It seemed as if someone had taken a shovel and dug out a hollow beneath my very heart, leaving that organ hanging perilously over a chilly breeze. Often in the early days of autumn, the weather, though it's already been spoiled at least once, suddenly clears, the sun reappears and the sky turns blue. But a heart once deceived can no longer trust what it sees. As Cho'lpon once said, it can no longer be fooled. It knows. The merciless autumn still lies ahead, and the cruel winter too... And the thought of returning to our homeland only reminded me of the rising autumn sun. Maybe that was why the rustling of my heartbeat reminded me, more than anything else, of the rustling of dry leaves in the breeze?

We weren't able to get any Moscow radio stations, but every day we listened to a station called Volga, which served the Soviet troops in the GDR. What was going on in the world? Something new seemed to happen every day. These were times when the world was changing rapidly. I was reading works by Turkish writers, from Tevlik Fikret's *The Broken Lute* to Fuat Köprülü, and in between I kept going back to Murad Muhammad Dost's *Field of Tulips*.

Those were the days when I first sensed an increasing separation from my motherland. Perhaps I still could have gone back to live and work there — but as I was here with my whole family now, and as we had been dropped into the hands of fate, I now felt, for the first time, truly detached from my native land.

—

During the daytime my friend Semih-bey would drive
over to take us on a jaunt to Nuremberg or sometimes to his own village, or to see a Turkish movie, or
sometimes just to a restaurant which had been set up
inside some other old mill. As we sat in his car and
saw all these good things in life, the state of our souls
grew even worse. That sort of affability, that sort of
benevolence, cannot last forever. After all, life is made
up of more sorrow than joy, and each of us separately
– both I and, in a subtler way, my wife – were tortured by a single question: what would become of us
later? Wherever Semih-bey went, things seemed less
strange. As a man of science, everything, for him, was
always well grounded, standing firmly on both feet,
and nothing could ever seem random or frivolous.

Semih-bey gave me a non-frivolous way to spend
my time, too. During the war, the Germans – or, as
we called them, the Fascists – recorded many stories and fables, legends and histories from captured
enemy soldiers. They figured they could use them
as part of their ethnographic research. The record-
ings had ended up in the hands of Semih-bey, and I
was working to translate them. I was reading things
in Karachay, and Chuvash and Tatar, then in Kyrgyz,
Uighur and Bashkirian. It all seemed, truly, to make
up a single whole. I don't mean because the prisoners

were detained under similar conditions or treated identically, but because in all those texts I sensed a commonality of consciousness, and of language.

I have a photo I saved from those days, of Semih-bey seeing me off at the train station. In the picture, the kind man seems to be talking something over with the autumn sunlight. I recall Semih-bey asked me then, 'My dear Sheikhov! Do you really want to stay in the West?' The question made me tremble involuntarily. Later I realised that my trembling resembled what happened to a leaf gone yellow, trembling, in autumn, on a tree.

My family was already in residence at our friend's house in Freiburg by then. From there, you could practically reach out and touch France. But I had lingered for several days at Semih-bey's place, because only he had the gift, like Aladdin, of breaking a person out of the prison of time. Sometimes even autumn shines brightly, for a few days. But a detached heart cannot trust it.

On the fifth day of Shawwal, the tenth month in the lunar calendar, when the sun had come into Aquarius, an extremely bright star appeared in the sky over the city of Bamberg. It seemed for all the world to be pouring down light over the city, pulsing in time with the sound of the church bells. The Stranger had pulled a fortune-telling stone out of his pocket as he sat in his field on the slope of the Michaelsberg hill, one of the seven hills over which the city of Bamberg ranged, and he waited for the breath of Capricorn to appear, bringing hope of sustenance. That bright star swam right up to him without the slightest disturbance in the air, and then it jumped up and touched the top of the cathedral, and its light immediately went out. A mysterious silence took shape. It seemed that even the lightning bird, which had hidden in the clouds stretching to the very horizon, was now spreading its wings carefully, gently, to allow the smooth surface of the earth to remain alone with this silence.

The stars in the sky seemed to have been nailed to it like the sun, but the Stranger, who had come from faraway lands in search of knowledge about the philosopher's stone, waited for the easterly wind – not out of any particular spiritual ruefulness, but rather in the hope that its power would lift off the ground the harvest of wheat he had raised over the spring and summer. Ever since some beast from the monastery forest had trampled over it, the stalks of grain had lain bent to the ground. This was the second year the Stranger had played the role of a mute, attracting no interest to himself, and thereby allowing himself to drink in the language and unpleasant traditions of this country. His first year, after the wheat had been gathered and threshed, a whole cart of it had been hauled to a mill called Walkmühle to be weighed. The mill kept one share of the flour they made. Two shares went to the monastery. The Stranger received the remaining four shares, which he sold to the healers in the marketplace. That was how this solitary, speechless man made ends meet, living out his life in a wooden hut near Michaelsberg.

But that year, probably due to drought, all the animals in the forest had been chasing one another across the fields. They had been rushing towards the river, or dirtying the only well in the region, and they had trampled his harvest like swine. The Stranger knew the names of all the forest's creatures, but recently, a few new ones had appeared. They resembled wild boars, though they were not boars, despite the fact that their bodies were covered with bristly hairs from head to foot. They resembled apes, but they were not apes, though they usually charged about on two limbs. They resembled goats, but they were not goats, though they had horns and beards, and were cloven-hoofed, too. They came up from the river and cantered towards Michaelsberg every evening as dusk fell.

On that evening, the fifth day of Shawwal, after the star had disappeared at the cathedral, the creatures seemed to have multiplied. Whole herds of them, screeching and yelping, chasing each other's tails and beards, paying no mind to the seedlings or to the young wheat, scurried towards the forest that grew on the hill, towards the cathedral that rose on its peak, leaving a flurry of black earth in their wake. So the poor Stranger gathered all his strength and flexed his tongue, which had pronounced not a word for two long years, and he prayed to his Creator, and then the lightning bird stretched out its wings in heaven, and Capricorn breathed from the horizon, and the sudden gust of wind lifted up the stalks of wheat, and *then*, after all that, silence reigned again.

On the path which led along the edge of the wood from the cathedral to the river, two monks approached the Stranger, breathing heavily. But their feet, hidden underneath their black capes, touched the ground soundlessly and did not disturb the silence that held court there.

'Come with us,' said one.

'We must arrive before darkness falls,' added the other.

The Stranger tucked the fortune-telling stone in his pocket and followed them. He had his own reason for doing so. Two years of observation had revealed to him that the Abbot of the monastery, Father Johann, was in fact the only person in the world who knew the secret of how to turn rock into gold.

They climbed hurriedly along the twisted path to the top of the hill where the cathedral stood. The two monks, their guard lowered before the mute Stranger, discussed how they might use him as a spy, and with his help gain access to this secret knowledge as the Abbot lay on his deathbed. And the Stranger, following diligently along behind these two Jesuits, listened to them discuss how Abbot Johann, already saying his farewells to this world, had had a dream in which, as he drew his last breath, he revealed everything to a man who did not speak. And the Stranger felt the fortune-telling stone turn warm in his pocket.

Finally they reached the cathedral. In the Abbot's cell, they found the monks gathered before him to receive his last will and testament, and Johann gestured with one weak hand that they should leave the room, and all except the last two monks walked out of the cell, one after another.

Just then the bells began to ring. When their music died out, the men heard the clock striking the hour. They may or may not have paid attention, but the Stranger caught the expression on Abbot Johann's face, and he realised that although it was still early, the clock was continuing to strike.

'Eleven!' whispered Johann.

One of the monks turned over an hourglass that stood in a niche in the wall. The sand began to flow downwards, rustling almost imperceptibly. Or perhaps that was the sound of the gentle rain that had begun to fall outside the window? Following the Abbot's gaze to the hourglass, the mute man saw an elegantly designed scale next to it. Could it be that this mage of the Western world used this balance to weigh his sundry stones before he turned them into gold? Suddenly the light from the single candle flickered and shook. Among the wavering shadows, Abbot Johann cast his gaze to the two monks, and called them by name.

'Benvolio! Frederic!'

And he gestured that they, too, should leave the room.

Their shadows, which had covered the icon bearing the images of the Virgin Mary and the infant Jesus, slipped across the floor and disappeared through the door.

Then the Abbot called the mute Stranger to his side. The fortune-telling stone in the mute man's pocket burned ever hotter, with a heat that was now unbearable. Suddenly lightning flashed in the open window. The dark sky cracked, and more shadows rushed inside the cell.

'I know you will not understand a single word you are about to hear, but I need a living soul to hear me,' the old man began, his voice a whisper. The silent man made no sign that he understood, and sat down next to him.

'There is no man in the world more steeped in sin than I. From head to foot, I am shrouded in sinful deeds.' Abbot Johann trembled as he uttered those words. 'Striving for sainthood through submission, I fell victim to a terrible pride. No matter how strictly I denied myself, no matter how much I strove for purity of the flesh, at night, even during times of fast, I could not help but spill my seed; no matter how I devoted myself to mastering all the sciences, in the end, I sank into the abyss of superstition, and wanting to surpass the laymen in their own ways, I turned to their idols; no matter how I strove for benevolence, in the end, I found myself surrounded by malevolence.'

He fell silent for a time, then continued.

'Though I desired to pray to our Creator, I sold my soul to the Devil. He is already here. He is ready!' the old man declared, pointing with one finger towards the door.

'Have you ever given thought to the very basest of

this life of sin? To the sweetness of succumbing to it? To disinterring and raping the body of your newly dead mother? Or to killing the child who calls you papa, who runs to you with open arms, and eating its flesh? Or on walking into an empty cathedral and shooting your seed over the face of the Virgin Mary, right there before the altar? Why does man choose to fall, to sink, to these depths? Why does he feel, in these rebellious temptations, a more perfect pleasure than he felt in the womb or in the cradle? Or could it be that he is not feeling his own self, but rather a godly force, the force which might stand firm before this lowness, which may just withstand this human failure? What must a man do to prove to himself that God's mercy is larger and more magnificent, still, than all this, that even the most fallen of all the fallen might find a place to shelter under the wing of this great mercy? Otherwise, what is the point of our journey through this frigid world?'

The old man foamed at the mouth and his fever rose.

But the fortune-telling stone in the mute man's pocket, dampened by the sweat streaming off his body, hissed and began to cool.

In his torment, the old man continued to speak. 'Look! There is a worm inside the hourglass! Has time, too, gone rotten? The worm does what he can to stop the current of time. If he wanted to, he could squirm through the sand, and lodge himself in the narrow passageway, and choke off the flow of the sand. If he wanted to, he could crawl lower and be buried in its grains, and if he wanted, he could stay at the top as king of the desert. I believe he was born of that sand. I believe he feeds on that sand. One fine day, that worm will turn into a butterfly – with one wing in the lower half of the hourglass, and the other in the top half. The worm is just like me.'

The old man was gesturing to the hourglass, as if to command that it be placed in his hand. The mute man, feeling somehow detached from events, handed the old man the timepiece, which had nearly completed its count. 'Probably none of us in this world are any better than this worm in its prison. No matter what we try to do, these two worlds, like these two bowls of sand, confine us,' Abbot Johann sighed.

At that moment, the clock began to strike news that midnight had arrived.

'There he is! He draws near,' the old man exclaimed, and he pointed this time not to the door or the window but to the niche in the wall. The mute man, alarmed, turned his eyes in that direction, but he saw nothing but the scale – and its empty pans unexpectedly rocked.

'Here he comes,' the old man repeated, his voice

now flat. 'Like a worm, he wants to chew through my soul!' he shouted. A beastly fear seemed to grip him, and he took the hourglass in his hand and threw it hard at the scale. Either the clock struck its last beat, or the vessel of sand sailing through the air like a butterfly hit one of the pans of the scale, or else the buttress separating the earth from the heavenly sphere trembled; but whatever the cause, in an instant, everything around them was covered in flames. The fire looked just like Satan or a demon: it exploded to life right there on one pan of the scale, which then dipped low.

Shadows danced around them, pulling the pan lower, shadows that resembled first the two monks, then the very demons or evil spirits who had trampled the harvest that night, and this mad dancing seemed to feed the fire so that it trembled and burned more strongly.

And then the Stranger, who had not heard his own voice for seven hundred days, spoke these words: 'Allah is merciful!' And he yanked from his pocket the fortune-telling stone, now completely cold, and flung it onto the second pan of the scale, and when an astounding flash of light lit up everything around them and the rays of light swallowed up all the visions of hell they had seen, the saintly and sinful old man, who had known how to turn rock into gold, let his soul depart his body.

⁎
⁎⁎

Again I am leaving for Bamberg, and yet again I am being escorted out of Frankfurt by Turks. The excitement of our pan-Turkic solidarity seemed to have been put on hold – or perhaps I just didn't want to interfere too much with their ideological commitments. Whatever the reason, we said our goodbyes rather coolly on the train station platform. As soon as the train lurched into motion, I remembered that I had left my umbrella behind. Devil take it, a thousand times! I had such a solid habit of losing umbrellas that my wife had bought me an umbrella as big as an enormous rolling pin and told me that even I would never lose such an umbrella, no matter how much I'd like to. And naturally, that was the one I left behind when I was on my way to visit my wife!

I was glad to be going, because I had missed her very much. I had envisioned every moment of this upcoming encounter in a thousand different variations. For that reason, I couldn't think of a single thing on the train ride other than that battering ram of an umbrella and my upcoming reunion with my love. As soon as we arrived in Bamberg, I got in a taxi and called out the address. 'Unterer Karlberg 26!'

My daughter was there, too, the daughter I hadn't seen for a whole year. When I rang the doorbell my daughter was the one to answer, and as soon as I announced it was me, she ran outside.

Then something oddly typical happened. You may think that the whole world is just about to come tumbling down because of whatever is troubling you, but when push comes to shove, you start off talking about something minor and completely unrelated. 'Why are you running outside barefoot? Couldn't you have put some shoes on?' I asked her.

'I said a prayer every day,' my daughter responded happily. 'I asked God to protect you.' She had grown noticeably: the top of her head reached up to my chin now.

Let me confess that my wife never meets me with an embrace. She needs a couple of days to conquer the doubts and suspicions that have grown inside her in my absence. After that, her heart gradually grows warmer. Sometimes this leads to misunderstandings and small quarrels. There's nothing to be done about it – that's just the way she is.

But I'll tell you everything from the beginning.

This time, in Bamberg, my family and I were staying in the home of our friend Michael, whose field of research was Uyghur history. Actually the house belonged to a certain Herr Brambrink, and Michael was only renting it. The building dated back to the turn of the eighteenth century. The part of the house that had once contained the kitchen and stables was given over to us. Now it had been transformed into two furnished rooms with a small bath tacked on. This time, too, Inga had taken the reins, and she had sent poor Michael out on long-term research assignments, first to Uyghurstan, then to Bashkortostan and Moscow. As a result, we more or less inherited the part of the house he had been renting.

I moved in during the summer. Soon autumn came, followed by winter, which did not make the bathroom any warmer. Every nerve ending in my body froze in that place. One room simultaneously served as kitchen, living room and office. When you walked in there was the stove, and across from that there was a big window looking directly out onto the cathedral. Without that feature, nobody would have paid a kopeck for those rooms. Lower down, under one side of that window, there was a wooden stand which held the computer that we would later use to write our articles and books. Under the other side of the window was the old sofa where our daughter slept.

The kitchen and office part of the room were divided by a door that led into the next room. These areas were each maybe a metre wide, and the rest of the space was taken up by that door. Our second room was just like the first: one window framing a view of the cathedral. This was our bedroom. There was a mattress that lay on the floor. One corner held Michael's books and things. A dozen spiders had the run of the ceiling, since they, too, had selected this room to be their bedroom. Every morning we woke up to the elaborate chiming of the cathedral's bells. The melody went on for fifteen minutes, mingling with the songs of bells from other churches and cathedrals around the city. This prompted the spiders to stir in their webs, and prompted us to stir in our beds and finally get up for the day.

I got there in July, and by September, our life was all blue skies. In the morning, if I had the energy, I went for a jog, and if I didn't I went out into the Brambrinks' garden and played table tennis with my daughter. In the afternoons, if my wife went to the university, I stayed home and sat down to work. If she didn't, I paid a visit to the university myself, to make sure they remembered me. Semih-bey was teaching me to use the computer. Sometimes he'd throw some work my way. In the evenings we visited friends and went to parties. Those were to celebrate my arrival, partly, but also because the academic year was almost over, and every instructor hosted a feast before leaving for vacation. We had a lot of fun in those days.

In August, Semih-bey himself departed for Turkey. Before doing so, he left me the keys to his office, and for no apparent reason, asked me to translate a work about languages, by someone named Melioransky, from Russian into Uzbek. He actually knew nothing at all about either Russian or Uzbek, but he said if I translated it I'd get a thousand German marks. Just another type of generosity! Really, the only other way to help me with money would have been to give it to me directly as a handout. And he probably thought that would be embarrassing for me, so instead of charity, he asked me to do this job. And as if that weren't enough, he was kind enough to leave me his computer!

At that time, when humankind as a whole was sufficiently well developed to put together such a machine, only a few rare specimens were sophisticated enough to use it. I explored every nook and cranny inside the labyrinth of that computer. Sometimes I'd emerge alive and well, but once in a while I'd find myself stuck in such a dead end that even my daughter, trying to rescue me, would be powerless to help, and the computer would start to make a terrifying screeching noise, making me think, 'This is the end for you, Sheikhov! You've destroyed Semih-bey's life's work!' In moments like these, when your heart nearly leaps out of your chest, and an ice-cold liquid rushes through your capillaries where the blood should be, you start to understand where your grey hairs are coming from, and you resign yourself to the decrees of providence. When you finally admit you have only two choices – you can hang yourself, or you can run far away from this room and this country – the noise from the computer stops, and some cryptic numeral, a 1 or an 8, appears on the screen.

What they say is true: once you burn your mouth on milk, you'll start to blow on water, too. So for the next few days I would be afraid to turn off that display of 1 or 8, not even allowing my daughter to get close to the machine. Then I would find a guy at the university who was a real computer ace, and he would come over and turn it off and on again very easily, clearing the way for me to conduct new experiments.

So I bumbled on like that. I gradually got used to the computer, and September sneaked up on me, unnoticed. I know I already told you about autumn, so let me leave aside, for now, the subject of how hard that season always is for our family. Let me tell you instead about how our visas ran out.

Montaigne had a famous saying: 'We live life as a

preparation for death.' As a matter of fact, this piece of wisdom had already been shared by Hoja Ahmad Yassavi, who said, 'You die before your death.' In this sense, our lives are always suspended, dangling off their end date. No matter which way I remember it, we were always counting down the days until our visas expired. It was similar to how people start thinking about next month's pay the day after pay day.

On one of those autumn days a sunburned Semih-bey returned from Turkey and handed me one thousand deutsche marks. After receiving that money, we had a difficult time answering him when he asked what we were planning to do next. I should mention that by that time the university directors had finagled a way for our daughter to study for a few weeks, free of charge, at the best gymnasium in the city. That was another reason to stay. I had come to realise that the Turkologists and Persianologists I encountered at the university were all Muslims on the inside, and they would never tell me to my face that it was time for me to leave. Instead they'd enquire in a roundabout way, 'What else can we do for you?' To which we always replied helplessly, 'We really don't know. Maybe you could help find some solution?' They were probably wondering why on earth they had taken it upon themselves to invite us here.

But as I mentioned, their Muslim habits never failed to prevail, and without telling us anything about it, they went to the town hall to quietly ask around. There was no excuse they didn't dredge up to help us stay longer. The first thing the local authorities asked was who would fund our stay, actually. But after some senior figure at the university put in a good word for us we finally managed, after a great deal of trouble, to extend our visas for another six months. Then the real autumn set in.

—

Oh, that autumn. It was the kind of autumn capable of knocking our yellowed hearts out from under our feet. A season that carries water straight to the transparent essence of the soul and does nothing to resist its current. Let that soul flow away, let this transparent life go, too, and we'll offer up a few detached, yellowed souls to that current as a sacrifice. Those hearts will float along, unable to either take off flying or to sink.

Every day we took our daughter to the river, to a place with no other people, and we spent hours singing songs about loneliness. One of them was Demis Rusos's sad song. 'Oh wind, my friend, you've come from the sea, and I'll show you my soul, oh wind, my friend.' It reminds me of other lines of ours, like, 'Hey, wind, give my love my regards.' But the wind never even thought to stir. Nor did our lives, there on the bank of the river.

Aside from that, during the day I sat in Semih-bey's office and hammered away at my unfinished translation of Melioransky, and when I got tired, I read Nasriddin Rabguzi's *Tales of the Prophets*. As I read I rejoiced. 'How wonderful it would be,' I thought, 'if I could translate this book into every language, so that other people could also luxuriate in such simplicity of soul and composition!' After daydreaming a little in that way, I would read a letter from Hamid Ismailov, or begin writing a review or commentary of some articles I had been sent, or do a little work on my own novel. When I stopped to look, the day would already be approaching noon. Then either my daughter would stop by after school, or I would go home myself, jogging past the town hall, crossing the bridges, walking the narrow alleyways, and finally climbing up towards Unterer Karlberg.

My wife is an excellent cook, and she put something new on the table each day – five-mark chicken, cooked according to one recipe today, another tomorrow, or fried, or baked or steamed. Sometimes my daughter, who was just starting to explore the culinary

arts, tried something that did not quite work out, and
we considered that a new dish, too. And then every
Saturday I made plov in the big saucepan.

After lunch we always got back to work on our
constant search for money. My friend Hamid Ismailov
had once told me, 'If things get really rough, you can
sell *this* – there are plenty of fans of this genre over
there,' and he had handed me five or six of his books
on remarkably avant-garde themes. Those were the
books I was sending out now to various addresses.
I'll tell you that when I tried to offer a book called
Postfaustum to a local collector of curious volumes,
who also happened to be a seller of books on Faustian
themes, he was inexpressibly overjoyed, and he bought
the book for a hundred and twenty marks. That was
half of our monthly income!

As you no doubt recall, after the brothers Abu Ali and
Abu al-Haris sojourned in the cave and learned the
teachings of Pythagoras, there was talk of punishing
them, but the brothers made use of the knowledge they
had gained about the power of magic and alchemy, and
disappeared without a trace. Now it just so happens
that Abu al-Haris later turned up in Baghdad, and Abu
Ali ibn Sino in Egypt.

Before turning to the tale of Abu al-Haris and the Padishah of Baghdad, we should make one thing clear. The two brothers were twins, born of one mother and one father, though Abu Ali was cleverer. During the years they spent studying at the madrassa, their teachers used to test Abu Ali's gifts by slipping a single thin piece of paper under the carpet in the cell before he came in. As soon as he entered the room, Abu Ali would perceive a change and exclaim: 'Either the earth has risen, or the sky has been lowered!' And that always brought his teachers great joy. In the cave, too, Abu Ali had absorbed all the knowledge of all the books with a single glance, while Abu al-Haris, despite his own considerable abilities, had taken a year to read just half of them.

And now Abu al-Haris had arrived in Baghdad, where he spent several days wandering the streets as a stranger, and then decided that it was improper to pass the time so idly, and that it would be better to get to work and earn a few gold coins. So he made a woodcutter of himself.

One day he was in the very deepest part of the forest, where forty straight pines stood extremely tall. The thought of chopping them down pained him, and so he pronounced the sacred words he had learned, and the forty straight pines transformed into forty strapping young brothers – tall, slender and mute. With the help of these men, he built a steam bath in an uncrowded neighbourhood of Baghdad. Soon, word of these baths spread throughout the city. Both rich and poor came to bathe, and the forty men were there to serve them.

Very soon news of the baths reached the padishah himself. He resolved that he and his viziers would go to bathe there, and afterwards, he invited Abu al-Haris to the palace. Abu al-Haris appeared for an audience with the ruler along with one of his pine men. The padishah asked the secret of the baths and the forty brothers.

'These forty young men built the baths, and this is the secret that explains their muteness, and how they are all so similar: they were born of a single mother and father in the depths of the forest,' responded Abu al-Haris. 'Each of them is master of forty trades, and building baths is only one of those forty skills. My young men move over the earth faster than water, and they move through the air quicker than the breeze. And no matter where they serve, East or West, they are always ready to complete any task.'

'Let East and West wait, for the ruler of a land called Sabo has a daughter of incomparable beauty. I am in love with her. I have sent my matchmakers more than once, but her father declines to permit our marriage. Solve this problem for me,' the padishah implored him.

'As you wish,' answered Abu al-Haris, and he ordered the young man standing next to him to go and bring the princess. The silent young man walked out the door. Just a few moments later he returned, holding the princess by the arm.

When he saw this, the padishah could not conceal his amazement, and he raised his arms to the heavens in astonishment. 'Am I dreaming, or am I awake? O wise man, share with us your secret! Tell us the truth! How did you do it?' he exclaimed. Abu al-Haris explained everything. The Padishah of Baghdad assigned the best rooms in his palace to the princess, and on Abu al-Haris's advice he sent ambassadors and gifts to the girl's father.

—

Now that the emissaries and matchmakers are on their way, and the lovebirds are enjoying each other's company, we will find out how things stand with the ruler of Sabo. When he learned that his daughter had disappeared, the ruler rent his garments in despair, and he collapsed senseless to the floor; but finally he called together the courtiers and the noblemen for a council.

One of the men assembled said, 'This is the work of a djinn.'

Another remarked, 'This is the power of magic and alchemy.'

'Most probable of all, this is the work of the Padishah of Baghdad!' they all concluded, and they conferred about what action to take against him.

'I'll send my soldiers!' declared the ruler, impassioned.

'No, your majesty,' one dignitary objected. 'He has an army of two hundred thousand men. We just barely held him off last time, and now, with your daughter in his hands, he is unlikely to be intimidated.'

So it was decided that the best course of action would be to join families with the powerful padishah, and let the ruler of Sabo be his father-in-law.

Meanwhile, the mission from Baghdad had arrived. The ruler of Sabo was given a letter from the Padishah of Baghdad, describing the great beauty of his city and the miracle of the new baths. And the letter invited the ruler of Sabo to come and see all these wonders himself. So he assembled a delegation of viziers and noblemen, ulema and wise men, and together they started off for Baghdad. Just after the emissaries returned to the padishah's city, the delegation from Sabo arrived there as well.

What a wedding it was! News of it spread around

the world. And for the service he had rendered, Abu al-Haris was named Grand Vizier to the court.

⁑

Just when I had begun cursing myself for ever deciding to become a writer, Semih-bey dragged me to the Frankfurt Book Fair, and fortune finally smiled upon me: at the fair I met the director of the Turkish Research Centre. And Semih-bey, of course, played a role in that!

'Here we have a genuine scholar from Uzbekistan,' he announced, by way of introducing me.

Actually, I'd never done any formal scholarship. I had just taught myself everything I'd managed to learn in this life, spelling it out not in publications, but in my own head – which would have to mean that I was an expert in language. And what I did write down had always been nothing more than a way to earn a crust of bread or a means of pouring out my soul. But the director turned out to be an indiscriminately greedy man.

'As a matter of fact, I have a need for just such a scholar!' he rushed to announce. 'What sort of a salary do you pay, where you are, to a respected hajji such as this one?' he asked Semih-bey.

And my friend, out of sheer simplicity of spirit,

answered with the truth: 'I paid him a thousand marks.'

The director, whose name was Faruch, spoke with an air of finality. 'Very well. For this hajji I will pay a salary of fifteen hundred marks per month.'

On our way back from Frankfurt, I said to Semih-bey, 'You've paid me much more than a thousand.'

To which the guileless man replied, 'I completely forgot about the small change!'

If only he had said that he'd paid me two thousand! What would my future salary have been then, twenty-five hundred? Oh, well. We would see what came next, I thought.

—

By February, the man who had invited me to work for him in November was no longer receiving my calls, and he kept telling his secretary to inform me the matter wasn't settled yet. In other words, he was giving me the runaround. At first I had taken it all very seriously, thinking that such a thing would never happen in Germany. Then I got a little angry, and started calling him on the phone every other day out of spite. But when nothing happened even then, I nagged Semih-bey. 'Can't you do something? Make him answer me one way or the other, yes or no.'

Semih-bey took a long time making up his mind, and when I was about ready to give up on our friendship altogether, he finally dialled the number.

He must have been mentally preparing for the conversation while he dialled, because his face was covered with hundreds of tiny beads of sweat. Faruch's secretary answered, and told him she would connect him, then disappeared for a long time, apparently swallowed up by the earth. When Semih-bey emerged from the ocean of that silence, he went right back to sinking into the ocean of his own perspiration. 'I'm sorry, he's just stepped out. I tried to catch him, but he's already in his car,' the secretary told him, playing innocent.

You should have seen how angry Semih-bey was then. The more his anger grew, the more courteously he behaved. This time he was excruciatingly considerate, using the sort of expressions you would never find in a textbook of Turkish eloquence. He conquered new heights of courtesy and generosity, and from those heights every sweet word he uttered flew from his lips straight to its chosen target. 'If only I could kiss you on each eyelid, you magnificent creature! Surely your sweet little tongue was dripping with honey when you said you would connect me. Now where have those promises gone, my precious girl? Little angel, would that I could touch your lovely hair; when you turned your head, it must have raised the breeze that swept your promises away!' He went on in these honeyed tones for some time.

My brothers, the Uzbek language is too crude to convey the fine shades of this passionate tenderness. You probably don't believe me, but that's because you've never heard Semih-bey speak when furious.

Even with all that impeccable courtesy, my soul still protested stubbornly against one point that Semih-bey kept repeating. Why did it have to be my own lack of success that was lit up in the glaring rays of this absolute politeness? And therefore I continued on, living as quiet a life as I could, keeping hold of my nearly empty cup of patience and guarding it meticulously.

Separation, followed by return, was surely the essence of this world, as true a slogan as 'There is no God but Allah', in the same way that Allah first created the great arena of nothingness and only later filled it in. So, too, did Sina remember every interval of his everyday life and began to understand that this workaday existence, labouring as a maid or a nurse, a builder or a bellhop, a guard or a gatherer of nectar, regardless of the presence or absence of any point in it, was nevertheless, in fact, his life in this world. For some people, even flight is just another daily job to do. Some people reach a long-cherished goal only to find that a new goal has presented itself. Forget the few select bees who had the good fortune to become pashas, and think about the drones! All they ever achieve in this world, actually, is to couple with the pasha bees, at the end of springtime, in the open air. They were akin to those who stayed close to the Teacher. But why did these thoughts grieve Sina so sorely?

Had not the Teacher blessed him when he had been the first of the newly resettled bees to carry a load of nectar and pollen into their new hive? It had been enough to make Sina's head spin. His legs had begun to buckle, and he had found himself dancing by no will of his own. It was a dance of the divine, a dance of devotion. All things had come together in that dance: his everyday life, plus the fields of flowers he had seen in flight, cultivated by this same unpretentious life, and the flowers in those gardens; the levels of life itself he had flown through and past, and the refuges he had left behind. The dance of the bees is akin to the dance of the dervishes.

Have you ever seen a real beehive?

In the city of Glasgow, in the Kelvingrove Art
Gallery, among the very old paintings and sculp-
tures, there is a living beehive on display for all to
see, encased in glass. They've built a glass tube leading from the hive to a window, a passageway by which
the bees can exit the building. The bees inside the
glass case enjoy just the same way of life they would
if they were outside in more natural surroundings.
The initial feeling of surprise a person beholding
that hive experiences comes from the complete
lack, in that hive, of any hint of emptiness. A person
needs at least a metre of space around him, or he
starts to suffocate. But bees climb over one another,
collide into one another, push each other around.
Their behaviour is like that of a person in a teeming bazaar, elbowing his way through the crowd on
a Sunday morning. But even then, not one bee ever
loses its sense of direction or forgets its goal.

Sina performed his divine dance among just that
sort of chaos, brushing up against someone else's
arm, stomping on someone's whiskers, colliding
into someone else's haunches and nudging right
up under the nose of someone else. But there were
miracles at work, of some kind, even there in that
pressing crowd. One bee took some pollen from
Sina's hand and got to work building a cell. Another

got ready to blow on some nectar to firm it up, and a third bee, following the elements of Sina's dance, put together the coordinates of the flower garden and started issuing instructions to some other bees who were looking for a job to do.

And the prayer-like dance continued all the while. Sina was now in a state of ecstasy. He had forgotten about everything in the world, and his heavy chest – no, in fact it weighed nothing, it was like air – inflated and relaxed again, and all the greater and lesser events died out in his memory for a while; in this state, all those memories took on an equal importance. Any bee on the dervish's path, experiencing moments so sweet they could never be experienced in life, would have been content to die there and then.

I will repeat this later, but I will say it now as well: they say that when Jesus wept, his tears turned into bees. That is probably the reason that no bee ever returns from its thirty-third flight. They all find their death in a place far from the hive. The prophet Jesus only lived thirty-three years, after all. The time for Sina's own thirty-third flight was now approaching. But he already knew what would happen during that journey, and in his heart, he accepted it as his due.

Before that flight, he would go again to the cell in

the centre of the hive, the one slightly set apart from the rest. Again he would pass through the ranks of the twelve close confidants and stand before the Teacher, and when the Teacher began to praise his name with a prayer, Sina would be released from the burden of that name, and he would transform into an ordinary bee, one of no rank or race. After the Teacher lifted the weight that came with his name, he would also relieve him of all his civilian duties, worries and cares, and Sina would have no more obligations or responsibilities to tie him to this world. Finally, the Teacher would release the bee of his memories of this world and this life. And now this solitary bee, free of both hopes and sorrows, would be ready for his thirty-third flight.

But there was still something stirring in his body, in his soul, which simply would not be still.

On the seventeenth day of the month of Sha'ban in the year of the Hijra 1413, I set out, having taken two hundred and fifty deutsche marks from the family budget which we had accumulated by saving money on absolutely everything.

First I will tell you about the evening preceding this event – that is to say, how I packed for my voyage.

My wife was busy laundering my clothes, my daughter was ironing them, and I, in the Uzbek custom, was getting a gift ready for my friend, a Turkish writer we had met at a vacation resort in Abkhazia who was going to escort me to my new job. There's a reason for the old proverb about how the poor are rich in imagination. We had a length of fabric we had brought from Tashkent. Now, I don't always understand the modern order of things. People had already reimagined the sumaklar they used to collect the night-time accidents small children had in their beds, and decided they could sell them as pipes for smoking. And in just the same way, from the bits of towelling cloth which had previously only been good for swaddling messy infants, people had begun crafting tea cosies and cushions to sell. So there I was, too, busy sewing a hem around the edges of a swath of some fabric. My wife dug around inside some plastic bags and came up with five or six scraps of satin (all pieces no bigger than a handkerchief) that I very methodically, one after the other, sewed onto the towelling fabric in the shape of a moon, sun and stars. The sewing skills they had hammered into all of us in kindergarten, girls and boys alike, truly served me well then.

My wife was making fun of me mercilessly, and

my daughter was getting angry that she was laughing, but I was determined not to go to a friend empty-handed, so I just sat there humming a song I knew about embroidery for queens, or reciting different poems on the topic, like this one:

> *'If I were the tsarina,'*
> *said my little sister Nina,*
> *'I would weave the world a blanket*
> *And make everybody share it.'*

Just your average family evening!

I thought I would nap on my journey, but no, sleep escaped me completely. My brain was racing with what lay ahead this time. Would I fail again, living out the proverb, 'He left like a bull and came back like a cow'? Would I return to my family, or might this adventure actually amount to something? Those thoughts pestered me all the way to Frankfurt, a route I knew well by now. After that, the unfamiliar landscape claimed my attention.

We passed through some gorgeous countryside from Frankfurt to Cologne. The rails ran alongside a highway and between two hills, and the great river Rhine, too, ran through that valley. That beauty continued to bewitch me for a hundred kilometres or more. On the hills and mountains, all covered in grapevines, people had erected castles. Real, historical castles, built in the medieval times and preserved carefully. To one side was the steep riverbank, and on the other were cliffs high enough to make you wonder how human beings, much less castles, ever got up there. Or had those castles been built purely for the sake of their beauty, meant to be seen only by those who cared to tour them in their imaginations? As it passed through the tunnels of the mountain, the train drew near first to the river, then to the highway. We were outpacing the racing automobiles. Only the river remained outside the competition. It flowed to meet us, and when the train picked up its pace, the river rushed ahead too; and when the train slowed, climbing a steep hill, the river bent, and sent its current under our wheels.

Yes, the banks of the Rhine are a fairy-tale place. We emerged out of that valley or crevice at the outskirts of the town of Koblenz, and after that came the capital, Bonn. Really, though, the name of that city deserved some sort of diminutive form. Bonnchik, for example. Because it was a tiny, cosy little town. Though of course the name Bonnchik makes you think of a ponchik, the doughnuts we all ate as children.

After we passed through Bonn, the cities came quickly one after another: blink your eyes and you're

in Cologne, then Düsseldorf with its public houses
right along the road, and then you come to Essen,
Dortmund, then the land of the Ruhr. Sometimes
this place is called the biggest city on earth: a whole
collection of towns blended into one giant metropol-
itan agglomeration.

But I've jumped ahead a bit. This time, actually, I
was not going all the way to Essen or Düsseldorf, but
just to Cologne. My writer friend met me at the station. We got in his car and rode to the edge of town.
There, cursing my own poverty for the hundredth
time, I handed him his present, my handiwork of the
night before, and to go with it, I declared, 'Especially
for you, from Uzbekistan!' And that present was, of
course, nothing more than a piece of towelling cloth.

The next day my friend decided to drive me to
Essen. Avoiding the perilous German highways, with
their exits of no return, we got there in good time,
and we even found the Turkish Research Centre.
We walked inside – straight into the busiest part of
a rollicking office party in honour of some Turkish
painter. The Turks call it a *sargi*, which you can translate either as an exhibit or a festival. Girls like angels
carried around wine, as the head of the Centre was
delivering a passionate speech and we applauded. We
soon realised we would not be granted any time to

rest, much less a dignified reception. Right away, the announcement was made. 'Now let's give the floor to our guest from Uzbekistan.'

I launched into a speech about this painter they were celebrating, and it was a good thing that the Uzbek language does not use gender as a grammatical category, because the artist I had been thinking of as a man turned out to be a young lady with long hair, and I was obliged to redirect all my hastily planned praise to her. I adapted my text along the way, changing phrases like, 'Masculine directness, a lion's courage!' into something that better fit this gentle young woman. I've already mentioned the local rules of the road: once you've chosen your route, you can't get off. You have to fight through to the end. And those words of mine were met with enthusiastic applause, and long minutes of clinking glasses! So that was my first work event at the Research Centre.

But perhaps you'll allow me to jump ahead to the next morning, my first full workday. I was supposed to show up by nine, but I had no idea how long it would take to get there, since the day before I had been driven around town and I didn't know where the train station was or how to get there. So I set out early in the morning, when it was still dark. It was February and very cold. I don't remember if there was snow on the ground, but I do remember an icy wind. And even if there had been no wind blowing outside, there was definitely one howling around inside me.

I walked where my eyes led me, and far in the distance I made out a woman's silhouette. I started combing through the daintiest German expressions I had in my arsenal so that I wouldn't frighten this woman in the dark. Still at a distance, I bowed deferentially, and asked her something like, 'Would you excuse me, kind Frau? Could I have just a moment of your precious time? Would you happen to know where in this neighbourhood there is a train station?'

The woman stopped, took a look at me, and shot out one question in Turkish: 'You're Turkish?'

I almost collapsed in shock. Then I asked, 'Are you Turkish, too? How did you know that I'm a Turk?'

This woman, who had surely never in her life heard such amazing words in the German language, who had surely never encountered such courtesy and tact, responded with confidence. 'You can't speak German.'

I wasn't about to argue with her.

Since she was also going to the train station, we talked along the way.

'So how should I have asked that question?' I asked her, by way of carefully beginning the conversation.

'You should have said, "Hey lady, where's the station?"' And she went on teaching me German from there.

It always astonishes me how we can study languages in textbooks for years, and then Turks and Arabs and Chinese people travel to another part of the world, and all they have to say is 'No understand!' in their own accent, and that's enough. Then they can quite calmly take advantage of the local blessings, earn their crust of bread, and manage their own affairs.

That's exactly how my own employment began at the Turkish Centre.

In Lorton Reformatory, which is in the state of Virginia, today was bath day. Not for everyone, of course. But A. Vissens had only just returned from the shower, managing to grab a newspaper from last week on the way back to his cell, and a couple of books they were passing off as new. Walking into his cell, he tossed his towel (it was short, so you couldn't hang yourself with it) into a corner, and stretched out on the vinyl cot nailed to the stone floor and began to page through the paper.

The headlines seemed to reflect the intestinal cramps of all humankind. As if the diarrhea had already passed, but humankind's arsehole was still itching. And it wasn't easy finding the reason for that itch. Really, what was going on? Was this all because of the unblemished state of the soul that only comes after a shower? But earlier, his daytime oblivion had seemed something like a dream, though it wasn't a dream; but if it was a hallucination, then how to explain his memories of the sweetest kind of satisfaction?

In prison, there is no sadder way to pass the time than by reading newspapers. You start to feel that everything is ephemeral, and if you look deeper, you understand that humanity itself is a prisoner, too: a prisoner of form, a prisoner of rules, a prisoner of ridiculous requirements, a prisoner of life, even... So it really wasn't worth taking the trouble. It would be better if you could keep yourself from reading those newspapers, just as it would be better if you could avoid drinking water after you eat an apple, so as not to get gas. But now your arse was itching, and something was niggling at you deep inside, too. The heartburn begins. Your tongue feels hot. Your breath fills with a strange stench.

Prisoner A. Vissens looked at the heap made by the damp towel in the corner. In the centre of his cage, the sun created a pattern on the floor like a soft Indian mandala, and from that spot triangular rays of light, sharp as teeth, shot upwards, interlocking with triangles of darkness. One thought awoke in his head: this meant that if the light was fighting through the dark, then the dark was also fighting its way through the light. But what we perceive with our sight and understand with our minds is that the light is striking a path through the dark. Then this thought, too, sputtered and went out.

What had that dream been about? The mood the dream had left behind was still affecting him, but he simply could not remember what had happened in it. Vissens let the newspapers slap against the floor and picked up one of the books.

———

The last rays of sun clawed their way down the chimney of the fortress of Farajan. To the right of the man sitting cross-legged on the floor was a ream of standard-size paper, and next to him was a bookstand; in his hand he held a pen, and to his left were sheets of paper laid out like the feathery wings of birds, just touching each other, still damp from his writing. This hut was locked from the outside, and it was checked twice a day by the guard whose job it was to look after the prisoner. This guard, in exchange for a ring the prisoner had given him, had promised to protect whatever he wrote, and he delivered fresh paper and quill pens every week, and secretly took the finished pages home with him when they had dried.

The prisoner had spent his whole life wandering from place to place, hurrying to some places, running from others, on one endless journey. There was no place he had not visited on his travels, no person he had not met and shared a plate with. He had been of one mind with them all, a buttress to some, a victim of others; he had taught some and learned from some, been trusted and been deceived, he had taken and he had been robbed... And now, in his forty-fourth year of life, when he had managed to concentrate his whole mind in this cell, he concluded that he'd passed down every one of these roads for the sake of this imprisonment, like the snare that was the last resting place for a bird always in flight. Could it be that he was simply food for his own mind? Once he accepted the creation of the world and the construction of life as equal currents of kindness, as a boon from Allah, it seemed likely that even this world, as created, was imprisoned inside his mind.

> We asked him to tell us more about this spring, and he said: 'You have probably heard of the darkness which forever reigns near the pole. The sun climbing into the sky shines upon it for the scheduled time once

per year; he who confronts the Darkness, and steps inside its boundaries, finds himself at the edge of a vast space, full of light. The first thing he encounters there is a living spring, whose waters make their way to a narrow isthmus. Whosoever bathes in that spring becomes so light and agile that he can float easily in water without being dragged to the bottom, and can clamber up to the crest of a mountain without feeling tired, and in the end, he comes to one of the two limits that circumscribe this world.'

As he wrote these words onto a tattered piece of parchment, he felt that his hand was not keeping up with his thoughts, that it was instead slipping off the charted path, and he was driving it onwards and onwards, as if spurring on a horse; but the thought had long since disappeared from view, and what remained from the movement of his hand was not even a breeze, but rather just four grains of sand, disturbed by the wind, and a clump of camel thorn.

———

Vissens laid the book on his stomach, spine up, and sank into thought. He was thinking of that dream again. They had returned from some sort of noisy party, and he was being crowded by girls on one side and, on the other, by some of the guys serving with him, and who were about the same age. Drunken, pointless conversations. Laughter. He had veered

off a little to one side. Maybe he was eavesdropping
on their conversation, maybe he was sizing up the
girls, maybe an argument had come up, one which
he wanted no part of, or maybe it was because of the
feeling of loneliness that had abruptly awoken inside
him; but for some reason he dropped out of the conversation, and stepped even further away from the
group. So they walked along in the same direction:
he and they, separately. And when, as they walked
through the darkness, they emerged from a shadow
into the light (it turned out it was evening, and the
sun was setting behind the forest, from where the
wind was blowing) – there was the jaundiced sky,
the grey road and suddenly, in the distance, among
the brown and green of the trees, a cupola appeared.
This cupola was shaped like an onion, and it was the
same shade of light green as an onion. The whisper
rose of another breeze, not too cold, and it was then
that his heart felt trapped: the edge of the city, the
end of the day, the conclusion of a life...

He remembered a tale he had read in one of those
tasteless paperbacks.

———

In his youth, he set out with a kinsman to travel and
search for knowledge. They passed down many roads,

and saw many different lands and different peoples, and many other things besides. One spring they came to a city, and there, a herald was blowing a long brass trumpet and informing the local people of an upcoming event, loud as he could. 'Tomorrow the cave will open! The cave will open! Let all men hear this news!' At the bazaar the travellers asked what that might mean, and a giant of a porter told them the story.

In ancient times, under King David, the famous philosopher Pythagoras had lived in that city. The son of King David, Prophet Suleiman, disliked Pythagoras at first, but when he realised Pythagoras's mind would be a good tool to use to examine his own concept of the world, Suleiman took a different opinion of him, and he offered Pythagoras everything he needed for philosophical enlightenment. Then Pythagoras said that all that was necessary for philosophy was a single cave – and rejecting the trappings of everyday life, he moved off into a cave outside the city, and there he wrote many, many books which he placed in a trunk. Soon after that, Pythagoras left this mortal world, and the devas and djinns who had been there to help him all parted ways and left, too. Some people said that Pythagoras had in fact disappeared along with them. But the things the philosopher had left behind remained in that cave, and nobody ever took it upon themselves to move his books from there. By and by, people began to fear that cave. Sometimes, someone would wander in and see those books, but an interdiction had been placed upon them. Now they only opened the cave one day per year. On that one day, the porter explained to the two travelling kinsmen, anyone who sought knowledge and who was not afraid could go inside the cave.

Then each of the two came to the same conclusion: 'Nobody can read that many books in a single day. What should we do? We shall trick them, and stay in the cave for a whole year,' they decided. 'But we'll need to make some preparations, and we won't be ready by tomorrow. Let's spend this year planning carefully, and enter the cave a year from now.'

So they agreed, and both brothers set themselves to work. Every time they earned two hunks of fried bread in a day, they sold one, and used the money to buy three hundred and sixty-five candles. They prepared provisions for themselves, too – rams' hearts, fried in almond butter, dried and mixed with dandelion greens. So the year flew by. Again it was spring, and again the herald announced the opening of the cave. Now the two kinsmen strapped their supplies onto their bodies, and walked into the cave along with everyone else. They hid in a dark corner and waited until all the other adventurers had left; and then, when the time had come and night had fallen, they lit their first candle and got to work. A spring bubbled in the middle of the cave, and around that spring were arranged trunks full of books. The traveller, even then, could memorise an entire book with one quick read-through, so he needed neither pen nor paper.

They spent one whole year in this manner. By the end of that year they had read and committed to memory the last volume, and they had burned their last candle and had seen it vanish in the darkness. Finally, the entrance to the cave was unblocked. Again a throng of adventurers and idlers came in. One of them lost patience even before the end of the day when he knocked his head against a low overhang; another started to yell and argue, while others started to whine and complain. Finally the day was over, the entrance to the cave was opened up once more, and the two kinsmen, together with the rest, walked out. But because they had let their beards and hair grow wild, shouts rang out among the crowd. 'Djinns! There are djinns coming out of the cave!' And they were immediately arrested, locked in chains and brought before the padishah.

The padishah wasted no time in summoning the executioner.

The executioner lashed them together and led them to the public square.

But no sooner had he drawn his sabre from its sheath than the two prisoners uttered the magic words they had learned from Pythagoras's book about magic – and disappeared from view, as if they had evaporated into thin air!

Outside the city's borders they threw off their chains, tossed them into a canal and said, 'Now we know that the best of the sciences is magic!' And off they went, continuing on their journey.

—

'Why would anyone have such sweet dreams in prison?' the prisoner wondered. Nothing but meaningless pictures and an imponderable mood.

Just the day before he thought he might have dreamed he was inside a cave, surrounded by people from who knows where. And in the middle of that cave, under an iron grate, there was a deep, deep well, he thought he recollected, and somewhere in there, deep down inside, the water under the earth was gleaming. But reaching it would have been about as simple as quenching his thirst with no water, or touching the light that shot into that well and made that water visible, made it material. The little children, however, who were hanging around there – *they* would be able to open the lock on the metal grate, get a ladder or a rope, then climb down into the well. Finally he caught one of the rascals. He followed the boy, who stayed near the door leading out of the cave, and from there he looked towards the sea, there beyond the dunes that stretched from the mountain to the water. 'Is that water much below sea level?' he asked, and, receiving no response to his question, he thought for a while about how applicable the laws of nature might be in this situation. As if there were some magical secret at work here, too. In the dream, time passed. The pipsqueak of a boy was looking for something. He knew something. And he found it. They returned again to the cave, and stepped upon the iron grate that served as a cover for the well. But something surprising had happened. Maybe as an outcome of those natural equations, the water which had been so low in the well now seemed just a wave of his hand away, and it was lapping over the sand like a swampy slurry. The sea outside was incomparably deeper and more boundless than this water... So what had happened?

Vissens looked again at his book. Had that been *that* dream, or a different one? He often dreamed of a stairway leading from a lower floor to an upper one, and at one landing, at a point when there was no turning back, the staircase ran straight into a wall, and then continued on again one floor up. He could see no way to get from this floor to that one, because the path was interrupted. How many times had he had that same dream? But in *this* dream, for the first time, as he looked at the wall he could see it was starting to crumble, and that inside that wall was a magical door. All he needed to do was to push that door, which was the same colour as the wall, and the path would be open to him! Could all previous riddles truly have come down to this?

—

The prisoner was still writing furiously.

Having rejected the shelter of any roof, they travelled further into the desert steppe, deeper than all the kings. Anyone who made an attempt to deduce the pedigree of this king would end up looking like a fool; any who thought to spread word that he was worthy would sound like a madman; and any man who searched for even the vaguest description of him would suffer in the most excruciating way. All comparison failed before him. He had no discernible features, but in his beauty his was a holy face, and in his magnanimity, his was a holy hand. His beauty made any other beauty pale, and his majesty of soul made any other such majesty lose value. When any one of those who crowded his carpet connived to see him with their own eyes, and let their astonished eyes travel the length of him, that gaze always returned in humiliation; it was sent back, you might say, before it ever reached him. His beauty was a veil to his beauty;

*when it found itself, it seemed to dodge away again,
and when it revealed itself, it seemed to be hiding. It is
the same with the sun: When clouded by smoke, it can
be more clearly contemplated; when the smoke clears, it
cannot be beheld by the gaze. As if its light is the veil
of its light.*

Again he dove deep down into thought. In the slice of
sky he could see through the chimney hole, the last
rays of sunlight were dying out, and the day was turning to face the night. Had he managed to write down
everything he'd wanted to, or was there more that was
unsaid the more he wrote? After all, there ought to be
some sort of conclusion to this! And what would that
conclusion look like? Or would the conclusion, too, just
like the mysterious path to prison, like the sought-af-
ter destination point to his journey, be yet another
yet unknown sensation? How long would he need to
live for that to happen? A thousand years? Or was it
that the longer you live, the more the pain of all those
years becomes compounded? What did you expect in
the end, after all? Primaeval peace and quiet? Even if
that peace and quiet were covered in sores, though,
wouldn't life, which you could never tear yourself away
from, just keep trudging along? Or do you expect the
most direct path, which would of course be the short-
est path, to be all that remains when you move from
the prison of silence to silence itself? In the end, is this

life a path or a prison? Or, just as you might be thrown into a prison cell to languish there, could you forcefully be thrown out again along the way? One could be free in prison and a prisoner on the path. All life's conditions seemed to come down to that. Ought time to be counted from the beginning of the common era or from the Hijra? Or do all our efforts come down to a return to this original starting point, like the sun's last glance over the dying day?

—

Vissens for some reason found himself recalling all the books he had read recently. This endeavour reminded him of his tortuous attempts to remember his dreams. A bee which had accidentally flown into his prison cell beat its body against the ceiling and buzzed, and Vissens was strangely stirred by the spectacle. After his shower today, no odours rose from Vissens that could reach that bewildered bee, and the insect buzzed indifferently overhead.

Ten or fifteen minutes later the bee swooped down and landed on a magazine, and its velvety feet slipped and slid as it wandered around some garish illustration. Finally the bee found the image of a flower, and when it recognised the shape but did not catch any scent, it sniffed the page suspiciously.

Vissens lifted one bare foot off the bed and let it hover over the magazine. The bee continued its ineffective efforts. Vissens was troubled. Why wouldn't it fly away from this pointless exercise? He kept watching the bee, even after his foot went numb.

Finally, the bee decided it had learned enough, and it drew nearer to that bare foot, which had started smelling of sweat. The bee sniffed, climbed aboard and began crawling upwards, towards the space between Vissens' second and third toe. It tickled, but he put up with it. The bee stopped, as if listening to something. It seemed these two living beings were sizing each other up, waiting each other out. Finally Vissens could stand it no longer, and he was just about to squeeze his toes together when the pain attacked – like a stinger had penetrated not into his foot, but throughout his entire body. Tears sprang to his eyes, the books were flung in all directions, the thread of his life snapped, and his soul – yanked up and around on the wings of the flying bee – quit his body.

EVENTS OF THE YEAR
OF THE HIJRA 1415

Between these two demoniac troops, however, there are some groups who haunt the frontiers of a certain clime lying next beyond that inhabited by the terrestrial angels; and letting themselves be guided by these angels, they find the straight road, thus departing from the aberrancy of the demons.

Avicenna, *Hayy ibn Yaqzan*

The more I tell you, the more remains untold. I feel I will be buried beneath these memories. They will overwhelm me. On the one hand, I would like to tell you about old Hakim's withering gaze, which used to flash at me on the road from Margelan to Yazyavan: he seats himself on the ground, crosses his legs and looks at me so penetratingly that either he will take off into the air like old Khottabych, or I will disappear from view myself, like the fragment of an explosive shell, lacking the strength to bear his righteous disdain. Is that what I wanted to tell you?

Or maybe it wasn't that at all, but rather how in

Essen, in the Turkish Research Centre, I shared an office with the former Turkish communist leader Guray-bey? Or I might have meant to tell you how this unassuming communist – and aren't communists in Turkey rather like dissidents in Uzbekistan? – had been engaged in bitter arguments, over the course of many years, about how to correctly pronounce the name Khrushchev. Was it Kroos-chev or Hrus-chi-yov?

What was it that I wanted to tell you? That at that Centre I found myself in a paradisiacal garden full of Turkish girls, and that among the modest young ladies I befriended there was a Portuguese girl named Dora Maria and a Norwegian girl named Undina?

Oh, yes, I do have things to tell you. But this spark will not last, and life is too short. So I will tell you about something else: my last trip to Germany. It could be that this, too, will seem frivolous, but the thinking reader may find some food for thought even here.

$$\overset{*}{\underset{*}{}}*$$

It just so happened that on that day I flew from Tashkent to Moscow and after spending the night with some friends, I loaded my sixty-kilo suitcase with twenty-five volumes of Pushkin and headed for Sheremetyevo Airport. Why would I need the Pushkin, you ask? My publisher had organised an exhibition in London, and had asked me to bring the Pushkin books, and since, being a true Uzbek, I did not know how to refuse, I immediately agreed to do it. Fortunately, some friends drove me to Sheremetyevo.

After that, there was nothing but trouble.

Our plane was flying through Riga to London, where I was supposed to surrender the books to my publisher and then head for Germany, to join my family there. The complications began with my very first step, right there at customs, where the agents insisted that each passenger was entitled to cargo of no more than thirty kilograms.

I tried to talk them out of it. 'Look, try to see it my way. I've travelled halfway around the world with this suitcase, and it was fine everywhere else, but not here?'

They responded with categorical refusal. 'Our agency was just created, and our rules are different. For your own safety, we do not allow more than thirty kilos per passenger.'

When I offered to pay for the extra weight, they answered, 'Oh, you'll certainly pay, but you'll need to unpack that suitcase, split it into thirty-kilo halves, and put the rest in a different suitcase.'

'And where am I supposed to get a new suitcase?' I enquired.

'That's your problem,' they answered, cruelly.

I was furious. I tore into them. 'You demand respect from foreigners. But you care so little about your own citizens, and even your very own Pushkin! So how do you expect people to feel?'

That didn't help.

Russians!

But sometimes, even among Russians, you can find good ones, the kind we can relate to. That meant natives of Angren or Kokchetau or Tursunzade. They're on our side, truly. They might say something like this, as an aside, for example: 'Those are Moscow Russians, you know. Don't pay any attention to them.'

I found one such Russian working at the airport: a pretty young woman, who turned out to be from Andijon. 'They won't let you out to get a suitcase, or even just a bag, now, because you've already checked in,' she told me, and she took my money and went off to buy me not just one, but five, plastic shopping bags. When she returned, she even helped me pack the five bags with thirty kilos of Pushkin. I plopped my emaciated suitcase down onto the scale. It now resembled a cow that had wandered away from the pasture and got lost in a barren field. Meanwhile, Pushkin, now transformed into a carry-on in the form of five plastic bags tied together with a scarf, looked something like a saddlebag slung across my shoulders.

And so I walked on, a saddlebag on my back, among those flashy, rich new-style Russians and new-style Latvians. If Pushkin had known what I was going through on his behalf, he might have risen up from his grave and shot at them all with the bullets he hadn't used up on that scoundrel d'Anthès.

It was the same story in Riga. They announced we must not leave anything on the plane for our own safety and tossed us out: everyone else with their little briefcases, and me with my thirty kilograms of books, in bags just starting to tear apart, over my shoulders. We walked into the terminal. Everyone avoided me, since they were apparently too good to talk to a black market mule. Should I tell you that there in the Riga airport a Pushkin fell out of one of the bags, and when I hurried to pick it up, the whole rest of the load tumbled off my back? I had no luck that whole day, that whole trip.

You can imagine what a sigh of relief I let out when we landed at Gatwick in London. Here it was, I thought, the free world, where you can do whatever you want! The first thing I did was to pile back into my suitcase all those disintegrating books. My suitcase took on its former appearance, and I transformed back into a friend and admirer of Pushkin.

Imagine how happy I was when, after handing the books over to the publisher, I received the money I had paid for them in return. I got into a taxi and flew off, light as a bird, to Heathrow.

There's one thing I forgot to mention. That day I didn't once take off my elegant black overcoat, the one that reached down to my ankles and had cost me some considerable cash, the one specially designed for travel abroad. So therefore, all day, anyone who might have wanted to call me a mule had to puzzle over my elegant overcoat, first, and then the awkward lump of a bundle on my shoulders. Put those two factors together, and there's only one thing they could have called me: I was a *new-style* black market mule, thank you very much.

Now, giving that coat of mine a satisfied pat, I climbed on board the plane that would take me to Berlin. I thought I would get there a little before midnight, probably by eleven, and the railway route I needed seemed to go right by the airport where my plane would land, so, technically, I could get on a train and be in Jüterbog in an hour, and there, probably, find a taxi – another half hour – and then, finally, I'd be in Wiepersdorf, reunited with my family again.

With Allah's help, I thought, I should be in the right
place by one in the morning. My daughter, of course,
would be asleep, but my wife would certainly wait up
for me if I called her from Berlin.

—

I really did land in Berlin at eleven, but the railway
station I had imagined ended up being next to a completely different airport, and getting there would take
at least an hour. A taxi driver informed me of that. As
I listened to his way of talking, which was not completely clear, I asked him, 'Are you a Turk?' And he
was. What a conversation we two compatriots had
then! In the end, he only accepted a third of the usual
rate from me in payment, and at a quarter to midnight
I walked into Berlin's Lichtenberg railway station.

At that point, everything in the ordinary world
took on a new, surreal sheen. And truly — just
imagine, please, walking into the waiting area and
running straight into a screen that covers almost the
whole wall. On that screen the local channel, RTL,
is showing a Hollywood film. Aside from the lovesick
people puttering around on-screen, you see nobody
else in the station. No — there, suddenly, two police
officers appear, with a pair of Arabs in handcuffs, and

they lead them off somewhere, after which silence reigns again.

When I looked around, I saw what looked like an information desk, and I walked up to it and rang the bell. When that bell rang it seemed to startle the whole station, frightening even the figures moving about on the screen.

After a short time a sleepy and unhappy-looking person emerged from behind a door. 'Is there a train to Jüterbog today?' I asked, trying to speak clearly in German.

'There's one at 12:20, but it terminates a stop before Jüterbog,' he told me.

'How far is that station to Jüterbog?' I pressed on, but the man shrugged his shoulders and disappeared behind the same door he had come from.

I was alone in the empty station. First I looked for a telephone. I called my wife. 'I'm here in Berlin,' I told her. 'I'm coming.'

'We're in apartment 76,' she said. 'I'll leave the light on outside.'

There were still twenty minutes until 12:20. I started wandering the station again. Every step I took was accompanied by flashing shadows and shouts from the screen on the wall, and as I walked past a metallic archway, I even heard a shoot-out. Past that archway a train timetable hung on the wall. I compared the time the morning train took to arrive from Jüterbog with the travel time for the trip I was planning to make, and calculated that the difference between the two stations came to thirteen minutes. About fifteen kilometres, I thought, reassuring myself. Certainly, where I was going, I'd find a taxi.

Two drunk German men walked by, spitting. It was a good thing they didn't notice me. The noise from that television show helped conceal me. Should I walk out into the light, or wait there in the shadow of the arch? Or should I ring at the information window again? But what if the man on duty called the police?

'The thing is — the thing *is*,' I went on thinking, and with those thoughts I put minute after minute to rest, until they lured me outside onto the platform. Again this emptiness, again an unknown city. And there, finally, came the train, pushing before it a wind shrouded in cold. Looking in from the outside, there did not seem to be a single soul aboard that train. Picture it, if you can. Even in the conductor's carriage, you could see nothing but the light in the empty window. I put my faith in God and climbed on. If there had been even one person in the car, even some hopeless tramp, like you find in the electric trains back home, that would have been alright; at least you can prepare yourself to deal with him. But here, there was only an eerie silence, as if Satan himself must be lurking unseen just around the corner. That was the mood I was in as I set off for the stop before Jüterbog.

Without so much as a rattle, the train swam through the darkness, not a single light visible on either side of the tracks. This was the former East Germany. It had been dumped by the Soviets, but not yet united with the West. Houses without windows, windows without glass, glass without light; only my eyes, and my thumping heart, which seemed to be radiating sparks, throwing them out in every direction.

At exactly 1:30 a.m., as the schedule had indicated, the train arrived with Germanic precision at the seemingly abandoned stop before Jüterbog. I gripped the handle of my suitcase and descended onto another absolutely deserted platform, and headed towards an underground passageway. Usually, in our train stations back home, even when nobody is there, you at least encounter some railway personnel, tapping away at the wheels of the train. But here, even those people were missing. I continued along the passageway. The dim lamps seemed to be leaking out their dull light into a depopulated place.

However, as I started ascending through that depopulated tunnel towards the waiting area, a growing noise of some sort came to greet me. When I finally reached the station building and opened the door, I realised what the noise was that was setting the waiting area on edge, but it was too late now to turn back. Here in the train station a bacchanalia was underway. Homeless vagrants, drunk off their rockers, one running after another with a knife, another pair kissing passionately, a third figure sucking on a bottle, barely detaching himself from it before passing it on to someone else – in a word, here the pandemonium before doomsday was in full swing. Satan's feast. A witches' sabbath.

I should mention that, in Germany, the tramps all feel drawn to railway stations at night. German tramps tend to be racists. And East German tramps are doubly so. Now there I was, walking right into that strained environment. I would have to very carefully choose how to behave. And I would have to walk out of there as if the mayor of the city was awaiting me, full of confidence, without a single glance at any one of them. But just then, for some reason, all the riotous noise stopped. Every one of them turned their shaggy heads in my direction, and froze, stunned. Someone in a long black cloak might as well have dropped down from the moon and confidently laid out a path among them. And I, counting my steps, tried not to interrupt that rhythm. My brain was urging me onwards like an electric motor, all the while analysing, vigilantly, whether there was anyone drawing a knife, or, lacking a knife, coming at me with a broken bottle.

Finally, and happily, I reached the main entrance, but I sensed that two people were following me. Then there I was outside, on the square in front of the station, and wouldn't you know it, the city's mayor was definitely not there to meet me. And what's more, worst of all, the square was empty. Not a single car! Failing the mayor, another solution in a situation like this would be to continue on at the same speed, to run straight ahead – but where? There wasn't any place to run! Here it was, the type of city I needed least of all: a dangerous, dark province of dangerous East Germany. And neither option was available to me.

So I chose something completely different. Option number three. That electric motor clicking in my brain caught sight of a telephone booth off towards one side of the square, and my feet, which felt as if they'd turned to wood, carried me in that direction. Who was I going to call, the mayor? The mayor of this city that didn't even seem to exist? Anyhow, it

was the telephone booth I walked to. My two pursuers – a younger man and an old woman, as I could
see now – stood off at a distance, waiting to see what
would happen next.

I walked into that booth, but as it turned out, the
telephone didn't run on coins. It was electronic, and
I needed a card. Here in this god-forsaken province!
I found a phone number for a taxi service, but where
on earth could I get a card to make the call with?

In the end, though, there is no situation that is
truly hopeless. I looked around and found a list of
emergency numbers, which were of course free, and
there was the number for the police station: 999. So
I dialled that number. And at the top of my lungs, to
make sure everyone outside could hear me, I began
to shout.

'Police? Is this the police?'

'Yes, this is the police station. What are you doing
shouting at midnight?' a tired voice answered.

I lowered my voice by about four decibels. 'Sorry,
I'm a guest of your city, and I need to get to a place
called Wiepersdorf, and I see the number for a taxi,
but I don't have a telephone card, so I needed to call
you. Could you possibly be so kind as to call this
number and order me a taxi? I beg of you.'

My German was suddenly coming out in torrents.

Out of sheer necessity, I suppose. When there's no need, there are no words.

'No. We are not a taxi service,' pronounced this defender of law and order, cutting me off decisively.

'If anything happens to me here at the train station, there will be an international scandal! Mark my words!' I warned them, my voice rising again.

'Fine,' the man agreed, and he hung up.

I wasn't sure what was fine: calling a taxi, or an international scandal?

In a word, it all ended with me standing there in that phone booth talking to myself. 'I called the police! They're coming right away!' Just like the Uzbeks do, when we speak to our daughters specifically so that the daughter-in-law can hear. The two people following me walked back into the building, and talked something over in hushed tones, and the noise in the station started back up again. That made me feel a little better. It meant they had forgotten about me.

Except that suddenly the two of them reappeared. The thought occurred to me that maybe I could make friends with them. Just in case. 'Is the Frau waiting for a car?' I asked the woman. I don't understand German all that well, but I was fairly certain that the inarticulate sneering she aimed at me then meant something like, 'No, thank you.'

I tried for reconciliation. 'There's a police car coming soon. We'll go together,' I said.

Hearing that, the man, from what I could tell, expressed himself in vulgarities. 'You and your police can go—' he told me, though I think I missed a word or two, and he and the old lady both walked away. Imperfect knowledge of a language really is fraught with difficulty. But in some cases, especially in the middle of the night, it can be useful.

Taking advantage of the fact that I had been left alone on the dark square, I took a good look around. The square was surrounded by apartment buildings, and a few cars were parked in front of them. A little late, I realised that I ought to head towards those cars, like someone ready to drive off. With nothing better to do, wondering what would happen, that's where I went. I looked, and thought I must be dreaming. There was a woman sitting in one of those cars. I walked up to it. It really was a woman, and she really was sitting in the car. And sleeping. She started to stir, and I knocked on the window. Lazily, she turned to me, then looked away again, unimpressed, and stared fixedly at the windscreen. I gesticulated to explain what I wanted. 'Take me to Wiepersdorf. I'll pay you.' The woman played dumb, and continued to stare straight ahead. But I could tell I had spoken too loudly. Those two from the station were coming up to me again, and they were getting closer this time. I quietly walked off.

I heard them say something in German to the woman in the car, and she rolled down the window. They talked some more, and the woman opened the back door. And it was two thirty in the morning! Those two were getting in the car. 'Maybe I could get in with them?' I thought, but another thought crept into my mind, too: they could put me in the car, drive me out of town, and, there, do whatever they wanted to me, which would be a fine way for this story to end. Believe it or not, though, the Germans revved up their engine and drove away without a word. Again I found myself alone on the dark, empty square.

In that sorrowful state, I watched a half hour, or maybe a whole hour, go by. I started shivering from the night-time cold, even despite the fact that my elegant overcoat reached all the way down to my ankles. And then suddenly, interrupting my thoughts about life and death, a car drove onto the square out of nowhere. Rejoicing, I ran to meet it, thinking this must be the taxi I had longed for with all my heart. The car, also rushing towards me like a lover who had yearned for this meeting, hit the brakes noisily right in front of me. It stopped, and the headlights went out. My first look told me this was no taxi, but rather a police car, in all its law-enforcement glory!

'Here I am! It's me!' I shouted gleefully. 'I'm the one who called you, I'm the guest of your city!'

I could tell they didn't understand. Not my words, and not the meaning they contained. Which meant these police officers were not the police officers I had telephoned. It was a good thing that one of the officers was a woman, I thought, and I tried to play on the most delicate strings of her soul: 'I'm going home to my wife and my child,' I told them, and on from there, describing how anxiously my loved ones were waiting for me.

The police officers exchanged glances, and the woman issued a command. 'Get in the car!' I got in.

'My wife is in Wiepersdorf,' I said, but I could see they were not driving me to Wiepersdorf, but rather to a building where the two of them got out of the car, walked up to the gate and rang the bell. After some time somebody responded in a sleepy voice. They told the owner of that voice to put me into his taxi and take me to Wiepersdorf, and after he agreed, they removed me from their car and drove off, to stalk the nocturnal streets some more. The noise from the train station was audible even here, and if I had known this place was so close, I thought as I stood there, shivering, I would have walked over two hours ago.

The taxi driver came out fifteen minutes later. He was tired, and not quite sobered up yet after what must have been an impressive drinking binge. 'The police brought me to you,' I began, just to cover myself. 'They told you to drive me to Wiepersdorf.'

My words did not seem to do much good. As if in scorn — fine, that's how it is, but you're gonna get it! — the haggard taxi driver accelerated with such speed that it took my breath away.

I haven't told you anything yet about the provincial roads in Germany. In both halves of the country, West and East, these are old rural roads designed for two-wheeled carts, framed on each side by centuries-old trees. And they turned along with the fields, following those trees. So now this taxi driver, to take revenge on me and to spite the police officers, was rushing us along at a hundred and seventy kilometres per hour, and I was terrified, praying to God that he had not let me live through that unholy experience at the train station only to die on these roads. I couldn't even fasten my seat belt, because the drunkard was sitting on the metal strap, and there was no way to pry him up at the speed we were travelling.

These lines are evidence that I managed to survive.

After half an hour, which meant it was maybe three in the morning, we were at the gates of Frau Bettina von Arnheim. My chauffeur stopped the car in the same abrupt style he used to drive, settled the fare as quick as he could, and just as quickly rushed back the way we had come. May God protect him, poor fool.

Thinking these thoughts, I took a look at the fortress in front of me. As my wife had promised, there was a light on in just one window. I picked up my suitcase and moved towards that light. I walked down a dark corridor and found what must be room 77, which meant the one my wife had referred to would follow. I tried the door and found it unlocked. I walked inside, set down my suitcase and breathed a sigh of relief. Then I looked around the room, and do you know what I saw? On a table under a lamp, there was a bottle which still held some wine, and next to that an ashtray and some cigarette butts. It was as if my happy mood after that sigh of relief had evaporated. 'Oh-ho, she had a little drink – I wonder where she learned to do that! Wouldn't have killed her to clean this up, though, I mean, she knew I was coming...'

I felt just about ready to file for divorce by the time I walked into the bedroom. In the semi–darkness I could make out two pillows: one big, one small. My daughter must be sleeping on the smaller one, and that shameless woman of mine on the larger pillow, I assumed, and I walked around the bed to her side. 'I'm here,' I announced, in a demanding sort of tone.

I heard my own voice, and then, immediately, a soul-wrenching scream.

She leaped from the bed.

'It's me, silly, your husband!' I said, and I was just about to shake her to bring her back to her senses, when suddenly the witch started babbling in German! I looked again. The woman I was intending to grab and shake was not my wife. It was some German woman!

'Entschuldigen Sie bitte, Sie sind nicht meine Frau!' I apologised, and I jumped back. She was still screaming in terror, and I tripped over my suitcase and fell down backwards near the door. I hurried out into the corridor again, and saw that the first door after 77 was 78.

Germans!

I walked back in the opposite direction, and found room 76. A light was burning over the door. I went straight into the bedroom. There they were, my own wife and daughter, sleeping and snoring sweetly.

The next day the news had spread throughout that fortress. According to the German woman, who happened to be an artist, and who had left immediately

the next day, an apparition black as death had visited her in the night, and said something to her in a
mysterious language, and then spread his long black
cloak, stretched out his wings, and flown away. 'But
he didn't look as if he meant me harm,' the poor
woman said, as she hurried to leave the place. I never
was able to wear my long, elegant black coat in that
fortress again.

Oh, those curved roads, carrying us along on their
crooked way to the truth... It's something like the
language of the birds. And the bees.

Now I understood something: all my searching
– whether for the right room, or Avicenna, or the
lost Stranger among the pages of old manuscripts or
in countries developed and developing, whether his
name was Vissens or Sheikhov, or whether they were
bees, drinking in the secrets of the eternal soul along
with their nectar – in truth, it had all been a search
for myself, for how I belonged to something more
important than the small, idle details of everyday
events in this inhospitable world. We find ourselves
only when we lose ourselves in the Other.

Look at a baby, how he drinks in the words and
gestures of the other to incorporate, to assimilate, to
integrate, that language, that behaviour, that culture
– or in other words, to make them his own. And at

the same time, like Sina the bee, carrying the immortal soul of the Sheikh, that child drinks in the entire image of that Other, and the Stranger plants his whole life inside him, now quiet and unnoticeable, now growing to cosmic proportions, sometimes a vexation and irritation, sometimes a torment, an interrogation… Some people will tell you the human soul is a battleground between God and Satan. Some will explain it all by way of what is conscious and unconscious, and some have other explanations. But I will hold my tongue and listen to the resonant silence of my Stranger, because in that, too, there is food for thought.

Let them stay there in Baghdad awhile, taking pleasure in life, and we will turn back to Abu Ali ibn Sino, or Avicenna, as he is known outside his own country.

Having disappeared without a trace from the gallows, he used his magic to reappear on the banks of the Nile, in Egypt. He shaved his face and cut his hair and nails, and, marvelling at the pyramids as he went, finally reached Cairo and walked into that city. Where else would a foreigner first direct his steps but to the bazaar? This visitor also went there, and when he passed down the aisles where tradesmen were selling honey, he caught sight of a young beekeeper who bore a very close resemblance to the Joseph of legend. The beekeeper, abashed by the dervish's steady stare, thought perhaps the old man was captivated by his beauty, and he offered him a spoonful of honey. Abu Ali ibn Sino put the honey in his mouth and immediately spat it out. Then the younger man thought, 'If he didn't like my honey, then maybe this dervish is a talented beekeeper himself!' So he invited the traveller to join him for a meal and arranged for a sumptuous feast.

The feast had already run past midnight, and the Stranger had spoken nothing but empty words. In the morning the young beekeeper would need to deliver his honey to the bazaar, but that honey had not yet even been collected from the hives. So the beekeeper put ceremony aside, the said, 'Father, you spat out my honey yesterday, which leads me to believe that you are a master beekeeper. In the morning I will need to bring honey to the bazaar, but since it is already dark, I cannot bother my bees. What would you advise me to do? Would you share your secrets with me?'

But the Stranger continued the conversation along the lines he had previously chosen. He told the younger man of the baths and dungeons of Istanbul, the old monks of faraway Granada, and the mysterious gardens of an island called Japan. The young man listened to what the old man said, but inside, he was growing impatient.

'I've been wasting my time with this old man. I'll just have to get as much honey as I can, and I'm sure I will see no profit today,' he thought.

Here the Stranger seemed to sense his host's discomfort, and he suddenly interrupted his own speech. 'Now then, since you ache over a cup of honey, bring me some offal,' he commanded, getting straight to the point.

'Where is it written that you can get honey from offal?' the beekeeper wondered, full of doubt, but he nevertheless brought his guest a sack full of offal.

'I had wished to deliver you from the cares of this life and introduce you to the secrets of the world, to teach you the magic of wizardry, to induct you into the mystery of alchemy. But you worry about getting your cup of honey. Well, then! Have it your way!' declared the old man. And, uttering a prayer of a spell, he covered a bowl full of offal with a lid. 'Tomorrow, you can bring this to the bazaar and sell it!'

With those words, the Stranger went off into a corner, and gave himself over to his own thoughts.

The beekeeper sat still for a while, contemplating what was what. 'This traveller must take me for a fool. He tried to trick me with his strange stories, and now he's covered a bowl with a lid and wants to pretend offal is honey. But calling offal honey does not make it turn sweet in your mouth!' The beekeeper walked outside, picked up the fire poker from where it stood in a corner, and walked back in, right up to the old man, his voice full of threat. 'Did you come here to rob me? Get out of my house, you mangy old fool!' he shouted, ready to strike him with the heavy poker. But Abu Ali ibn Sino turned to look at him with such a gaze that the beekeeper fell backwards from the sheer force of it, and then tumbled and scrambled through the door.

When the young man had gathered his wits again, some time later, and opened his eyes, he found he was lying outside in the very heart of the desert. He jumped to his feet and started to run, first in one direction, then in another, and as he fled through the desert he did not encounter another living soul, nor any desolate human structure. Not even a wandering bee was to be seen. Finally, a solitary haloxylon shrub appeared in the distance, and he moved towards it. The sun was high in the sky now, and he barely managed to reach the plant and collapse in its paltry shade. Even he himself did not know how long he lay there, but when he opened his eyes, he saw a caravan of soldiers moving in the distance. The beekeeper yelled out with all the strength he could still summon. Although the soldiers had wrapped their heads to protect them from the sun, they nevertheless heard the heart-rending cries of the honey-seller, and they came to where he lay, and without speaking a word they bound his wrists and tossed him into a cage that was lashed to a camel's back.

'I have heard, somewhere, of mysteries such as these,' thought the beekeeper, and unhappily he remembered the Stranger and he sobbed in remorse.

After a couple of days, the soldiers delivered this young man, who was as handsome as Joseph, to a particular city. When he asked what city this was, they told him it was Baghdad. The soldiers were peacekeepers returning from Palestine, so when they stumbled across any sort of booty along their way, they always picked it up and brought it to their padishah. Therefore the young honey merchant, too, after all his travails, was delivered to the padishah, and after endless questioning, he was appointed assistant beekeeper of the padishah's apiary.

Here, as he took care of the bees, he met and befriended a scribe called Abu al-Haris, who was copying out the *Tract on Bees*, and who was also collecting honey for his experiments in alchemy. One day the assistant beekeeper was even invited to the magnificent hammam Abu al-Haris had built. There they had a grand feast, and recited ghazals, and were served by forty young men who did not speak. In the midst of the mirages formed by vapours from the baths and the wine that took the shape of beautiful maidens, and surrounded by the melody of the ghazals that reminded him of the songs an enchantress would sing, he bared his soul to his new friends.

'What a fairy-tale place you have here in these baths! It reminds me of how I was transported overnight from Egypt to Baghdad,' he confided in them.

The people around him were astounded, and asked him what he meant by that. Could anyone truly travel from Egypt to Baghdad in a single night?

So the young beekeeper told them, in detail, everything he had experienced.

The next day, with some assistance from his friends the scribe and the vizier, soldiers again brought him before the padishah. The beekeeper had only a foggy memory of the previous evening's events, and he hoped he had not let his tongue run too freely.

In the palace, reclining on some pillows, was the padishah, and Abu al-Haris was there to his right, telling the padishah the beekeeper's story. 'O Padishah, this young man, who has undergone such unusual adventures, must be a sorcerer or an alchemist, and he is hiding from us knowledge that we do not yet possess.'

'What is the difference between sorcery and the miracles of alchemy?' asked the padishah.

'O great ruler, sorcery is an evil force brought about by desperation, but the miracles of alchemy cannot be wrought without pure and kind intentions.' The padishah stroked his beard and reflected while Abu al-Haris continued. 'O Padishah, if you issue the order, there will be no difficulty in dispatching this young man back to Egypt.'

'What use is it to us to keep this unhappy foreigner here, deprived as he is of his homeland? If he wants to return to his own country, then let him return! We will not keep him,' the padishah declared. The beekeeper, as if expecting just that, immediately agreed. And then Abu al-Haris pronounced an incantation known only to him, and the beekeeper, in the blink of an eye, found himself in Egypt, at the door of his own house.

—

And now we will hear what had been happening to Abu Ali ibn Sino.

After he sent the beekeeper off on his magical road to Baghdad, the Stranger, wishing not to subject the young man's mother to grief, whispered a spell and turned a bee into a man, and gave him the beekeeper's appearance. The next day that young man went to the bazaar to sell honey as the beekeeper always did, bringing with him a whole bowl of honey created out of offal.

That honey surpassed all the other honey sold at that marketplace. Nobody ever bought honey from the other merchants any more, and within three months their honey had all crystallised, and the beekeepers were bankrupt.

The beekeepers decided to take revenge on their young competitor. They gathered in a particular apiary, and invited the young man to be their guest, as they told him, and they set upon him all the bees that had gone rotten and wild. The young man was stung by a whole swarm, and his body swelled up and he fell to the earth. After three days of suffering in his mother's arms, he released his soul from his body, and together with his soul a bee flew out of his mouth.

The mother summoned the best imams and muezzins to accompany her son on his last journey, and after they recited all the proper prayers in the best way they knew how, they set the young man's body in his grave. The unfortunate mother arranged a funeral banquet, gave alms to the poor from the wealth her son had amassed, and laid the rest of his things in a trunk and locked it up tight. One evening, when she was deep in mourning, stricken by grief, there was a knock on the door. 'Who could be knocking on my door at such a late hour?' she wondered.

But a familiar voice came from behind the door. 'Open up, Mother! It is your son, the beekeeper!' And indeed it was her son's voice.

'O light of my eyes! Tell me, am I dreaming? Do not torment the mother who buried you, the mother who is deep in mourning, with your miracles! Do not bring my soul back to life, only to murder it once again!' she begged, but nevertheless, she opened the door. And what did she see but her own son, alive and well, standing before her! 'Help me, Allah! Yesterday they put you in the ground, and today you stand here before me alive and unharmed, as if you've just woken up! Am I losing my mind in my old age?' the mother cried.

Her son the beekeeper, seeming to understand what had happened, asked her, 'If I am dead, then where are my things? Where did you put them? Show me.' The mother opened the trunk and looked inside, but there, instead of her son's clothing, was a heap of offal, and a single bee crawling around on top of it.

'Mother, what did you do with my stand at the bazaar?' asked the beekeeper, as if realising something.

'It is still there as it always was, and a dervish is looking after it,' his mother told him.

And then the son told his mother everything that had happened to him, and everything he had gone through. The mother was a canny old woman, and she immediately gave her son some advice. 'Son, there is nothing simple about that old dervish. He must be a great wise man, a mage. You should not have offended him! Go and ask him for forgiveness. Become his pupil and his follower! Perhaps he will share some of his knowledge with you.'

The son carried out his mother's wishes. Like a bee obeying his queen, he went to Abu Ali ibn Sino and greeted him respectfully. The Stranger looked at him kindly, smiled and said, 'Where have you been, young man? You disappeared for a long time.'

The beekeeper, tears in his eyes, fell to the Stranger's feet, and kneeling before him, he asked for his forgiveness.

The Stranger extended a hand to him and lifted him up off the ground. He embraced him, kissed him on the forehead and explained, 'My dear child, for your rudeness I cast you into the desert of Baghdad. Tell me everything you saw there.'

The beekeeper told him how he had run across the desert, been taken prisoner by the soldiers and been brought to Baghdad. He told him how he kept the padishah's bees and met his courtiers, and he told him how, at the padishah's orders, he had been sent in some miraculous manner back to Cairo. He shared the remarkable impressions he remembered of the pleasures of his time in that foreign kingdom. His tales did not simply teach Abu Ali ibn Sino about the everyday life of a beekeeper in far-off lands. They also allowed him to guess who it was, exactly, who was serving as vizier to the Padishah of Baghdad and by whose hand the beekeeper had been sent miraculously back to Egypt. Without a doubt, this was Abu al-Haris, Abu Ali ibn Sino's twin brother.

The beekeeper also had questions. He asked the Stranger about his double, who had been buried just days ago. Abu Ali ibn Sino praised Allah for the knowledge He had bestowed upon him, and told the beekeeper that for the sake of his mother, so that she would not suffer, he had turned a bee into a young man who closely resembled him, and that man had been put in his grave, and the bee had regained his former appearance. Then he added, 'But everything that you have seen and heard is just a drop in the ocean, a particle of the light of the sun.'

The beekeeper was amazed beyond all measure. It was in this state that he began his schooling. He became a pupil of the wise teacher, and he coaxed out of him his ways of making honey from offal, and he learned something about alchemy, too. The Stranger, for his part, treated the beekeeper like his own son, and built a whole row of buildings for him in the centre of the bazaar, complete with residential quarters where the two of them lived together. His business flourished as never before, and the other honey merchants, realising that they could not hope to compete, that even murdering the beekeeper had not helped to get rid of him, decided to find other work. One of them began making halva, and another crafted sweet candy on a stick. Meanwhile, the fame of the young beekeeper's honey spread across the land. Some called him a honey miracle man, and others called him king of the bees. By day the beekeeper ran his honey shop in the bazaar, and by night he listened to the amazing stories the Stranger told, and tried to riddle out the wisdom they contained.

One day the beekeeper was out selling honey in the city and found himself at the king's citadel. There, looking out over the city from a window in the fortress, was the king's daughter, a woman of incomparable beauty. The princess caught sight of the beekeeper, handsome as Joseph, and she summoned her nurse, and told her, 'That young man is selling honey, and my mouth is watering. Bring him to me immediately!' And the next instant the beekeeper and his honey were delivered to the palace.

When she saw the beekeeper enter, the princess lifted the veil from her face and moved her fan aside, showing the world her beauty (which was more dazzling than the stars and more blinding than the sun), and she said, 'Good sir, are you selling that honey, or are you only here to tease me with it? Would the sweetness of your honey set only my lips ablaze, or would it penetrate my very heart? May I taste it, my sweet young man?' Blushing at her words, the beekeeper was unable to lift his gaze from the ground, and he feared he might drop the vat of honey he carried, but he offered the princess a spoonful. The princess did not reach for the spoon, but instead simply touched the honey with the gentle tip of her finger, and lifted that finger to her mouth, and licked it, and sucked it.

Then the princess handed the beekeeper a feather from her fan in payment for the honey; but the other payment the beekeeper received was the particular suffering they call love.

After returning home, the beekeeper poured out all his sorrow to his teacher, the same way bees carry all the nectar they collect back to the hive. 'I am so confused!' he cried. 'And I cannot decide which is true:

does my life have meaning now? Or has it lost all meaning?'

The Stranger, too, was plagued by troubling thoughts.
He uttered a spell, the door opened quietly, and the
incomparable princess herself walked into the room.
She had also fallen in love with the young man who
sold honey. When he had left her, she had ordered that
he be hunted down, but her guards had not found him.
And now, seeing the young man before her, she blushed
like the morning sun. That evening the Stranger left to
wander the mysterious night-time streets of Cairo, leaving the two young lovers alone.

In the morning, Abu Ali ibn Sino came home, and
in the same miraculous way as before, he returned
the young woman to the palace. When she awoke in
the castle that morning, she remembered in detail
everything that had happened the night before, and
she was overcome by shame. What a scandal it would
be, and what would she say to her father if he were to
find out? She castigated herself, and she decided to
tell the padishah the truth. But too ashamed to meet
her father face to face, she wrote everything down on
paper, sealed the letter with a stamp, and sent a servant to bring it to her father.

After reading her letter, the padishah convened
a council. The viziers and military commanders, the

ulema and wise men, all came to the same conclusion. Orders were given to guard the palace on all sides, so that even a mosquito could not fly in unobserved, and to set an especially vigilant guard around the princess's chambers. Evening fell, and the guard detail went to work.

The beekeeper, meanwhile, had passed that day with great difficulty, and in the evening he again poured his sorrow out to the Stranger. Abu Ali ibn Sino again spent some time deep in thought, then uttered a spell. That same instant, the sleeping princess stood up in her bedchamber and moved towards the doors, but when they saw her, the servants guarding her slumber raised the alarm. 'Stop her! Stop her!' And they rushed at her, reaching out to her from all directions. But a miracle occurred, and the princess disappeared right before their eyes, like smoke dissolving in the breeze. The palace was in an uproar. They checked every room, every nook and cranny, but the princess was nowhere to be found. Then, when morning came, the princess was back in her own bed again. As soon as she opened her eyes, she exclaimed, 'Save me from this ordeal, or I shall kill myself!'

The Padishah of Egypt was terribly worried. 'Do you remember the door of the house you entered?' he asked his daughter.

But she answered, 'I was not myself, and I do not think I would recognise it.'

The padishah decided to resort to trickery. That night, while the princess slept, he dipped her fingers in saffron, so that traces of the spice would remain on any door she opened, and they would be able to find it the next day. But Abu Ali ibn Sino knew everything that went on in the palace, and by the next morning he had woven another spell. When the padishah sent the captain of the guard into the city to find the door coloured by saffron and arrest the owner of the house, he found every door marked the same way. Much distressed, the captain of the guard returned to the palace and reported this disgrace to the padishah.

And so the miracle repeated itself for forty days: as soon as night fell, the princess disappeared from the palace, and at dawn, when the golden-winged bird of the sun had devoured the stars, she reappeared in her bed.

Finally somebody mentioned that the Padishah of Baghdad had a vizier who was a great wizard, and the Egyptian king sent an emissary to him, bearing a letter to the ruler and to Abu al-Haris. When he read that letter, the Padishah of Baghdad remembered his own past misfortunes, and he took pity on the Egyptian king and ordered Abu al-Haris to prepare for a journey. Abu al-Haris cast a spell and appeared in Cairo that very night. Upon his arrival in Egypt, Abu al-Haris took a miracle board from his bundle of possessions and dove deep into thought.

But Abu Ali ibn Sino's servants had already informed him of his brother Abu al-Haris's arrival in Cairo, and so he had also prepared himself for a battle none would ever see. By reciting just one spell, Abu al-Haris's miracle board showed Abu Ali ibn Sino to be located not in Egypt, but rather on a far-off island, in the middle of the sea, surrounded by a wall of fire. And now, according to what Abu al-Haris's miracle board told him, it seemed as if every night the princess flew across the seas and the oceans to that distant island, to spend hours in a picturesque palace. But no matter how hard he tried, Abu al-Haris simply could not discern where in the world that island was located. And that was because – though Abu al-Haris and Abu Ali ibn Sino were indeed brothers, though they were born of the same father and mother – Abu Ali ibn Sino was twice as intelligent as his brother by blood, and, in that cave, he had been able to read all of Pythagoras's books, while Abu al-Haris had managed to absorb only half. Abu al-Haris's knowledge of magic and alchemy drowned like a drop in the ocean compared to Abu Ali ibn Sino's wisdom.

One day, Abu al-Haris entered the princess's chambers and handed her an eagle, and he said, 'Hold tight to this bird. When you wake up tonight in that other place, release him. The bird will peck out the heart and the brain of the one who has caused you such suffering. And pick up something you find in that place, and keep it with you.'

Abu Ali ibn Sino, knowing what had occurred in the padishah's palace, gave the beekeeper an enchanted hood, and he warned him, 'Tonight the princess will bring an eagle with her. As soon as she enters your room, throw this hood over the bird's head, or else you will die!'

That evening, before the girl arrived, the Stranger decorated the room like an island in the Indian Ocean, hanging seashells on the walls, and corals, and models of small golden sea creatures. On the table he laid a dish of elephant fish, oysters and other delicacies.

Now night fell, and Abu Ali ibn Sino, as always, recited his spell, and after a moment the girl walked through the door. The beekeeper was ready for her, and he threw the enchanted hood over the eagle's head, and the eagle immediately dropped dead.

'O most beautiful of all beauties, why would you wish me dead? Are you not the creator of all this suffering?' the beekeeper rebuked her.

Seeing that her plot had failed, the princess tried to

assuage his anger. 'O sweet boy, strong and powerful as you must be, you still lack the confidence to tell me who you really are! You have disgraced me before my people. If that was your goal, then you have achieved it! But if you ever thought to spend your life with me, then ask for my hand in marriage and perhaps my father will give his consent.'

They came to no agreement. When they sat down to eat, the princess barely touched the amazing delicacies before her. But just after midnight, before she left, she slipped an elephant fish and an oyster into her pocket.

In the morning Abu al-Haris examined the elephant fish and oyster, and using his miracle board he determined that these sea-dwelling creatures came from the Indian Ocean, near one particular island. 'Consequently, the princess must be visiting that island every night,' he concluded, and he reported as much to the padishah.

That very day the padishah, wasting no time, outfitted a delegation of emissaries. Abu al-Haris uttered a spell, and in an instant the emissaries found themselves in India, where they were received by the ruler. He read the message the Padishah of Egypt had sent, which described how, on an Indian island, specifically one surrounded by a wall of flame, an Egyptian princess was being treated in an absolutely unfitting manner.

'What nonsense!' laughed the Indian ruler. 'How could anyone get onto that island if it is surrounded by a wall of flame? I'd like to see this ridiculous letter-writer try to find it. Send him to me!' It was in this spirit of disdain that the ruler of India composed a curt missive in response. He did add, however, that if necessary, he would be prepared to render all the assistance he could.

The ambassadors accepted the insulting missive and set off for home.

While they travel from India to Egypt, we will return to Abu Ali ibn Sino.

———

On this particular morning Abu Ali ibn Sino awoke very early, and, perhaps because his head hurt, or perhaps for some other reason, he went to visit the bathhouse. He felt better after a bath and a good comb, and he searched his pockets for money, but discovered he had not brought any with him. So he drew a handkerchief out of his pocket and handed it to the bath attendant, and asked him to hold it until he returned with the money; but that made the attendant angry, and he began hurling insults, calling the Stranger a beggar and a dervish and a miser, and he tore the handkerchief in two and threw it away. The Stranger did not say a word this whole time, but a man walked out of the baths and scolded the attendant. 'How can you speak to a dervish in such a way? Are you a man or aren't you? Here, take your filthy money, and don't you dare insult him again!' commanded this kind man, and he paid what the Stranger owed. Abu Ali ibn Sino thanked this cordial gentleman, uttered a spell, and left the bathhouse.

As soon as he spoke the words of the spell, the baths froze over. The men bathing there felt their hair and beards turn to icicles, and they rushed outside, knocking tubs of water over on their way. When he saw the chaos, the bathhouse attendant was furious. 'This must be the work of the dervish. God is punishing me!' he said, and he ran after the Stranger, but by then his trail had gone cold.

News of this unprecedented event spread throughout the city and finally reached the padishah's palace. Abu al-Haris hurried to the padishah. 'Without a doubt, a master of magic and alchemy is at work in this city,' he said. 'A man who can freeze a hot bath would have no trouble bringing even a frozen heart to a boil and lighting the fire of passion within it. This event and the whole ordeal with the princess must be the work of the same man. If the bathhouse attendant can help us seek him out, then I believe we will also find a way to unravel what is happening to the princess!'

At just the same time, the ambassadors returning from India arrived at the palace. The padishah had been freshly inspired by Abu al-Haris's logic, but when he read the insulting letter from the ruler of India, his mood turned, and he lashed out at Abu al-Haris.

'You are not the wise man I took you for! There is no knowledge in you, nor is there wisdom! How could you err so severely, counselling me to send ambassadors to such a distant realm? A truly wise man would have foreseen all that would happen, but you cannot predict even the simplest of things!' Abu al-Haris was crushed. But the other viziers, realising that something similar could very well happen to them one day, moved to defend Abu al-Haris. The padishah took mercy on him and decided to give him one last chance.

Abu al-Haris, much relieved, returned to his task with new determination, and he ordered that the bathhouse attendant be brought to the palace.

'Would you recognise that dervish if you saw him again?' Abu al-Haris asked the attendant.

'Certainly, I would!' the attendant answered.

Then Abu al-Haris assigned some of his own men to the attendant and sent them into the city to search for the dervish. The attendant looked everywhere, in every home and teahouse, and, finally, in one very intimate gathering, he caught sight of the Stranger.

'There he is! The dervish!' he called, pointing the man out to those accompanying him. They immediately notified the palace.

Soon the captain of the guard arrived, and picking the dervish up by the scruff of his neck, he dragged him outside, growling scornfully, 'He's wanted at the palace, and here he sits, enjoying himself!' The Stranger protested that he was a poor, humble man and could not imagine what the palace might want from him, but the guard paid him no attention.

Then the Stranger uttered another spell, and he took on the appearance of the captain of the guard, becoming his twin, and he grabbed the collar of the man's uniform and began to scream at him. 'Where have you been hiding, you bastard? Now you come with me!' The people around scratched their heads in bewilderment. Sure enough, here were two identical captains of the guard, wrestling and dragging each other to the palace.

When they reached the padishah, the true captain of the guard begged him pitifully, 'Your majesty, here he is, the man you ordered me to apprehend! While I was bringing him here, he used magic to take on my likeness, and now he is passing himself off as me and trying to take my place!'

But the Stranger did not hesitate, and spoke decisively. 'Be careful, my Padishah! Do not believe this sorcerer! *He* is the dervish! The devil has used magic to make himself look just like me!'

The padishah, confused, did not know what to do, and he turned for advice to a local judge who had just walked in.

'What shall we do with these two?' he asked.

The judge did not think long before answering. 'Do not listen to them, your Highness! Order them both to be hung. It's no great tragedy to lose one guardsman, if we rid ourselves of a sorcerer in the process.'

An order to do just that was immediately written up, and both men were handed over to the executioner. In the centre of the city, where it could be an example to all, gallows were erected, and drawn by the blaring of horns and the beating of drums, the people gathered.

The unfortunate beekeeper was there in the crowd, too, despairing. 'What will become of me now? Can such a wise man truly die?'

But Abu Ali ibn Sino, standing under the noose, had one more spell to use. He transformed himself into the executioner, and turned the executioner into the captain of the guard. Now the real executioner began to scream. But nobody in the crowd paid any attention to his cries. The order rang out. 'Hang them both!' And both of those bloodsuckers were yanked upwards in their nooses that instant, while the people watched.

Having carried out his orders, the executioner walked away, to all appearances going home. Along the way Abu Ali ibn Sino uttered his spell again, and transformed into an invisible man. He walked back through the crowd until he reached the beekeeper, and he whispered into his ear all that had occurred. Soon the square was empty. A few vagabonds wandered up to the gallows to get a closer look at the convicts. Hanging there were the captain of the guard and the executioner.

The news reached the padishah very quickly. He had just begun to breathe freely again. In fact, he was just sitting down to a celebratory feast. When he heard the report, he turned his wrath on Abu al-Haris and the judge. 'Because of you two good-for-nothings, I've lost two pillars of my state! Get out of my sight!' Clearly, no meal could meet his approval that day.

To spite him further, that night the princess disappeared from the palace, as usual. And this went on for quite some time.

But the more the beekeeper saw his beloved, the more his heart demanded. Now he found himself unable to wait for night to fall. So he made a new appeal to his teacher. 'Share just a little of your knowledge with

me! Teach me just a small bit of wizardry, I beg of you.'
He especially wished to learn to be invisible.

'Being a wizard would be of no use to you. Every
person is worthy of his own trade,' objected his teacher.

But the beekeeper would not be dissuaded. 'I have
followed your path. Now you owe it to me to teach me
your trade,' the impatient beekeeper insisted.

The Stranger felt sorry for his young disciple, and he
told him one of the instructional legends from the time
of the great plague, the one about the teacher and his
pupil, and then he said, 'All right, I will teach you the
very simplest type of wizardry, which is turning someone into a bee by spreading pollen from a flower over
their eyes. But only on the condition that you promise
never to use this knowledge except in your greatest
need. Promise me you will not forget this! Because in
life, old age, inevitably, is what lies ahead, and there is
no returning to youth. In the same way, in the science of
magic there is only wizardry, and there is no way back.
Always remember the consequences, and weigh your
choice a hundred times before you use the knowledge
you are about to receive.' And so Abu Ali ibn Sino heard
the beekeeper's vow, and he introduced him to the
secrets of his art.

In those days the Stranger often used to visit the
Library of Alexandria, where he engaged in profound

debates with two Catholics and a Jew. Taking advantage of his absence one day, the beekeeper smeared his eyes with pollen as he had been taught, and uttered just the right spell, and when he looked in the mirror, he saw, instead of himself, a tiny, velvety bee. He had a bee's shape on the outside, but on the inside, he remained himself.

In that form he paid a visit to the palace. He flew in right past the guards and the servants, and made his way to the princess's chambers. He waited off to one side for a while, relishing the girl's indescribable beauty. As he watched, some servants set the table for the princess, bringing out unusual delicacies and uncovering delicious-smelling dishes. The beekeeper's mouth was watering, and he settled down on the tablecloth across from the princess, so as to have a better view of her and at the same time to have a taste of the wonderful food she would feast on. Habit rules everything, and so the beekeeper started straight in on his meal. His human form was invisible, but the delicacies on the table started to disappear one by one. As the servants watched, each dish seemed to rise up into the air of its own volition, move towards the tiny bee, and then simply dissolve. But they were too afraid to chase the voracious insect away. After all, if it could eat this much, imagine what its sting must be like! So, after whispering to each other, they continued to bring out new dishes. But one of the servants was rather quick-witted, and while making a show of going to fetch another dish, she instead stopped by the chambers of the vizier Abu al-Haris, and told him what was going on in the princess's chambers. Abu al-Haris immediately guessed who was behind it all, and he went straight to the padishah and told him his plan. The padishah approved.

One by one, all the slaves and servants were summoned from the room. The princess and the beekeeper were now alone. His belly full, the beekeeper felt it was time to relax. He flew closer to the princess and whispered in her ear that he was there. The princess was frightened, but once she had recovered her senses a bit, she marvelled, 'I always said you were a djinn! I was right!'

When the princess found some excuse to leave her room, Abu al-Haris, who had been standing on the other side of the door, immediately slammed it shut, and then, just as he had planned, he began pumping smoke into the room through the keyhole.

And so the room filled with smoke. Some might think this would cause the death of the troublesome bee. But Abu al-Haris's cunning was more elaborate than that. First tears began to drip out of one of the beekeeper's eyes. The more his tears flowed, the more the pollen was washed away from his eyes, and a curious picture emerged for those peering through the keyhole: there in the room stood a naked being, half man, half bee!

Abu al-Haris piped in more smoke, until the pollen had been washed out of the man's other eye. In the end, the bee had disappeared completely, and in his place stood a young man: the honey merchant. They threw a sheet over him and brought him before the padishah.

'What shall we do with this one?' the padishah asked his advisors.

'He must be driven out in some humiliating manner, and then executed,' came the answer.

They sat the young man on a donkey facing backwards, and to the blaring of horns and the beating of drums they led him around the streets and squares of Cairo. When they reached the bazaar, they erected gallows. But suddenly, from out of nowhere, a swarm of crazed bees swooped in and started stinging everyone they could find: the executioner and the guards, the vagabonds and the voyeurs. Everyone took off running. And there among them, the beekeeper again transformed into a bee, and he disappeared with the rest of the swarm.

Abu Ali ibn Sino gave the young man a severe

scolding after that. But the beekeeper apologised so profusely that his teacher finally forgave him. 'You are mixing up two worlds: the surface, and the secret. One of these worlds is the world of vanity and deceptive daydreams, and the other, invisible to all, is a secret world. If you have entered one, you must forget the other! But do not forget that you are only a guest, no matter which world you visit,' said the Stranger, and he went on to recount one of his parables.

The young man seemed to understand his words, but he was unable to absorb them, because he was not educated enough to do so. Besides, the voice of his disobedient heart always prevailed over the voice of reason. Once again he missed his beloved desperately. Once again he begged the Stranger for help. Once again the princess disappeared from the palace. Once again the padishah summoned the vizier Abu al-Haris.

The next day, steering the young woman before them, the vizier and a contingent of guards walked the streets of the city. By evening, in one particular neighbourhood, the girl pointed out one particular door. 'I think that is the one,' she said. Some of the men immediately escorted her back to the palace, to her own chambers, and the rest stayed behind to keep an eye on that door.

As soon as night fell over Cairo, the princess disappeared from the palace again, and the news was reported to the men lying in wait. They burst into the house with a noisy clamour. In they came, and in a particular room they saw the beekeeper, the princess, and there with them the foreign dervish. The guards meant to seize them all, but just then the dervish uttered a spell, and each guardsman immediately went limp, lost the gift of speech, and found he could no longer move his arms. Abu Ali ibn Sino saw that the padishah and Abu al-Haris were among the men who had burst into the room, but he made sure his brother did not recognise him.

'Greetings, my Padishah! Welcome to our table!' the dervish said with a bow, and he passed him a hunk of fried bread and a cup of honey. The padishah, without meaning to, dipped a piece of bread in the honey and placed it in his mouth – and he tasted something the likes of which he had never tasted before. 'My son harvests this honey,' said the dervish. 'If you do not object, then your visit here, as our guest, can mark our children's betrothal. Will you give your daughter to my son in marriage?' he pressed.

But the padishah was still eating honey, and he could not talk.

'Look how attentive he is, after so many words!' thought the Stranger. He glanced at a bee which had appeared in the room from somewhere, and smiled almost imperceptibly.

The guests also noticed the bee, and as they watched, it seemed to be drawing nearer and therefore increasing in size; but in fact the bee was moving further away, and now it touched the ceiling, broke through the roof and grew even mightier. The padishah and Abu al-Haris sensed that they, too, were being lifted up, following the bee. They thought of jumping down, but it was too high; they looked up, but they could see nothing above them but the enormous bee. Behind it the mountains and valleys, and indeed the earth itself, could no longer be seen, only darkness, and even the enormous stars hummed quietly like a thrumming beehive.

Finally they passed through a door shaped like a blossom and into a garden. This garden was like paradise itself. A heart unaccustomed to such serene peace and quiet might be frightened by it, and beat worriedly, making clear its desire to return as quickly as it can to a more ordinary life – and so the padishah, much perturbed, began searching for the door by which they had entered. And when they found it they rushed through it, and found themselves back in the palace in Cairo.

The padishah was bewildered by this strange turn of events, but Abu al-Haris had long since realised what was happening. 'This is the work of my twin brother Abu

Ali ibn Sino. He is the only one in the world with the knowledge to do it. Other than Pythagoras, no man has ever reached his level and understanding – not Aristotle, not Plato. My advice to you is this: submit to your fate and my brother's demands!'

But the padishah grew angry and would not listen to his vizier. 'Your brother tried to intimidate me with that gigantic bee! I will never make peace with him! I am issuing the order right here and now: capture him and bring him to me!' he demanded, and he sent twelve soldiers to the now-familiar house at the bazaar.

The soldiers burst into the house, shouting threats, and moved to seize Abu Ali ibn Sino – but he uttered his spell again and turned them into the twelve beasts of the oriental horoscope, then led them through the bazaar to the delight of all the people there. Then he turned them back into men and sent them to the palace, telling them, 'Go, and tell the padishah that he must cease his foolishness, and permit the two young people to wed!' The soldiers made a detailed report of everything that befell them, and they passed on what Abu Ali ibn Sino had said.

The padishah grew even more furious. 'So he still dares to threaten me! I will teach him a lesson!' And this time he sent a force of two hundred thousand men against the Stranger.

When he heard of this, Abu Ali ibn Sino walked out into the beekeeper's garden, uttered a spell, and turned all the bees in the apiary into warrior bees, well-armoured and ready for battle.

And what a battle it was! The blue waters of the Nile ran red with blood as the river reached the sea. As a matter of fact, that is why that sea is called the Red Sea. And the padishah lost his army of two hundred thousand men. With that, he was forced to send Abu al-Haris to Abu Ali ibn Sino to beg for peace.

The two twin brothers finally met again! They embraced, and told each other everything they had seen and done over their long period of separation. On behalf of the padishah, Abu al-Haris invited Abu Ali ibn Sino to the palace. 'I will go not for the padishah's sake, but for the sake of honouring your request,' the Stranger told his brother, and the two kinsmen went together to the palace.

The padishah received the Stranger with every possible sign of honour, and to flatter his guest, he even called him the Pythagoras of his time. Then he asked him a question, out of curiosity. 'You have brought us so much trouble, and you are so powerful in the arts of magic. Could you demonstrate those arts to us here and now?' The Stranger laughed, and asked to be given a bowl full of water.

They brought him an ordinary bowl and some ordinary water, and Abu Ali ibn Sino turned to them and said, 'All right, any man who wishes to see a miracle should look into this water!'

One courtier said, 'Your Highness, allow me to look.' The padishah gave his permission. The courtier looked into the bowl of water and saw himself, walking into the desert, disguised as a woman. There was sand all around him and not a single plant. And the sun was tacked up high in the sky. Suddenly, out of nowhere, a black man like a deva appeared, and he mistook the visitor for a woman, and began chasing after him. He ran this way and that, and when the man had almost caught up to him, Abu Ali ibn Sino appeared before him, also out of thin air.

'Help me!' the man disguised as a woman beseeched him.

Abu Ali ibn Sino laid out two conditions. 'First, what you have seen here you must never, under any circumstances, reveal to anyone. And second, I am going to ask the padishah to give his daughter to my son in marriage, and you will agree with me and help me to convince him!' The man agreed. Then Abu Ali ibn Sino led him to the exit.

When the courtier had recovered from his ordeal, he found he was still sitting there with the bowl of water.

Everyone asked him what he had seen, but he did not speak.

Now another nobleman expressed the desire to look into the bowl. 'I shall certainly tell you what I see!' he promised. This man also found himself in the desert, though he maintained his masculine appearance; but he was pursued by a soldier who wanted to arrest him. He took off running, but the soldier chased him, and seemed just about to catch him when there in front of the fleeing man Abu Ali ibn Sino appeared, and told him what he had told the previous man. This man also agreed to all his conditions, and when he returned, despite his promise, he did not speak a word about what had happened to him.

Several more people looked into the water, and each of them saw terrible things – cloven-hoofed beasts running wild, and narrow-eyed beasts tearing apart their stomachs – and not one of them said anything at all about what they had seen.

Then the padishah himself decided to look into the water. He looked, and other than the water, he saw nothing at all.

'Look very closely, my Padishah!' said Abu Ali ibn Sino.

He looked closely, and the padishah suddenly saw himself inside a well, naked. He wanted to plant his feet at the bottom and look up, but his feet did not reach. He wanted to reach out his arms to touch the walls of the well and look down, but the walls were too slippery. Very carefully he looked up, but the padishah saw nothing but the sky. And his heart compressed with terror. While he was still trying to come up with a plan, he began to sink. Then the padishah began waving his arms through the water with all his strength, but there was not enough room to tread water. He was frighteningly exhausted, and he had just about given up when suddenly a bucket struck the top of his head. Somebody had sent that bucket down into the well to collect water. The padishah grabbed it.

The person up above began to raise it, and found that it was heavy. He lifted it closer and closer until suddenly he saw a naked figure clinging to the bucket! 'A water spirit!' he screamed in fright, and he thrust the bucket away, back down where it had come from.

Again the padishah found himself at the bottom of the well, and again he was fighting for his life.

After some time, another bucket came dropping down, and again the padishah was pulled up. This time there were soldiers waiting for him, itching for a fight with a water spirit. They spoke a language he did not understand.

Hooting and hollering over the padishah, they delivered him to their commander. This man treated the padishah considerately; he gave him food and wine and a place to sleep in a separate room. The padishah fell asleep, and when he awoke, he found he was sitting in the desert with nothing but sand all around him, and nothing but the sky overhead. He ran this way and that, but he found not a single sign of life. Now evening was settling in, and finally he caught sight of a twinkling light in the distance. He walked towards that light, and found two ogres gobbling up a skull. The padishah jumped back at the sight. But the ogres had already caught his human scent, and they lunged after him. They caught up to him and they grabbed him, but then they turned on each other, each one shouting 'He's mine!' – and taking advantage of the confusion, the padishah fled.

He ran until he reached a place where a dragon was puffing out fire in all directions. The padishah very much wanted to wake up from this nightmare. But what would be waiting for him in real life? Just as he had reached his wits' end, the Stranger appeared before him.

'Save me!' begged the padishah.

But first the Stranger laid out his terms. 'You must tell no one what you have seen here, and you will go on living life as you lived it before. Second, you will give your daughter in marriage to the beekeeper!'

And the padishah agreed with no arguments whatsoever.

—

But vows made in the world of magic are one thing, and the realities of everyday life are another. The padishah found himself staring into the water again, and he shuddered, and said with a smile, 'Did I lose consciousness for a while?'

To which Abu Ali ibn Sino, standing off to one side, responded, 'My Padishah, I did not reveal to you my modicum of knowledge to show off. My purpose was to bring two lovers together, so that distance does not stretch like a desert between them.'

'All right. Let us consider it,' the padishah grumbled, and he retired to his chambers. Abu Ali ibn Sino returned to the bazaar.

The padishah may have lost this battle, but he had no plans to surrender in war. Once alone, he summoned Abu al-Haris, and scolded him. 'I spared no expense in bringing you here from Baghdad. I have fed you and coddled you. And you have repaid me by shaming me before the people! You have no knowledge and you demonstrate no initiative! Curse you and what little you know!'

Abu al-Haris could not think of how to answer, and he was embarrassed. Sure that he would soon be banished, he invented one final intrigue.

Determined to demonstrate some initiative this time, he applied his knowledge of wizardry and built another magnificent bathhouse, this time in Cairo. It was even better than the one in Baghdad. And one day he invited his twin brother to visit it. Not expecting any ruse on his brother's part, Abu Ali ibn Sino packed his things in a bundle and came to bathe, and when he walked into the room, Abu al-Haris, again using his knowledge of wizardry, transported Abu Ali ibn Sino to the very heart of the desert.

Abu Ali ibn Sino looked at the position of the sun in the sky and chose a route to follow, and soon he found himself in an unfamiliar city. He did not want to enter the town stark naked, so he uttered a spell and was soon clothed in some old rags. He walked into the city dressed like a dervish.

The ruler of that city was someone by the name of Dikyanus. As soon as they caught sight of the Stranger, the ruler's spies reported the intruder. Dikyanus had a wizard in his employ, and this man, named Jolud, received an order to bring the dervish to the palace.

Jolud found the dervish at the bazaar, and told him, 'Come now, friend! You are expected at the palace.' But the dervish refused. So Jolud uttered a spell, and a fire broke out in the bazaar. In response, the dervish uttered his own spell, and the bazaar was soon filled with water, extinguishing the flames. Then he uttered another spell, and Jolud turned into a bumblebee. The dervish picked him up, put him into his snuffbox, and slipped the box into his pocket.

Dikyanus, meanwhile, grew impatient as he was waiting for them. He decided to go out into the city himself. When he reached the bazaar, he saw it was flooded with water. People were wading around trying to rescue their goods, and Abu Ali ibn Sino, holding his cloak up around his knees, was pushing through the crowd and hurrying away. When he noticed Dikyanus, the dervish uttered yet another spell, and suddenly scores of reflections trembled across the water. Now instead of one dervish, there were forty. Neither the ruler of the city nor his guards could tell which one they needed to catch. 'And that is the whole point!' declared the dervish mysteriously, and he disappeared to who knows where.

That was the last anyone knew of Dikyanus.

For now, let this be all we know of Abu Ali ibn Sino, too, and we will return to Abu al-Haris.

—

Abu al-Haris, having dealt with his brother, hurried to see the padishah.

'My great Padishah! Your enemy is no more! You will never again find anyone strong enough to challenge you – or me!' he boasted. And he promised, 'From this day forth, I will work to change rock into gold, and sand into pure crystal.'

The padishah was not dreaming just then of changing rock into gold, but rather about how to erase the memory of his daughter's shame from the minds of the people he ruled. 'In that case, let's kill the beekeeper first,' said the padishah. 'He enchanted my daughter with his honey, and I will not allow the people to lose their minds over him the same way!'

'My Padishah! The secret of that honey had something to do with Abu Ali ibn Sino's teachings. Abu Ali ibn Sino is no more, so the honey ought to be finished, as well.' Abu al-Haris hoped to reassure the padishah with his words. 'Now the people will pay no more attention to the stories of the love between your daughter and the beekeeper, and they will go back to their usual affairs.'

'That's enough of your arguing! The beekeeper must hang as an example to the others!' insisted the padishah.

Abu al-Haris still objected, 'If you kill the beekeeper,

everyone will still remember his honey. But think: what will he be able to accomplish without Abu Ali ibn Sino's sorcery?'

—

While the two of them argued, Abu Ali ibn Sino was using that very sorcery to bring himself back to Cairo.

He immediately went to the bazaar to find the bee-keeper. When he discovered that he was absent, he became very worried.

The beekeeper had in fact already been seized by the padishah's soldiers and thrown in jail, and now everyone was awaiting the padishah's orders. Abu Ali ibn Sino's heart beat full of blood. 'No matter what you teach a padishah, it does no good at all! I can see there is no changing him. The only option left is to punish him!' Abu Ali ibn Sino told himself. He pulled his snuff-box out of his pocket, caused a bouquet of flowers to grow out of the bumblebee inside it, dressed himself as a flower merchant, and headed for the palace.

But before he saw the padishah, he caught sight of Abu al-Haris. Enchanted by the beauty of the flowers, the Stranger's brother did not even glance at the one who carried them, but instead remarked, 'What a wonderful scent!' And he took a bouquet from the flower-seller's basket, inhaled deeply, and immediately fell down dead, poisoned by the bee's venom which those flowers had absorbed.

He who sows evil, dies from evil. There is nothing to be done about that.

Abu Ali ibn Sino grieved for his kinsman. He had lost his twin brother, and now he was all alone in the world. In the past, as he had wandered the world, he had always been comforted by the thought that somewhere out there was a kindred soul. But now, as he wandered, he would be burdened by the additional weight of his solitude.

With these sad thoughts, he left the palace, but just outside the gates some guards fell upon him and dragged him back inside.

Whatever for? Well, the princess had been watching from her window, and she saw the flower-seller shuffling sadly away, and she was enchanted by the beauty of the flowers he held – so she had ordered that he be returned. The guards steered the merchant to where the princess waited and delivered the flowers to her.

'Only once before have I experienced such pleasure: when I first tasted the honey made by the young beekeeper. These flowers must be the source of that honey!' she marvelled, staring, enchanted, at the flowers. And truly, in those flowers, there was none of the paleness of pink, none of the yellowness of orange, no velvety notes of darkness, and no deep shades of burgundy. They were the clean scarlet hue of a young child's blood. And their shape was just as enchanting as their colour. There are certain types of roses that resemble wide-open tulips, except with no seeds. There are others that look like mushrooms from the outside, or immature bolls of cotton. There are blossoms that resemble curved teeth, some are like sets of coquettish lips, and some look like something caught and splattered in a mill. But this flower was like a road leading to an extraordinary world. Or into the very depths, the very core, of this one.

The Stranger was just walking into the princess's chambers then, and he wished to stop her, but she was so drawn to the flowers that she would not listen to anyone. No spell would be of any use, first because he was bound by a curse, and second because of a strict law of wizardry: a spell already uttered is an arrow released from the bow. Who can call either one back again?

'The flowers that made my honey!' whispered the princess, and her soul left her body.

And they threw the flower-seller into the dungeon where the beekeeper was already being held.

But what is a dungeon compared to lacerations of the soul? Naturally, when he saw his teacher, the younger man was glad. 'Father, say a spell and save us both! I long for my beloved. Let's get ourselves home at once,' he urged. What spells could deceive the poor boy now? Is there any such spell in the world? So Abu Ali ibn Sino, there in the dungeon that resembled a cave, told the beekeeper not his latest tale, not a parable, not a story, and not a slice of the philosophy of magic, but the most honest truth of all.

—

Is there any burden in this world heavier than a ruined soul? Plato compared this world to a cave, and our lives to the shadows inside a cave. But there is no pain in shadows! Is there any scale strong enough to measure the weight of spiritual agony? And is there any sorcery powerful enough to conquer it? Might that not be the reason that Pythagoras walled up the truth inside his cave? Back then, when he had first stepped inside that cave, Abu Ali ibn Sino had seen a spiderweb that covered the trunk where those countless books lay. There was a tiny bee caught in that web. He had released the bee immediately, then hurried, thirsty for knowledge, to open the trunk and read the books. But might that have been the greatest wisdom of all? Who was the spider here, and who was the bee?

And who would ever know where the honey ended and the poison began? At what point does poison become more valuable than honey? Why do suffering and pain contain such sweetness? Why does bitterness still linger, even at the height of pleasure? What makes the sweetness of a question bring about the sour after-effects of doubt? What did this proud science, this high-minded knowledge really mean? And a beehive, as perfect a structure as it is... does it not in some way resemble a spider's web? The Stranger had sensed, in one instant, the trembling bee, struggling in the web of a hidden spider. But not knowing whom he could compare to whom, with a feeling of profound helplessness, he uttered his very last spell.

Some have said that Abu Ali ibn Sino brought down from heaven a deluge of toads, and others have said that he unleashed a horde of mice to chew through all the books in that country of Egypt. But the very oldest tale has it that at that instant the sky filled with black storm clouds, and lightning struck. With every flash of lightning, a spider's web fell to earth. Soon the land was completely covered in cobwebs. Every person who tried to escape brought agony down on another. They all suffered as one. When all the suffering was done with, there was no living being left in that land. Then, like a living spark, a bee rose up from the morass – a confused, homeless, unspeaking bee.

Until this very day, for a negligible fee, local diggers

in Cairo point visitors to the hardpacked clay beneath
the eternal sands of the desert, and they tell you that
that is the spiderweb from all those years ago.

But that is not our story.

END

And your Lord inspired to the bee, 'Take for yourself among the mountains, houses, and among the trees and in that which they construct. Then eat from all the fruits and follow the ways of your Lord.' There emerges from their bellies a drink, varying in colours, in which there is healing for people. Indeed in that is a sign for a people who give thought.

Quran (Sahih International Version), Sura 16, ayahs 68–69

The bee, having now flown out of that prison into the freedom of the open air, saw how everything was crumbling to tiny pieces in the landscape it was leaving behind: the iron grates, the cell, the four metal columns – and, as if trusting his memory to this infinite space and this blue sky, it shuddered one more time, and the whole disappearing landscape was reflected in its tiny body and blood, in the endless path along which it knew it must fly.

—

In Khotan, if you walk along the aisles in the

marketplace, and exit through the grated metal door, and then turn right, you may find yourself under an overhang. In its shade you will find two people resting next to an old outdoor grill and an oven for baking samsas and a boiling samovar: they are the owners of this enterprise.

Khimka-Levoberezhnaya, at the outskirts of Moscow. A nine-storey brick building. A balcony hanging over a dark-green door, plywood nailed up where the glass should be. If you take the path to the left of this door and circle the building, you might see a telephone booth, where an apple half-eaten by some university student lolls on a shelf; to the right, a double-wheeled track leads to the electrical box. That box sits between two buildings. One is nondescript. The other houses a department store on the ground floor. Off to the left is an unfinished construction site fenced off by a concrete wall. In another building, across from that concrete wall, is a bookshop. The concrete barricade ends at a mental hospital. The merely abnormal and the completely loopy all look out from its barred windows, sometimes sticking a finger through, coated in sticky porridge, or reaching out with a bowl.

The snow melting on the sloping alleyway between the Jarrah-Pasha mosque and a little shop.

The grey wall of the mosque, gone purple from leaks and smudges. Vapour rising over the road. During your descent from the attic of the pink four-storey building the sea is visible just for a moment, but at that instant your attention is distracted by the sellers of mineral water in the courtyard of the neighbouring building. A guest is climbing up into that house, over the snow. But the road bends low like a springboard. The rocks, the walls, and for some reason, there at the doorway onto the wide avenue, the water, rushing furiously with melted snow. On the corner to the right some sort of Turk is selling fruit and vegetables out of a cart.

The road leading to the cathedral in Naumburg. The narrow path between two rows of poplars that leads from Vereschagino to the cemetery. The apricot trees, the earthen ramparts, and the impenetrable mud of Balkh. The lazy current of the Sigulda, its surface reflecting the cool forest. The mature persimmon trees in the palaces of Shiraz. The neatly arranged train tracks of Philadelphia. The transparent waters of the Black Earth region. A lonely village on a hill. A sunlit bee on a cloudy-looking blossom.

—

Perhaps his body, deprived of its stinger, had been

sucking in the poison of life, or perhaps it was the bitterness of the wine or the astringency of the juices, but whatever the cause, the bee was very aware of the flapping of his wings. He could feel the small nicks lower down his torso, where the waist was connected to the lower part of the body. Clearly this was the end of his blossoming, and the end of the paths leading to his blossoming, and the bee's body, for the first time, was filled not with nectar he had collected, but rather with the life of the man he had borne away...

—

The daily needs are taken care of. All habits and cares are perfectly clear, all customs well-defined. You walk out of the house and hunt for beauty: I remember the aul in the foothills in Azerbaijan, the stone cottages, the hollow cables, the metal columns brought in from who knows where, meant to prop up electrical wiring. Hanging up the laundry seems too high to reach. Playing tightrope walker seems to take too long. I remember the boy on the donkey, and the pomegranate he has started to eat, lying on the ground with its scarlet spill of seeds. The rooftops of houses, red with corrosion, over the earth.

Or the endless sandy shore of Rio de Janeiro.

Young and old, chasing a ball over the sand, morning to night. At a certain time an old man dressed all in white comes to this place, and remains here until the ocean waves lap over the sandcastle the children have built. Then he walks away into the darkness. He brings sweets for the children, and the children, busy with their games, forget and lose them. Melting in the seawater and shining like gems, the sweets begin to give off a strange bitter smell.

And in that, for a thinking person, there is food for thought.

—

Now the bee has been deprived of all of this. The road to the hive, to which he had always carried the fruits of his labours, has been closed. The scent of the flowers no longer attracts him. Small drops of sweat, through the noise of his flight, break through his velvety coat and spread the odour of alarm. And now the bee has felt the weight of a human being's spiritual pain. After all, he has been flying around burdened by the human soul which has settled inside of his body. Could it be true that the life of the most delicious beast on earth is in fact so bitter? Even the crisscross veins of his transparent wings ached with that pain. Where was it carrying this soul?

The bee seemed to be remembering his own life
– without a stinger, from now on. A life like a cell
constructed to perfection. His existence had been
shaped in harmony with his flights and affairs. His
community, knowing its own worth, which buzzed,
swarmed, and arranged its whole self around the
queen. Everyone knows that bees love nobody other
than their queen. Their historical leaders had liberated their memories from romantic catastrophes.
But what torment awaited this bee now, now that he
was tied to a human soul? What was beating inside
his velvety torso that could not fit inside his body?
What was making it bang and twist and crash there?
And what sort of sudden memory was this? The old
stories say that bees were created from the tears of
Jesus on the cross. Could it be that this was a return
to those very tears?

The bee flew on and on, not stopping. His feet
had long since gone numb, and exhaustion suffused
his wings, now heavy with moisture, but his head
was as awake as before, and it was buzzing as if his
brain was a beehive. Could it be that the human soul
had penetrated even into his head?

Before the bee's bewildered gaze, forty-nine pictures presented themselves at once. In the first, a
young man was dreaming, and running after that

dream along the edge of a cobblestone bridge. In
the second, a mullah was sitting cross-legged and
rising up, detached from the earth. In another, a
bicyclist set out on a long jump with his bicycle over
his shoulders. There was a fire at the edge of the sea
and there were snorting stallions; there were balls
knocking around a billiard table; there were two
portraits on a wall cosying up to one another; there
was a garden built of stone; there was a black sea; an
empty jail; a road, a sky, a night awaiting the day; a
dead tree; a river flush with water; roads like a memory of a crowd; air fastened tight to a foot; there was
honey that had lost its fire, like the receding dawn.
Foreign flashes, like a ripple in the water, fleeing a
central point and travelling over the surface. The
bee suddenly felt his head spin. Maybe his left wing
had grown weak from the pain in its leftmost nerve,
and that was why he had been flying in a circle for
so many hours now. Could the source of these pictures appearing to him actually reside somewhere
outside of him, rather than within? Or did each of
these forty-nine pictures of the world fit with one of
forty-nine truths of that Stranger who had planted
a human soul inside him?

They say that witches and wizards, before being
sent to burn, used to eat a queen bee. Then neither

the fire nor the curses of their faithful kinsman could take them. Did the human soul which had settled inside him know that secret?

Nerve fibres and all the nodes along them stretched from his brain to where his stinger once sat. There were air sacs under his wings and a honey sac extending all the way to his waist. He had a gland that held poison, and a honey stomach that moistened the pollen from flowers. All of that, perhaps in concert with this soul, was becoming more and more foreign to him, and other feelings now seized his whole being. This tiny creature, bearing the burden of ninety-eight truths, lost its connection with the only truth of its prior existence, and since the bee did not know the way to the single truth of this disembodied soul, he wavered through the air, from side to side.

How could this soul be avenged? Could it be conceiving of itself as a blossom of nature? Had it confused this fuzzy creature with an angel or a mystical maiden? Or perhaps, in the end, it did not wish to depart this last, warm body, as tiny and insignificant as it was? Just look at what this body has, after all: wings! Or had it grown accustomed to living between poison and honey, and chosen this reality as a last symbol for itself? Could it be that it had built up these truths, detached in life, only to return them to the perfectly constructed monolith of the cells in the hive?

'Why,' wondered the bee, 'do dreams leave no pain?' Only life did.

To the left was the setting sun, tumbling over the sand, rolling along a sandbar. A place to rest. That is where the bee turned in a last burst of energy. The wind caught up with him and made his wings useless. The flow of air which seized his little body and the soul settled inside it carried them, in a rush, to their last refuge. As he crossed into the ray of light from a flower blossom, this tiny creature, in his last agony, sensed that he was no longer hauling that soul after him. The soul was carrying him. Is not the flower perfect? Just as every cell in a hive, modelled from the nectars collected over an entire lifetime, is in tune with the melodious songs of the East, or else with the pragmatic logic of the West? But which of these songs was woven into this artificial flower, yes, yes, a flower, a flower, or more precisely the seeds of that flower? The seeds of life?

And then a vortex of light, thrown despite itself from the other side, seemed to embrace both the heavens and the earth. This brilliant shining was something like the niche in the cave, and like the lantern it held, the lamp whose light was brighter than the first stars to emerge in the dome of the summer sky. This luminescence, flowing outwards like a fountain, resembled an olive tree for just an instant, though he had never encountered such a tree either in the East or in the West; the flame in the lantern flickered, like a light which had just stirred the silver leaves of the trees, and in that small flame there was a surprising transparency. A ray of light flowed within that shining... And this tiny, faceless, insignificant bee also flew into that shining, and now the intrinsic qualities of any beam of light reminded him of the cells of his past, but light raced at such a speed that even that image could not remain in his memory, and it dissolved and disappeared.

Once upon a time, he had landed in a web woven by a spider, and he had experienced fear and inspiration similar to this, a fight for his life.

The last ray of light hit the ninety-eight cells of his eyes, eyes that were black as cauldrons, and from the life still present within them, as if from a particularly fine honey, something radiated outwards – light? a final pain? Or perhaps the soul fought free of this bee, and rose up into the Universe, which knew nothing of East or West.

And on this page, upon which the ink has not yet

dried, a secret has fallen like a seed, unknowable as a face with a hundred names, and perhaps even I cannot understand it: the gnarled small body, half light, half dark, of a bee, which this time has lost for good its ability to roam between the heaven and the earth, between life and death.

The sage, Hayy ibn Yaqzan, said: 'Were it not that in conversing with you and inciting your awakening I was at the same time approaching that King, I should have to perform duties towards Him that would take me from you. But if you like, you may follow me to Him. In peace.'

Avicenna, *Hayy ibn Yaqzan*

This edition published in the United Kingdom by Tilted Axis Press
in 2019. This translation was funded by Arts Council England.

tiltedaxispress.com

First published 2001 in Uzbek by Editions L'Harmattan (Paris) as *Hay-ibn-Yakzan*.

ISBN (paperback)   9781911284369
ISBN (ebook)   9781911284352

A catalogue record for this book is available from the British Library.

Edited by Theodora Danek
Copyedited by Saba Ahmed and Deborah Smith
Cover design by Soraya Gilanni Viljoen
Typesetting and ebook production by Simon Collinson
Printed and bound by Nørhaven, Denmark.

Supported using public funding by
**ARTS COUNCIL
ENGLAND**

ABOUT TILTED AXIS PRESS

Founded in 2015 and based in London, Toronto, and Seoul, Tilted Axis is a not-for-profit press on a mission to shake up contemporary international literature.

Tilted Axis publishes the books that might not otherwise make it into English, for the very reasons that make them exciting to us — artistic originality, radical vision, the sense that here is something new.

Tilting the axis of world literature from the centre to the margins allows us to challenge that very division. These margins are spaces of compelling innovation, where multiple traditions spark new forms and translation plays a crucial role.

As part of carving out a new direction in the publishing industry, Tilted Axis is also dedicated to improving access. We're proud to pay our translators the proper rate, and to operate without unpaid interns.

We hope you find this fantastic book as thrilling and beguiling as we do, and if you do, we'd love to know.

tiltedaxispress.com

@TiltedAxisPress